The Trade

The Trade

FRED STENSON

DOUGLAS & McINTYRE
VANCOUVER / TORONTO

Douglas & McIntyre Ltd.
2323 Quebec Street, Suite 201
Vancouver, British Columbia V5T 4S7

CANADIAN CATALOGUING IN PUBLICATION DATA
Stenson, Fred, 1951–
  The trade

  ISBN 1-55054-816-6

  1. Fur trade—Canada—Fiction. I. Title.
PS8587.T45T7 2000   C813´.54   C00-910872-6
PR9199.3.S72T7 2000

Editing by Jennifer Glossop
Copy editing by Naomi Pauls
Design by Val Speidel
Map by Stuart Daniel / Starshell Maps
Cover: Hudson's Bay Company coat of arms reproduced courtesy of Hudson's Bay Company
        Archives, Provincial Archives of Manitoba; Dakota Buckskin Pictograph, (AF 96),
        Glenbow Collection, Calgary, Canada
Printed and bound in Canada by Metropole Litho
Printed on acid-free paper ∞

We gratefully acknowledge the financial support of the Canada Council for the Arts, the British Columbia Ministry of Tourism, Small Business and Culture, and the Government of Canada through the Book Publishing Industry Development Program for our publishing activities.

FOR PAMELA BANTING

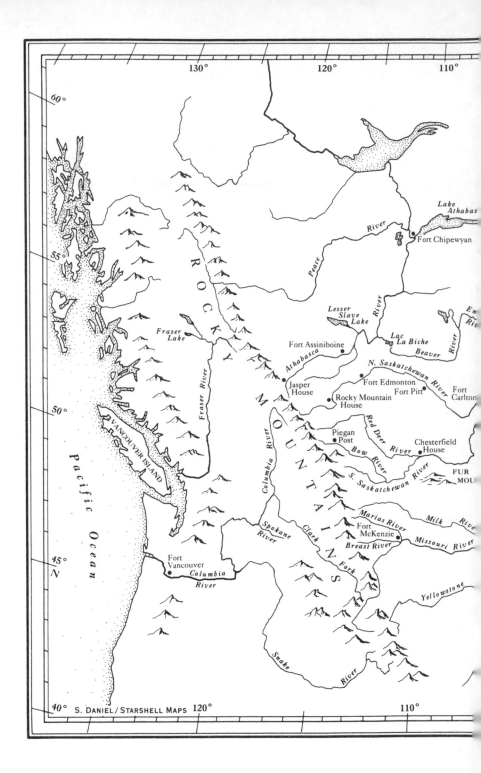

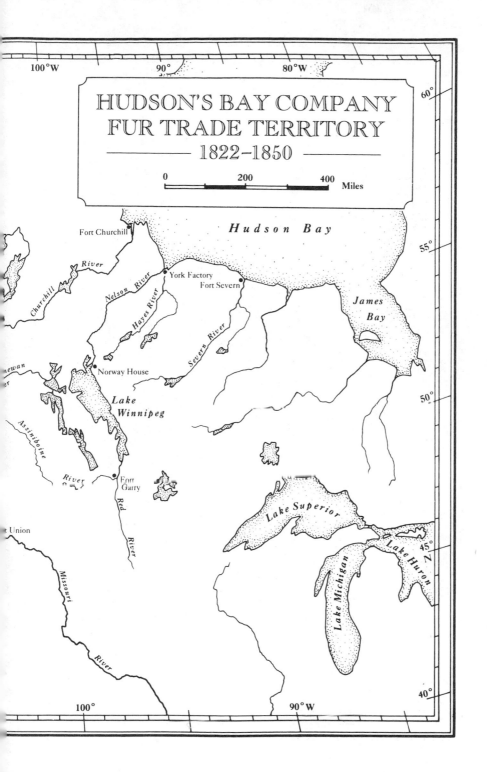

HUDSON'S BAY COMPANY
FUR TRADE TERRITORY
—— 1822–1850 ——

0   200   400 Miles

Hudson   Bay

Fort Churchill

River

Churchill

York Factory
Fort Severn

Nelson   River

Hayes River

Severn   River

*James
Bay*

Norway House

*Lake
Winnipeg*

Assiniboine

River

Fort
Garry

Red

River

Lake Superior

Union

Missouri

River

Lake Michigan

Lake Huron

60°

55°

50°

45°
N

40°

100°W   90°   80°W

100°   90°W

PROLOGUE

*A*n old woman cooked the flesh from the trader's bones for pay. The pay was good because the trader was greatly feared. The story goes that foul curses rose from the cooking pot as it came to a boil. Many said so. Generations did.

They put the clean bones into an empty keg. Rum was added as a preservative and it was sealed with lead. The old woman got her purse then. She earned more later from the soap she made with the rendered fat.

Inside the keg, the bones took to the river and began their journey to the sea. At each fort, people gathered on shore, some taking off their hats, others praying, still others cursing aloud. At least one said it was his happiest day to see the man dead.

A few would not speak to, or look at, the voyageurs who had hired on to take the bones to Hudson Bay, in case they were doomed. When a storm rose on Lake Winnipeg and lightning showered down with the rain, the voyageurs threw the keg overboard to save their lives. It was found again, in all that watery expanse, the swish of rum and the thump of bones still inside.

By fall the keg made York Factory, in time to board a ship for England. After wintering in a Liverpool shed, and full four years after the death of the body they'd lived in, the bones came home to Montreal. There, not far from their birthplace, they were buried.

All this is true. It is the end of one of the stories about to begin.

The Bow River Expedition

1822–1823

Mill Creek, 1900

Dear Editor of the *Rocky Mountain Echo,*

I read your letter about wanting me to write some fur trade memories. I thought I was beyond flattery but I'm not. The list of names you sent along interests me. I knew or met everyone on it. I saw how you put a line under the Governor's name. I said to myself that's how history gets started. Some young fella putting a line under a name and leaving other people off. I was a working stiff in the trade. What you call history looks upside down to me.

As for when to start your story, I'd go back before my time to 1822. That's after the two old companies stopped fighting and joined. They picked your Governor to lead the Northern Department and first thing he did was send an expedition west to find beaver. I'd start the story there.

William Gladstone

Open the Bay! What cared that seaman grim
For towering icebergs or for crashing floe?
He sped at noonday or at midnight dim
A man, and hence there was a way for him
And where he went a thousand ships can go.

—CHARLES MAIR

There are roads in the ocean along which the ships of deep draft sail, past floating cathedrals of summer ice and through the neck into the bottle of Hudson Bay.

A Home Guard Indian sitting beside the crooked ship's marker at Point of Marsh saw them first. He saw the ships with his ears when the horizon of water was shimmering and empty. He fired his musket, and ragged children ran with the news along the trail to the stockade and the old octagon. Indians and voyageurs pushed back the flaps of their tents, rose from the circles of their dead fires. They flowed like the rippling grass to the sea.

That evening the ships stood at anchor in the Five Fathom Hole, two miles beyond the river mouth, masts bare. The sun set into the raven profile of bog spruce, and the ebbing tide caught the last shore-bound schooner and held it fast.

Inside the old octagon, the Governor dined with his guests, a formal meal with china plate and silver on white linen. Buffalo boss and moose tongue, ptarmigan pie. They toasted with brandy and Madeira, and shrub for the ladies.

In the bachelors' hall, within yellow walls and around a cast-iron stove, the lesser men did what they could for pleasure in the absence of women. Smoked the air blue. Drank and bragged. Joked, argued, sang. Later, they wrestled and jumped over a chair, wagering on each result.

Beyond the stockade, where the brigade men camped, the coming of the ships meant a regale of rum, a pint per man. As darkness came, their bonfires bloomed along the broad foreshore. Most sat in circles, but a few were up and walking in dandified gangs: pint porringers held before them, clay pipes in their bearded mouths, hats full of coloured feathers they claimed were ostrich, but were chicken soaked in dye. Bear teeth hung on leather. Beads inscribed *fleurettes* on buckskins greased with beaver fat and sweat. In the red woven sashes at their waists, they'd tucked lengths of lace and silk: presents for the ladies.

Down the fire-illumined corridors of sand and river wrack, they swaggered and they crowed, devil faces grinning. Where knife points had scored their cheeks, the skin puckered. Other scars were straight as a knife edge, the seam healed with a line of soapy skin never the colour of the rest. In one man's face, a dead eye looked disinterested in whatever excited the living one. Another man's nose was slit on one side and the flap remained unjoined. From under every hat flowed a greased mane, kept long for sweeping off mosquitos and flies, as a horse does with its tail.

The loudest bunch came from the Saskatchewan brigade. Their name was Blaireaux, or Badgers, and they strode in the wake of a feathered and tasseled bully named Michel, who, two days before, upon the arrival of the last brigade, had fought the Taureaux bully for the title of *chante la coque* and won. He stayed standing when the other man lay bloodied and still.

Taureaux means pemmican pounded out of old buffalo bull, and when Michel led the Blaireaux past a Taureaux fire, he crowed and taunted that the Taureaux weren't so tough to chew this year. He and the others lured their women with presents and promises of what younger bulls could do.

Some of the younger men wrestled and bloodied one another, but that was without consequence. Few watched or bothered with the result.

Late that night, above the bonfires, the stockade gate swung on a screeching hinge and a mouth of light opened in the upper darkness. A column of men filed out, their servants holding lamps. Bottles winked in the lamplight and a laughter of false hilarity rained down on the heads of the boatmen and their Home Guard women. The Blaireaux bully stopped at the sound. He watched them come, like an Easter procession profaned, and the grin on his face relaxed away.

Most of those who came from the upper fort were clerks and apprentices from the bachelors' hall, but the ship captains were there, too, and a few Hudson's Bay Company officers who'd left the polite drinking in hopes of something wilder. Frock coats wagging open over coloured vests and lamb's wool cravats, some with shirt tails hanging, all drunker than they knew.

Pushed to the front of their column was a giant in common seaman's dress and a greased pigtail, his gait the rolling ocean one. Said to be the toughest English sailor off either ship, he had been brought to shore to prove that an Englishman, hardened by sailors' work, can best a Halfbreed riverman, even the *chante la coque* himself.

The Blaireaux bully and the sailor stripped to the waist. Painted in yellow firelight, the hammered flesh and furrowed scars caused silence until a drunken Englishman yelled that he hadn't come to see a fashion show. At that the betting resumed and each side prepared its man—drammed him, coaxed him, massaged his knotted back and arms.

Inside a ring of onlookers, the bully and the sailor circled. The sailor stood upright, back arched, fists raised and curled towards his chest. The Blaireaux bully hunched low and shuffled sideways with his hands down, as if his fists were made of stone, and heavy.

The sailor poked a few times, scoring on the bully's face. He got little out of it, not even surprise. The sailor danced and the bully chased until, with a grunt of impatience, the bully charged, swinging and kicking. At close quarters, he jerked the sailor's foot up and knocked him flat with his shoulder.

The crowd shuddered silent, for the sailor was on his back and still. He reached one hand across towards the top of the other shoulder. He kept reaching but the hand would not go where he wanted it. The bone at his collar was broken in half and he could not continue.

For some time the officers and the men of the bachelors' hall stood gaping. One or two had made bets with the rivermen, and as these inched closer, intent on collecting, they dug out beaver tokens and threw them on the sand. Then, as one, the Company officers turned to go, leaving the matter of the fallen sailor to the bachelors.

Silent now, the spell of happiness broken, they climbed the rise for the stockade on stubborn legs. It was a procession still, but funereal. Behind them, a noise of furious pleasure was building. A firework, exploding, wrote a golden spur on a blue-black sky.

❧

YORK FACTORY, 1822

The next day the Governor sat in the stifling heat of his office, a pile of account books open on the desk. The leather top was too high, so his forearm and writing hand were pushed near his face. The chair made his feet dangle like a child's at school. He had complained a year ago and still it had not been fixed. Drawing a page towards himself, he wrote:

Cut this desk. I will not ask again.

Bulldog flies emerged from cracks in the painted timbers. They crawled in slow bewilderment, fell on their backs to buzz and spin. In an adjacent building, tinsmiths were cutting and tapping porringers. Elsewhere blacksmiths plucked red teeth of iron from the coals and hammered onto them the square and taper of nails. The fur press screamed.

Last evening's drinking, and the Halfbreed commotion in the night, had left the Governor too alert to sounds today. He felt tense, poised and watchful, as if he were hunting. It was all out of proportion given he was here in this office, hot and still, grappling with the problems and uncertainties of the Bow River Expedition.

In the night the wind had failed and the air turned swampy and warm. The Governor preferred chill air and a breeze on his skin, and when the Halfbreed racket started, he woke on the edge of fury. The brigades were singing and cheering, igniting fireworks, and the Governor despised them for it. By any standard approaching fact, these Canadians lived and died like dogs. But as far as they were concerned, they were kings, superior in their freedom to all mankind. Hearing such ill-considered optimism expressed onto the night's sodden warmth, the Governor raised his foot and pushed the woman from his bed. Go. Take your stinking heat with you.

It was only a mistake that she was there to begin with. His normal practice was to have it over quick and neat. Take them once, take them twice, send them off. The Governor wanted no heater for his bed. He liked to be alone afterwards to feel his satisfaction properly, the cold night air like delicate fingers through the hair on his naked skin.

The Governor grabbed a second page. He shot his hand out of his shirt cuff, freshly dipped his pen:

> The Bow River Expedition will leave as soon as the pieces are moved from the supply ships to the river boats. This expedition employs labour from Red River, formerly of the fur companies and found to be surplus at the time of amalgamation. Some believe they are *back with the Company* and every officer's duty is to disabuse them of this notion. *They are hired for this season only.* Afterwards, they go back to Red River and see to their own survival. The Company may hire them again, if needed and if worthy, but there will be no charity.

The Hudson's Bay Company, whose Northern Department he governed, had only last year absorbed its rival, the North West Company. The two, become one, had much too much of everything: rivermen, labourers, hunters, trappers, traders, clerks, plus far too many old people, women and brats.

He believed the London Committee had made him Governor at age thirty over others of longer experience because they spotted in him an aptitude: an ability to cleanse these rivers and forts of their human debris. For this job, his newness to the country was an asset. He had fewer friends to reward, no debts to repay, and absolutely no sentimentality about the people.

Nor was it a matter of vengeance or prejudice. Rather, it was economy. The Governor's longest working experience had been as a sugar broker in London, and to the present task, he brought a sugar broker's meticulousness. Under his leadership, every beaver trap and pound of powder, every bolt of cloth and musket ball, would be numbered, weighed and accounted for. Pilferage and waste would be punished by the lash. If a score could not be settled in that quick fashion, he would let the clenching fist of Arctic cold do the job more gradually. Economy without mercy and no exceptions.

Economy, the various ways a few pence could be shorn from department expenditure, was a pleasure for the Governor. The exercise made him feel vigorous, exacting and strong. In that mood, when he imagined his enemies calling him a bastard and a usurper, it was as if they were tossing little pebbles which he could bat away or not, as it pleased him.

But whenever the Governor stopped in his work, even for a minute, to take a cup of tea or to study himself in the looking glass, or if he stepped outside for a breath of cooler air and then returned, the other side of the ledger confronted him.

If you considered the trade as a game, and the Governor sometimes did, then economizing was his strong suit. But because every ledger has two sides, expense *and* revenue, he could play that suit only half the time. What's more, revenue was trump, for without revenue, economy is worthless.

Revenue, meaning the supply of beaver, was the Governor's weakness. Having been on this side of the Atlantic for only two years, he knew less about the country's sources of beaver than most of the men he governed. When the London Committee had decided that the Bow River Expedition was the answer to all the problems of overhunting, depletion and scarcity in his department, he filled with doubt to the point of bursting—but could not argue. In the absence of any real evidence to support his concerns, he could only pretend to embrace their view, while hoping they knew what they were talking about.

Without having to look, the Governor reached out and tweezed the edge of a document that lay folded and flat on top of the ledgers. He pushed back the other books, gently unfolded the document and spread it out on the desk.

A map, brown and water-stained, minutely covered with spidery rivers, lakeshores and mountains. A great deal of the map had been surveyed by David Thompson, a capable mapmaker. The rest was copied from other maps, less scrupulously made.

Rupert's Land.

The Governor pointed his finger and tapped inside an egg-shaped space east of the Rocky Mountains and north of Lewis and Clark's Missouri River. The land of the Blackfoot-speaking Indians, the Piegan, Siksika and Blood. The problem with the space was two-fold. First, it was into that space that his Bow River Expedition was about to probe, and second, it was blank.

About the space the Governor had not one kernel of personal knowledge, nor did any of his trusted compatriots. Bay Company traders had been staying out of the space for more than a hundred years because the Blackfoot-speakers preferred it so. All the Governor *did* have was rumour: theory and hearsay supplied by men he would not trust to cook his food.

In all his decades of exploration, David Thompson had not acquired the evidence to make one mark in that egg-shaped space. How could any of these men presume to know more?

For the remaining hours until sunset, and later by candlelight, the Governor continued to search the post journals, letters and account books. Sometimes he looked at the blank space on the map and tried to push his mind up the rivers he imagined there. The candles guttered. The handwriting blotted and blurred, and all he found with which to jab himself awake were occasional entries where the Piegan and Blood Indians brought sudden abundances of beaver to Fort Edmonton or Rocky Mountain House from the south. On these rare prosperous days, his hopes lightly rested.

Later still, the young Governor slept across his work, coils of red hair curving near a licking flame in a puddle of wax. He slept and dreamt of the uncharted southwest. Dreams of a castor El Dorado where dams like mirrored staircases rose up every watery defile, and every beaver lodge crawled inside with life-stuffed skins.

❧

HAYES RIVER, 1822

The Bow River Expedition left York Factory in late July: six giant Orkney boats loaded above the gunwales and eighty-four men. A light canoe stroked ahead of the larger cavalcade, and in its bow stood First Officer Donald McKenzie, tricorn hat pointing like a second prow and one arm curled behind him, the fist in the small of his back. Lounging on cargo bales behind him was his son, still a little drunk and trying to play a wooden flute he'd bought from a sailor.

Donald McKenzie was a stranger to few rivers in this country, but the watery path before him was one of the least familiar. He had been a Nor'Wester out of Montreal when he started in the fur business more than two decades before, and this, the heart of the Hudson's Bay Company domain, had been enemy territory then. It became something else, more alien than enemy, when he switched to Jacob Astor's company out of St. Louis in 1810.

In another sense, a river was a river and all fur trading roughly the same. Standing in the canoe, watching the play of light and shadow in the current's riffles, McKenzie was in truth more comfortable than he had the ability to convey.

What his men saw when they looked at their leader was a man like an old stag, all hawky at the nose and split below the cheekbones as though some taloned beast had ripped him both sides of the nose to the jaw. The eyes were an unlikely blue and, close beheld, were inquisitive and innocent. They suggested a fear he did not own, which had always been to his advantage.

McKenzie stripped off his tricorn to smooth the thin hair over his skull and the picture changed again. His dark hair had begun to drain white on the roof and temples. Where a weakened musket ball had creased his skull while glancing off it, he wore a scar the colour of his mood.

York Factory had disappeared by now, sheared off by the low walls of the Hayes River, and for a time the tide rolled up the river as if God's hand were delivering them on their way. But the tide weakened steadily until the river's force was finally greater. The river began to push them back.

McKenzie ordered half the men over the sides to begin tracking, and they splashed to shore with the *cordelle* lines. The strongest went to the front and fitted the sweat-stiff tumplines to their foreheads, then walked into them until the lines were taut. On a signal they heaved together and the giant boats drew forward against the current.

They climbed the Hayes for two more days. Then they entered the Steel, coming to Rock Portage on the fifth day: a ten-foot waterfall round which the trippers ran with bales while the strongest of the rest dragged the boats over the rock sill.

Then came the black rocks and a more difficult ascent. Up a rapid and a waterfall, then another and another—days of continuous labour, until twenty-two cataracts had been scaled. Hill Mountain, they called it, and its summit the Dramstone. Reaching that point, McKenzie called for rum, and they drank deeply, each man trying not to think too much about the thousand miles remaining or of the murky destination, some place the bosses had already named Chesterfield House.

The next day, spent rowing and sailing across Knee Lake, saw Joseph Roi fall into a deathlike state. The bosses said it was from drinking the river water, and McKenzie sliced a vein and bled the *meilleur*, but still he did not revive. They put him in the light canoe and sent him back. When the canoe caught up a few days later, it was to say that Roi had died.

McKenzie drammed the men more than usual that day and worked them harder on the lines. Let their superstitious fear mingle with salt and pour forth as sweat.

❧

SOUTH SASKATCHEWAN RIVER, 1822

Where a long coulee widened into the valley, an open stretch of grass stood above the river. Three spotted cayuses hobbled leg to halter, and a dun walking free, cropped the tawny grass. Lazily they ate their way around a pair of travelling tents and a cooking fire that gave up its smoke to a cloudless sky.

The grass dome, a swell of alluvium that the coulee had been building for a thousand years, allowed a view of the river through the tops of poplar and over willows that extended to the river bends in both directions. There, Ted Harriott and three Halfbreed families from Fort Carlton waited to join the Bow River Expedition.

They had waited three days now, eating off a buffalo cow that cooled in the river. Most of their time had been spent sitting as still as possible in the shade of the tents, smoking to keep off the mosquitos and drinking tea to produce a sweat for the river breeze to cool.

The fact that the Halfbreed families were there intact was a contradiction of the Governor's orders. For some reason known only to him, the new Governor had requested that all free men contracted to hunt or labour be *single*. Unless he wanted twelve-year-olds, it was hard to know what he was after. The Halfbreeds, who were the only employable hunters, never left their families for fear of losing them, and if the Governor thought being single would make them cheaper, he was wrong again. The hunters, if alone, would dip into the Company provender far more often than if they had their wives along to dress meat and cook for them.

So they brought their families, and their nod in the direction of the rule was to keep an eye on the water. When the brigade finally did appear, the women and children would run for cover. Once the hunters had been counted by First Officer McKenzie, they and their families would trail behind or flank the brigade on the prairie above the coulee mouths, doing their work of hunting out of sight of the rest. Later, at Chesterfield, if weather or danger compelled them to bring their women and children inside the fort—well, they hoped the nonsensical rule would be forgotten by then.

As for Harriott, the Halfbreeds weren't worried about his telling or making a fuss about it. They knew him, and they fed him from their fire to cement the bargain.

For Harriott himself, the waiting was much different. He was a Company man, a junior officer, and this was the greatest opportunity he had ever enjoyed in the trade. At twenty-two, he was eight years more experienced in this country than the Governor, but at the same time was one of few who did not feel superior in knowledge to that man. Partly it was that Harriott looked like a youth even to himself, a set of manlike shoulders from which a boy's slenderness depended. Beyond appearance, he had his Uncle John Peter Pruden to thank for an insecurity he felt in most matters of the trade. Pruden had brought Harriott from England when he was twelve, to Fort Carlton, where the older man was master. Like any boy, Harriott had started by doing labour around the fort, even helping in the kitchen. Later, when he was old enough to do more, he noticed how his uncle preferred to restrict his orbit to a couple of days' ride in any direction. Harriott asked why and was told it was for his own safety.

Nowadays, Pruden admitted young Harriott was a polished trader, able in Cree and well liked by the Indians, but he still held that his nephew was pliant and soft, lacking in the harder traits called upon the farther you moved from shelter and allies. In the recently concluded fur war, thanks to his uncle, Harriott had fired no gun, nor even raised a fist in anger.

Then came the letter from the Governor—actually from Second Officer Rowand on the Governor's authority—instructing Harriott to join this exploring expedition as one of its junior officers. The letter was presented to him by his uncle, already opened and read. When he read it himself and looked up grinning, he saw no echoing pleasure on his uncle's face.

Uncle Pruden's Halfbreed daughter Margaret, Ted Harriott's cousin and lover, was also present when he read the letter. She stood behind her father, visible past his shoulder, wearing an expression of fear. Young clerks did not receive Company letters, so in her eyes it was something awful. An Arctic posting or a death in his English family.

His uncle's stony expression was harder to read, but after Harriott had considered it awhile, the meaning fell out. Jealousy. Harriott found it funny how something could come clear like that, a thing whose meaning had been obscured for years. John Peter's claims that Harriott was soft, too passive and the rest, had never been anything but a handy lie. In truth, Uncle Pruden had been holding him back not for safety's sake at all, but from a fear that he might succeed. If Harriott got beyond Fort Carlton and was noticed and admired by another trader, Pruden might live to see himself surpassed, which he would accept from a son, but not from a lowly nephew.

Later that night, the night of receiving his commission, Harriott had tiptoed from his bed in the bachelors' quarters, and Margaret did likewise from the bed she shared with a sister in her father's house. They met near the hay pile and proceeded out the back gate to their trysting place by the river.

They made love, of course, still discovering the dimensions of that hunger, but afterwards the talk ran long and awkward. Harriott explained at pious length why he must go for the good of them both, how if he remained here, he would stay the same unworthy person in her father's eyes. A boy. In service.

Margaret's first response was to argue. Although it meant something close to incest between them, she liked to think that Harriott was like a son to her father, and that her father was famous for being hard on all his sons.

"You should have seen him teach them to read and write. He made them read the Bible. He stood behind with a switch and, every mistake, he hit them on the ear. He never hit you once, so maybe he likes you best."

Her conclusion was that her father would stand up for Harriott, when the time came.

"But *now*'s the time, Margaret. I can do something now for myself. I don't have to wait for him."

For a time neither of them spoke, and the river and the little wolves, and all the other sounds of night in summer, clamoured from the shadows. Then Margaret was furious. Cried and wouldn't speak. Harriott knew the reason, too. It was because he was lying. Even though the expedition did mean the opportunity he said it did, that alone didn't account for his excitement tonight, or the fact that it was so much bigger than his love. Two seasons apart, maybe more. A possibility that he would never return. Other times, he had agonized over two days apart from her. Tonight all he felt was elation.

"I love you," he told her. "You know I do."

But she struggled out of his embrace and hit him as hard as she could with a closed fist on his neck below the ear. Then they made love again.

Now, on this grassy swell, a day's travel away from Carlton and Margaret, Harriott's feelings were more balanced between adventure and desire. Already the journey was presenting itself more as things really were and would be—the waiting, the hunting, the fires, the rolling into a blanket for a cold night's sleep.

He probably knew more about the expedition than most others about to embark on it, because of the gossip between his Uncle Pruden and his old cronies in the trade. John Peter had been with the Company so long (he'd given Edmonton House its name in 1799) that he knew all the oldest veterans: stalwarts like former governor James Bird and the comical but revered Colin Robertson. By extension, Ted Harriott was familiar with them too, a young fly on the wall as they recounted their legendary accomplishments.

The Bow River Expedition had been the talk of two winters and a summer already, and Harriott knew from his uncle that Bird was greatly for it and Robertson just as vehemently against it. (Uncle Pruden was for or against, depending whom he was talking to.) Robertson knew the old explorers Fidler and Thompson, who had both been out this way before. On their evidence, he claimed there was nothing much to be gained from forts in this country.

What they all agreed was that the new Governor, whom they didn't respect or like, would use the expedition to build his reputation and to test his men. He was anxious to be rid of his experienced advisors, people like themselves, and was on the lookout for younger men of talent and limited ambition whom he thought he could trust and control. Harriott wasn't about to say so, but that part sounded good to him.

Harriott had been sleepily eyeing his dun mare while he thought, and now he saw Small's head jerk up. She stopped chewing and the grass hung limp from the green corner of her mouth. Her ears were shot forward and her intense eye shone with some complex idea. Before she nickered, Harriott knew it meant other horses. Several riders, Cree, appeared out of the brush from downriver. Backs round and faces sullen, they passed below the camp and continued into the bush on the other side. They did not speak, nor gesture, for they knew what they needed to know already. Angry heralds, they proclaimed the brigade boats on the river: boats that would soon enter the country of their enemies for purposes of trade.

❧

CHESTERFIELD HOUSE, 1822

A league below the forks of the Red Deer and South Saskatchewan Rivers, a month and a half of hard travel from the Bay, the Bow River Expedition stopped to build. The valley was low-walled and spread, and only the crooked poplars were stout enough for lumber. Poor as they were, these trees were the best they'd seen since the prairie opened and emptied south of Carlton.

Donald McKenzie took a quick gallop upriver to the confluence itself and found the wood there poorer still, not yet recovered from Fidler's and Garth's winters at Chesterfield a score of years ago. He rode back to where he'd left the rest, confirmed the choice of site, and gave out the first orders regarding the fort they'd build.

Since leaving the Bay, McKenzie had never mentioned any previous Chesterfield House, but during his first speech to the Indians at the building site, he mentioned it often. For a week the number of Gros Ventre, Siksika, Blood and Piegan tracking the brigade along the valley roof had risen daily. Now he spoke to a big crowd that hemmed them in along the river's edge.

"Last time this Company built a fort for you here, so you would not have so far to travel, and wouldn't need to cross the country of your enemies to trade, you did not treat us with respect. Our hunters and trappers were killed. But the Hudson's Bay Company is good to you. Even though you behaved badly then, we have returned to help you because you asked us to. But hear my words: Mistreat us again, we will leave."

While McKenzie spoke, the Indians suddenly became distracted. They stared past his shoulder on the upriver side. They talked eagerly and pointed. McKenzie turned and saw that the river was black with the carcasses of drowned buffalo. Close by, one rolled and fixed him with a wide-open eye. Buoyed by air, it rolled like a seal and danced east atop the current.

The Indians, male and female, forked past McKenzie, splashed into the water and grabbed the buffalo by hair and horn. They dragged them to the water's edge and started harvesting what they could while the white men looked on stupidly, letting the opportunity pass.

While the Indian women made camp in the shady willows, some of their men walked up a low rise to open ground and sat on sweet-smelling sage. From there, they had a clearer view of the frantic scurry of white men, Halfbreeds and foreign Indians below. They watched as, first, the workmen cut and fitted axe handles, then as trees began to fall and horsemen trailed them to the deepening saw pit. A few of the whites with carpentry tools were throwing up a trading shop so crooked a man could jump through the cracks. Then a larger group set to work in lines. With shovels and bars, they cut the prairie open in the shape the fort was to be.

After two weeks, only a few of the nearby trees were left standing. The rest had vanished into the partial palisade of the fort. The axemen ranged far afield, and the leaves on the trees they cut and hauled were yellow from the first nights of frost. Even then, with fall advancing, more Indians arrived, until the valley was full of tipis and smoke. At the end of each day, the Indians lit their fires, drummed and sang.

Around some of these fires, the talk was of killing the English. The presence of Iroquois among the whites and Halfbreeds was the most often repeated reason. To bring foreign Indians to trap here was an enormous affront. It made them wonder if the English actually wanted a war. How else had this Company changed since the two old ones collapsed into each other's arms?

A few among the Gros Ventre were old enough to remember when the English were here before, and they said the practice wasn't new. There'd been Iroquois then as well. They had requested to hunt south on the Fur Mountains, and they had been lured there and killed. An opportunity should be sought to kill them again.

The counterargument ran that the English were here because the Blackfoot had asked them to come, to bring their forts closer. But that did not forgive the bringing of foreign Indians, and so the arguments continued, round and round.

What kept the peace each night was how outnumbered the whites were. They and their Iroquois could be killed so easily. Harmless ants scurrying around the valley, so busy and serious that not one Metis played a fiddle or plucked a jew's-harp, or even sang beneath the jewelled hand of night.

In the white camp, the men worked and slept in an atmosphere of hatred and fear. The men who had come with the brigade were the sourest because of the way McKenzie's son and Pambrun, the harshest of the foremen, had driven them on the river. Forced to track at a run. Lashed along the shore paths and portages. Skimped on drams even as rum splashed beside their ears in countless kegs. In the moments closest to mutiny, the bosses hinted at a regale, but McKenzie's feet were not yet dry when he bawled the first orders to the woodcutters and saw pit diggers.

Now that they were camped and building, and with fall gaining, the hours of labour increased. They were made to rise in darkness and to work by firelight at the other end of day, often without enough meat in their bellies to keep their flesh from burning away.

What kept their anger at the level of talk, and of fighting amongst themselves, was fear. Few of these boatmen and trippers had ever been so far out on the prairie. They were born in, or within sight of, the strong woods, and as the hills grew bald around them, an echoing nakedness chilled their insides. Talk of desertion was one thing, but who would actually ride into that place so barren of cover, where your life was worth infinitely less than the horse between your legs?

Day after day, the fear held them fast. The words they whispered during the long workdays were often about it. Nobody had known of other forts here, but short hours after McKenzie revealed their existence, there were stories. Peter Fidler, the first bourgeois of Chesterfield, was still alive back in Red River, but in the stories that went around this camp he was not. The limbs of his body had been cut from the trunk. His fleshless scalp wore a cap of ants as he died slowly under a pitiless sun.

The talk was also about recent omens. These were more fear-begetting because no one could deny them. Everyone had seen Roi fall into a sleep like death, the river in his belly turned to poison. Later they'd seen Hugh Munro, an interpreter and capable horseman, fall from his saddle into the river. The horse kicked his head as he fell so he arrived in the water unconscious. If Henry Fisher had not been there to drag him out, Munro would have drowned. Then, as if fate were angry at Fisher for stealing its prey, his own gun exploded in his hands while he hunted buffalo a day later.

The oaths and threats against the bosses, who kicked any man found resting and cursed you no matter how hard you worked, in truth concealed a fear that the bosses were not tough enough. The men saw how often their captains' eyes went to the top of the valley where the Indians sat watching. There were so many, it was like the line between land and sky had grown hair.

They remembered the day the toughest boss found a man asleep. He had jerked him up and grabbed his jaw as you would a dog's, twisted his head so he looked at that horizon.

"You blind ass," he said. "Those aren't fort Indians. They'd take your worthless life."

Trapped here, the men wanted their masters more arrogant than that. If the Indians raced into camp tonight, the bosses were all you had.

At night when the men could talk freely, safe from being overheard and whipped, they often said nothing at all. McKenzie had lately estimated the number of Indians surrounding them at several thousand. Noise poured continuously from their camps, music and the firing of muskets, dogs fighting and a thousand horses snorting and milling. It came to their ears in a tangled mess, the pulsing of some great beast's heart.

Few among them credited Indians with being human, and each night they paid a price for it. When their leaden bodies stretched on the ground, the only lullaby was that heartbeat split through by keening, like a wolf's howl shaved thin. In their exhausted sleep, fearsome images rose from the murk to stare. Warriors fanged and wolf-eared. Hollow bellies heaving, fringed in silver.

In the leather tent he shared with translator Hugh Munro, an Irish officer named Francis Heron and a trader called Henry Fisher, Ted Harriott concentrated on the other men's snoring to keep himself awake. Like an expectant lover he waited for a tap on the leather door, the almost nightly signal that One Pound One needed a parley.

"One Pound One" was Second Officer John Rowand, and the nickname, used everywhere but in front of him, came from his having a limp. It was the sound he made walking the hollow boards of the Big

House at Edmonton. That he came tapping after Ted Harriott at night was the strongest of several signs that the young man was more highly regarded than the other junior officers on the expedition. When the older officers needed someone to supervise a work crew, Harriott was their choice. The same when they wanted to share a bumper of rum.

What seemed funny to Harriott was his belief that it owed less to his own character than to Margaret. What the old hands liked in him was his cheerfulness on a plain day and his calm on a turbulent one, and the source of both was the smiling spectre of Margaret that never failed to walk with him or to shine life-size in his mind. The hard-boiled traders were like urchins seeking out a street lamp in the midst of a London fog.

This idea was doubly funny when applied to One Pound One, or "John," as Harriott was now permitted to call him. John Rowand's huge face would pucker sourly just to hear a word like *love*. He had a Halfbreed woman named Louise back at Fort Edmonton, but he never mentioned her here, never seemed to give her a thought. But whatever drew One Pound One to Harriott, he was drawn, and a certain part of Harriott's job had become to listen to the man's angry confidences most every night.

Tiring of the vigil and a surfaced willow root against his backbone, Harriott rose from his buffalo robe and picked his way to the door flap and out. The night was windless. Indian firelight plumed through the bush in both directions and across the river, too. The air smelled of smoke he could not see. In the upriver direction, one of the big Indian drums was still booming. From around it, voices lifted. The sky above was starry purple in the west and flannel grey to the east. A gibbous moon lit the line between as yellow as a streak of egg yolk.

Harriott took out his pipe and considered how to light it. Having smoked the evening through, his desire wasn't strong enough to make him fumble in the dark for flint and punk, especially when, given a little patience, he could soon light it off One Pound One's. That one's pipe never stopped.

Harriott was certain of the Chief Trader's arrival because of the day's events. At noon, a Fall Indian had waved a musket and shouted outside the trading shop that he meant to kill the next white man he saw. One Pound One enjoyed that kind of challenge and, being in the shop within earshot, he charged out and wrenched the fuke from the Indian's hands. Enough discipline, likely, but One Pound One was never so subtle. He gave the Indian the stock across the jaw.

The Fall Indian had not come alone. He had several more of his people with him. A bunch of Company men had likewise been drawn by the commotion. Now the two groups stood clutching their guns and cutlery, waiting to see who would move.

Luckily, the Indian got up, dusted off, and left, the rest of the Indians following—which was the signal for the Company panderers to crowd around One Pound One, thumping his back for fine bravery and bold action.

All through the afternoon, the Indians were upset. Shouting outside the gate. Shooting their muskets in the air. Galloping by the palisade walls. Come evening, Donald McKenzie declared that no more rum would be traded until a proper palisade was built and a gate hung.

It would be funny, that declaration, except for its also being dangerous. Like telling your opponents in a war that they must stop fighting until your breastworks are dug. As it was, the men took their fukes to bed, and One Pound One would surely come looking for Harriott so he could blow off steam.

When Rowand finally did show, he was at first only a bulky shadow that Harriott could identify by its lurching step. Then One Pound One pulled on his pipe and his square face lit orange. He was a man forever in disguise. Only by his quickness could you guess he was as young as thirty-three.

Seeing Harriott was outside, One Pound One veered and made for the blacker dark beyond the last tent of their leather village.

Coming to the place where the saw pit glowered in the ground, the Chief Trader called "All's well!" lest they be taken for Indians and shot. Beside the pit was a cottonwood log bent as a harp, and in the deepest swale, he planted himself, already beginning a rant about the quality of wood for building at this locale.

"Like a dog's leg, Harriott! Except for cowardice in some quarters, we could have gone two more days up either river and found spruce trees. Imagine that, eh? Thirty foot long? Straight from end to end?"

In this way, like climbing a rope, he hauled himself to his favourite topic.

"Bloody mistake giving rum to these Indians in the first place. They have next to nothing to trade. His Nibs thought they'd come for it if it wasn't offered, but where's the proof? You never look a greater fool than giving an Indian what he didn't ask for. Make them earn everything. You know that yourself." He took a pause to drag smoke. Sucked more than the slender pipe could give.

"Mind you, Harriott, what can you expect? My own orders were full of strange ideas. Thinking you can get Halfbreeds out without their families. Telling me to summon trappers after I'd already given them their outfits and sent them north. As if they were cutting hay in my backyard. Foolishness. But you've not heard a word of this from me, mind?"

Harriott knew most of One Pound One's opinions by now, either because he'd heard them many times or could deduce the unsaid ones from the rest. Even though he was only a chief trader, same rank as Uncle Pruden, One Pound One thought he should have been first officer here. As to how McKenzie ran things, One Pound One always knew better. Particularly, he hated what he perceived as cowardice and servitude on the Company side. In McKenzie's place he'd have left off the dainty diplomacy in favour of force.

The temperature of One Pound One's tirades was hotter of late because of their orders for the first subexpedition. About to leave Chesterfield any day, it would be led by Donald McKenzie. Meanwhile, he had assigned One Pound One to stay behind and boss the fort. Harriott could measure his friend's disappointment by gauging his own excitement. McKenzie had chosen him as one of the officers, and all of his tent mates were going, too. The Irishman Francis Heron, who held himself distant as though he were of much higher rank than the rest of them, finally had some justification. He was to be McKenzie's second in command. Hugh Munro, being a capable translator into Blackfoot, was badly needed, as was Henry Fisher, the most experienced trader of them all.

"Of course, McKenzie was all buttery flattery. The force I leave behind must be strong, John. There must be stout defence, John. The only one I'd trust. Blah, blah, blah. But you know the truth. He thinks he's going to find the Queen of the Beavers down there, and all her immense tribe, living in a beaver city the size of London. He wants the glory of that discovery to be his and none for One Pound One. Pah!"

In addition, One Pound One was sharing a tent with McKenzie.

"He makes all manner of noises in his sleep! Must be scalped four times nightly. On account of which he's always praying and telling me how he's willing to die in command. If you die in this command, pox, dysentery or mosquitos will get you, not Indians. You know that."

Harriott listened calmly, with one ear turned to the night lest someone wander close and eavesdrop. He seldom spoke in these sessions, and if he did it was to echo One Pound One's sentiments, encourage him, flatter him. In fact, he agreed with little One Pound One had to say. As for McKenzie's cowardice, Harriott had often heard the reverse. From Carlton gossip, Harriott knew that McKenzie had gone over the mountains from St. Louis to Fort Astoria on the West Coast in 1811. That was for Jacob Astor's fur company, and it was a voyage few white men had ever attempted. It seemed doubtful McKenzie would have become a coward since.

But knowing that One Pound One wouldn't care to hear it, Harriott kept the story to himself—and others, too, such as the one Colin Robertson had told him about the older Chesterfield House of 1809, a mission led by John McDonald of Garth. The Indians had besieged Garth that winter. Finally, in desperation, he'd made a kite and flown it. When the Indians saw the thing rise, they turned in a rout. The siege was lifted and Garth went home. If Harriott were to tell One Pound One that story, the Chief Trader would be bound to say he needed no damn kite to scare this bunch of cowardly Indians, and so on.

One of his few mistakes in handling One Pound One had been the night they talked about Jimmy Jock Bird. Jimmy Jock, or James Junior, was ex-governor James Bird's oldest son, a Halfbreed like the rest and a particular favourite of Harriott's. The nickname Jimmy Jock had probably come about to set the boy apart from his father, but various permutations had arisen. Jimmy Jock was handsome and humorous, good at dancing and whatever else he tried, and people, both men and women, worked hard to get his ear or catch his eye. Playing with his name was one method. Some called him Jimmy Jock, some Jamey Jock, others Jemmy Jock. He came to be known by any and all of these names, seeming not to care which.

When Harriott was twelve and just out of England, Jimmy Jock at eighteen had made a fuss of him, conferring a much needed status on the new boy. Jimmy Jock treated Harriott as a good-luck charm and liked to take him out on hunts and trades if Uncle Pruden would allow it. One of the many things Jimmy Jock was good at was translating, and from him Harriott had learned his Cree, some Assiniboine as well.

Thinking One Pound One would share in the general enthusiasm about his friend, Harriott said several flattering things about Jimmy Jock one night, before detecting a rising anger in his listener. Then he had to sit through a rant of half an hour, about "Jamey Jock's toffy English accent," and "him thinking himself so talented and educated," and how, now that his father was no longer governor, Jamey Jock and his tribe of Halfbreed brothers were all without a scrap of power or distinction.

"You'll notice *not one* of Bird's sons is along on this expedition. That's how highly the Bird family's regarded by the Governor!"

Luckily, occasions as unpleasant as that one were rare, and not hard to steer out of when they came. On balance, Harriott was glad enough to be making this growling friend. The bit that he didn't like was a small price to pay for the good favour of someone so obviously rising in the world.

One Pound One paused in tonight's critique of Donald McKenzie long enough to pour the ember from one pipe onto the tobacco of another. Another Indian camp had commenced drumming and the two were answering back and forth. One Pound One scoffed at the notion that these Indians could storm their camp and kill them, but Harriott knew by their songs that they were at least thinking about it. If that desire broke loose into widespread intention, it would be over in an hour. They would die, One Pound One in his bravery as quick as the next man in his cowardice.

But although he thought it possible, and certainly believed the

Indians capable of wiping them out if they wanted, Harriott found he didn't believe it would happen either. Their English clothes, stinking as they were, and their English flag were amulets of protection still, strong enough to get them home.

They sat smoking in silence for a time, then One Pound One heaved himself to his feet. He knocked the tobacco ball from his pipe and scuffed out the splinters of orange fire in the grass. Straightening, he bobbed his head once at Harriott and once in the direction of the tents. Friendship done the Company way, the senior officer was declaring their meeting at an end.

❧

POST JOURNAL

October 11: Today the men hung the gate.
The Indians pressed around the palisades and laughed at them through the gapes and cracks as they did so. Some with fukes pointed them in to emphasize the jest. Meanwhile the saw pit howled, squaring boards for the bastions. The search went on for wood to line the holes and cover the laughing faces.

October 12: Second Officer Rowand went to trade ammunition for horses.
A costly trade for horses they might wind up eating if the hunters could not find more game. With so many in the valley, all needing to eat, the wildlife for miles and miles had been destroyed.

October 13: Fort still porous as a fence. Camp still hungry.
An Indian thrust his musket through the wall and called that he would shoot these white dogs.

October 14: First Officer McKenzie's expedition readies to leave.
A cavalry of fifty-five men, with mounts and pack animals and very few extra horses, crossed the river. On the far side they made camp and waited for McKenzie. A day later, that man was still at the fort bribing

Indian chiefs, promising not to assist the Americans, promising not to trade guns or ammunition to their Indian enemies. Whole twists of tobacco were burned and gifts given, but when the last smoke rose into the October sky, McKenzie had only five Indians with whom to travel.

October 16: The McKenzie expedition is on its way south to the Fur Mountains.
Three blasts from the fort's cannon cheered McKenzie and his Indians as they stepped into the river.

🌿

THE FIRST EXPEDITION, 1822

Travelling south was easy as long as they stayed within sight of the Saskatchewan Valley just outside its steepest coulees. Then the river bent west and they had to leave it. They aimed for a black cap across the southeast horizon. The Fur Mountains: their first destination.

After leaving the valley, the land before them went in sweeps so vast it took a day to cross one. The journey into open country began calm, but by midday a west wind rose so hard their faces were peppered. The horses curved from the path, not wanting the sandy wind on their tender noses. Where the wind had worked rifts in the grass, their hooves raked up a line of fine dust that marked their place in the sky.

The land ahead looked rich and velvety, the grass like the fur backs of animals, dimpling rhythmically. Upon approach, it turned to twists of dusty brittleness, clubs and spurs of cactus, mats of buckbrush, binding soil the colour of ash.

Below the wind, the cavalcade kept up a foreign chant of metal. Steel traps clattering and lodge chisels ringing. In the saddlebags of each officer nested a vial of castoreum, carefully wrapped. Love juice of the water-loving beaver, while beside them the gullies ran with dust and the pothole bottoms were gaming boards of broken grey.

🌿

CHESTERFIELD HOUSE, 1822

One Pound One looked often at the sky above the valley's southern edge, the way you'd bite a canker to feel the pain. The half-built fort with its single bastion, the malcontented workmen, the interpreters who spoke none of the local languages but were experts in the tongues of the enemy—he looked south to remember the man who'd left him in this mess.

Pambrun and Feistel, the two men McKenzie had given One Pound One to boss the crews, were good but intemperate men. At the best of times they were inclined to brutalize the men, and these days, being in as bad a mood as their boss, and for the same reason, they were worse. They whipped the men like dogs for the twenty-one vertical feet of bastion McKenzie had asked for, and the job would be done in record time unless there was a mutiny.

Last night, an Indian had climbed the wall past some sleeping fool. Walked up to giant McKay, who was up having a piss in the square, and said, "Rum." He wanted it, not in trade for anything, but just because he wanted it.

McKay was a vast man, like a house, and he easily collared the Indian, who promptly began to scream. He screamed and he wailed exactly as if he were being put to death. One Pound One and the others were roused by the sound, and so were half the Indians in the valley. Hearing their fellow's cries, and assuming he really was being tortured or killed, they came on foot and on horseback, clamouring at the gate.

One Pound One had taken the Indian in hand by now and was frog-marching him out, when a different thought occurred. He pushed the Indian off on Feistel and grunted up the ladder to the primitive first bastion where the cannon was. He loaded her and let go a blast into the darkness.

That put an end to things. The Indians rode off pell-mell, crashing their horses into one another to escape the golden belch and thunderous roar. That provided time to turn the rascally Indian out and show that he was no more than a little bruised.

In the aftermath, One Pound One was left wondering what he often wondered: if he'd been tough enough. When you lay into a man, an Indian especially, you must beat him so he knows he's beat. A half-beaten Indian can nurture ambitions, can fool himself into thinking he might have bested you. It was too late now, but One Pound One vowed to give that Indian a real drubbing if he ever showed his face inside the fort again.

❧

FUR MOUNTAINS, 1822

Two more days and McKenzie's army reached a running stream, just before the land began to rise. By then, the expedition was down from five Indians to one, a defection for each morning, and only the Piegan left.

When McKenzie asked the Piegan why he did not go as well, the answer was not reassuring. The others went because it was not how they wished to die. He himself had lost a favourite son to the war with the Americans. He accepted the present risk for a chance to injure them.

The land beyond the stream rose in hills, all naked and tawny and fleshlike, as if an animal of bizarre musculature were swelling the skin from beneath. The Piegan said it was the beginning of the ascent into the Fur Mountains, a series of hills each taller than the last until finally you rose into cool forests, almost unimaginable from the perspective of the arid prairie below.

The Indian described the Fur Mountains that lay ahead and above as a place of icy streams and hill-cupped lakes with forests of big spruce and little doghair pines no bigger than your arm that you could scarcely squeeze through. The top was flat as a skipping stone, and this is where the buffalo grazed in surprising numbers and the biggest grizzly bears in Old Man's creation stood up out of the tall grass to survey their surroundings.

Off the hills, the water ran in two directions. It ran north to the rivers that drained into Hudson Bay, and it ran south to the rivers of the Crow and the Sioux, and the hated Americans.

More fanciful still, the Piegan called the Fur Mountains the *light-ning breeding hills,* a place where storms raged when the surrounding prairie was dry, where eagles lived, both the white-headed ones and the brown. It was so like the western mountains that surely a stretch of their foothills must have broken off and been carried here by God.

When McKenzie asked about beaver, the Indian grew impatient. What a question when he was talking about important matters.

Restored by water and several antelope killed, the men were anxious to see this place. They began the climb briskly. The going was not difficult except for their horses wanting to feed on the softer grass. The land went up gradually, hill then valley then hill, so that the feeling of ascent was frustrated. You thought you had not climbed at all until a look back from a hilltop showed hazy prairie behind and below in the distance.

Each hill they topped, they hoped for a view of a lake or a river, or of the piney crown itself, but long before any of these, their scouts came racing back on lathered horses, trying to tell news that was told for them by a sudden filling of the horizon. Against the sun, a ragged silhouette rose, a long, narrow shadow bristling fukes and spears, with golden light winking among horses' legs. McKenzie's fifty-five men were all on foot, leading their mounts and pack animals, and they froze before the sight like startled rabbits.

McKenzie consulted the Piegan, who said the Indians were Big Bellies, and the scouts confirmed it based on tipi designs they'd seen in a camp between the next two hills. Eight hundred tents, they said, and counting heads against the sky, McKenzie saw it was no exaggeration.

Calling Hugh Munro to interpret and the Piegan to vouch for them, McKenzie rode up the hill to parley. For a time the Indians above made no corresponding move. Finally a group of six detached and rode down zigzag. As the Indians descended McKenzie saw that they and their horses were painted for war. Yellow lightning strikes and plenty of black. One, probably the chief, had hair to his pony's back hanging out of a buffalo horn headdress. Another wore a badger on his head, which might have looked humorous except for the severity of his expression. A younger, bareheaded warrior riding behind wore a red-flannel shirt, unbuttoned, and just below the flint blade of his spear, a blond scalp twisted on a string.

None of this worried McKenzie at first. They would dress like this and show these things given many intentions, it being in their interests to inspire fear even if they meant only to exact a price for passage. McKenzie had gifts, promises and concessions ready. He addressed Hugh Munro.

"Give tobacco to the one in buffalo horns. Tell him we'll sit and smoke."

Without dismounting, Munro took tobacco out of his saddlebags already carefully wrapped in red cloth and blue ribbon. Munro was no more Indian than Harriott, but he wore his hair in two long braids. Some treasure in a leather bag hung from a stroud around his neck, and his greasy leather coat was dense with beadwork. At some point Munro had assessed the Company hierarchy and knew he would never rise above clerk. Instead, he took a Blackfoot wife and learned her language and her people's ways. He was careful nowadays not to disrobe in front of other whites, but rumour had it he wore a two-holed scar in each breast where bone skewers had been inserted. The chests of many Plains Indian warriors bore the same.

Munro urged his horse forward and handed the ribboned package to the Indian in the buffalo horns. He made no move to accept it, so Munro offered it to the one in the badger head veil. No good either. Finally, the buffalo horn chief spoke a few words, taking care not to look at Munro or at any other white.

Munro backed his horse and turned it so he could talk to McKenzie out of sight of the Indians.

"They won't smoke with you."

McKenzie was reaching to wipe dust from his eye. The hand stopped between the pommel and his face. If the Indians would not smoke, they would not talk. They had made up their minds already.

McKenzie's best hope now was to get away unharmed but, his mission weighing heavily, he tried again. He instructed Munro to ask why the Big Belly chief had taken this attitude. He hoped it was out of belief that the expedition meant to trade guns in the south. If he could get the subject around to that, McKenzie believed he might still win the day.

Munro translated. This time before the Indian answered, he raised an arm and aimed down it at McKenzie's face. The Indian spoke a few more words but didn't wait to see their effect. He spun his horse and ran it up the incline, followed more sedately by the others.

"He says he knows you," said Munro.

"That's ridiculous. I don't know him."

"He says you used to work for the Americans and that's why he won't smoke with you. He says they'll kill us if we cross this hill."

McKenzie turned to ask the Piegan's advice, but the Indian kicked his horse into a trot and rode away. He made a space between himself and McKenzie, then pulled the horse back to a walk. He did not ride to the Big Bellies but rather aimed due west along the flank of the side-hill. He kept his eyes fixed where the foothills and mountains would be if you could see them: the place where his own people lived.

Returning downhill, McKenzie gathered his officers and interpreters. Francis Heron, Henry Fisher and Ted Harriott. Sinclair, Welch and Munro. He explained the Big Belly position.

"Of course I worked for the Americans. I crossed the mountains south of the Missouri for Jacob Astor in 1811. Damn few have made that crossing, damn few who lived. It's why I was chosen to lead you."

Sinclair, one of the interpreters, suggested they drop back to the foot of the hills and wait a day or two, see if the Big Bellies stayed around. But McKenzie wasn't interested. Eight hundred tents could outwait them, could easily outflank them.

"What we'll do now is retreat," he said. "Ride back to Chesterfield with a whole skin and be glad."

The council was over. To one side of it stood a man with his ragged hat bunched against his chest. He stared at the ground except for one glance up at Harriott. While the others filed by to their horses, Harriott stopped to hear him.

"What then?"

"The men want to know if we're to fight, sir." He was one of the older hands, an Orkneyman named Flett who could speak English and whom the other French and Gaelic ones trusted to speak for them. He risked another glance up. "The men have a right to know, sir."

"Tell them, no fight. We're leaving. Tell them to keep their fukes empty and pointing at the ground. Tell them to go slow and not look back."

❧

CHESTERFIELD HOUSE, 1822

Before knowing for certain that the McKenzie expedition to the Fur Mountains had failed, One Pound One had a prophetic thought about it. Without Harriott to confide in, he told it to himself.

"They go out all piss and vinegar and they'll come back like whipped dogs."

He rehearsed other statements for their next audience.

"You are always outnumbered in Indian country. The moment you leave the fort, you are. Did McKenzie believe he could smile and bow, and the Indians would part for him all the way to the Missouri?"

Beyond prophecy, One Pound One knew for certain the thing had failed when news came of the Indian defections. From the foot of the Fur Mountains, McKenzie had sent a messenger back to explain this state of affairs. Premonitions of doom? Wanting to leave a record should he be killed? Whatever McKenzie's reasons, the news did not surprise his second officer.

"They saw they had a weak leader and they bolted. Simple as that."

The next indicator came in the night. A tumult of yelling, chanting, drumming and musket fire—all that passes for applause in an Indian camp. By this, One Pound One knew it was a reversal but not on what scale. The complete story he did not know until Harriott came riding in on his grey mare the next afternoon, with the interpreter Welch following a half mile behind him.

Between Harriott's arrival and that of McKenzie was an interval that One Pound One intended to use for his own devices. First, he tidied up the fort and got the cannon into the new bastion. Then he made arrangements to wring Harriott's information out of him, detail by detail.

Late that night, One Pound One led Ted Harriott to the saw pit again. This time the Chief Trader carried a loaded pistol and a cask. As they approached the pit and an Indian ran off, One Pound One took mock aim at his back.

"That would be an axe head or hammer gone. Lazy bastards leave 'em lie about. We'll be driving nails with rocks soon."

Seated on the logs, they fumbled in the dark with their pipes and tobacco. They lit them from a tallow candle brought by Harriott. The Indians were making a ruckus still, celebrating their victory, while in the hilltops the coyotes sang. As he worked the cork with his knife, One Pound One gave his opinion that the animals were the better singers of the two.

He tipped the rum into his own mouth before handing it on. Then, while Harriott took his pull, One Pound One asked the first question, which was if McKenzie showed fear when the Big Belly spotted him for an American.

Harriott hadn't noticed any—an answer One Pound One found disappointing.

"During the retreat, did the Indians follow?"

No, again. Not that Harriott could see.

"That surprises me. That they didn't try and steal the horses? After such a weak showing."

On his side of the conversation, Harriott was still excited from his ride. Small had easily distanced Welch's horse. He was also greatly enjoying the rum. He tried to think how to twist his answers so One Pound One would like them better and maybe allow him to drink more on that account.

"They might have tried to steal the horses after we left," he said. "After Welch and I were sent ahead."

Inside Harriott an emotion was building that was almost frightening in its strength. It started like a headache in the back of his neck and spilled in cascades over his shoulders and down his arms. It made him want to talk, and he couldn't seem to get in front of it to head it off.

"It seems to me that the command around here has changed," he said.

"What?"

One Pound One swung his bullish head around and stared. He stayed that way, staring, for some time, then jerked himself straight. He made a fist and knocked himself on the forehead.

"Damned if that ain't true."

He turned and faced Harriott.

"You're saying McKenzie can't lead any more, is that it?"

His tone was gloating but only for an instant. Harriott saw the shoulders sag soon after.

"If you're right, and you might be, it won't change damn all for me. I could be the last man here with legs and he wouldn't let me budge."

The Chief Trader looked wildly around. Harriott thought it was an Indian, but then he understood that One Pound One was angry and wanted something to smash. What he found was a dry branch on the log, which he broke off and threw in the saw pit. He turned his back and the whole broad square of it spoke clearly enough.

You're going to get something I want and I deserve it more was what it said.

After a time his temper cooled and he spoke almost calmly.

"It's good luck for you then. If McKenzie can't show his face around the country, and if he won't send me, then it's you. He won't let a Halfbreed lead, or a clerk. Out of the gentlemen, you know Indians best."

"Not me," Harriott said softly but with assurance. One Pound One had the keg tucked under one arm, and Harriott looked at it with longing.

"Who then?" One Pound One asked.

"Francis Heron."

One Pound One laughed, a wet laugh like sobbing.

"Heron? Good lord, man. That Irish git?" One Pound One took a noisy drink and offered the cask. Harriott drank deeply.

"I heard what happened when this expedition was discussed at Council," Harriott said, wiping his mouth on his sleeve.

"Go to hell! You weren't there and neither was your uncle."

"James Bird Senior was, and Colin Robertson. Colin told my uncle the man from the London Committee wanted Heron for the job you got."

"Nicholas Garry wanted that? Christ, no!"

"It's true. Heron wrote a report on how the Bow River Expedition should go. It impressed Mr. Garry and the Governor, too."

One Pound One grunted annoyance. Harriott charged on.

"That's why Heron was second-in-command of McKenzie's expedition and that's why he'll command the next one. The Governor probably told McKenzie to give Heron a command and see how he does. McKenzie wouldn't give him the first command because he wanted it himself."

Something in One Pound One's silence suggested he was beginning to believe what Harriott said. Again Harriott succumbed to his own excitement, charging headlong into that silence.

"You think you're up against McKenzie but that makes no sense. He's a chief factor already. If you're being tested, it's against Heron."

"But the Governor likes me!" One Pound One said it explosively, shoving the rum keg at Harriott at the same time. "Why give Heron a chance and deny me the same?"

"The Governor's not here. The decision's made here. The choice is you or Heron, and I say McKenzie picks Heron."

"I've done my duty! I've respected that damn fool's orders!"

"But you don't respect him and he knows it. So why should he help you?"

This time when One Pound One swung towards Harriott, his eyes were deep sockets, his brow clenched.

"You know a lot suddenly."

The Indian sound rose around them, bristled across the top of the night.

"Maybe I know nothing," Harriott said softly.

The singing pierced upward, through the shaft of itself and into the ear like a needle.

"All right," said One Pound One. "I'll listen."

Harriott had a good long drink this time. It was still burning his throat when he excitedly continued.

"McKenzie can't lead. He can't take credit either if someone else succeeds. Maybe he wants the whole business to fail as proof it can't be done. Or if he still wants success, he'll want it to belong to someone he controls. Either way, it's Heron, not you. Heron's more likely to fail, and he's more likely to share credit with McKenzie if he succeeds."

"You've a mind on you, Harriott. I wish to hell you'd given me the benefit of it sooner. So, which is it? Will McKenzie want the thing to fail?"

"I don't think so. It goes harder on him than the rest of us if it fails."

"Aye to that."

Finally, the talk between them stopped. For a time each disappeared into himself, where the rum had started to give a lunging rhythm to their thoughts. In that aloneness, Harriott started to feel afraid, a cold, white feeling that stole in and occupied all the places the red excitement had just been.

Talking as equals when they never would be. Making such a big show of his opinions for a long suck on the rum tit. If he could have recaptured his words, stuffed them back into his mouth, he would have.

"You'll do better than anybody if it fails," he said finally.

"How the devil could that be?"

"You're the only one who can't be blamed. If the Indians don't overrun the fort and take the trade pieces, you've done your duty. In the end, you might be the only officer who can say that."

"And what do you think? Do you think it will fail?"

Harriott considered what he had to say, then said it.

"Colin Robertson told my uncle something else. He tried to tell the Governor, too, at Council, but the Governor wouldn't listen. He wanted to tell him that Peter Fidler had been out here twenty years ago and lived a winter with the Piegan along the mountains. I don't know if he went to the Missouri, but I do know he didn't think much of the rivers he saw. He didn't think there was enough beaver to warrant a fort."

"By God. I almost wish I didn't know that."

One Pound One sat solemnly a moment. Then he put his hand on Harriott's shoulder in a ceremonious way. "I make you a promise, Harriott. If it does fail, and if as you say I come out smelling better than you, I'll see you right. As a friend."

A smart friend too, One Pound One was thinking a few hours later when Donald McKenzie returned. Once across the river and through the gate, the First Officer paraded about on his horse, then on foot, majestically. Acting the king in defeat more than he had before, he insisted the whole fort be roused and that the officers meet in his house. I will tell you everything, he kept repeating.

When the meeting convened, McKenzie made his proclamations,

the part about his American service and almost boasting how this meant he could not lead any more expeditions.

"The point is this, gentlemen. Winter won't wait and neither should we. I want a fresh expedition out of here in two days. Francis Heron will command it. Edward Harriott goes as his second-in-command. Go up the Red Deer River and, when you near the mountains, take the south arm at every fork. Then head south to the Bow River and follow it home. We'll try to get a Big Belly or Piegan to go, but you may have to do without. Godspeed and bring back beaver!"

❦

THE SECOND EXPEDITION, 1822

Between Chesterfield and the river forks, the Heron expedition camped for several days. The weather was warm in the afternoons but frozen before dawn. The sky was bright and whitish blue. Each morning an order came to pack the horses. Each afternoon a second order countered the first, and they took down the packs and allowed the horses to graze.

The problem was that McKenzie could not find an Indian to accompany them. He and Heron interviewed and courted several, but without result. McKay brought an old Big Belly named Flesh Eater who he claimed had agreed to everything. But once Flesh Eater smoked and listened to the plan, he too remembered other places he needed to be.

In the camp by the river, the horses grazed perfect circles around their picket pins. In circles of their own, the men tossed marked knuckle bones. The women boiled antelope in kettles for present needs, and jerked and smoked buffalo meat for the trail, watching that their fires did not creep away between the stones and ignite the papery grass.

Harriott sat apart from the others at the river's edge, staring down for hours at the same upraised rock and the riffle that poured over it. He trusted Small to graze without hobbles, and when she tired of eating, she came and stood over him. She lowered her Roman nose to an inch from his shoulder, closed her eyes and slept.

All the while, Harriott was busy inside with regret. The smart thing to do on this expedition, the best opportunity of his fur-trading life, would have been to spread his attentions equally among the officers, as he had done at the beginning. But One Pound One had chosen him and that was that. It had the potential of being a good thing, if One Pound One stayed in the Governor's good books and rose accordingly.

The real problem was what he had done to himself, with no greater provocation than a little excitement. Like a careless fool, he'd unburdened himself of his true thoughts into One Pound One's ear, showing off what his mind could think and his mouth could say. Now that he had done so, would One Pound One ever be satisfied with less? And being bound that tightly to one man in the trade, would any others trust him again? Heron and Munro already looked at him that way, as the Second Officer's spy, and they only knew the half of it.

The greatest danger, considering One Pound One's temper, was that the man would turn on him. It was a short haul from there to disaster. "I have heard from young Harriott that the Governor used the Bow River expeditions like a horse race, testing his men against each other." "Young Harriott seems to think Donald McKenzie handed out expedition commands based on who could outshine him least."

This putting of all his eggs where one boot could smash them made Harriott nauseous. The expedition had been going well for him, but now there was danger of a complete reversal, thanks to his wagging tongue. When he thought of Margaret now, she was frowning at him in disappointment.

On October 30th, the order to pack the horses was not rescinded. At four in the afternoon, a party came riding from the fort led by McKenzie and Heron, with a tall thin Indian less than twenty years old in tow. He was a relative of Flesh Eater's and had come to the fort to see if the offer of a new fuke and ammunition might apply to him as well. It was unlikely he'd seen much of the country they were entering, but McKenzie took him anyway.

Heron and his men mounted and took to the trail away from the noisy mob at the river's edge. Muskets fired behind them. Women waved and wept.

They rode the north shore to the forks and kept to that side beyond it, pursuing the Red Deer River west. It was a "Hudson's Bay start," meaning with the sun already low in the west. If the horses proved lame, or if something were forgotten, they could return in the morning and make up the deficit.

As the journey commenced next day, the valley was broad and ill defined, a confusion of old channels, some with water in them, some grown full of willows. Travelling into the wind, hidden by it, they came to an old mule deer buck raking his antlers in the willow, working furiously to lose his itching rack. The wind and his own noise let them walk close, and the deer's first notification of their presence was a hot musket ball in his brain.

Then the hills grew taller, shouldering up into the sky, and the river was a sinew of blue reflection in the valley's depth. There were Indian camps along this stretch, Siksika and Blood, a main camp by the river and a second on the valley roof for vigil. The tents were weighted heavily around the edges so as not to blow away in the powerful winds.

Towards these Indians, Heron was unfailingly rude. Once the question (beaver) had been answered (no), he dropped all pretence of pleasantry and moved on.

Throughout these days, Harriott kept a close eye on his leader. He had never met the man before this expedition and didn't care for him much based on what he'd seen. Though neat in dress and quite good-looking in a small-featured way, Heron was a cold fish, distant and superior, as if intent on pushing people back from any familiarity. Now that it was his business to study him, Harriott soon noticed how little there was to see. Instead of a character, Heron had ambition. Sitting bolt upright in his saddle, he hardly looked left or right. He never turned in his saddle to see how those behind him fared. He wore his hair closer cropped than was usual for a fur trader, and Harriott grew sick of the sight of it bobbing below his hat brim square as the end of a box.

What was most obvious to Harriott was that Heron was burning up his horses and seemed powerless not to. As each vista lacked beaver dams, he muttered curses and pressed on. At the short stops he allowed, he went beneath a tree to write in a book he kept in oilcloth in his saddlebag. Pages he shared with no one.

Two camps at this pace brought them to another change, a place where the sun burned hot and intense, and the grass thinned until the earth's ribs stood out. The valley here was an ashen cage with smaller hills inside it, smooth hills the colour and shape of wasp nests inverted. Still farther, the beehive hills were striped sideways, purple between the grey, and some bled orange as if packed with rusting iron.

Second-in-command meaning nothing, Harriott spent his time looking and remembering. He cached what he saw for later and for Margaret.

> Rocks point up and balance other rocks. A rock like the sail of a fish sticking out of sand. Cutbanks textured like the skin of the elephant my father took me to see at a fair in London. In one of those sidehills, a reddish-brown thing I swear is a bone.

Leagues of distance passed, and days, and the good weather held. They left the dry, skeletal valley and entered a cooler part where evergreens grew in the shade and aspens on the benches. The grass was better but Heron wouldn't let the horses graze sufficiently, and their ribs began to show. The faces of the men caved in against their teeth. Sometimes they ate pemmican while deer grazed in sight. Heron would rather starve than stop, rather scoop cold grease than hunt and make a fire to cook.

His disappointment continued. No castor and not even the broken dams and pierced lodges and gnawed stumps of departed castor. When they finally did find a mated pair about their busy work, Heron said to leave them. It was the first of his orders Harriott approved. Only insanity would harvest the rare mother and father of a vanishing breed.

By the time they'd been on the trail a week, the Red Deer River had swung such a turn that it no longer came from the northwest. The mountains were visible like polished saw teeth, and the river pointed to an origin somewhere in the southwest. For a week they went towards the mountains, and on some days those rocks looked smaller than they had the day before. A hand could have been picking them up in the night and placing them farther back along their trail as a joke.

Once inside the mountain foothills they followed McKenzie's orders, taking the south arm at each fork. By the compass this swung them south. It also meant that the river they followed shrank, becoming just a worm of water ploughing deep black loam and inscribing the letter *S* over and over. In time there was no river at all, just a wet meadow under the stone backbone of a tan hill.

Along valley bottoms dry and treeless, they continued, the going easy except that their horses were ruined and had to be led. Even Harriott drew his mare, though she needed it less than the rest. Harriott led her so as not to excite envy, so as not to lose her. The mountains flanking them were massive now, the largest things Harriott had ever seen.

In that humble way, on foot, the expedition met its first Piegan, a dozen boys who rode parallel on fit horses, just out of musket range. Harriott watched with interest how squawman Hugh Munro began to act differently when the Piegan arrived. Immediately, he left the fur traders and led his horse to walk among the Indian boys. He came and went often, and each time upon returning, he claimed to Heron he'd been spying. But Harriott noticed he had nothing significant to tell.

More likely Munro was acting the free man before his tribe and distancing himself from this half-starved crew. The Company believed it had every white man's allegiance, no matter who they married or fathered, but watching Munro and consulting his own bridegroom feelings, Harriott knew otherwise. Many ideas like this one, born in the old country, did not work here.

The next morning, they broke camp early and had not ridden an hour when the Bow River Valley opened below them. The whole country dropped away, and whether they had guided themselves or been drawn by the Piegan boys, they came to the river within sight of a large Indian camp.

Munro went to parley and came back to say the Indians were a mixture of Piegan and Siksika and wanted to smoke. Heron asked if the Indians had peltries. Munro said he did not think so.

"If they have no beaver, then no parley."

Harriott was there. He met Munro's eyes, and the two of them knew what must be done.

"There's many headmen in camp, sir," Munro said. "We'd best stop."

Heron seemed not to hear. They were all mounted now, to cut a better figure, and Harriott noticed how Heron listed east in his saddle. In a sense he was barely present at all, having moved on to that time and place where he would have to explain his failure. Seeing how he was, Harriott urged Small ahead so her neck went under that of Heron's horse. He turned the two horses as a way of breaking Heron's entrancement.

"Mr. Heron. I wish to talk as your second-in-command."

The Irishman woke angrily. "What?"

"This country may have few beaver, sir, but the Piegan have at times come to Edmonton and the Mountain House with considerable skins."

"Don't take me for a fool, Harriott. I know why we're here."

"No disrespect, sir, but this many Blackfoot must want to tell us something. If we don't listen, they could kill us."

The last phrase altered Heron's mood. Maybe it came to him that, even facing failure, he did not wish to die.

"I know how they get their beaver, damn it. They steal them from American traders and other Indians."

He stopped talking, looked across his horse's quivering shoulder at the ground.

"Oh, very well," he sighed. "If you think it's so important that we hear their nonsense."

The council tipi was tall and broad across the base. It smelled of leather and spruce, tobacco and burned sweetgrass. On a padding of boughs, men of all ages sat in half-circles according to rank, and to Harriott's eyes, all seemed prosperous and in polished good health. The desperate quality now general among the Big Bellies at Chesterfield was absent here. Except for guns, they do not need us, was Harriott's thought.

He also looked for Jimmy Jock Bird. Like Munro had with his Siksika woman, Jimmy Jock had married a Piegan, whether to secure a trading advantage for the Hudson's Bay Company or for his own purposes no one seemed to know. But Jimmy Jock's Piegan lived near the Missouri River, and this bunch were probably not the same ones. In any case, he was not present.

Munro was already translating the Indians' speeches. They had no beaver and they seemed impatient to get that subject out of the way. What they were more interested in were the rumours about the Bow River Expedition.

"It is said you bring eastern Indians to hunt and trap the beaver," said a powerful-looking man with a chest like a slab. "You think we can't kill beaver ourselves?"

In his reply, Heron was, as usual, rude. Harriott knew enough Blackfoot by now to hear that Munro was turning some of it into more diplomatic language.

"If you have no beaver, how is it you bring beaver to the Saskatchewan forts?"

When Munro translated this, the Indians laughed. They passed the question back so the ones behind could laugh, too.

"What, Munro? I said nothing humorous."

"I said what you said. I don't know why they're laughing."

The laughter died and a handsome square-faced man in the front pointed south.

"He means the beaver, sir," said Munro. "They get them south is what he means."

"Tell him I think the truth is they steal the beaver. *There* and *there* and *there!*" Heron stabbed the air with a finger. East, west, south.

"Are you sure I should say that, sir?"

"Of course I'm sure! You're my interpreter, not my advisor!"

Said in Blackfoot, Heron's accusation caused even louder laughter. Heron tried to stand but Harriott, sitting on the opposite side from Munro, held him by the arm.

"Has everyone gone mad? Get your hand off me!"

"We've only smoked one round, sir. It's their country and we're their guests. Let them say when it's time to go."

"I won't be laughed at by damned Indians."

Harriott looked at Munro, kept looking at him until the interpreter met his eye.

"Mr. Munro, you hear the Indians talking. I think Mr. Heron should know what they say."

Munro's face soured.

"Go on, Munro," Heron said. "What are they saying?"

"They're talking amongst themselves, sir."

"I can see that. I want to know what they say."

"They're saying whether they should kill us. It's only joking and bragging. They probably don't mean half of it."

"What do you make of it?" Heron asked Harriott.

"It might be talk and it might not. What I'd do is flatter them. Tell them how badly the Company wants their trade, not just in beaver but for the buffalo and pemmican they bring. Tell them what good hunters they are and so on. How we're here to build them new forts that will make things safer."

"Oh, hell," Heron sighed. "I'm not repeating all that. Munro? Say what Harriott wants said. Butter it on thick."

So Harriott spoke, at length and with many flourishes, and Munro translated, and though he did not know a lot of Blackfoot, Harriott made the man repeat any time he sensed his words being watered down.

Later, when they smoked again, the square-faced chief gave Harriott the pipe first among the whites. Some women entered with fresh-cooked buffalo meat on hides, and by the way Munro behaved towards one, Harriott understood she must be his Siksika wife. She was on her way to her husband when the square-faced chief intercepted her with a word. Eyes cast down she turned to Harriott, offered him the meat. Taking a rib, Harriott could see Munro's face past her hip, and how he was offended. Then he looked at Heron and saw a similar look there.

As with One Pound One two weeks ago, Harriott felt cold and wished to put his words back where they'd come from. Everything he'd said here was true, and the diplomacy of it would probably gain them the horses they needed to get back to Chesterfield.

In another way it had been unwise. Heron's pride was injured. Munro's feelings hurt. Down the road, if he needed either man, their backs would likely turn.

❦

CHESTERFIELD HOUSE, 1822/POST JOURNAL

November 2: Trouble with the Indians.

An Indian fired through an unlined crack in One Pound One's stockade. The ball missed Alexis De Eu by a margin so small his capote was burned. Later, the Indian sent a friend with a robe and his gun to ask forgiveness, but One Pound One refused.

November 10: More trouble with the Indians.
Two men out squaring wood were shot at. Neither was hit.

November 11: Mr. Rowand traded with the Big Bellies for food.
Again it was necessary for One Pound One to trade guns and ammunition to the Big Bellies. McKenzie feared to do so because he needed to investigate the Missouri country beyond where the Big Bellies lived, but he made the trade regardless.

Heron's expedition was not back but an express rider brought their news. No beaver and no significant trade. The messenger said that Heron's horses were spent and his travel slowed further by poor hunting and snow. The snow had come to Chesterfield as well, a depth of more than a foot under heavy skies. The river was a slice of black, along which the ice grew thicker every day.

When the snow came, the Indians began to leave. Tents struck, goods lashed to travois, and gone. A slow attrition and a sense, overall, of disappointment. Not much good or even interesting had come of Chesterfield House as far as the Indians were concerned. The dispersal of rum had started out generous but had been grudging of late. The range of goods for trade was never exceptional. The Indians left to hunt but also out of boredom.

The Indians who stayed, some going hungry to do so, were those who feared seeing the fort abandoned. There was a rumour that Edmonton and Rocky Mountain House might close as well, which, if true, would leave the Blackfoot and Big Bellies at the mercy of the Americans with whom they were at war. To protect themselves, they would have to trade across the mountains, or east into Cree country, danger either way, and if the trade failed entirely, all their enemies would have more guns than they.

An outbreak of pox, Cupid's Measles, added to the tension, both sides blaming the other.

Then, on November 16th, Heron's expedition returned. The horses, even the few gained in trade from the Piegan, were skeletal and stone-bruised. Several horses had been eaten when a blizzard made it impossible to hunt.

On both sides of the river men worked to smash a path through the ice to open water. Then the expeditioners led their stumbling horses into the ice-filled torrent. Coming closer, the men's faces were fierce with grime and fatigue. The horses' eyes contained a gelid terror. The water was frigid, the current deep and strong. As it lifted the horses off the rocky bottom, the weakest ones floated away. McKenzie sent canoes in after the floundering men, but all that was rescued from the drowning horses were their saddles and a bit of tack.

Later, when seated across from McKenzie and giving his report, Heron talked of prospects for river navigation. He showed in his book, on his little maps, places well suited for building. Outside, the packs sagged empty. They and the starved horses and men told a different tale. Navigation to what end? Forts for what purpose? And if Heron was embarrassed that day, it was worse for him the next.

In the grey dawn of November 17th, the fort lookout announced a trading party. Indians fired a salutation from the south hills, and within the hour, they came to the river's far edge pulling travois round with skins. Well-fleshed horses towed bullboats from shore to shore on ropes of woven horsehair. The Indians were Piegan. In a day of trading and a night of drunkenness, four hundred beaver crossed the counter at Chesterfield.

As to the source of their peltries, the Indians pointed south. To the Fur Mountains and the Missouri. The land of south-flowing rivers. The places Donald McKenzie's Bow River Expedition had yet to set foot.

One Pound One's winter house was half built. Over the shell, he had rigged a leather roof, making it a tent with wooden walls. The night of Harriott's return, they sat inside it, without a fire, drinking rum.

Astride stump chairs and wrapped in robes, they had been drinking and smoking for hours. Getting drunk for no reason Harriott could decipher. Save for its guards, the fort was asleep, and Harriott wished hard that he were too. Even this drunk, the pain in his back and legs would not die. His joints shouted their position with pain. He was cold to the bone.

The topic of Heron's expedition had been exhausted hours ago. Not much to tell that Heron himself had not told McKenzie earlier. Francis Heron could have, and should have, handled the Indians better, but it was doubtful he would have gained many skins even if he had.

It was harder to say what they were talking about now. From the leather roof, One Pound One had hung a buffalo horn full of tallow, and the shaking light echoed the shivering in Harriott's core. If he could only sleep, his strength would return, but One Pound One would not release him.

The Second Officer tipped the rum keg and overflowed his mouth, most of the black gulp running down the crease of his jaw onto his neck. Harriott had never seen drink finish this man, but it seemed certain to tonight. His eyes were dim and swimming. His upper body wove circles around the base of his spine. Out of some monologue inside his brain, occasional mumbles surfaced.

"Murdering bastards . . ."

For comfort in this cold and pointless waiting, Harriott tried to compose the face of Margaret. But the image so available to him a month ago was a struggle now, a shadow passing that he could not hold. What came instead was tramped snow jolting in front of his feet, dead claws of poplar trees gripping the woollen sky. Every thought played to Indian drums, even now when the night was calm. Feathered tail fans brushed his face. Anklets of dew claw rattled the doors of his ears.

When he next looked at his companion, One Pound One's eyes were closed and his back was round. Finally asleep, Harriott hoped, but then a hand flung out and caught him on the shoulder. One Pound One's eyes startled open, sulphurous in the livid face. As if it were the last angry bellow in a long argument, he shouted, "I can't stop it! The bastard means to send you, that's all."

Harriott tapped his ear, meaning quiet, meaning there might be listeners.

"Damn them! I've been quiet too long."

The eyes closed, the crimson face working as if it had something to chew. The entire flesh shrugged and Harriott reached to catch it. But again One Pound One jerked himself upright and reopened his eyes, wherein all had turned to sorrow. Rage into maudlin affection. Harriott watched the black-haired hand come groping across the space. It dropped dead-weight on his leg.

"He means to send you, Ted. He trades 'em guns and sends you down their middle. When he loses you, he'll say he tried and you're the proof it was not possible."

A thistle pricked on Harriott's back.

"Where? Send me where?"

"Fur Mountains. Missouri. Straight at the Big Bellies, and McKenzie's given 'em the stuff to shoot you with."

"When?"

"Tomorrow."

"That can't be. There's no horses."

"That's the worst. He'll make you go on foot. I tried to get him to pick Pambrun. Pambrun's mad for adventure. I told him you're no fighting man."

The words stopped and the whole being behind them went out like a snuffed lamp.

"John. Wake up. I need to know what you know. Tell me what you know."

The flesh was like flour in a sack, spreading over the edges of the stump. The eyes were closed and the lips slack. The stem of the pipe slipped from One Pound One's mouth and fell. The clay bowl split on the hardpan and a greasy ball of tobacco lay stranded between the halves.

🌿

THE THIRD EXPEDITION, 1822

Thirty men and an Indian guide. Harriott in command. Sinclair to translate.

Their trade goods consisted of tobacco and rum. For defence: fukes and daggers. To eat: two bags of grease.

"You're meant to hunt" was McKenzie's explanation for the small quantity of food.

Meant to hunt their way south. On foot.

Choosing Harriott's mare for his mount, McKenzie rode south with the third expedition for part of the first day. Along the roof of the South Saskatchewan, the men cut lines through the snow with their moccasined feet. Their packs were heavy with tobacco, rum and grease, and the barrel of a fuke, wagging, poked from the top of each. The valley was a reassuring shadow close by to the west.

After two hours, Harriott called a halt and drammed the men two rounds. He never looked at McKenzie to see if he approved. As they drank, McKenzie eyed the packs beside each man and noted something missing.

"Bourassa, you have no fuke."

"No, sir."

"Why is that?"

"She burst, sir. When I was hunting for Mr. Heron."

"And why did you not replace it on your return? Mr. Rowand could have furnished you another."

"Too expensive, sir."

McKenzie tapped his quirt against his pant leg. Then, as if on a whim, he drew it back across his shoulder and swung it sharp at Bourassa's ear and again onto the neck by the collarbone.

"You are useless. Get back to the fort."

Bourassa rose. Though his ear was split and feeding a line of blood, it was his neck he held on to. He bent to the side that hurt, but not cowering. He stood close to McKenzie, facing him.

"I'm happy to go. But I won't buy a gun. I'll quit."

McKenzie let Bourassa finish and watched in silence as that man took a few small things from his pack and left, walking back down their trail in the snow. As if dreaming, McKenzie climbed onto Small's back and twisted the horse's head so it looked north.

Harriott and all the men were facing that way, after Bourassa, their shadows pushing towards him. McKenzie's shadow on top of Small was the longest, nipping at the heels of the *engagée,* who still held his collarbone and walked bent to that side.

The situation was oppressive and McKenzie could not stand it. He bent his bearded face to Harriott, who stood by Small's shoulder.

"All done then, Harriott. Godspeed. Good luck."

Harriott turned to look but the sun was in his eyes. He felt Small's side grow round with air against his arm. Her winter hair was frosty at the tips. He went back to watching Bourassa, already small and getting smaller.

"I said, do you need anything, Harriott?"

Harriott reached and placed a hand on the soft skin of Small's nose where breath was steaming.

"Don't eat this horse."

Then he heard a snap, the quirt on Small's hip, and the mare burst by him. She galloped down their long shadows, the longer V-shape of their footprints, flinging her head in protest at the tight way he held her. The frogs of her hooves packed fists of snow that flipped in the blue air.

As horse and rider came down on Bourassa, a tension gathered in the backs and shoulders of the men. Harriott felt it in his own. McKenzie's words chiming. *Godspeed. Good luck.*

Yes, if God is fool enough to walk His prairie in winter loaded with weight. Godspeed, certainly, if the life flies out your opened skull.

Then the distance between rider and man on foot closed, until you couldn't tell one from the other. A sound came from the men, as if they'd all taken a blow. But McKenzie did not cut Bourassa a second time. Just passed him by.

Directly after, Harriott called his men to circle around him.

"If we want to get home to our forts and our women, we must be smart," he told them. "I don't care if you think me a good leader, but when there are Indians around, act as though you think I am. We'll go where we're told to go. We'll look for beaver as we're told to look. But we'll do each thing in the way most likely to get us home."

Led by Flett, the men gave him three cheers for what he'd said. They liked the sound of it and the idea, repeated, of home. They began to walk with spirit in their legs.

That first day south, Harriott called the halt as the sun came plumply to rest on the horizon. They made camp on the eastern edge of the valley, on a cliff between coulees commanding a view, and when they'd settled, he made a strange announcement. He told them their chore for the night was to drink every drop of rum. If they could not drink it all, he would pour the remainder on the ground and break the kegs. They would do this drinking here where there were no Indians, before they took another step south.

It was the oddest night of many of their lives—those who could remember it. Like New Year's at a big fort, except the rum never flowed nor the tobacco burned as freely then as now. They had but one jew's-harp, but they sang and played, clapped and danced regardless until they were tired. The gambling and the dancing and the fighting went on long after the moon had set.

Harriott got as drunk as the rest, but when two men drew knives over an argument, he was quickly between them.

"No dead men," he said. "No half-dead men."

They posted no guard and slept how and where they fell.

When the next day's dawn came pink to the horizon, a foraging party of Big Bellies approached from a long ways off. Only Harriott, grey-faced and eyes bloody, was awake to see them. Rather than cross a coulee and present a target, the young men circled far to the south and came with the dawn behind them. Harriott let them come most of that distance before he woke the others. He told his men to ready their weapons, to load and point them, but not to fire unless he gave the order.

Himself unarmed, Harriott walked beyond musket range to meet the Big Bellies—boys, it turned out—and he stood without flinching as they came at a gallop. They let loose shrill cries and waved their spears. One had an arrow on the string. Then, before Harriott's curious act of bravery, they skidded their horses to a halt in the snow, sat on the winded mounts and stared. In the trader's hand, held out to them, was tobacco. While the two leaders dismounted, the others stayed in their saddles, ready with bows and spears.

Harriott stuffed his pipe, lit it, offered it. After they had all smoked a couple of turns, he spoke the bit of their language he knew. He said he had a message and would need another to translate. He beckoned Sinclair, telling him to leave his fuke behind.

What he wanted said was that this little expedition was no stronger than it appeared. The Big Belly boys should go back to their people and say how these white men travelled without horses and without rum, without any trade goods at all. He showed them the broken kegs.

"We're like a wolverine, when you corner him. All we have is our claws to sell our lives dear."

The young Indians watched as Harriott wrapped a bit more tobacco in a piece of cloth and tied it.

"Our last," he said, giving it to them. "Now we truly have nothing."

❧

FUR MOUNTAINS, 1822

Dear Margaret,

You said once I was a fool to show my love for you so much. How very foolish you'd think me if you could see me at this letter tonight.

There is a big prairie here, close to the sky and level like a table coated with snow. The moon is so bright I need a fire only for heat, not for light. On the plain a single tree has the moon in its branches. Right behind me it's all forest and I suppose I shouldn't have camped that way. Defence seems hopeless so I thought we might as well be close to wood.

When we came here this morning, there were buffalo. The wind was such they couldn't smell us. A Halfbreed covered himself in a robe and crawled among them. He shot a cow where she stood. We were starving and devoured much of the meat raw.

Since then we've looked around for beaver and found a few lodges. My men would have cracked them but I followed Heron's example. There are no beaver save these few, contrary to all the lies. Let somebody else kill the rest.

I am no longer quite a human man. Here I take the time to write you a letter, thaw ink for the purpose, and what I write about is buffalo and beaver. But I have to try. Even as the other men are sleeping and snoring, I will keep this watch and write this letter in hopes it will breathe life back into my memory of you.

It occurs to me that I can say more in this letter than I could if you were here. I can talk about what I remember of you as a child, when I was a little older child and fresh out of England. You were a powerful mystery to me, my cousin and yet a Halfbreed, as though I could become an Indian myself if I stayed in the country long enough.

I remember you best of your family because you were cute and talkative, and peculiar. That's why I picked you to come hunting prairie chickens, because I knew as soon as we were in the trees, you'd start in about your Windigos. Creatures once human that ate human meat. Your mother had you convinced you were in special danger on account of being beautiful. "Even a rabid wolf picks the one it likes to bite," you told me once, and you were very angry when I laughed.

That was how I saw you, my cute and funny Halfbreed cousin, until that time I found you picking berries, or stems out of berries, on the river slopes at Carlton, the day I think of as the beginning.

Hot day in late July and you had your skirts up and tied around your legs to feel the breeze. You bent forward over the berries, on the watch for worms. Your legs were smooth and brown, and the muscles tensed as you pushed onto your toes to hold the berries in the basin of your lap. There were wires of red where the thorns had torn you and I found I wanted to kiss those places, run my tongue on them.

You looked up. I suppose I made a noise, and small wonder, as I was never in such an uproar. Helpless to move or shift my look. Sweet face, framed in brown hair, and the bow of your lips smiling, and a woman's shape pushing out your dress. I knew you were mostly amused by me but my heart was stolen anyway.

If it weren't for the books I read, I wonder if I'd have any words for this. Those books talk about love as coming but once. I trust I have that for you.

Ever since that day on the river, at every regale, every time you dance with a man, I almost go mad. Even though I know it's nothing to you, I can still barely stand it. Even when you share a joke with one of your brothers and lay a hand on his sleeve, a ridiculous anger comes over me.

I knew it was different for us when I saw you looking for me during the brigade dance last spring. I caught your eye and you weren't laughing any more. That's why I went outside to wait. When you came out, I walked ahead through the back gate and down to the river. Where the sound of the river was loudest, that's where you caught me up. I put my arms around you and the heat through your dress was like a fire. Your lips were the softest thing I ever touched.

I told you I was afraid to have you in case it harmed you. You told me you wanted me. For all the men sniffing around, I was the first.

Together, we found a place soft enough to lie. You took off your dress and walked around me. You weren't ashamed. Then we mated and I burst inside you. That left me lonely until your fingers started tracing figures on my skin. I looked at myself, half expecting to see something there, maybe some kind of old writing.

But I am not there on that riverbank now, much as I wish I was. I am here on top of the Fur Mountains, this cold high place. The fire has died. I don't imagine you will ever see this letter. I only write it as a means of seeing you, in case I never see you again.

We could have been killed many times by now. I keep that to myself so the men go on believing they're safe. Right this moment there could be loaded weapons in the trees. Why not? Much as I want to come home and lie with you again, why not?

That's enough said. I don't like to think how I'm probably

meant to die, how I'm drawing these men farther from home towards a likely death, and how I'll never see you again. One thing for sure is, if I am allowed to return to you, no man living will take you from me.

Written this 14th day of December, 1822
Edward Harriott

❧

CHESTERFIELD HOUSE, 1822

Harriott and the others had been gone a month and no news. Christmas would soon be here and New Year's after that. One Pound One supposed there would be a rum-soaked attempt at making it homely. He himself would drink no joy if news from the expedition had not come. A good young man and thirty more gone and likely dead, crow and coyote bait in some place of ambush. Their story lost.

A couple of weeks back, on the 2nd of December, McKenzie had sent his first express to Edmonton. Three officers, eight men and an Indian guide. One of the main purposes was to apprise the Governor of the findings of the expedition, and One Pound One had seen McKenzie's letter before it went under seal:

Prospects for Chesterfield House and posts planned in this area poor.

Harriott's expedition south was mentioned only as:

Fate unknown.

In other words, McKenzie admitted sending those men with no expectation of results. *Prospects poor* in spite of not knowing what they'd seen or found.

One Pound One's mood was so dark that, when he heard a Blackfoot threaten inside the fort, he stripped him of bow and arrows, broke every piece and tossed them on the fire. He put his pistol to the man's ear and marched him to the gate and out.

Two days later, there was a scuffle outside the fort between the interpreter Welch and some of the Indians. If Pambrun hadn't come along just then and used considerable force, the interpreter's days could have been over.

After that, the gate was closed and barred.

Two nights of siege followed. McKenzie, in private, scolded One Pound One. Said it was his extremes of behaviour had put them in this mess. We are almost finished here, he said, why threaten our safe return?

That was when One Pound One came closest to grabbing his boss by the throat, the slimmest distance from calling him a killer and a coward and throttling him on the spot. What right had he to speak of the endangerment of lives, meaning his own miserable life, when he had cast off a good young trader and thirty others like so many packs of rotten grease?

❧

THE MISSOURI, 1822

Starving their way south. There was no other way to describe it. Harriott dreamt of past meals. The buffalo ribs in the Bow River camp of the Piegan. He would begin to chew, his jaws moving, his teeth clenching and grinding, a sea of spit welling in his mouth. Sometimes he found himself on his knees in the frozen deer path with no memory of falling.

He hated to look at his men, so little had they eaten since the day they crossed the first south-flowing river. Since then the country had soured, or more so, their luck had gone bad. In high, well-treed hills south of the first river, they had seen game enough but always out of range. One of the men kept firing at a deer beyond reach, firing, reloading, firing, reloading, until Harriott had to hold his own musket to the man's head to make him stop. That was the day they licked the corners of the last grease bag clean and threw it away.

They were to that point of starving where food made them sick. On a shallow wintery lake, they cracked a beaver house for the meat, and that night Harriott awoke several times to the sound of vomiting.

They were now so far from Chesterfield they could not turn back. It would take a starving week just to return to the Fur Mountains, and Harriott could not imagine making it that far.

The Indian guide was consistent in his advice. He kept leading them in a southwest direction where he said they would find a river and buffalo. Harriott believed it was the only way. Find buffalo and wood. Make shelter. Wait for warmer weather.

They were too weak to walk far at a stretch, so he stopped often to rest. The sloping land glittered in the sun. There were only the tracks of small animals in the snow, and few enough of those. To keep the men from eating snow, Harriott carried coals and dry dung and built a fire at every stop.

A rabbit tops the nearest rise, freezes white on white.

The explosion of a fuke.

A puff of snow and then a mourning silence when the snow settles and the rabbit isn't there.

White patches on cheekbones, soon to pain and fester. One man with a rag around his head to keep the light from his snow-blind eyes.

Hopeless.

But Harriott tells them to rise. Makes another speech of hope from his broken lips. A sound like snapping twigs as he unbends his knees, stands as an example. They walk up the side of another bowl of diamonds. Dream a buffalo, a river, a biscuit, the worst meal they've ever eaten. Boiled owl. Hemlock-poisoned beaver. The bright snow is soaked with the sky's pale blue.

When light came pale to the next cold morning, they saw two things that had not been visible the night before. Far ahead, just short of the west horizon, was a curving smudge: the promised valley, the guide said. Closer was a black hump atop the snow, the familiar shape of a buffalo.

They walked to the buffalo and it was no mirage. An old bull, exiled by age but not killed by it. The blood in the snow traced to two close-set wounds fired expertly into the heart. A single horse trail led away.

The carcass was frozen to its core, and the men had to wait for the fire even to eat the first bits raw. Harriott policed the eating all that day, limiting them to what they could digest with their unpractised stomachs, saving as much as possible for the coming days.

Why someone would kill a buffalo in the dead of January and leave it Harriott could not imagine and spent little time wondering. What the buffalo meant to him, beyond immediate salvation, was the possibility of returning to Chesterfield alive. One old bull, carefully husbanded, eaten to the skin and marrow bones, might sustain them to the Fur Mountains. If they could make it that far, they could make it home.

When he shared these thoughts with his men, the Blackfoot guide was adamant against him. A bad plan, he said, a plan that would kill them. The Indian stabbed repeatedly at the smudge near the horizon. There they would find buffalo and fuel and shelter from the north wind. If they holed up there for a week or two, they could fatten themselves. They could jerk meat and journey home without suffering.

When he thought about the guide's words, Harriott saw a further advantage in this plan. If he went to that valley, he could describe a second south-flowing river. That would add to the illusion of his having explored the Missouri watershed for beaver.

So they followed the guide and came to that valley, dense with willow and grey cottonwood. They descended to the river and took a well-tramped trail downcurrent. The guide spoke of a fine camping place less than an hour away.

Sooner than that, they were joined by many mounted Piegan, armed riders who stepped their horses from the trees and began herding them like cattle. A league farther, the trail bent off the river where smudges of smoke marked the pale air above the trees.

They emerged into a meadow, a triangle formed by a recess in the river hills. Fifty tipis or more were arranged in a half-circle, doors to the sun's rise, the area trampled and dotted with horse dung. The Indian horses grazed the edges, pawed the crusted snow.

Told what was happening, the snow-blind man started weeping, tears rolling from the bottom of his head rag. Harriott slapped him hard across the jaw.

"If they meant to kill us, we'd be dead."

Which was more than he believed.

The council tipi was off the curve of the other tents, in the centre of the circle they partially inscribed. Harriott and Sinclair were taken there while the rest of the men were corralled outside. Inside the tent they were told to sit beside an old Piegan who was readying a pipe. When it was given to Harriott, he sucked on it gratefully.

The Indians were in no hurry to talk, and while he waited, Harriott studied every man in every row, hoping to surmise their intention. In so doing he found something better. Near the centre of the farthest ring, against the lodge skin and not far from the seam that marked the door, was Jimmy Jock Bird.

When the speechmaking did begin, it went on for a long time. It was as if these Indians had not spoken to a white trader for a long while and had saved up much to say. They told Harriott of their hatred for the Americans who were trying to come into this country. They were like rabid dogs and the Piegan treated them as such. They spoke too of their displeasure over the Canadian and English companies becoming one. The one simply did not trade as fairly as the two had done before. What if the Americans and the English were the next to marry? How high would the price of a fuke rise then? To *twice* its height in skins?

They told Harriott that sometimes the Piegan thought the best practice might be to kill all the whites, including the English, and go back to the way things were before. If there were no white traders or guns, the Piegan would still be numerous and brave. They could still hold their hunting lands.

In all this speechmaking, Harriott had time to think of his reply. He supposed he would be talking for his life, the presence of a friend notwithstanding. But even if he accepted that his life was at stake, the range of response was limited. If he went beyond the truth and said the Hudson's Bay Company would fight beside the Piegan against the Americans, they wouldn't believe a word.

When the time came, Harriott said what he always said. His

Company wished to continue trading with the Piegan, on whom they relied greatly for buffalo meat, pemmican and beaver pelts. He would happily carry back their request for a fort nearer their hunting lands and farther from their enemies.

During his talk, the Indians became suspicious of, or at least dissatisfied with, Sinclair's translation. They called Jimmy Jock to take over. When Jimmy Jock stood and walked forward, Harriott watched his one-time friend closely. The young man had vanished into an older one. Taller than his father and his brothers, deep in the chest and well developed across the shoulders, he was the finished version of himself. His hair shone with grease, and the beard from his father's bloodline, though shaved, was an erratic tattoo under the skin.

As Jimmy Jock translated, Harriott was struck anew by his friend's gift. Compared to Sinclair's simple words—there was no comparison. More than just translating, Jimmy Jock became Harriott and the other speakers, somehow retaining their personality in his words, even down to the hand gestures.

When the talking was over, Harriott was tied up, dragged to a small tent and thrown inside.

That night, Harriott lay on the ground, so cold under a thin trade blanket that smelled of dog that he thought he might freeze before morning. His hands were full of blood from the tight leather that bound them. The fingers were numb, while his wrists above the string were paining. He longed to be able to rub his aching knees.

On the far side of the tent, a young man sat cross-legged by the door. Harriott could not see his face or much else. When the wind moved the tent flap, a shaft of moonlight over his shoulder winked on the knife held unsheathed across his thighs. He was awake. No one could be that quiet and asleep.

The speeches in the council tipi swirled in Harriott's brain. He was no longer sure what had been said to him, or even what he had replied. He thought of his men sleeping on the frozen ground outside and hoped none would lose his nerve or try to be too brave. He had not been allowed to talk to them after the parley but had seen how the women and children were gathered, reaching out to swat them with sticks.

Then he thought of Jimmy Jock.

Harriott had studied how the Indians had looked at their translator, and it seemed to him they were well pleased. The Piegan, and all the Blackfoot-speakers, were said to regard learning white languages as beneath them. At the same time, they needed someone who had that ability. A good interpreter, if loyal, could acquire status and power in an Indian tribe.

It was nice to dream that Jimmy Jock would be his salvation, but Harriott recognized how foolish he would be to believe it. For whatever reason, Jimmy Jock had left the Company to come here and make his life. Being half-white, it would take him a long time to gain the Piegan's confidence. Time and deeds of bravery were needed. All of which could disappear in a moment were he foolish enough to show favour to someone from his former life. Why *would* Jimmy Jock take that risk for a friendship so ancient and unused as theirs?

Harriott must have gone to sleep, because his next recollection was of two voices speaking Blackfoot in the dark. The younger voice of the two was slurred, a fact explained by the smell of rum and the slap of liquid against wood. The other he knew. Jimmy Jock, talking smoothly, seductively to the guard.

Harriott lay still and listened. Each time the young man spoke, his drunkenness had deepened. He wanted to do something with all that strong feeling. He tried to sing but Jimmy Jock stopped him. Then he got up to dance and Jimmy Jock let him do so. One foot shuffled then the other one stamped, over and over, as he tried to portray his fights and acts of bravery. Once, Harriott heard a swish through the air above his ear. A knife. He was being used as a theatrical property.

The Indian was still at his dance when the rum rose up and drowned his mind. He toppled. Then Jimmy Jock's voice, in Blackfoot still and gentle, murmured for a time, probably reassuring the boy that he, Jimmy Jock, would keep guard while he slept.

Even then, with the boy asleep, Jimmy Jock said nothing. He opened the tent flap, crawled partway out, came back. Looking directly at Harriott for the first time, he put a finger to his lips. Struggling into a sitting position, Harriott turned to show his bound wrists, but Jimmy Jock paid no attention.

When Jimmy Jock did move, it was to conceal the rum keg inside his blanket coat above the sash. Reaching behind Harriott, he caught hold of the leather string and jerked him onto his feet. He dragged him out into the brittle cold.

Held this way, the prisoner had to walk backwards across the camp, in a curving path close to all the doors. The dogs snarled and darted out. Faces came into view in the tipi doorways. It was the opposite of secrecy. Jimmy Jock wanted to be seen and heard by all.

On the far side of the village half-circle, light shone inside a small tipi. A figure moved within. Jimmy Jock shoved Harriott through the door flap and a woman tending the fire shrank back, until Jimmy Jock entered and said something in Blackfoot. The woman looked at both of them, back and forth, then hooked the water kettle over the fire. Jimmy Jock's Piegan wife.

At first, neither the woman nor Jimmy Jock paid Harriott any attention. He used the time to study her. *Pretty* wasn't quite the word, though she was shapely and attractive. What she had was unusual self-assurance, which probably meant she was of a powerful family and had never had to worry about status—until now, when by marrying a Halfbreed interpreter, she'd pushed herself from the centre of the village circle to its edge.

Her eyes when she bothered to look at Harriott were full of contempt. Jimmy Jock had brought home a beggar and offered him tea. She was not pleased.

Now that he was in his home, Jimmy Jock had a more confident and luxuriant air. He removed his capote and arranged a willow backrest so he could sit by the fire facing Harriott. He called his woman and she sat beside him. She poked at the fire with a stick as he stroked her hair. Still it was a long time before a word of English was spoken.

"You look poorly, Ted," Jimmy Jock said finally. "Like a rat in a rubbish pile. This is my bride. She has a Blackfoot name but she permits me to call her Sally."

Sally looked up abruptly. She stared at her husband, puzzled and annoyed that he would disclose her pet name to a lowly white. Jimmy Jock talked to her in Blackfoot, and whatever he said made her bristle and turn away. Jimmy Jock laughed.

"I've just told Sally you were like a little brother to me once. She doesn't care for that at all."

"Why did you get the guard drunk?"

"He was being a nuisance. He wouldn't let me take you to my tent. And I didn't want to talk English in front of him. Now that he's gotten drunk on duty, we share a secret. He'll say what I want him to."

Jimmy Jock lifted a piece of wood in the fire and propped it to burn closer to the kettle.

"I'm not happy to see you, brother. You're trouble for me and you're trouble for yourself. Tell me why you've come to this country like an orphan on foot."

"I'm meant to look for beaver."

Jimmy Jock studied Harriott. The pot over the fire had begun to growl.

"Do they not understand that you can't impress Indians by coming begging into their camp?"

"Maybe I wasn't supposed to get this far."

Jimmy Jock leaned back on the willow rest, stared up at the smoke hole. His one knee was raised, leaning on his wife's slender back as she sat forward watching the fire. Something came to Harriott that should have come sooner.

"It was you who left the buffalo for us."

Jimmy Jock acted as if he did not hear. He became interested in a line of quillwork on his wife's sleeve, and he traced it with a long finger. He was still doing so when he spoke next.

"You stayed young longer than my other brothers. Maybe too long. Now, from what you tell me, you've grown up weak and your uncle can't or won't save you." Jimmy Jock looked away from the quillwork, straight into Harriott's eyes. He was very angry. "The moment you got your orders, you should have gone to your tent and cut your leg with an axe."

"If you've had a hand in keeping me alive, I thank you for it."

"Don't assume I'd take the chance."

Jimmy Jock picked a stick out of the fire and gestured in the air with its fleshy end.

"My father served your Company his whole life. He thought I could go to England and become a gentleman, but they laughed at me there. He couldn't help any of his sons. Now they're all back in Red River hoeing potatoes."

He thrust the stick back into the fire.

"Is that why you're here?" Harriott asked. "Because you couldn't rise in the Company?"

Jimmy Jock looked around the leather room. Something made him laugh.

"You're not the first to think I'm here out of disappointment. Maybe I'm here for the opportunity."

"If you have influence with the Piegan, you have influence with the Company. I understand that."

"Are you such a Company man as all that, Ted? That you can't imagine opportunity that isn't about them?"

The kettle was roaring and Jimmy Jock pointed at it. Sally looked in the pot but wasn't satisfied with the boil.

Watching her, Jimmy Jock said, "I like this place more every day. Part of what makes it so fine is that your Company isn't here. And that we kill the Americans on sight when they try to come."

The boiling water shook the kettle now, and Jimmy Jock's woman took out a leather pouch and sprinkled tea from it into the water. Jimmy Jock took a wooden cup from beside the fire rocks and indicated that he wanted it filled. Sally shook her head. It wasn't ready. But Jimmy Jock insisted. Disapprovingly she poured the cup full.

"But that's the point," said Harriott, "we're here because your people want us here. They want us to build forts. Dammit, Jimmy Jock, untie me!"

"You may be right, Ted. And that may be what you owe your life to. But know this." He struck himself on the breastbone. "I don't want your forts."

"Like everyone else here, you need our guns . . ."

Jimmy Jock reached and grasped Harriott by the coat. With amazing strength he drew him up until the two of them were face to face.

"It makes me angry, little brother, when you talk to me like that. When I hear a trader talk, a Piegan answers."

The wet hit Harriott between the open halves of his shirt. He knew the pain before he felt it, and he wrenched away and curled himself as tight as his back would bend. Then, for a time, he knew nothing.

When he could again open his eyes, Jimmy Jock's face was low beside his, staring at him across the ground.

"Never trust me again," he said.

Jimmy Jock set the empty cup on one of the fire stones. He hauled Harriott to his feet. Saying nothing to his woman, he threw back the tent flap and pushed Ted back into the cold. They crossed the camp as they'd come. At the prison tent, Jimmy Jock pushed Harriott inside and flung him down beside the unconscious guard. The tent smelled of vomit.

Jimmy Jock withdrew but there was no sound of his going. After a time he pulled the leather back and stood in the opening, a faint shadow unmoving.

"Remember that the Company tried to kill you. The Piegan let you live. But if you come back here, I'll kill you myself."

❧

FORT EDMONTON, 1822

The Governor spent the first half of the Bow River Expedition winter in the Athabasca country, sorting out its brigade routes, portages and timetables. Travelling by dog team from Lesser Slave Lake, he arrived at Fort Edmonton just before Christmas.

As the exhausted dogs pulled the final mile, the valley was revealed, with Edmonton's frozen fort giving up a few curls of smoke. But the flag was down and the only musket fired belonged to the man who opened the gate. At the sound a few sleepy-looking individuals stepped from their cabins into the square. Temporary Chief Factor Mr. Colin Robertson was not among them.

The Governor strode past the brainless onlookers to the main house of the fort and knocked heavily on its door. It was a long time, minutes, before Robertson opened it, a tall loose-built man with a mane of white hair, a ruddy face and round, comical eyes set too close together. There was a smear of chocolate in one of his muttonchop whiskers, and in his hand he held an open book. He looked back across his shoulder as if trying to account for why it was he who was answering the door. His legs were naked and extremely white, an absurd sight.

"Mr. Robertson."

"Good heavens! Governor! When did you arrive?"

"Didn't you hear your own fort's gun?"

"I thought it was some lesser event. Pardon me. I was engrossed in my book. Please, come in."

The room was a mess, dishes still on the table, mud on the floor. There was a smell of mice and milk gone bad. The woman of the house was nowhere to be seen. Robertson pointed at a chair near the fire, but the Governor preferred to stand.

"That must be a very good book. What is its subject?"

"Us, sir."

"What do you mean *us?* The English? The Scots?"

"Fur traders, sir."

"I'm sorry. My mind wanders when you're being witty."

"Not trying to be funny, sir. They do write books about us now. I received this one in the fall mail. The Company men are shown as noble chaps, vigorous and brave, fighting for England among the blood-thirsty savages."

"And you find that humorous."

"I find it inspiring."

"I'm glad you have something with which to occupy your time. I find mine is much taken up with business. Are you drunk, by the way?"

"No, sir. Though I find chocolate has a heady effect."

"What do you hear of the Bow River Expedition?"

"Not a peep. I wonder some days if they're still alive."

The Governor felt a flush of heat come over him. He was recalling the Department Council meeting in the summer and how Robertson had tried to interrupt him during his explanation of the plan for Bow River. He had been trying to say something about Peter Fidler, another Company ancient who was presently dying at Red River.

"Mr. Robertson, every time you speak on the subject of the Bow River Expedition, I find you are pessimistic and that you hint at information none of the rest of us has. I would be much obliged if you would speak up once and for all, if you know something I should know."

"Only an opinion, sir. It seems to me that if there were a great many beaver on the Missouri, we'd've heard by now. If this expedition had found them, they'd be more anxious to brag. That's all. If you'll excuse me, I'll put on some clothes and find Theresa. She can get us some tea."

"No. I am not finished. I'm going to be blunt with you, Robertson. We are grown men. I don't see the point of being otherwise. I know you resent being sent here this winter to replace One Pound One. I suppose this greeting is your way of signifying it. I suspect as well you think I was a poor choice as governor. But whatever my experience and yours, I will have the respect of every man in my department, one way or the other."

"Well said, Governor."

As Robertson turned and walked away, the Governor saw the man's eyes lower to the page. He read his way from the room.

A few days later, on December 21st, McKenzie's express from Chesterfield House arrived at Fort Edmonton. The Governor was still present and went down to the river as the gaunt messengers were brought over the ice and black water. Manson, Munro, Douglas and the rest, all reduced to skeletons. They had come on foot in bad weather and had slept several nights on the prairie without food or fire.

The Governor took the letter they had brought and read it quickly. He thrust it into a pocket, turned, and started brusquely up the trail.

Back in the fort, he crossed to the main residence. He entered Robertson's house without knocking and walked through to the office. When he opened that final door, Robertson was carefully blotting a letter at the desk.

"I was about to come out, sir. How are the fellows from Chesterfield? Something wrong?"

The Governor pulled the letter from his coat and spread it flat on Robertson's desk. He knocked on it lightly with his fist but said nothing.

Holding it close to his eyes, Robertson read it twice. Then he set it down and lowered his head as if to pray.

"Too bad. I hope young Harriott isn't lost. I've known him since he was a boy."

The Governor had been standing back two steps while the other read, tapping the floor rapidly with the toe of one shoe.

"I find I have had enough of this, Mr. Robertson."

"What on earth are you talking about?"

"The last of your smugness and cheek that I will tolerate."

"Now, sir, let's not have . . ."

"You would be well advised to shut up right now until I have spoken. I do not lose my temper. It is my rule. But you push me near it today."

"But I have done nothing."

"Normally, that's what you do best."

"I have fought duels. I have defended Company forts with hot musket balls whizzing by my ears. But, in terms of your being my Governor, I do as I'm asked. For example, I am here this winter."

"Then do as I ask one more time and tell me how you knew this expedition would fail."

Robertson was silenced. He turned his chair to face the Governor, slumped back deeply in it with his legs splayed. He closed his eyes and opened them, sad as a dog's.

"I've not been on the Bow River or the Missouri."

"Don't evade me. You knew something."

"I knew only what Mr. Fidler told me."

"What are you saying? That Fidler knew these rivers?"

"I'm not sure how many. I'm not sure he went as far as the Missouri. I doubt that. But he spent the winter of '02 with the Piegan somewhere near the mountains."

"And what had he to say?"

"That the country was extremely beautiful, but not abundant in beaver. Not sufficient to warrant forts, especially since at that time the Blackfoot didn't want them."

Some men when they feel most compelled to violence will force themselves, as a discipline, to do something precise and small. The Governor picked up the letter, folded it neatly, and put it back in his pocket.

"And you felt no responsibility to tell me this."

"I did, sir. At the Council last summer. I tried to turn your attention to it, but you were busy with other matters."

The Governor stood with arms folded. He stared at Robertson, unblinking.

"You know that's a lie. You should never challenge me on memory, as mine is near flawless. What I remember is asking you near the end of the meeting to have your say. But you, Mr. Colin Robertson, were too vain to repeat yourself. I had told you earlier to be quiet, to hold your comments. This wounded your pride and you decided to wound me back. But you cannot hurt me. You lack the power. What you have done instead is hurt these other men, this Harriott of whom you allege to be so fond and some thirty others. A high price to exact for a small insult."

Robertson closed his eyes again. He stroked a hand through his long white hair, fondly.

"What do you plan to do with me, sir?"

"Nothing."

The Governor said the word through a grim smile, then waited as if to exemplify what nothing meant.

"Yes, nothing. I expect that in itself will become an adequate punishment. Given sufficient time. After that, we'll see."

❦

CHESTERFIELD HOUSE, 1823

The New Year's regale was a week behind them, as drunk an occasion as One Pound One could remember. It proved that men will drink the same in reunion or loneliness, happiness or sorrow. With laughter and bragging, it began. Jig dancing followed: the men taking turns beating their feet on a noisy plank. Then argument: who was the best dancer, hunter, fucker, fighter. After which the fur began to fly.

As predictable as cattle.

The sole exception were those in whom liquor fired lust more than violence. These he tried to collar on their way out to the Indians, but really it was like catching sugar in a sieve. They left with their hair greased to gleaming, feathers in their hats, and trailed in next day with their eyes punched closed, and probably poxed. One Pound One wished them Happy New Year by putting them over the cannon, to make them that bit sorrier still.

Mind you, One Pound One had settled scores of his own at the New Year's regale. With those who thought themselves clever. He hated men laughing behind his back and felt it was happening more the deeper they sank into winter. One by one, he chose them out and showered them with verbal abuse until they could stand it no longer. They came at him with a kick or a wild roundhouse punch. His art was to walk inside, close with them, chop them down with blows to the body. It never hurt to prove to the enlisted men that they hadn't a prayer against you. When they fought a man of higher rank, they fought their fear as much as you. It made them distracted and weak. They all but worshipped you for half killing them. They made no further trouble afterwards.

Undeniably, his mood had been blacker that night for the business with Harriott, who was nothing now but a silence to the south, a little something missing beneath the brief arc of the sun. But when the New Year's ache in his head subsided, One Pound One discovered that his feeling of loss over Harriott had disappeared.

Nor did he struggle to bring it back. Death was common in this country. It did not pay to mourn for long. Why risk catching whatever it was that slowed people enough for death to catch them? A pity about Harriott and his men, and always would be, but two days into 1823, One Pound One ceased to brood about it.

Then the express returned from Edmonton. A pathetic sight. Manson and the others, with a pair of Indian guides. They had seen no game for nine days and had eaten that number of dogs to stay alive. One Pound One and McKenzie extracted their news while they fed, then let them sleep. They had almost nothing to say, despite the Governor's having been at Fort Edmonton to receive them. He had met the news that the Bow River Expedition had failed with near total silence.

Winter's fastness began to settle heavily. Blue days, cold as iron, where the devotions of daylight were scrounging wood and checking traps. The buffalo were long gone except for the odd ancient bull, the hun-ters having scorched the earth to every horizon of all other hoofed beasts.

Darkness came early, ushering in a half-hungry vigil before each smoking fire. Looking at the faces of the men as sleep stole upon them, you'd think crows had come and pecked out their brains.

Then, in the afternoon of January 11th, the bastion lookout saw a cluster of specks against the snow. He squinted hard into the sun before shouting down.

"Men! On foot!"

Then, moments later:

"Men with beards!"

But how many?

After counting and recounting, he proclaimed a number that caused a roar of approval from the people clustered below. Rotten hats flew up. In all that time, only one man was missing. Even that deficit did not mean a death, it turned out. The missing one was the Indian guide who had betrayed them and stayed on the Missouri.

The gate of Chesterfield swung open. A crowd descended to the riverbank. A pair of frozen bull boats were thrown into the black water and poled across to the three-foot crusts of ice along the far shore. One by one, Harriott's men were lowered into the boats and fetched across. Stinking, bearded, ragged. They were mobbed and kissed none the less for that. A horse was killed and some of the blood and raw organ meat was fed to them, their teeth so loose they could only suck, not chew.

The cannon pounded and echoed until McKenzie ordered it stopped, lest it overheat and split. The muskets kept blasting, though, until the air was putrid grey.

Last to cross was Harriott. One Pound One smiled his brown smile to see his friend and how he sat, slim and straight, fragile hands gripping the round rail. His head was bare and his wispy hair fanned backwards. Where the other men had arrived all desperate, clawing the air for the slop of bloody horsemeat, Harriott rode like an angel, his sunken grey eyes soft and pleasant, blurred as if he had seen God in his travels and had his earthly worries erased.

Looking for a hero, the men of the fort crowded around Harriott. They tossed him, light as hollow bones, to their shoulders, many hands reaching up to hold him balanced. They set him down before Donald McKenzie, who clasped his junior officer's hand between both of his, eyes sparkling tears.

"Is my horse alive?" said Harriott through split lips.

McKenzie turned and gestured towards a corner of the palisade, and there stood Small, chewing eagerly, ears alert, and in better flesh than most of the men. A pile of grass lay atop the snow, pulled for her by someone. She nickered at him and went back to her food.

"You have missed the New Year's regale, Mr. Harriott," McKenzie said. "There will be another punishment of the rum tonight. In your honour."

Everyone cheered. The gate slammed shut to keep the Indians out. Two of the last kegs were fetched.

One Pound One lit their way with a tallow candle, a weaving progress across the tramped snow, aiming for a rock-chimneyed house across the yard. He had his arm stretched comically around Harriott's taller shoulders, while Harriott sang off-key, replacing most of the words of an old sea shanty with his own nonsense.

"They can think us bum boys if they like, Ted, but from now on you live with me. I'll sleep on the floor. You take the bed. Tomorrow I'll put a couple of these lazy bastards to work. Build you a bed of your own."

One Pound One kicked his door open, staggered into the stinking dark. He hung the candle from a nail in the beam, then scrabbled on his shelf. He knocked a tin plate to the floor before he came away with wooden cups. His keg was under a false floorboard. He lifted it out and gave it a shake.

"Oh well. Enough to blow out the lamp."

"I'll be sick," said Harriott from his chair.

"Go on, then. Go out and puke. Feel at home."

One Pound One slapped the door shut.

"There, ya big-eared gits."

Ignoring or forgetting what Harriott had said, he spilled the keg's contents into the cups. Harriott, just as forgetful, thumped his cup against the other and took a swallow. One Pound One sat on the bed.

"Ah, Ted. What a jump it gave me to see you walk in here. *As back from the dead.* That's exactly what I said out loud. Ask Pambrun if you don't believe me. Old McKenzie's heart must've give out at the sight."

"He was relieved to see us."

"Aye, maybe. Bury the hatchet. But goddamn if you didn't flummox the bastard anyway. You'll make chief trader out of it. First parchment same as your uncle, in half the time. And better earned, since it'll be for bravery."

Harriott shook his head to clear it. It was full of birds.

"I'm satisfied to be alive."

"Don't be humble, goddamn ye! Go to hell and back? Come out with all hands?"

"And with bad news."

One Pound One flopped back, had likely forgotten that he meant to offer his bed. He tensed and pressed out a fart.

"Fucked if that's your fault. You're a good man just to have survived. You must've had more scrapes than you're admitting."

"Not really. The guide betrayed us, I told you that. I had to talk our way out of a camp of Piegan on the Marias River . . ."

"A river no Bay Company man knew existed! That's like Fidler. Like Thompson. That's exploring."

In the middle of this speech of praise, One Pound One began to snore. Harriott watched his friend's bulk rise and fall, the loose lips flapping. The cup of rum stayed hooked on his finger, just off the edge of the bed, a little rum spilling each time the body filled with air. Harriott pulled it off and set it on the floor.

Alone and drunk, rum screaming in his brain, he still did not sleep, would not let himself. He held on to a shore just this side of oblivion and, carefully as he could, thought over what he'd told McKenzie. *No beaver. Not enough to warrant forts.* Not a lie. But a little less than the truth.

As to motive, that was simple enough. As Jimmy Jock had said, the Company, or McKenzie at least, had tried to kill him. If he needed more reason, Jimmy Jock had provided that as well. If Harriott said there were no beaver, there would likely be no forts. If there were no forts, he would never be forced to return, and Jimmy Jock would never be obliged to kill him.

Harriott tried to lie down on the wooden floor next to One Pound One's bed, but all balance deserted him. He pitched face first into the floor. He smelled pine sap and his own blood, but he waved away the pain and let his muscles turn to sponge. He merged with the cold plank while staccato visions of his men darted in his brain. They danced and humped the air for lack of women, and somewhere in the same picture, Margaret knitted and played with his unborn children.

Let the Company keep its parchments. All he wanted was Margaret. Given charge of some insignificant post, he and Margaret would live happily. He would mould his men with kindness. He would turn them human. He would give the Company no excuse to try to kill him again.

❦

It was March, and the frozen stillness at Chesterfield was altered by occasional blizzards. The storm before the calm. Some days the season forgot itself, and strong warm winds blew in from the west, enough to wet the snow. McKenzie and One Pound One had everyone working on the boats, making compounds from pitch and cloth and riverbank clay to render them riverworthy again.

At night, the expedition officers sat around a table in the main shed, sharing an inkpot and a candle, penning their reports. How many Indians lived in the lands they had visited? How many beaver? Each man in his own way skirted the issue of why the Governor thought there'd be so many beaver where there were so few.

A similar diplomacy was at work when the reporters commented on each other. The summaries were brief and flattering. The place to look for truth was in the slightest qualification, such as when One Pound One complimented McKenzie's reasonable leadership, considering the delicacy of his health. One Pound One showed that comment to Harriott across the candle they were sharing and winked.

Looking at them all at their work, Harriott felt he could almost divine the future by the physical attitude of each man. One Pound One, who wrote slowly and with difficulty, was at the same time jubilant. On the Bow River Expedition, he had been allowed to look for nothing and therefore could not be faulted for finding nothing. The reverse was Francis Heron, who wrote on pages torn from his journal, three

destroyed for every one kept. He could have been writing his own obit-
uary, given the gravity of his appearance, and perhaps he was.

At the head of the table board, Donald McKenzie didn't seem
bothered by the task, though he certainly filled many a page. In a career
as long as his, maybe this winter's events were not so uncommon. At
worst he might have no more expeditions to lead, and was that such a
bad thing for a man his age?

In his own report, Harriott strove to be as mundane as possible.
Even the revenge he took on the Company was quiet. When it came to
talking about how many beaver he'd seen on the Missouri, he sub-
tracted about half of the not very large number. Beyond that the only
thing he kept back was the number of beaver skins he'd seen in tents
and stretching on hoops in Jimmy Jock's camp. "No forts in this region
seem warranted" was his conclusion, when the foothills of the Missouri
watershed and its mountain headwaters could have been crawling with
beaver for all he knew.

Of the actual departure, not much need be said. The ice began to
move. The boats were arrayed along the shore. To the last, McKenzie
believed in an attack and, even as they were loading, sent One Pound
One to smoke with the Indians and tell them pacifying lies.

Don't worry over the abandonment of Chesterfield. A bigger and
better fort will rise. Somewhere. Sometime.

In late April the boats took to the river, and Harriott on his robust
mare led a string of men overland.

Behind them, the third and final relic of Chesterfield House began
its decay. As the boats rounded the bend, and as the land brigade topped
the valley rise, the first of the palisades came down, to feed Indian fires
or to be loaded onto travois for the crossing of the treeless plains.

THE
GOVERNOR'S
MISTRESS

1823–1825

PRO PELLE CUTEM

Dear Editor,

I've got a grandson chases cows near Medicine Hat. I told him about Chesterfield and where it was and he decided to ride up there and have a look. He told me he scouted up and down the north shore for a day and found nothing. Time had wiped the place out. There should have been some hearthstones in the grass but he didn't find them.

The story of that expedition disappeared in a way too. On account of it was a failure, the first big one on the Governor's head, there was a curse on it. Folks saw what happened to the ones blamed and they learned to button their lip.

Francis Heron was one who said there would be a lot of beaver and for years afterwards he was posted to the coldest northern forts. His career came to nothing. Colin Robertson was blamed too for something to do with it, I don't know what. His punishment went on for decades. If there was a dirty, thankless, hopeless job, Robertson got it.

The one I don't understand is Mr. Harriott. It seems he should have been a hero but I never heard anyone say he was. And trouble seemed to follow him forever after.

The only officer that Bow River did any good for was One Pound One, which proves the saying that the devil likes to leave his manure on the biggest pile.

William Gladstone

YORK FACTORY, 1824

In the summer of 1824, One Pound One was invited to the Northern Department Council. He had been to York Factory with the brigade three times, but the invitation to sit with council was new. He took it to mean that his promotion to Chief Factor was ready for announcement.

Council convened at nine in the morning following a drunken spree, and wearing a head like a canoe, One Pound One ran into the meeting chamber at quarter to the hour to meekly take the only seat left save the Governor's throne.

The Chief Factors ignored him. Having pushed themselves back to make room for their bellies, they sat with legs crossed, tugging at pipes and muttering smoke in one another's ears. The sound of them together was a growling like sled dogs at breakfast.

The first signal that the Governor would arrive was a bunch of boys with urns and mugs. They ran in, poured coffee and left. A churchly silence fell. When the door opened again, it was the Governor's secretary, a monkish, soft man who twisted at the waist when he walked and held a bushel of loose paper trapped to his fatty chest. He set the paper down by bowing flat over the table board, and the view of his tonsured scalp was embarrassing, like a sudden glimpse of a bared ass. The secretary went back to the door and stood by it at attention.

The Governor strode in briskly, high colour on his cheeks, red hair tufting upwards, chest bigger than a barrel. He nodded to this one and that one, made noises of greeting to them all. He walked in front of the chair at the table's head, flapped his coattails and sat. The secretary's job was to get the chair under him before he dropped.

One Pound One thought himself primed for whatever the Governor said today. He had vowed to learn everything. But when the Governor spoke, the sudden burst of speech panicked the Chief Trader entirely. It was like a horse race when you think the field is matched. Then the gun fires and one explodes away. The Governor must have been speaking thrice normal pace, and try as he would, One Pound One could not absorb it.

Fool, he castigated himself, nitwit. Damnye, think!

The first part, as far as One Pound One could tell, was about a personal undertaking by the Governor for the coming outfit. "A transcontinental voyage," he called it, from here to Fort Vancouver, leaving as soon as possible. He so emphasized the need for hurry, repeating it several times, that you expected him to jump up and bolt at any second.

What it was to be was an "investigation of the Lac La Biche route to the Athabasca," after which the Governor would cross the mountains, travel down the Columbia to Vancouver, and spend the winter there with Chief Factor Dr. McLoughlin. Come spring, he would return by the Athabasca route.

"My intention is to be back at York Factory in time to chair the next sitting of this council."

One Pound One looked around to see if anyone else was as dizzy as he was at this amazing traverse of territory. If they were, they weren't letting on. They continued to stare and puff their pipes, trying to look grave and intelligent.

After an hour, One Pound One was sweating with exertion, but he was also beginning to keep up. The Governor's rapid talk had a rhythm, and the trader was acquiring a feel for it.

Go fast. Stop. Look around as if for comment. Move on quickly before comment comes.

If the Governor reared back and slapped himself on the chest, that was the signal to laugh. The Chief Factors readily responded, and their attempts at mirth were pathetic or frightening. Glowering mouths full of black sticks of teeth, a laughter that expelled a stink into the room.

The sight reminded One Pound One of how dogs will grin in imitation of the human.

One Pound One had met most of these men before on their own ground, in their own forts, and there they were individual and formidable. Each had his own superstitions and cravings, and the violent nature they seemed to share was tapped in different ways that you had to learn for your own safety. This one was religious; that one more like the devil himself. Several had a studious bent, a devotion to something useless. The naming of plants. The taming of wild animals.

The interesting thing was how, in the presence of the Governor, they were all rendered mute and similar. Like monks at Catholic service, they nodded and bowed in unison, burst into laughter all at once. When they weren't laughing, they furrowed their brows in pensive study that was also laughably false. By the force of the Governor, they had been made witless. They could not think but only imitate.

Two men stood out as different from the mob: James Bird and Colin Robertson. Robertson would have stood out anywhere, mind you, save in a circus or on a London stage. His Halfbreed wife had put all manner of beads in his white hair, and he'd found some military trousers with a scarlet stripe down the outside of each leg. The trousers were too small, in the ass especially, and this, in a caricature way, seemed to account for his red face.

Given the rumours of how out of favour Robertson was, the old fool should have sought the protection of silence, but instead he butted in frequently and even tried a joke in contest with the Governor's own.

It came when the Governor was onto his favourite topic of department economy, speaking long and passionately about every sixpence snipped from debit. This turned into a harangue—under a thin pretence of humour—against the Chief Factors for keeping Indian and Halfbreed women, and putting endless babies inside them. This "all-too-bounteous crop of Halfbreed spawn," he said, was the greatest threat of all to Company economy.

You could feel a chill go round the room. That he was talking about their wives and children, and not some bunch of tarts and urchins, was either lost on the Governor or made no difference to him.

"Why not take a page out of Nature's book?" he said with a smirk.

"Be a buck to your heart's content but return to the bachelor herd when the breeding's done. Find yourself another prime female when the rut resumes."

That was when Robertson popped up with his joke.

"A page from Nature's book," he said, "*and* from the Governor's own."

The remark drew no laughter, not a sound. One Pound One might have laughed himself except for how hard he was thinking about this bachelor herd and rutting business. He was desperate to please the Governor, would have jumped off a cliff into a lake had he been asked, but this bachelor edict didn't appeal to him.

Like a towering hail cloud, his country wife Louise rose in his mind. He could not see past her. She blocked the sky. From behind her skirts, his Halfbreed children peeked out and grinned. His cheeky girls and the toddling son he had named after himself.

The thing about turning Louise away was that she would not go, not calmly. If One Pound One made her go, she'd return and take a dangerous revenge. Add to that the fact that he was passing fond of his children.

The truth on this subject, which even Colin Robertson wouldn't speak, was that the Governor was turning out bastards at as fast a rate as anybody, more, probably, because he didn't confine himself to a single woman. Though he had a favourite mistress, a Halfbreed named Miss Margaret Taylor, whose children he acknowledged as his own, there were several more mistresses and children he would neither confirm nor deny.

At any rate, the moment passed and the Governor moved on to another aspect of Company business: Red River and what a seemingly useless accumulation of people it was. As that district's Chief Factor, James Bird Senior was eventually jabbed into a rebuttal.

If possible, Bird was even more damned in the Governor's eyes than Colin Robertson, for having strongly advocated the Bow River fiasco. But as Bird rose to speak, he had the old stately air of the governor he'd once been. Fearless, as only those beyond ambition can be.

"You put half the people in the Northwest out of work and coax them to my district. And you tell them to farm. First of all, they know nothing about farming. Second, there aren't enough implements in the settlement to plough a garden let alone feed thousands."

The Governor smirked in response.

"It was my understanding, Mr. Bird, that you had more farm implements than that yourself." The Governor looked at the others for appreciation of his witticism.

Bird did not flinch, nor swerve from his argument. "I bought those implements with my own savings, from years of service to this Company. I'll be damned if I will donate them to the charity of Red River. What I'm asking is for some sensible plan for what these Halfbreeds are to do with themselves, short of starving or robbing me."

The Governor waited for Bird to stop. He stared up into the corners of the room, first one and then another, as if two swallows were building nests. Then, waking from his dream, he shook his head slightly and spoke.

"I have no such plan for Red River, Mr. Bird. And I rather hope you do not either. You solved the problem of Red River unemployment last season with your Bow River Expedition. If you have another such scheme up your sleeve, leave it there, as the Company will never afford a benevolence on that scale again. As I said earlier, the Company did not ask its men to produce endless Halfbreed bastards, nor is the Company under any obligation because you went ahead and did so. We will hire them as we need them. And no more."

One Pound One felt the point of these barbs as if each one were meant for him. But Bird took them easily, as if they were no more than what he'd expected.

"I wonder if you'd be so calm," he continued firmly, "if you were living at Red River and could smell the stink of rebellion as I do."

The Governor cocked his pug nose and snuffed through it. "I quite agree that Red River smells. I can almost smell it from here. But unless rebellion and manure smell alike, I'm not sure I understand your point."

The Chief Factors exploded into laughter. While they were still chortling and shaking their heads at the Governor's wit, the man himself consulted his secretary's timepiece. When the laughter died, he insisted they move on.

At long last they came to the place on the agenda One Pound One had been waiting for: appointments for the upcoming year. If he was going to get his promotion to Chief Factor, it would be announced now. It took forever to get down the list to Edmonton, and as it approached, One Pound One felt his breath catching. He could not seem to get air both into and out of himself without struggle. At the words meant for him—*will continue in charge of Edmonton House as Chief Trader*—he snorted, a sound he had not intended to make.

No promotion. No promise nor hint of a promotion. At very least, he must wait another year.

As the recitation went on, One Pound One did not listen or try to. He sat alone in the silence of his disappointment. If the others saw him at his brooding he didn't care. He didn't care because he didn't want them thinking he accepted this setback calmly. The truth was he had all the duties of a Chief Factor without the title or the Company share. His career stood still.

Only one sentence from the remaining litany was heard by One Pound One, and that was the news that Harriott again remained a clerk at his uncle's emporium of Fort Carlton. If there was ever proof of the folly of taking disappointment well, Harriott was it. After Bow River, he had trotted home to Carlton, smiling and happy to take up his old duties, happiest of all to be back at kissing distance from his cousin Margaret; and seeing such joy, the Company saved sixpence and left him be a clerk, possibly forever.

As the meeting was about to break up, Colin Robertson rose and asked if they might observe a moment's silence for the explorer Peter Fidler, who had died the previous winter. The Governor complied, but if anyone was counting, his head stayed down nowhere near sixty seconds. He was impatient with this moment of solemnity, an unexplained irritation aimed at Colin Robertson.

As always, there was plenty of hubbub before the brigades left the Bay. One Pound One was out on the river shore, pushing taller folks aside to watch a fight he'd bet on, when a sharp tug pulled his sleeve. Lucky for him he didn't swipe back and bash whomever it was, for it turned out to be the Governor.

The Governor drew him away, a long ways away to where he could speak in a normal voice and not compete with the shouting. He had a proposition for One Pound One, he said, a challenge.

"I'm on my way west to test the Lac la Biche route to the Athabasca River. As you're headed west as well, what say we race? You with the brigade and I with my north canoe racing for Fort Assiniboine."

One Pound One grinned back so hard it made the corners of his mouth sore. He tried in every way to act pleased. Inside himself was a painful welling of the opposite. At a glance he could see what it meant. He would have to hurry the brigade more than usual, which was unpleasant to start with. Then, when he made Edmonton, he'd have to trade boat for horse and ride through the muck to Fort Assiniboine. Was there a man in his right mind would welcome that?

"If I precede you at Fort Assiniboine, which logically I should," the Governor continued, "I will not wait. That would waste time. We can simply mark the dates and compare them by letter. On the rare chance you get there first, you must stay, as I could not possibly be far behind."

The whole thing was ludicrous, as a contest particularly. While One Pound One and his men started upriver the next day, loaded with trade pieces, the Governor and his picked paddlers stayed behind to enjoy a day or two more of York Factory's festivities. While they ate and drank their fill, One Pound One and his racing side met the river current at the end of tidewater, cast out lines, and tracked.

The low country gave way to rocks and the staircase of rapids called Hill Mountain. At the Dramstone, One Pound One let the men drink and enjoy a few hours' rest. Damned if he felt like bringing out the lash in the name of some contest he was certain to lose, which he was probably wise to lose.

Somewhere in this stretch of time, the Governor would have gone whizzing past on a river to the north of them. One Pound One imagined him sitting in the canoe like a little king as his paddlers dug up the current like fools.

FORT ASSINIBOINE, 1824

Weeks later, One Pound One and his brigade made Edmonton. Dropping with fatigue, he staggered from river to fort, his bad leg so tight and frozen it practically dragged behind him. The pain in it made him furious. At the dinner table, Louise demanded to know why he was eating so fast. He hadn't told her yet that he was leaving again.

"After a thousand miles of river, can't a man eat in peace?"

"If you call that peaceful eating," she said.

Still chewing the last mouthful, he got up from the table and went out to the stable. Louise followed him, and the whole tribe of their children behind her.

"Where do you think you're going now?"

"To London, England. Where I intend to be a duke."

He chose a horse and the stable hand saddled it.

"You're a fool not to spend the night, no matter what you've been told to do."

"I'm keeping the Governor waiting as it is. Should I tell him for an excuse that my nagging woman demanded I stay the night?"

"If you sleep in a mud hole, that will make him happier?"

"Back now. I don't have time for this."

He stood by the tall horse and signalled for the stable hand to hurry and give him his hands as a step. His children were all around the gelding's legs.

"Get back, you rabble!"

He swung at them with his riding crop, twisted the horse around and goaded it into a gallop. Out the gate and away to the northwest.

Dismal journey. Picking his way through gloomy muskegs and places where deadfall blocked the trail. His back was tortured, and he filled the broody silence with the fustiest oaths he knew. All he wanted was the business over so he could get back to Edmonton and more important matters, but it wasn't possible to make Assiniboine in a day. He camped in the shallow valley with plenty of wolves for company, sleeping light with his hand on his fuke lest a rabid one sneak in and bite his face.

Late the next day, he swam his horse across the Athabasca, to the opposite shore where Fort Assiniboine stood. The few inhabitants were drowsing in front of a fire. He kicked the chair out from under the lazy clerk in charge and demanded to know how many days ago the Governor had passed. The troubling answer was that the Governor had not yet been.

The days that followed were idle and nervous. One Pound One could think only that his leader had met with disaster, and he was not sure what to do in that case. Each day he took the clerk and rode along the river east, as far as they could go and get back at night to sleep. By the sixth day, he was packing for an expedition, a search party. He was not yet under way when the Governor's north canoe rounded the river bend into sight.

Watching the voyageurs fight with the current to get the north canoe ashore, One Pound One was almost pulled apart by contrary feelings. In one way he was profoundly relieved; in another he felt sorry dread. The Governor took such pride in his speed on the water that One Pound One feared this "victory" might cost him the Governor's friendship.

But as the Governor's paddlers carried him up from the gravel shore, the man was grinning. He greeted One Pound One heartily, clapping him on the back, and after hearing how long One Pound One had been waiting, his mood rose further into euphoria. The only thing that darkened him at all was when One Pound One asked the reason for his delay.

"Damn fools who recommended that direction should be flogged! The Beaver River is hardly a river at all. Light as we were, we had to drag. It meanders all about and is full of sand."

Cheering up again, the Governor knocked One Pound One on the chest.

"I wonder if you know what you've discovered."

In truth, One Pound One had no idea.

"*You,* my good man," the Governor spoke dramatically, "have inspired me to revise the entire transportation network from the Athabasca to the Pacific."

One Pound One was attempting to look both canny and curious.

The Governor grabbed a stick and began drawing in the gravel and sand.

"Now that I know what speed can be made to Edmonton, I will cut a road from there to here. The brigades will come direct to Edmonton, then by horse train direct to here. Here at Assiniboine, we reload onto a second set of boats, some of which will go to the mountains, and the rest the other way, to the Athabasca."

At the top of his drawing he made an oblong shape and stabbed it. Lake Athabasca.

One Pound One grunted enthusiasm and tried to keep the man-killing rapids on the Athabasca River north of Lac la Biche out of his thoughts. The Governor continued in the same schoolmasterish way.

"Do you see how this plays to your advantage, John?"

One Pound One still had no idea what his boss was talking about. The Governor held up his drawing stick and wagged it in front of his face.

"You must think quickly if you are to be my man at Edmonton. This change will make that fort a bustling place. If you can handle the responsibility, a good deal of power will be yours."

Ten days after his departure for Fort Assiniboine, One Pound One returned to Edmonton. He returned so puffed with pride he could barely see out of himself. Escaping Louise and his children, he walked his palisades that night, trying hard to imagine the new fort that would rise. Soon he would tear down this rickety agglomeration of forts Augustus and Edmonton and build something really grand. Something high up that you could see for a long way.

Horses, he was also thinking. To meet the proposed portaging plans, Edmonton would need a herd several times as large as the present one. Almost certainly the Company would give him its blessing and resources to buy good animals, until all the best equine blood in the country was present here.

A hot excitement rose in One Pound One to think of what splendid runners a plan like that could produce. Above this spot, on a high plateau, he would build a racetrack. He would start having it cleared and levelled this spring. The reputation he'd make among the Indians by beating their best horses—the Company had to see the utility in that.

One Pound One looked around at the old fort and he asked questions aloud.

"Why does a fort have to be colourless? Featureless?"

Indians loved decoration. Why not bring them into a trading hall that was painted gaudy colours and whose ceiling was done up in fancy forms of plaster, like the big buildings and churches in Montreal?

"Why not paint pictures on the damn walls?"

Since the prairie Indians went in for triangles and such, pictures of actual creatures, ordinary and fanciful, would be a great novelty to them. Who knew how far they would journey to see such wonders?

Ah yes, with the power in his hands, what couldn't a good man do?

❧

FORT EDMONTON, 1825

Near the end of February, the outfit of 1824–25, One Pound One sat at his desk in a corner room of the Edmonton Big House that he called his office. His wife and children were strictly forbidden to enter there. The fire was smoking badly and diamonds of frost glittered on two of the walls. On the tabletop, between a porringer of steaming tea and a line of clay pipes arranged according to heat, sat a letter.

During its cariole ride to Edmonton, the letter had soaked up damp from a leaking keg. It had dried in waves that crackled each time he pounded them flat. The letter was brown. Its lines wept ink. He blew fans of pipe smoke across its surface.

One Pound One hated this letter. If you could burn a letter and incinerate its consequences, eliminate the cause of its being written, this one would be ash.

Ft. Carlton, January 1825

Dear John,

Another winter for me and Margaret at old Carlton and my duties much the same. It's hard not to dwell on it, having been here every season since a boy, except for our time at Chesterfield. Then again, if I turn my mind to better tidings, I suppose there are some. We're healthy if a little hungry.

I hear when it comes to buffalo it's the same for you. The earth has swallowed them and the Indians say it's God's displeasure over something. We laugh but I haven't a better explanation for why they surround you one year and disappear the next.

Whatever else, I should be glad Margaret and I live in the same fort. If there was bell, book and candle, I'd have married her by now. As there's not, and as her father objects, I'll wait, for what I'm not sure, maybe until a promotion or some heroic deed proves me worthy.

Enough of that. I know how little interested you are in romance.

Actually, I have to say one more thing about Margaret. When the Governor passed this way on his return from Fort Vancouver, two falls ago (1823), he was enchanted by Margaret. He spent a good part of his time here in her company. Since then, hardly a letter from the Governor arrives without a note inside just for her. He says one day he will return to visit her. I suppose that could mean this summer.

I almost ended without thanking you for the books you sent. I have added them to my library. The more books I have, the more Uncle John Peter shakes his head. He blames my lack of promotion on my reading. Says it shows a mind unfit for business. Anyway, I have read all three books at double speed with John Peter away. Lewis and Clark's I read with special interest, as I was not far off their trail when I went south to the Missouri. They are lucky they survived.

I have probably extended your patience with the length of this letter. I hope you and yours are well.

Your friend,

Edward Harriott

Soft fool!

One Pound One struck the table so hard one of his pipes fell and broke. He could hear Louise approaching from the other side of the house to see if he was drunk or having a seizure. When she stuck her head in, dressed in flannel for bed, she delivered a wordless rebuke. Did he have to wake the house, him and his foolish rages? And just as needless of words, he answered. Enough out of you, woman. Be gone.

Watching her go, a bulk that filled the door frame and blocked the light, he said to himself, *that's* the kind for this country. Tough as whalebone. No love talk. You put a roof over her, babies inside her. See to it she isn't slack in feeding you. *That's* enough to venture.

Old John Peter was right to shake his head at Harriott's books. Reading was not a fit pursuit for a grown man unless it was documents pertaining to the trade. One Pound One could think of four men in the Company who were given to reading: Archibald McDonald at the Coast (who swanned around giving plants names and whom the Governor could hardly stand for his tedious small talk), Alexander Ross (who thought himself a writer, for God's sake), Colin Robertson (who had as good as read himself out of Rupert's Land). And Harriott. Fine bedfellows all!

The only reason One Pound One had added to the vice was he had three books, wanted rid of them, and didn't know where else to send them. During the outfit of '23–24, Blood Indians had brought the books along with their peltries, two volumes by Lewis and Clark and something called *Arabian Nights*, plundered from an American trading party. Every time One Pound One looked at them, he got a chill. A picture in his head of some fool beside his campfire, peering through spectacles at the tiny print, when boom! Down comes a stone axe and puts an end to his reading for all time. Lewis and Clark started the war with the Blackfoot by killing one of them in 1806. Now a man reading their book about it is killed in the same war.

One Pound One hated that sort of superstitious thing. He got rid of the books as fast as he could to the only person he knew who would want them.

But the damnable thing in this letter, the part that pricked sharpest, was this business of Harriott's woman. Thank God again that

Louise was fat and plain, and that some of his daughters promised to be the same. Harriott would soon enough learn to rue his woman's beauty and the *enchantment* he saw on the Governor's face.

Was the man completely deaf to gossip? Blind to the ways of the world? By God, if the Governor could find nothing else, he'd stick his thing in a nest of bees. But given he was who he was, he stuck it where he pleased. For Halfbreed men the Governor had nothing but malice, wouldn't tolerate one above the office of clerk, but Halfbreed women? That was different. He was always on about their beauty.

Almost up to the standard of the European.

And the particular type he liked best was the tall, slim sort with the doe's eyes and an oval face—which is to say, the spit of Harriott's Margaret.

Nor did the Governor exactly stoop to courtship. What he preferred was for the cowardly fathers to pimp their daughters to him. He would sit at business until all hours, then God help the post procurer if the woman of choice was not warming his bed when he got into it.

But the worst thing, the thing that rankled most for One Pound One, was how he himself had been made accomplice to this business.

Last summer at Fort Assiniboine, when he and the Governor had been toasting the Governor's discovery (the chance to save a few dollars, a few hours, just the thing to put him in a good mood), the talk had turned ribald. In his cups and anxious to please his master, One Pound One had dredged up every salty story he knew, every tale of men caught with their trousers at the ankle.

With the topic of women raised, the Governor put a question.

"You know the Saskatchewan well, John. Who would you say is the prettiest piece on it?"

Without thinking, One Pound One answered.

"That would be John Peter Pruden's daughter at Carlton. The one called Margaret. Least that's what everyone says."

The Governor looked out the open door, at the summer twilight, and smiled.

"Margaret. Yes. I met her at Carlton in '23. Exquisite, really. I must see her again."

One Pound One gave his head a knock, trying to make the damn thing think. Harriott must be warned. He must be told. But what to tell and how? What he should be told was to marry the woman by whatever ritual. Bell, book and candle or burning grass and tom-tom. Just do it! Get her moved into his house before the Governor passed through again, an event scheduled for this summer.

One Pound One had seen the Governor at it before. If he had that woman in mind, he'd find a way to make Carlton a stopping place. Old John Peter, Margaret's father, wouldn't let the Governor have her for nothing, though he might be enticed into some more elaborate arrangement, but he was on furlough in England and wouldn't be there to do anything.

That was the danger. If the Governor had his mind set on Margaret, he would create a way to get her. If Harriott made too big a fuss trying to prevent it, that would be the end of all promise for him in the Company.

Warn Harriott, aye. But would One Pound One risk a letter to do so? A letter that could easily get into the wrong hands? You don't save a drowning man by jumping in and drowning with him. It was also possible that Harriott did understand and the stupid letter was some kind of code, but even given that, it implied he expected some action or response.

The more One Pound One thought about it, the more certain he was that he would not risk a letter or anything else. The more he knew that, the angrier he became. Letter, table, candle, fire—he hated everything at this moment, and most of all, he hated the memory of his arm on Harriott's shoulder and his lips speaking drunken words of promise.

If I come out of this well, I will see you right. As a friend.

One Pound One grabbed the candle and porringer off the table, threw the tea dregs on the fire.

"Go ahead and smoke, you bastard!"

He stuffed the pipes into his pockets regardless of their heat. With his hand on the door, he looked back. The letter, tea-spotted and grimed with pipe ash, stood on the table an inch high on its wavy pages. He returned to it, picked it up, threw the crackling mess onto the fire.

He had decided one thing at least. Either in the spring when the Governor came to Edmonton, or later when Council sat, he would recommend Ted Harriott for promotion. He would recommend he be put in charge of Fort Assiniboine, being a place in One Pound One's domain and at the same time out of the way. If there was powerful objection, he would drop it. He would not fight the Governor over it. And never, under any circumstance, would he mention Harriott's confounded woman.

One Pound One hoped that would be enough to put the scales of conscience right, but lighting his way along to bed he felt in his guts that it wasn't so. The gnawing was still there, anxiety dining with its old insistence.

"Get a baby on her," he shouted at the darkness ahead. "Take that girlish prettiness out of her or, by God, you'll pay."

🌿

FORT CARLTON, 1825

The spring of 1825, and the people of Harriott's home fort were busy preparing for the Governor's visit, his first to Carlton since 1823 and second ever. It might be a week yet, or two, but much of each day's activity went to that purpose.

Urged by their women, the men were cutting shingles and filling gaps on the toothless roofs. Inside the houses, the women fixed and decorated things the Governor would never see. Every day a boy was dispatched to the bastion to restore the cannon's brass gleam while a whole detail of youngsters worked through the horse herd, trimming manes and pulling tails. Even the fort half-wit had a chore as he took daily practice ringing the flag up the pole. At night the activity continued. Behind glowing window parchments, the women sewed new flourishes on old finery.

Chief Factor John Stuart, John Peter's furlough replacement, burned midnight oil himself, trying to solve the riddle of how lavish an entertainment to provide in the Governor's honour. Regales and dances for passing brigades were currently out of favour with that man, and Stuart had to decide if the rule applied when the Governor himself was among the travellers.

All through this bustle, Ted Harriott did no more than what he was asked. He did not like Stuart, a lumbering, posturing man of limited imagination and countless opinions. Whatever chore Stuart thought up for him, he did it the quickest possible way, then returned to his own spring project, which was doubling the size of his bachelor cabin. Stubbornly, Harriott was making his house into a home fit for a Company officer, a place where an officer could have a wife and raise a family.

When the frost left the ground, he had dug his cellar. Since then, he'd placed sills, ordered boards from the saw pit, and raised them. And every day, while he worked, his thoughts marched along a path that never changed. Each day he began by remembering the Governor's arrival at Carlton in the summer of 1823, and after constructing that two-year-old day and night, he would move along to each of the interferences since: the damage done each time a note arrived addressed to Margaret in the Governor's hand.

The first picture in this gallery was the Governor's north canoe bearing down on Carlton's shore, crew and boat so perfectly enmeshed as to look like one smooth-flexing machine. Like everyone else that day, Harriott stood bouncing and craning for a glimpse of the Governor, the chimney of his tall beaver blinking in the sun. Not enough of the crowd's energy could be expended into the sky as burned gunpowder, and finally the line of men on shore had breached, half a dozen spilling into the water. They took the canoe by its sides and ran with it to shore.

With the north canoe pulled up and the Carlton men looking apt to touch the Governor, his paddlers formed a circle that kept them off. Two of these Iroquois made a chair by crossing their arms, and the Governor sat in it so lightly and arrogantly as to turn it into a throne. He was set down in front of John Peter (who hadn't left for England yet), and Harriott's uncle stuttered out an obeisance so grovelling only a Governor could dignify it. All the while, Harriott was pushing and driving himself forward through the crowd, burning with a desire to shake the Governor's hand.

There had been a time (recent, too) when Harriott would have been in the little group at the front, standing at John Peter's side along with his sons. Back then, he would have been the third or fourth man introduced. His exile to the back of the crowd dated to his return from the Bow River Expedition, to the moment when he had asked his uncle for Margaret's hand in marriage. In answer, John Peter's long, weathered face had turned to stone.

"I will have no incest in my family. Just because we live in a wilderness, we will not mate like animals nor savages."

And so it stood. His uncle and he rarely spoke.

Harriott was still chasing his introduction to the Governor that evening when the dance began. But he was also distracted. Margaret was there with her family, so concentration on any other object was difficult. She was wearing the dress she had made for his return from Bow River, a beaded white deerskin she intended to wear the day she moved into his house. She had made it while he was away.

For the first hour they did not approach each other. John Peter would have stopped them, even now with the Governor in attendance.

The dance itself began shyly. The fiddlers completed the first tune with not one couple taking the floor. John Peter was furious. He went to the fiddlers and demanded more music, then he stomped around the dance floor shouting for people to get on their feet, to dance. The music seemed too slow when it came and the jiggers were awkward, as if they were trying out new feet.

Making use of the diversion, Margaret left her mother and stood in a vacant place along the side wall, in shadow. Before John Peter could notice, Harriott joined her. They pretended to watch the dancing, but their real attention was where their fingers met in the folds at the side of her dress. In whispers they planned to meet later, in their trysting place beyond the rear gate.

In this way, both failed to notice the Governor's approach. He had been walking back and forth in front of the crowd, darting occasionally at someone with a greeting and a handshake. It was all the shy deer of Carlton could do not to run away. Then, noticing a handsome young couple standing separate at the side, the Governor veered towards them.

Taken by surprise, Harriott fumbled with the Governor's hand, caught only his small, soft fingers, and probably squeezed too hard. His mind emptied of all the things he had wanted to say. The Governor knew who he was and was making some comment about his walk south to the Missouri last winter. Harriott had expected congratulations, but what he saw in the Governor's eyes was a skepticism that chilled him.

"I'm sorry, sir. I missed that last part."

"I said, rumour has it the Americans are very interested in the upper Missouri, that and the Snake River country. I was simply saying that, by your testimony, they're wasting their time."

Harriott started to say something about not having gone very far up the Missouri but stopped when he felt the Governor's attention leave him. The hand in his became gripless and slid away. The barrel chest brushed by. The Governor was standing before Margaret and his voice had filled with sugar.

"Who might this fine young lady be? Margaret. Oh, John Peter's. I should have guessed. What a lovely dress. Did you bead it yourself?"

Harriott could not hear Margaret's replies. The Governor's bursts of words shaped themselves around silence. The longer the Governor stood with Margaret, the more attention flowed their way, until finally everyone in the room was watching. As for the older women, they had seen it before and were resigned to it. They soon went back to tending babies. But the younger women, instinctively jealous, could not as easily turn away. The men, young and old, watched because they watched everything the Governor did.

John Peter was a special case. On his uncle's face, Harriott read great pleasure, also excitement and rekindled ambition. The Governor still had hold of Margaret's hand, and trapped in that connection of flesh, John Peter, the old Chief Trader, could likely see his elusive second parchment fluttering. When the Governor finally did release Margaret and spun to the crowd, his face looked greasy. Shiny with greed.

The Governor danced only once that evening, and he chose Margaret for his partner. He took her by the tips of the fingers and led her onto the floor. It cleared before them. The fiddlers sawed out a jig, and while Margaret executed the foot stitchery of the dance, the Governor stood still with one hand cocked to his waist and the other in the air, the fingers turning—as if he were presenting her as a spectacle to the others. The Governor's eyes drifted down her body once, then rested politely on her feet. Just when it seemed he would make no move to dance himself, he rose on tiptoe and did a brief balletic canter abruptly applauded by everyone.

Harriott looked at his uncle again and saw how his hopes were rising still. John Peter was not fool enough to imagine a marriage. That was not a question he would even put to himself. More likely, he was asking if it was not better for his girl to be the Governor's mistress than a poor cousin's wife. The families of the Governor's mistresses fared well in the trade. If John Peter had moral qualms, he must set them aside for the general good of his kinfolk.

It was a hot summer night the night of the Governor's ball at Carlton, 1823. The mess hall door stood open, exhaling heat and smoke. Harriott stepped past anyone's notice and crossed the square in the direction of the small gate. Darkness had filled the fort along the ground, but the sky was still alight and blue. A few charcoal smudges slanted through it. Beyond the first cabin corner, Harriott stopped and turned to watch, trained his eyes on the smoking golden rectangle of the door.

He had no idea how long he waited. Any amount of time would have seemed long. When Margaret finally did come out, she stopped to smooth her dress. Harriott coughed and she started his way, the small steps under the long dress making her seem to sail. She crossed into shadow and Harriott embraced her, but only briefly, as both were anxious to watch the doorway again for what would happen next.

He did not make them wait long. As Margaret had done, the Governor stopped as soon as the night air hit him. He had dispensed with his jacket in the heat, and now he pulled his shirt out of his trousers and let it hang. For one more moment he studied the shapes and shadows. Then, with uncanny accuracy, he started towards them. Trying not to make noise, they retreated, to another set of shadows, another cabin corner.

When the Governor stood where they had just been, he stopped to listen. Hearing nothing, he made a huffing noise like a deer will make when startled out of a good hiding place. The Governor turned his back to them, gathered up his shirt, and they heard the fizz and roar of piss hitting a solid log here and a hollow board there.

After that, the Governor returned to the dance and Margaret and

Harriott completed their walk out the small gate to their willow lean-to. When they got there, they mated, but it was urgent and distracted. Both were happier back in their clothes. Shoulder touching shoulder in the dark, sitting in the grass and neither saying a word, they listened to the wild orchestra of night and breathed its thick perfume.

In many ways the two years from then until now had been but a prolongation of that evening, as they awaited the inevitable day when the Governor would return.

During the vigil, they were forced to continue mating in the woods, and the lovemaking was never as good again as it had been before. The Governor had gotten between them, was always there somehow.

The first of the letters had come in the next westbound mailbag. A little envelope inscribed with Margaret's name. It was placed inside a business letter to John Peter, and John Peter broke it open and read it himself before handing it on to Margaret. Margaret brought it to Harriott because she could not read and did not trust what her father had read to her.

> I will return in the not so distant future. I look forward to pursuing our friendship at that time.

After two years, the letters numbered five. They stood on edge trapped between cups on the shelf in Harriott's cabin. They were legendary. Everyone in the fort knew about them. Possibly everyone on the river did. Nor could Harriott do a thing about them, except build his house and wait.

Behind the walls of her father's house, Margaret also found something to create out of frustrated dreaming. She beaded and she sewed. On the nights when she and Harriott were not together, most nights, she took out the dress in which she had hoped to be married and into it wove more coloured thread and trade beads. The floral garden grew and overgrew, became unruly, unpretty. Her mother turned her eyes away.

Up and through the skin and beads, she pushed the needle. Into the oozing wood, Harriott drove his nails. Some nights he lay in his roofless cabin annex and stared at the piece of sky framed by the half-risen walls. Sometimes, when her family was sleeping, Margaret let the wedding dress fall onto her naked shoulders, just to feel its amazing weight.

❧

FORT EDMONTON, 1825

On May 2nd, 1825, the Governor stopped at Edmonton on his return trip from the West Coast. He came from the northwest on horseback, riding the new Fort Assiniboine road that One Pound One had built the previous winter, and, once past Edmonton, would proceed to Carlton and onward to either Norway House or Fort Garry.

On the gallery, One Pound One stood watching through his spyglass as the Governor appeared and disappeared among the aspens on his descent into the valley. Every step the horse and rider came closer, a braid of worry tightened in his chest. Having ridden the new Assiniboine road, was the Governor satisfied with the work? The oval racecourse he had just passed on the upper plateau: did it strike him as a trade-inspiring attraction or a waste of Company time and money?

Then there was old Fort Edmonton itself. As he came close enough to see it in detail, did the Governor know how old a fort it was? Did he understand about the flood, and no time as yet to repair the damage or clear the debris?

The Governor's horse appeared tired. Its weight fell hard against its front legs as it descended the trail. Then the Governor gave it a few sharp kicks and quirts and brought it in at a gallop, a showy ride the last hundred yards that caught One Pound One by surprise. He was still labouring down the ladder when the gate split and the Governor passed under. One Pound One bellowed for a man to catch the Governor's reins, for another to assist his dismount, but the Governor hopped down neat as a pin without help, leaving his horse behind with its reins dragging, too blown to escape.

The Governor and One Pound One came face to face, the Governor already smiling and talking. He bore himself with his characteristic swell-chested, roosterish pose, but One Pound One was struck by the greyness of the man's face behind the robust display. The Governor swept his hand across the dilapidated inner wastes of Edmonton and complimented its tidiness. One Pound One thought it might be sarcasm but did not know for sure.

"We're too low in the valley as you know, Governor. Damn flood catches us every few years."

The rest of the Governor's entourage had passed the ridge by now, and one by one they straggled through the gate. A dusty, exhausted crew, man and horse. Chief Factor James McMillan was in the lead, an old friend of One Pound One's from Nor'Wester days who was part of the Governor's inner circle now, then Tom Taylor, a boat captain's Halfbreed son and brother to the Governor's principal mistress. Last in line was Alexander Ross, a lean and handsome individual who, rumour had it, was being relieved of his duties in the Snake River country. Ticketed for Red River as a headmaster for the new settlement school. Trader to schoolteacher: a perilous drop.

Returning his gaze to Tom Taylor, One Pound One felt his mood begin to brighten. He was thinking of Harriott's confounded winter letter, to which he had never replied. He was thinking that with the brother of his country wife in tow, and that particular wife being the mother of children the Governor admitted were his, the Governor was a lot less likely to play the ram along the way. This was good news for Harriott.

The three travellers were peeled off their horses with the aid of some Edmonton men. McMillan's and Ross's knees were locked from riding, and they had to be carried off and propped against buildings like dummies.

The Governor meanwhile had concluded his introductory pleasantries and was anxious to talk shop. First topic was the buffalo shortage. He wanted to know precisely how short of the mark provisions were.

If there was a word in the language One Pound One hated more than *precisely,* he didn't know it. His mind did not work precisely and the answer he gave—*down by half, about that*—was bound to irritate his boss. The Governor began to pace a square. He reached for his face and tweezed his chin between thumb and forefinger. He pinched and released, pinched again, as if it were a means of milking the brain.

"What of Carlton then? Same thing?"

"Mr. Harriott wrote from Carlton, sir. Said the buffalo had failed there as well."

Wanting badly to counter bad news with good, One Pound One mentioned Henry Fisher's harvest of beaver from the Piegan. Fisher was an excellent trader, like a secret weapon, and One Pound One had sent him down with a big outfit. Though it had taken Fisher the best part of a winter, the mission had come up trumps.

"Two thousand beaver from the Piegan this winter, Governor . . ."

The Governor made a complimentary noise but was not listening.

"I need a boat, John, to get me to Carlton. Best get it ready immediately. And pick me a good crew. I've got far less time than I thought."

Inside himself, One Pound One felt a flutter like panic. Louise and his three daughters had been sewing and cooking for weeks, preparing a great festive ball in the Governor's honour—which it now appeared the Governor would not attend. One Pound One hated it when his women were disappointed. They always found him to blame.

One Pound One mumbled something about it, a night of dancing in the Governor's honour, words mainly for his own sake so as to be able to answer Louise when she demanded how he had phrased the invitation. The Governor studied the Chief Trader's face. He had a way of looking at you as though the face were a thing in motion. His eyes went all over, peppered you, and that's exactly what they were doing now, with the mention of the Governor's ball hanging in the air.

The Governor shifted his gaze to his travelling companions, who except for Taylor were sitting like lumps in the dust. Finally he spoke.

"A dance. Good. But I want no drunken paddlers come morning. Arrange me a crew and tell them they can have their drams at journey's end. None before."

That decision made, the Governor's mood lightened. Having made time, he could now afford to be pleasant during it. He put his hand in One Pound One's back, exactly like a man at a fair animating a hand puppet, and he steered him by it to the big house. Suddenly, in his own fort, One Pound One was a visitor. You had to credit the Governor. When it came to high-handedness, he could not be outdone.

Inside, One Pound One had a basin and pitcher fetched so the Governor could wash, which he did with thoroughness and meticulous care for his clothes. Afterwards, the two men sat across the table waiting for tea. The Governor stared into the empty cavity of the hearth and drummed his fingers on the table. It was hot as hell so he wasn't hinting for a fire, only resting his eyes somewhere while he thought. Only when One Pound One's daughter Isabella came, poured tea, and departed did the Governor turn to face his Chief Trader. Same thing: the look that roved and stung like salt.

"What caused the Norway House fire?" he asked. Then, before One Pound One could attempt an answer, he asked about the buffalo shortage again. What was the cause?

One Pound One's face filled with blood till it was so tight it felt explosive. If a subordinate had asked him such questions he would have given him a clout on the ear. Why would anyone, having burned Norway House by design or accident, tell One Pound One? And who the hell knew why buffalo came and went? He was not a soothsayer.

In hopes of a topic he could expand upon, One Pound One tried again to bring up Edmonton's beaver returns, being largely composed of Fisher's harvest from the Piegan. This time the Governor listened.

"That is a fine haul. Piegan, you say. Now which Piegan? The ones close to the Missouri or the more northerly ones?"

"South Piegans, Governor."

"That would be Mr. James Bird Junior's terrain, then, wouldn't it? Jamey Jock? Do you hear anything of the man? Does he visit?"

"No visits, sir. Not all the years he's been down there. He's cut himself off."

"Am I right in thinking that you don't trust Jamey Jock?"

The Governor wore a slight smile. Where he'd got this idea One Pound One did not know, but it was exactly right. Now the trader didn't know what to say. His real opinion of the Halfbreed verged on hatred. He considered him a haughty bastard and had never had any use for him. But what if the Governor had taken a liking to him? The fact the Governor was smiling implied a deliberate mischief, that he knew he had his Chief Trader in a vice and was twisting the screws.

"I was a Nor'Wester before the amalgamation. Jamey Jock was Bay Company like his father. I haven't had much dealings with him since."

"I was Bay Company too, John. Does that mean you bear me a grudge? We're to put that feud behind us. You know that."

"Of course I know it, sir. And I do for the most part . . ."

"But you make an exception of Jamey Jock. That was rather my point."

"Well, he's not exactly a Company man any more, sir."

As if deciding his victim had sustained enough pain for the present, the Governor leaned back and lifted his eyes to the ceiling timbers. He placed his thumbs back of his lapels and drummed his fingers on top.

"You will have to get over whatever it is you have against Jamey Jock, John, because I intend to use him in ways that involve you. I wish to use him because I believe he is signalling a desire to be used."

"I hadn't heard . . ."

"Neither have I. That's not what I mean."

The Governor reached for the teapot, and One Pound One lunged to get it first. Where were those damn women when you actually needed one? When One Pound One had finished his clumsy pouring, the Governor threw half of it into the hearth to make room for milk. He kept on talking while he did so.

"It seems significant to me that, while James Bird Senior gathers his sons at Red River to turn them into farmers, his eldest son stands a thousand miles aloof. As the father forsakes his lifetime connection with the Company, his one son pursues a career among the Piegan, one of the tribes we are most interested in expanding trade with. Do you see what I'm getting at?"

One Pound One's face was wet with sweat. He pulled his coat sleeve over his fist and wiped it. What the Governor was saying could mean a lot of things.

"My point is that you perhaps don't understand Jamey Jock's potential importance to us."

One Pound One signified with a shrug that perhaps he did not.

"As you see, I have Alexander Ross with me. Until this season, he was in charge of our trade south of the Columbia River, the so-called Snake River trade. His returns were good but he was unaggressive. He sat back at Flathead Post and let the furs come to him. If he could get four thousand beaver by that measure of effort, I said to myself, what could an energetic man accomplish? A man who would push harder and farther."

Great Jesus, One Pound One said to himself, fearing the Governor meant to replace Ross with Jamey Jock Bird.

"So I have taken Mr. Ross away from that duty and put Peter Skene Ogden in his place."

One Pound One made a loud noise and gave up trying to mask his surprise. Ogden, like himself, had been a Nor'Wester during the fur war, but one who had pursued his part with a nasty fondness for blood. At the peak of the trouble, Ogden had been wearing double daggers and committing murder. When the war ended and the two companies joined, no one wanted him. He had been passed over for every commission.

"A bloody man for a bloody job," the Governor said, as if completing One Pound One's thought. "I lured him into the proposition with a parchment and gave him a crew of devils every last one of whom is working off a Company debt."

One Pound One scratched in his hair. They had been talking about Jamey Jock Bird but were now talking about Peter Skene Ogden and the Snake River trade. He could imagine no connection between the two. This time the Governor did not so quickly oblige him with an answer to his unspoken question.

"I had other reasons as well. Some Americans out of St. Louis are active in the Snake River country again. It's far enough south that it will likely become American territory someday. Therefore, I have instructed Skene Ogden to scorch and bloody it. I told him to take the life of every beaver, male or female, in or out of season, adult or kit. I also told him, ammunition permitting, to slaughter every other kind of animal he finds."

One Pound One was gaping. Every principle of husbanding a beaver ground was confounded by what the Governor had just said.

"I know, I know. You shouldn't be so polite either. However, there are excellent reasons for pursuing this policy. First, if the country is to become American, let's take out every skin we can, while we can. As well, why not injure the future industry of the United States? They would ours. But the third reason is the most important. If we temporarily ruin the beaver grounds south and west of the Columbia, it becomes a less pleasing prospect. By impoverishing it, I might actually save it for England. The longer view, do you see?" The Governor sat back, admiring himself. "Yes, yes," he said. "A bloody man for a bloody job."

One Pound One could not stand this a moment longer. "What does this have to do with Jamey Jock?" he asked, and as he feared, the Governor pounced on him.

"That shows you are not thinking geographically, John. In the Snake River country, west of the Rockies, Mr. Skene Ogden is our means of challenging American competition. But who will do the job on the east side of the mountains, on the Upper Missouri?"

"I thought the Blackfoot were taking care of that. They still make war on the Americans."

"That's better. But what if the Americans manage a treaty with those Indians? It could happen, and think of the trouble we would be in then. Suddenly it's much closer for the Piegan, the Blood, the Blackfoot, the Big Bellies—all of them—to trade south. We would lose their beaver and their pemmican, and we can't run the Northern Department without it. Properly prepared, Jamey Jock might be just the weapon we need to ensure the Piegan make no such treaty and continue to trade with us." The Governor paused dramatically. "And one more thing, John. Having told you what I've just told you, you know more about my intentions with respect to Jamey Jock Bird than I want anyone else in the trade to know." He put his finger to his lips as you would to a child to emphasize what silence means.

At that, One Pound One understood that the real business of their conversation had ended. As he often did in such a situation, One Pound One sat like a lump and wished he had the slightest gift for small talk. Finally he took a gamble and asked if there was truth to the rumour that the Governor was headed for England this coming season.

"If you've heard that, I expect you've also heard that I go in search of a white wife."

One Pound One flushed scarlet. It was exactly what he had heard.

"I'm not desperate for such an article, but if the right lady should present herself . . ." The Governor pursed his lips and made a little sideways nod.

One Pound One kept firmly silent on the subject. He could think of nothing more useless than an English wife.

"Thing is, John, and this is also a bit of a confidence, it seems very likely that the old Governor Pelly, the only man who stands above me in this country, will give up soon. He's got a sick wife. I believe that the London Committee intends not to replace him but to give his responsibilities to me. Country wives are good for what they're good for, I suppose, but they command no respect. If I'm to be Governor of two departments, I must have a wife who can adorn and dignify my court. A *white* wife, you see."

One Pound One did not see at all. It seemed to him that the Governor already had a wife back in Red River, or a mistress who bore him children, which was all any of them had. What was he planning to do with Miss Margaret Taylor, the boat captain's daughter, and his children by her? To say nothing of his other mistresses and their bastards strewn around the country.

"No matter," said the Governor as if in answer. "What of your dance, sir? Do you have any pretty specimens on display? Edmonton usually does."

"A few, of course, Governor."

At the same time One Pound One knew the question would have been asked quite differently if the Governor seriously meant to have his pleasure.

The dance that night was an occasion belonging to the Governor. For the last hour, the music stopped and all of Edmonton crowded around to hear that gentleman's stories.

"So I overtook McLoughlin still in camp at seven in the morning. Standing there in his nightshirt, wearing two days' beard—I wouldn't want to encounter the likes of him on a dark street in London. From York Factory to the Pacific Ocean, my men and I made it in eighty-four days. That's weeks off the previous record, and if it hadn't been for McLoughlin, I'd've done it faster . . .

"And there they were: dining on English beef and English biscuit brought round Cape Horn while salmon lay flipping on shore. I said to them, if we on the prairies can feed on buffalo and pemmican, you can most certainly get by on salmon and other victuals of the Pacific Coast...

"Nothing for it, given the poor arrangements, but I had to walk across the mountains . . .

"If my meeting with Pelly is cancelled, and given the shortage of buffalo, I expect to go from Carlton to Fort Garry on horseback. I realize it is five hundred miles and crawling with Big Bellies and Sioux, but I believe there is no choice."

🌿

FORT CARLTON, 1825

Never had the ritual for celebrating an arrival seemed as empty to Edward Harriott. John Peter Pruden's furlough replacement, John Stuart, had been fussing for weeks about how best to greet the Governor, but now that it was happening, it was a mirror held up to every other such occasion. The men in their gaudy vests, sashes and head rags; the women in hair ribbons and old dresses with new bits of frippery sewn on. The air rank with gunpowder and your ears wincing at the noise.

Standing near the back of the crowd, Harriott was the only one in everyday clothes, his head bare to the breeze. Seeing that he had failed to dress, Stuart had left him with the children and the old women, rather than dragging him forward to represent English blood and manners in the official greeting party. Primed by John Peter, Stuart disliked Harriott and, since he'd arrived, had taken sinister pleasure in keeping him away from Margaret. Now he had fresh evidence to report of the clerk's insubordination. *Did not dress properly for the Governor's visit.*

The Governor's canoe was halfway from the river bend to the fort, and a man in the bow was firing back to Carlton's salvo. Harriott would not look at the boat, but kept Margaret in view instead. She stood with several other women her age a few rows forward. Though they had never discussed it, Harriott had assumed she would dress like him, shabbily in protest, but she had not. She wore a summery dress he had not seen before, and there were vermilion ribbons plaited into her hair. She laughed and looked as expectant as the other girls. She looked beautiful, and in that moment, Harriott hated her for it.

The Governor was on his feet now, in the prow of the canoe, one hand holding his tall beaver steady. When the boat scrunched gravel, he crouched comically, a caricature of a man about to leap or fall. Then, to everyone's surprise, he did jump—for all his majesty unafraid of making a slip in the mud or some other unintentional comedy. Of course he landed lightly on a dry spot and skipped another few steps to where Stuart stood waiting. The hearty handshake, the routine compliments. Then the Governor's eyes found Margaret.

After a brief speech, he dove into the crowd, shaking all the hands he could find, but really he was only going hand-over-hand like a man climbing a rope to a single destination. Reaching Margaret, he stopped. He took her right hand in his, and he brought it up and gallantly kissed it, drawing a sigh from the crowd. Then the Governor went into his pocket with his left hand and pulled something out. As a finale to their greeting, he clasped Margaret's hand in both of his.

When the Governor finally moved on, Harriott kept watching Margaret. He watched her drop what the Governor had given her into the pocket of her dress.

Harriott was the very last person greeted by the Governor. The scruffy, unhealthy appearance of the clerk, his fishy handshake and seeming indifference were noted.

"So, Mr. Harriott, you haven't taken it into your head to walk to the Missouri again?"

"Once was enough, sir."

"Our American competitors do not seem to share that view."

"What view is that, sir?"

"Come now, Mr. Harriott. That once is enough. That the Missouri is useless for trapping. The Americans are suddenly very anxious to go there, even despite their war with the Blackfoot."

"I wouldn't know about that, sir."

"Funny, I thought you were our authority on the subject."

That was all that was said, but it was enough—enough to give Harriott a feeling at the temples as if the skin were pulling itself back, retreating. Just then, Stuart caught up to the Governor and confirmed to him that both hunting and trading had failed, and that Carlton had little to contribute to the brigades.

"In that case, I must go to Fort Garry immediately. If I don't order pemmican from the Halfbreed buffalo hunters soon, it will be too late for them to hunt. Did you hear me, Mr. Stuart?"

"Immediately when, sir?"

"What does immediately usually mean, Mr. Stuart?"

It seemed like no time at all since the last cannonade that the fort guns were booming again, this time in farewell for the Governor. His horses were swimming the summer river on their way to the prairie. Among those pouring musket smoke and noise into the air was Harriott. In fact, he exceeded all others, firing his fuke until it was too hot to hold. Shouting hurrahs.

To see the Governor go, already gone so far you could blot him out with your thumb, and unlikely to return for years—what happier time in Harriott's life could there be?

In that moment he forgave Margaret for dressing up, and he forgave himself for doubting her. It was simple and natural for her to dress up and be pretty. She would only have drawn attention to herself by trying to be drab. As for himself, what could he have been other than jealous to see her adorned in honour of another man?

With Stuart present and in a foul mood over his failed dance, Harriott ran up the path to Margaret, slid his arm around her waist, and held her tight all the way to the fort. He swept her to his house and sat her on the log bench outside while he went inside to make tea. Coming back outside when the fire was lit, he saw she had a slip of paper in her hand. She was holding it up to her eyes. The Governor's handwriting was easy to identify. The individual letters bent forward, lunging, so that they looked about to fall flat.

Harriott drew the page from her fingers. He read it once silently and then a second time aloud.

My Dear Young Lady,

I am sorry things have turned out as they have. I will see you sooner than you think.

Harriott went back inside and quietly closed the door behind him. He folded the slip of paper and placed it among the envelopes on the shelf.

🌱

FORT CARLTON, 1825

A few weeks after the Governor's visit to Carlton, One Pound One came down the river in charge of the brigade, bound for York Factory. The snow had finally melted in the mountains, and a week of rain had swelled the river so the York boats sped out of the distance like so many corks shook in a jar. The steersmen were aiming aslant of the current, trying to hit the spot among catkinned willows and drowned aspens where Carlton's path had recently plunged beneath the flood.

Standing there in wait of them, framed by the golden morning, were Stuart and Harriott, unmoving, unspeaking, their eyes locked on the river in silence.

The recent excitement of the Governor's visit had spoiled Carlton. The fort's capacity for jubilation was so exhausted that hardly anyone had followed the Chief Factor and his clerk to see the brigade land. Up the trail a few labourers leaned on trees in the shade, but they had been ordered to attend. The sole volunteer was an old woman who pushed on Harriott's shoulder and squinted past him, trying to decipher through the river's glare if her nephew was among the crew.

Then confusion. Ropes were thrown to shore that Stuart and Harriott wound around the nearest aspen trunks. The current drove the boats past this mooring and their sterns collided dangerously. The ropes sawed at the trees, wheeling off wet ribbons of bark.

In the lead boat, One Pound One reeled with each collision,

bellowed orders for the ropes to be cast off, for the men to get in the river among the heavy boats and guide them to the nearest eddy. It was where Stuart and Harriott should have called for them in the first place, if either had used his brain. When the boats were moored and the crisis over, Stuart fumbled his pistol from his sash and fired it once in the air.

One Pound One lowered himself from the moored boat and splashed to the gravel, cursing at the top of his voice. He was the colour of a brick. Harriott stayed back and let Stuart do the greeting, and when it was his turn to shake One Pound One's hand, he did so without looking the man in the eye. All he could think of was the failure of any reply to his midwinter letter. All he saw was a man who had fattened in a time of hunger, the evidence hanging from his jaws and pushing out the tail of his coat.

One Pound One turned away from them then, to harangue his men. Not many years ago, One Pound One would have been into the river with his men, using his bulk to buffer the boats. Now he cursed and drove them to hurry with the pieces, and he made no move to help. One of the men, in his panic to go faster, tripped on a bale and fell. One Pound One hobbled forward and kicked him hard in the ass. It wasn't a scene foreign to Harriott's experience, but he was disgusted by it. His sympathy was with the men, and none for their master.

Once he had his men falling all over themselves in fear and confusion, One Pound One returned to Stuart and Harriott and began the customary coarse drolleries. He also began to brag.

"Two thousand beaver. Don't suppose Carlton has anything like that in these few bags."

In giving the details of the Piegan harvest, he managed to make Henry Fisher sound like a puppet that he had skillfully manipulated on long strings.

Finally, One Pound One turned to Harriott and asked how he'd been, commented on his skin-and-bones appearance. "It's just like you, Harriott, to starve a little more than necessary when the buffalo fail."

With most of the Carlton pieces on the boats, Stuart went to fetch his luggage, it being his plan to travel with the brigade to Norway House and Council. When he was out of sight, Harriott and One Pound One were struck dumb. Then something in the Chief Trader's manner changed. He grabbed Harriott by his sleeve and towed him out of earshot of the others.

"What happened?"

"What happened when?"

"The Governor!"

"Nothing happened."

One Pound One clapped his hands. "I knew it! I saw Tom Taylor along and I said to myself, there's Harriott's worries past. Have you taken her into your house yet?"

"John Peter won't allow it. Stuart's preventing it in John Peter's absence."

"John Peter's holding out for better. The skinflint. His own nephew not good enough."

"Listen, John, before he comes back, I have to ask you something. Would the Governor be planning a trip back this way?"

One Pound One frowned ferociously. He found the question stupid. "Christ, how would I know? In a couple of years . . ."

"I mean this year."

One Pound One opened his hand and slowly slapped Harriott across the head, laughed at him.

"You're soft as an egg. Ted, That's not possible and you know it. Besides, he's for England before the Bay freezes. After an English wife is the rumour."

Harriott's lean face had a foggy, daffy look, and then he laughed. Laughed and laughed. He punched One Pound One's shoulder with his fist.

"Easy there, you fool. You're mad."

That was how Stuart found them, on the shore of the eddy, laughing and jostling like children. Disgusted, he passed to the boat. He dragged his box off his man's back and swung it to another on board.

Red from laughter and not even sure what he was laughing at, One Pound One followed. He grabbed a Carlton labourer and forced him to his hands and knees in the water, then stepped in the swale of his back and got purchase enough to haul himself over the gunwale and in.

Happily, Harriott threw all his weight against the bow, fought alongside the others to get the boat off the gravel and back into the current. He waded in until he was waist-deep, steadying it while the oars were unlimbered. All around him, they fell like trees, slapped in unison. The crewmen dug hard while the mad current grabbed them and threw them downriver.

Standing at the edge of calm water, close enough to touch the braiding current, Harriott waved them out of sight.

That night under the roof of his finished cabin, Harriott and Margaret made love until the light started to return. When they gave up to their drowsiness, she curled at his side so sweetly she hardly seemed to breathe. He wished he could be like that, silent to the soul. Too long in the habit of unhappiness, he stayed awake, biting on old sores. The way he had doubted her, his misjudgement of One Pound One.

Like a drunk repeating things, Harriott tried to apologize to Margaret, waking her to tell her things.

"I'll marry you, darling. Never think I won't. We'll go to Red River. There's a chaplain there."

His own fervency kept bringing him to tears.

Then the silence erupted. Margaret, laughing, calling him a fool, telling him to shut up. She jumped up and pushed him over onto his back, straddled him with her smooth thighs. She grabbed his wrists and pinned them above his head. She grinned and waited, her teeth glowing in the coming light. She waited for him to speak, and each time he tried, she smothered his words with her lips and tongue.

❦

YORK FACTORY, 1825

That summer, the Northern Department Council met twice: at Norway House to survey the damage caused by the fire, then at York Factory for the usual items of business and the trial of Bouché and Ossin. The two were Company servants accused of deserting an expedition in the Peace, of killing Company horses for food and stealing supplies. They would have been better off accused of murder.

The trial was brief and the first part of the sentence immediate.

The two were taken to the roof of the Factory and exposed in manacles. The punishment would continue at the Factory for another week, confinement on bread and water, and would be completed at Forts Churchill and Severn. Across a winter of darkness and bitter cold, they would have much time to rue their misdeeds.

Beyond that diversion, the biggest news was the recent retirement of old Governor Pelly, the young Governor's only superior in Rupert's Land. Other business included Alexander Ross's posting to Red River as schoolmaster, John Peter's reposting to Norway House upon return from England, and the punishment of John Clarke, who had left his brigade to conduct a "domestic duty"—a woman, in other words. The Governor fined him the amount he reckoned lost in time and resources.

At both meetings, toadies made efforts to praise the Governor for his remarkable transcontinental round trip, the speed record he'd set that would never be broken. Unprecedented. Would go down in the annals of Company history. They laid it on thick and found themselves curtly and coldly ignored. In fact, anyone on any subject taking a few seconds too long was cut off sharply.

All in all, the Governor was in as sour and impatient a mood as any had ever seen him. Given there was no apparent hurry, they assumed two years of travel had infected him with a restlessness that no longer needed a cause.

Outside the fort, the men of the brigades milled among the tents thrown up for their commerce and amusement. They went in groups defined by brigade and searched for women, presents for women, liquor, unusual clothes to buy. When Bouché and Ossin were pushed onto the roof, the majority responded with jeers and stones. If any felt compassion, they kept it to themselves.

When the Chief Factors adjourned after their final dram, they joined them, and soon enough, the brigade bosses had the bullies stripped to their breeches and fighting.

Like another time, the Governor found One Pound One in the thick of things beside such a fight and drew him away. With the Governor leading and One Pound One trying not to look back at the fate of his money, they walked up the strand between the shore grass and the river. There, with the tide making the river run backwards beside them, the Governor confided his wish. He asked the favour that his Chief Trader had little choice but to grant.

❧

FORT CARLTON, 1825

It was still summer and hardly an aspen leaf had turned when One Pound One returned to Carlton. His fall brigade was weeks early, and only by luck was there a man on the gallery to spot his flags. The lookout ran to find Harriott, who in turn rushed around gathering labourers and a greeting party.

Coming to the river's edge, Harriott could not see anything at first. He turned to the man who had announced the brigade's approach and made a questioning gesture.

"They're tracking, sir."

"Then run down and help. All of you. Double quick."

The men ran along the shore path, closed off from view by a tangle of berry bushes. Harriott followed at a walk. Why they would be pulling their boats was a question that should have perplexed him, but he was smiling, rehearsing what he wanted to tell One Pound One about the pleasures of domestic life.

Coming to a spot on the path where the shore was clear of brush, he got his first glimpse of the brigade and its crew. The Carlton men had joined them on the lines, and the contrast between the two groups was striking. His were laughing and asking questions; the brigade crew were grim-faced and not responding. They trudged with the *cordelles* over their shoulders as if each step weighed like lead.

As the first boat came closer, Harriott made out One Pound One sitting on trade pieces in its middle. Looking down from his perch, his face was like his men's, but blacker. An expression that did not change at sight of Harriott.

An hour later the brigade boats were pulled up, the sorting and off-loading of bales under way. One Pound One lay in the shade of some willows with his hat over his eyes. He paid no attention to whether his men were finding the right packs or correctly reorganizing the remainder.

Harriott sat beside him, wondering at his friend's sullenness and unwillingness to communicate. Even questions about the trade and about Council did not stir him. Harriott's own buoyancy was thwarted, and he reminded himself of a puppy trying to get an older dog to play.

Finally One Pound One sat up and shouted a command for the men to rest. "Dram them," he yelled and pointed to the boat where the keg was stowed. As the rum went around, some Carlton men crept closer to One Pound One and Harriott, hoping to overhear some news. One Pound One swiped at the nearest with a closed fist.

"Can't a man have a word in private without some dog's ear listening?"

When they cleared back out of earshot, he was almost forced to say something as justification.

"I hate hurry when there's no damn hurry," he growled.

He was careful not to look at Harriott, directing the comment at the river.

It began to irritate Harriott to be treated this way. For the second time he asked why they were tracking. It seemed to him that the answer to why they were pulling their boats must contain the cause of everyone's agitation.

"I was mad at the bastards, that's why. They were rowing so feeble I thought they could make better time on the lines. Not their fault, though. This damn fool's errand."

"What errand?"

One Pound One finally shifted his gaze to Harriott. He was angry about something, could have been angry with Harriott by his manner, though that made no sense.

"The Governor picked my brigade to go first, and not just first in the normal rotation but first by days. I had to pull them out of their booze, which makes them ugly to begin with."

"What is the hurry then?"

Harriott began to sense something here he would not like.

One Pound One received the keg and tipped it, rubbed a dribble of brown from his unshaven chin.

"The Governor's orders are these. I'm to unload and get out. John Peter's family, with the exception of your woman Margaret, is supposed to take a canoe and go to Norway House, where John Peter will be this winter. That's also to happen immediately, by which I mean today. Also today, or first thing in the morning, you are to take every able-bodied one of your men and go to the prairies. You are to contact the Plains Cree and the Assiniboine and ensure they come north with their peltries this winter."

Harriott felt a prickling on his scalp, as though someone danced a needle there, then a deeper feeling like an iron comb grooming him neck to tail.

"Those Indians come north anyway. What would he have me do? Take the men and leave the women undefended?"

"The Governor *says* he fears the Americans. He wants extra care taken that our Indians don't go to them."

"I still don't see the need."

One Pound One ripped grass from the ground and threw it at the river. "Fine, you don't! Then you stay here and in a couple of days you can tell the Governor himself why you've decided to disobey him!"

The iron teeth rode his spine.

"The Governor is coming here?"

"I wasn't to tell you. There it is. For you, I betray the Governor's confidence."

"Why?"

"Don't torment me with stupid questions, Harriott. We both know why."

Harriott closed his fists on some of the long shore grass. He held tight.

"What should I do?"

"There's no sense my saying. You and me, we're not the same. Just don't do anything mad."

One Pound One dropped back on the grass, stared through the edge of the tree canopy at the pale sky. He continued to talk.

"I know you, Harriott, yet I don't know what you do when roused. Quiet men are sometimes the worst. You've got to remember it's the Governor. Cross him and you're done. You'll spend your life in the

Arctic or you'll be cast back to England. Back there, you're just another man without a trade."

It was late by the time the goods were stowed and the brigade crew fed. One Pound One gave the order for the men to board the boats. Some kicked the ground to let him know they preferred to stay the night. One Pound One knocked down the biggest, set his bully on the rest. They were back on the water soon enough.

Onshore, Harriott watched the boats struggle into the current. The river was silver and the sky above bled the colour of distant fires. He stood as if his feet were buried. As long as the boats were in view he could not seem to move.

The red evening darkened into night, and by then Harriott was in the fort at work. He had chosen men and horses. All around was a bustle of packing. He went through the familiar routine of putting together gifts and taking guns and ammunition from the store, writing everything down in the ledgers.

Margaret came to find him as it got dark.

"My family is going to Norway House and I'm to stay here? Or am I going to the prairie with you?"

But he would not talk to her. He worked on silently until she went away.

It was late when he finished. Even the dogs had settled by the time he crossed the square. His uncle's big house was one of the few still lit as Margaret's mother and her brothers and sisters packed for Norway House. The place was full of noise, excited laughter from the younger ones and the mother's monotone Cree unceasing in the background. Margaret was there, helping. He shouted her name at the door. Not waiting, he turned and went to their house.

When she came in, he was sitting on the edge of the bed with both hands in his hair. Seeing her enter so quietly and carefully, like a deer into an evening clearing, the feeling came back, the hatred of how pretty she was.

Then it was time to talk, and he did so with uncharacteristic frankness.

"The Governor has given me orders to leave and go to the prairie.

I'm to take all the men of the fort and go talk to the Indians about this season's trade. He specifically wants you to stay and your family to go, so it will only be you and the other women here. It's because he's coming here, any time now. He wants you. We know that. Now's his time."

As she listened, the only change was a deadening in the eyes, a light behind them getting small and going out. Then she sat at their table, staring at the candle. Its flame guttered. She made no move to trim the wick.

Hardly aware of whether he was speaking aloud or in his mind, Harriott listed things he thought they might do. He could stay and pretend he never received the order. He could go and she could ride with him. Or she could go missing. That way she wouldn't be here or with him. Though the Governor wouldn't be likely to believe it, Harriott could tell him that he didn't know where she was.

Margaret picked with a fingernail at the cloth that covered the table. In the centre under the candle was an embroidered *fleurette*. She was picking a thread loose, lifting it out from between the other strands, careful not to jerk and spill the candle wax. The thread grew longer. The flower shrank.

"That wouldn't satisfy him," she said.

Mesmerized by what she was doing, it took a moment for Harriott to understand that she had replied.

He imagined himself jumping up, jumping at her. *Damn the Governor's satisfaction!* But it never got beyond his mind and, even there, was just a lantern show. A little Harriott, who was not quite Harriott, performing on a little stage.

"If I go," he said, "what will you do?"

"I think the Governor wants to trade," she said.

Harriott had a sensation like being turned inside out, the way you do with a skinned rabbit. He was mad. Or worse, he was bursting out of delusion into sudden sanity. By the blurred image of Margaret, he understood he was crying.

"You are not a thing to be bartered."

In the lantern show he was up and shouting. In the room itself, he had barely whispered.

She shifted around in the chair to face him. The sight of Harriott in tears did not move her.

"You can't trade me. But I can trade myself."

"Margaret, no. I don't care if I rise in the Company. This to get that? It disgusts me."

She was on her feet. With quick movements she had the trunk off the rug and the rug off the trap door. She pulled the board away, lowered herself in and came back with Harriott's winter rum. She lifted it above the edge and rolled it along the floor.

When she got down a cup from the shelf above, the envelopes from the Governor fell over. She pulled the wooden stopper from the keg and slopped the cup full.

Harriott rose, obedient. He walked two steps and sat at the table. He looked at the *fleurette* under the candle base, small now, and the long, still-attached thread, a crimson line from its shrunken petal over the table's edge. He lifted the cup and gulped it. She filled it again as soon as he set it down.

She went behind him and he heard her taking off her dress and the frame of the bed cracking. He looked once and saw the slim shape of her back under the buffalo robe. He finished the second cup. Poured more.

❦

SASKATCHEWAN RIVER, 1825

The breeze along the river's course was sweetly cool on the Governor's face. It took away the heat of the midday sun and fanned the closed eyelids through which he watched a delicate web of his own veins. By the cool of the wind, the season was beginning to turn and he was glad, preferring fall and even winter to summer's sticky heat. *The cold element is male,* he thought to himself. *Heat is female.* It seemed an important thought. He would write it down at the next stop.

Lying comfortably back and feigning sleep, the Governor experienced fully each pulse by which his north canoe drove forward. The clean, mechanical power made him think of an old resolve, how he had once plotted a revenge against old England in the form of taking hand-picked Iroquois to challenge the rowing teams of Oxford and Cambridge. The desire had never left him, and again he thrilled at the idea of a bastard like himself with a bunch of savages in tow beating the pale products of the best of British blood at the sport they thought they had invented.

The power of the canoe on this particular voyage was like nothing he had ever felt before. All it was costing him was Company rum and presents he had promised to bring back from England for each crew member if they made the round trip in time for him to take ship for Gravesend. A bargain price for their never mentioning this journey and for pulling like madmen with little rest in both directions.

What an adventure, thought the Governor. Greater than anything he had attempted before, and greater too for the fact that it would never be found in anyone's journal, letter or history.

The feeling of such haste, the bucking surge of the fine canoe, was a sexual feeling really, and no wonder the alert good friend inside the Governor's trousers had decided to jump up and stand to attention. The Governor saw the familiar face shining on the inside of his sun-painted eyelids, the face that had tortured his sleep for how long now? Almost two years?

Margaret.

Don't worry, Peter, my boy, he told his prick, at this pace she'll be ours soon enough. All was made ready and she wouldn't escape again.

The Governor smiled to himself then, for it occurred to him that the Iroquois must be noticing the stout evidence of his ardour. All the same, not one of them would risk a hand off a paddle to make a joking gesture, nor would they speak a word about it in any language. They thought him a god, these men, and he missed no trick to enhance that view. Keep them off balance. Keep them amazed.

One of his tricks was this: pretending to sleep when awake, then commenting the instant there was a change of motion in the canoe. Never pass up a chance with savages to push your stature above that of a normal man.

It was the same with his practice of stripping naked and plunging into the river at the breakfast stop each day. That keen explosive feeling—like coming, really—and the lesser men felt their inferiority just to watch you do it. They stamped and flapped their arms by the fire all the more pathetically. The fact that the morning plunge itself had raised his tolerance to cold was a trick he kept secret from all.

A man created to rule in a winter land.

But good friend Peter did not care for the wanderings of the master's mind. To change the topic back, he gave a twitch, reminding the Governor why they were making this excursion. That it wasn't to prove a point about travelling speed.

Yes, a comely bitch to be sure. She would have to be something extraordinary indeed to make worthwhile this gamble: coming back inland and risking a delay in the ship bound for England. To avoid that embarrassment would take perfect luck and unprecedented speed. The annals of Company history, indeed. If the fools only knew the half of it.

There were slight worries, of course. The clerk in charge at Carlton might see fit to place romance over duty and common sense. The trader's family might have dawdled a fatal few days. All such things were possible, but the Governor's experience was that, fairly warned, people would not often choose to stand in his way. Rather, they made themselves scarce as possible.

And God help them if they didn't! The Governor did not care for flogging and caning. Leave that for those like One Pound One who lacked the wit to come up with anything better. For the Governor, punishment was an art, and his culprits sometimes waited years for their penance. Ossin and Bouché, the men tried not long ago: they stole and ate Company horses so he forced them to winter in the dark, where cold and hunger would bite like the lash. Another example: Ross, the trader who wasted his time reading. The Governor fired him and rehired him as a lowly schoolmaster. He had done a few things to Colin Robertson but was still unsatisfied. That man deserved something really masterful.

The worst was if they failed to understand how neatly their punishments fit their crimes. The Governor hated that. An artist likes his appreciation.

"But don't worry, Peter, my boy. They will all be out of our way, one senses it, and the night will proceed as planned."

The only mysteries left worth considering were what sort of girl she'd be. Would she be like the majority who quietly submitted? Or was she the rarer kind who would resist? No matter, really. As in the Greek myths, Zeus did not much care if he took his pleasure in the form of a man or in that of an angry swan. The old gods and the Governor shared the knowledge that only the fucking mattered.

Some slight change in the motion of the north canoe woke the Governor from his reverie. The roar of the river came back into his ears as if he were removing his hands from them. He did not open his eyes to look but with the stealth of a snake lowered his right hand from its position on the rail down to the water. His hand entered the cold current and pushed in farther until the surface of the water was level with the base of his wrist. By how high the current rode up, he could tell exactly how hard the Iroquois were pulling.

What it told him now was that they had slackened their effort the slightest bit. Without so much as a blink, and not raising his voice above the level necessary, the Governor told them to make speed. Abruptly, the canoe jumped to its human engine. As the breeze quickened across the Governor's face, fanning him cool, his features loosened into a smile.

❦

THE PRAIRIE, 1825

The land was bleached a thirsty tan. Even the expanse of sky was faded white at the horizons. A parched look, but the weather was cool, the sun having begun its winter slide down the southern sky.

Two of Harriott's riders had fanned out from the rest to hunt, and now they returned, a pronghorn doe slung over a saddle, the blood from its cut throat running black down the horse's side. Food, but Harriott would not let anyone stop to eat it. He pushed them all that day and beyond dark that night. Soon they were riding by a sliver of moon that barely revealed the horizon. Harriott kept Small ahead of the others, trusting her feet in the dark, as he scanned the night for fires.

Later they rode under clouds that screened even that tiny light. The horses and men could barely see at all. A wind rose and the more nervous horses began to shy at sounds. Sage rattling, the denser sound of buckbrush. When Small tripped in a badger hole and fell to her knees, it woke Harriott to the danger of what he was doing. With little regard for where they were, he shouted to stop.

On the other side of night, with just the slightest smudge of grey in the east, he raised the camp and insisted they go on. Even Small resented this, walking backwards as he pursued her with the saddle.

Leaving that camp, Harriott set the pace too fast for the little rest they'd had. He felt as though his night's dream were continuing. He had dreamt that he was riding and had lost all sense of compass. He would ride only to cut his own trail coming back at him. He would change direction and come to a river that he was supposed to have already crossed. As daylight returned, he could not shake this sense that he had gone astray.

Later that day, when the sun was near the top of its arc, they found their first Indian camp, in a shallow valley by a trickle of stream. There were thirty Cree tents, a group dispersing after the summer dances. Led in by the camp's guards, Harriott read the mood of the place and did not like it. They sat around their fires, no one working. Like Englishmen after a wedding, they knew they must return to their duties but were in no hurry to begin.

Harriott could not keep his mind pointed at any one thing, and he found himself in one of their lodges without much memory of how he had got there. He could not remember what he'd done with Small or what his instruction had been to his men. The tobacco-cutting board was out, and the lodge owner's woman was finely chopping a twist of tobacco for the pipe. Harriott supposed he was the source of that tobacco.

The tent filled. The smoke ceremony, the prayers, the speeches. The ritual. Harriott could do nothing to make it go faster. Moment by moment, he fought his own impatience. White and Indian were alike in this: if they sensed you were anxious to go, they would hold you longer.

Outwardly passive, he listened to their cordial complaints: why the Company, which had told them so often they were its favourites, its best hunters, continued to arm their enemies; why the cost of a fuke was so high. His answers came out of nowhere, like memorized prayers.

The fact that it was all such a ritual, a rote, made a silence in Harriott's head where he listened to his last conversations with Margaret. The unsettling one in the night, and the brief and simple one next morning when she'd woken him from his drunkard's sleep. His eyes opened to her eyes watching him.

"It's time you were going," she said, and the way she smiled broke his heart. Her bravery was so much greater than his own.

"Don't worry," she said. "I'll hide when he comes. I know many places around here where no one can find me. When you see him, you'll tell him I was here when you left. Then he won't blame you."

Even with that recollection, Harriott could not stop the wheel of worry. He could not fashion her words into a stick to jam its spokes. Instead, he imagined the Governor arriving at Carlton and Margaret being found. The story, as invented by him, began there.

One version was that she was taken by force. It vied against another where she did not hide, but simply presented herself when called. He could not choose between them, even though the latter suggested a betrayal.

Once or twice during the drone of speeches, Harriott imagined more than Margaret or the Governor. This was a vision of himself leaving camp in the coming night, abandoning his crew. Instead of a mad rush back to Carlton, he would go the other way, south. He saw himself hiding in valleys and gullies, riding the mare by the moon until he crossed the height of land into the Missouri country. Still in secret, he would traverse Jimmy Jock's territory until he found an American trading post somewhere beyond it. He would offer his services. He would start anew.

But this story was just the wheel of worry in another form, turning in a different direction, turning above the ground.

By the end of the first day, the Cree were not done with Harriott. In his travelling tent he lay warm beneath a robe but could not sleep. The night with its sounds and beasts was vivid as a lightning flash. The

Governor on the river, then in his fort, then in his house. Harriott also dreamt of rum. If he'd had the foresight to smuggle a keg along, he could have obliterated these images the only way he knew how.

Pour rum to a depth that conceals. Swirl until the words and pictures blur, until the mind gives up its concerns and grows tired. Sleep.

❧

FORT CARLTON, 1825

Since early morning, Margaret's family had been packing the canoe. They started for Norway House at midday. From the boat, her mother made a final speech in Cree. "Forget about him. Come with us. He can look after himself." Her stern-faced mother made a gesture with her hand and wrist, shaped the two into a device like a crook, as if to catch her in its bend and pull her. A woman beginning to be old, almost hidden among the many bags she'd spent the night packing, inviting her daughter back to childhood.

Margaret thought about it, then she did not think about it. She made no answer to her mother because the invitation, or question, was not real. A person's life does not run backwards.

The canoe slid into the water, the final farewells were slapped out by the paddle, drowned out by the river's roar. She watched them out of sight before heading back to the familiar palisade.

Once inside the fort's gate, Margaret did not return to Harriott's house. She made instead for her other, older home, what passed for a Big House in Carlton's modest terms. The door stood open. When she entered, one of the women from the fort, a labourer's wife, was combing the house for something to steal. She took fright when she saw Margaret and ran past her into the day.

Margaret went to the centre of the room and stood. Here her family had spent their time together. The present nakedness of the room, save for the smoke-stained hearth and chimney, and one crooked chair too damaged to save, was frightening. Her whole childhood seemed erased, removed from the floor and walls, from atop the mantelpiece.

The only thing that hadn't gone was the smell of her father's pipe, and starting with that spoor, she pieced the room back together from memory. Standing in front of the fire, with his back to it, her father smoked and read aloud from his Bible. He did so every evening. Or there, where the table had been, he often stood ranting over the shoulders of her brothers, the lessons about A, B and C. His determination to teach this thing stopped short of his girls, and Margaret had always been glad of that. Like most men, her father believed knowledge was like a nail, to be driven.

While that was going on, Margaret had sat with her sisters and her mother on the far side of the room, making strouds, dressing leather, beading and sewing leather and cloth. Something boiled in a pot over the fire. Her mother would talk to the girls in Cree with the same insistence as their father spoke to the boys: practical things about skinning and softening leather, about sewing moccasins and gutting fish; and what she thought were equally practical things about how you protect yourself from what you cannot see. The old idea about how the beautiful ones in their family were often destroyed by evil; and, cited as proof, Margaret's favourite story, about a beautiful great uncle who had decided to sleep beneath the stars one hot summer night. He closed his eyes on the moon, a completely happy man, and while he slept, a rabid wolf crept into camp and, finding him, bit through his beautiful face.

An ox was also attacked that night and bitten. In the next days it went mad and raged through camp and had to be shot to keep it from destroying tents, carts and people. The uncle with his ravaged face wrapped in clean cloth saw the ox and understood something that was gathering inside him. He packed, kissed his loved ones good-bye, and told them, if they ever saw him return, to shoot him as they would a rabid wolf, for that's what he would have become.

The poor man walked in the strong woods for days, feeling himself grow to the height of a walking grizzly and transform into some other being. He became a Windigo, and his sole desire was to return to his camp and eat the people he had left there. The urge was pitiless but somehow he was not. Such was his courage that he starved himself to death rather than give in to it, and though his spirit form wanders that forest now and forever, he in life did no one harm.

Later that night, the night of her family's departure, Margaret returned to her and Harriott's house, and she sat on their bed with the wedding dress spread out beside her. The other women who had been left behind would be together in one house, gathered around a candle, doing handwork and talking, maybe about her. What her mother had imagined and feared was now at hand. When the Governor first showed his interest, the women had drawn nearer. Then they drew back. Nowadays, none of them, not even the closest friend from childhood, would speak to her. She was the measure of what they were not, and their consolation was that, even at this moment, a kind of trouble neared for her about which they need never worry.

She smoothed her hands over the pebbled surface of the dress, imagined designs that could still be woven into it, smaller flowers that could be made into the petals of still larger flowers, angles like roofs or treetops over, under and through.

So many beads on that dress already. It was an expensive thing, senseless, beyond fixing or explaining. "People dress the way they feel," she'd told her mother once, her one answer to countless questions. That alone was what the dress meant, and she knew of no other way to explain it.

She licked her fingers and pinched out the candle flame. The darkness filled with sound. A wind had risen, just enough to work the palisade poles. She heard a horse stamp and a distant wolf howl. What she could not hear were people and that was very strange. Not to hear people in the fort.

❧

THE PRAIRIE, 1825

By noon the next day, Harriott felt he was free to go. The morning's speeches, some of which were repetitions of the night before, had been listened to. He had fought to keep silence inside him so that they would not intuit that he had things he regarded as more important to think about. All was said and all was done with proper protocol, and the Cree had agreed to pass his words along to everyone they met in the weeks to come. "Come to Fort Carlton. Better trade than ever at Fort Carlton." They were his agents and would tell the other Indians. That would be his excuse to the Governor for stopping only once.

He was giving the ropes on the packed horses one last pull when an old man came walking across the stamped ground, a shambling gait made of creviced arrow scars on both his thighs. Harriott waited and the other Indians, seeing the old man's progress, came as well.

What the old man said was that he knew of a thing, a very strange thing, in an Assiniboine camp a half day's ride to the south. The old ones here would value Harriott's opinion of it.

Harriott tried to control his face as his heart crashed through him. He saw the way the others stared. Be it a two-headed buffalo calf or a stone fallen from the sky, he knew he was obliged to see it.

On the trail to the Assiniboine camp, the pace was slow. Two of the oldest Cree rode on the travois. The riders made their horses walk to lessen the old men's discomfort. It was more than half a day by the time they came to the Assiniboine camp, before they sat in its council tipi, waiting.

The custodian of the thing brought it wrapped in a clean and supple deerskin. He set it down in front of Harriott, then pulled the leather string that held it covered.

Spreading back the leather, Harriott revealed a length of bone the colour of dried blood. A leg bone by the look of it, but exceptionally large. Also, though a bone in shape and construction, the thing was made of stone.

Harriott had seen wood that had turned to stone, but he had never seen a bone that had done so. Bone made into stone. A valuable curiosity, and Harriott panicked inside to think of how much these Indians might have to say about it, how long that talk could last.

The Assiniboine owner explained how the bone had been found on the Red Deer River by his son, who had ridden that way with some other boys, looking for horses. This bone had been stuck in a cliff and, being reddy-brown against the grey, had drawn their attention. They found no horses so they brought the bone back instead.

The old men began or, in the case of the Assiniboine, continued their debate. The two Cree elders, after viewing, touching, weighing and smelling the bone, said it was from a buffalo, a giant one. There might have been a time when all creatures were larger, men and buffalo both. The speakers on the Assiniboine side found this doubtful, citing that no such human bones had ever been found.

A second theory, backed by several Assiniboine, was that the animal was not a buffalo because the bone was not like a buffalo's in ways other than size. These believed that a race of giant animals had lived here once and then moved away. Either they had moved to a place without people, or they had moved so far that the Indians here had never met or heard of the people among whom the animals now lived.

The Assiniboine had obviously been arguing this amongst themselves, and one stood up immediately to denounce the idea. How was it then, he said, that they had heard so many other things from far away? The red pipestone. They had heard about it long before they were able to acquire it in trade. What about the people who danced with snakes? Why would they hear these things and not hear the most amazing story of all, of an animal as large as this?

Finally, Harriott was asked to state his opinion. He told them that in England, the country of his birth, many animals had once lived that no longer did. As the numbers of people increased, the animals were killed or pushed out. Many kinds were entirely gone, but their bones were occasionally found. Perhaps this animal, being such a big animal, with so much meat on it, had been wiped out by their ancestors.

One or two of the Indians nodded, but most looked at Harriott with disappointment. Avoiding his eyes, one Indian said he knew of no animal killed this way. The people would take care not to kill that many of an animal this useful.

On and on, round and round. When the debate threatened to go into a second day, Harriott could stand it no longer. Without bothering to explain why he'd kept back such important news until now, he told the Indians that the Governor was coming to Carlton, and he must go right now to meet him. When he saw how readily they accepted his words, he could have screamed or taken a knife to his arm. The trouble now was that many here wanted to meet the Governor and hadn't on his previous visit. They wanted to go with him.

Not possible, said Harriott. Not this time. The Governor had to come and go quickly because he would take ship for England before winter. At this, they laughed. How could that be true? Harriott countered that it was possible because the Governor was an extraordinary man. When he travelled, he did so at several times the speed of an ordinary person. Harriott vowed that next time the Governor visited Carlton, he would endeavour to tell the Cree and Assiniboine long in advance. But for now, he could not help them and must go.

The sun was almost to the horizon when Harriott went to his crew. Showing an irritation none had seen in him before, he commanded them to pack and mount. They must leave tonight and not camp or stop, nor even build a fire, until they were home.

"The fort is undefended," he yelled at them. "The women are not safe."

A broad and powerful middleman named Paulet, a leader among the men, said in French he would not do this crazy thing. He was tired of being pushed like this and being made to travel at night. He would eat, sleep, then leave in the morning.

The others stayed seated on the tramped grass, showing that they supported Paulet in this opinion.

They were roasting a shoulder of antelope, and the dripping fat made a hushing sound as it landed in the fire. Hot, rhythmic sluice. Harriott felt himself changing, as if the dripping fat were the cause. There was a heavy surging across his chest, down his arms and into his hands. It twisted in the braids of his muscle, taut and red. He had Small by the reins and he dropped them, to pull the fuke from its scabbard. By the barrel he swung it, driving the wooden stock into the Frenchman's face. Paulet had been climbing to his feet. Now he collapsed backwards, gingerly touching his crooked jaw.

"Broken," he said, the sound squishy and bubbling.

Harriott stripped off his sash and handed it to the nearest man.

"Tie his jaw onto his head. Put him on a horse."

Through that night, in moonless shadow, they rode as hard as the horses would let them, a dangerous pace in daylight made horse-killing by night. Their mounts galloped and shied, and stumbled in half-blind pursuit of the North Star. Inevitably a horse rammed a foreleg deep in a badger hole, crashed and spilled its rider like a ball. The horse flailed on the ground, unable to rise. An almost human sound of agony came from it.

Harriott pulled his fuke and dropped from his mare, loading as he came. He saw what he expected—the unnatural angle, the quivering. He put a ball in the horse's brain.

The rider was on the ground still, feeling his parts, and Harriott told another with a stout horse to take him. He gave them last instructions, what star to follow and what precautions to take. Then he left them. He whipped Small to her fastest gallop, knowing that she would give him more than she had if he kept asking. He thought only ahead.

❦

FORT CARLTON, 1825

The Governor gave the Iroquois a small keg to share with the Carlton women. Not enough rum to seriously hurt anyone or delay their morning departure, but enough to fuel a dance and keep them minding their own business.

He asked after Margaret and the women pointed to a cabin, the only one with light in its window. He went and knocked and a woman's voice said, "Come in."

The room was mostly dark. A log glowed pink on the hearth but the candlelight he'd seen came from beyond, through an arch in a second room of younger-looking wood. There on the bed she sat wearing a dress gaudy with decoration, dense with beadwork and hanging on her slender shoulders like a sack of shot.

The Governor stood for a moment beneath the arch, taking her in. Pretty in the half-light, in spite of the ridiculous dress. The face smooth-skinned, like cream made flesh. Rare to see that unmarked a skin in this country. The heat rose in him and he spoke to it schoolmasterly, instructing it to be patient. Take this moment at least to assess her mood.

That proved no simple business. Where the Governor had expected fear, or perhaps the other, the cowering adulation that some affected, he saw a calm that was not entirely flattering. The dress and the carefully plaited hair at this hour also confused him. Could she possibly have been expecting someone else? But if so, where was her surprise? How often does the Governor of the Company walk into a woman's bedroom?

So it must be the note. The enterprising little tart had figured it out and was expecting him. Hence the clumsy effort at dressing for the occasion.

"You are able to read, then," he said.

She did not answer.

"Listen, Miss Margaret. I have had a long trip. Can you find a drop of something for your Governor to drink? And for yourself, of course."

The question was rhetorical given that he had seen a keg and a cup on the table. He did not care for rum, but a clerk was not likely to have brandy or wine. Even in his condition of anticipation, the Governor noted the position and condition of the keg.

The clerk in charge, our Mr. Harriott, takes rum when no one's looking.

It had to be the clerk's doing and not the woman's, because he smelled no rum on her. She smelled very clean. The Governor raised his hand as she passed to fetch his drink and brushed her, the dress giving back its hard feel of beads.

"Mr. Harriott is gone, then?"

She was reaching down a cup and did not reply for the seconds it took her to straighten some papers on the shelf.

"One Pound One sent him to the prairies," she answered.

"I'm sorry to miss him. Oh well. Another time."

She handed the Governor a cup well filled with rum.

"You take none?"

"I hate the taste."

"That's good. So many acquire the taste to a troublesome degree. Come. The bed seems the most comfortable place to sit."

The Governor saw with satisfaction how she sat. Close enough that their arms touched.

"Here, Margaret," he said. "I have brought you a little something."

From his pocket he produced a silver brooch, a better class of bauble than he usually offered. What a prize she was, so cool. The brooch would have excited greed in most women, but she only gazed on it casually. It would have offended him, this, except it excited him more. The unusual is always the most enticing.

At length she took the brooch off his palm. She glanced at it briefly, then put it down beside the candle on the stump beside the bed.

"You don't like it."

"I do."

"But you don't put it on?"

"It will look better on another dress."

"I believe you're right. You haven't space on that one."

He laughed. She did not.

"You're very serious, my dear."

He reached up and touched the side of her face, ran his finger to the corner of her pretty mouth. He was searching for tightness, found none.

"It is rather exciting being here with you alone. You must have known from my notes that I fancy you. Or do you still contend that you don't read my letters?"

"Mr. Harriott reads them to me."

"Oh my. That must have caused a problem or two."

"No."

"Is he so understanding a man as that? Your Mr. Harriott?"

"He isn't here. Why talk of him?"

The Governor laughed again.

"Quite right, my darling. Why indeed?"

He leaned around her then, kissed her lips. She did nothing. The lips cool and unmoving. The first small surge of anger passed through him.

"You don't seem pleased by me."

"I've seen a man before."

The heat surged into the Governor's face. He hated her to see him flushing. Impertinent. He drank and slammed the rum cup down beside the broach. Sometimes it was a waste of energy to treat them like ladies. He unbuttoned his flies, spread the cloth, released Peter into the cool air.

"There now," he said. "Maybe I go too slow for you. Why don't you take off that absurd dress and then you can touch it if you like. Or lick it. That's what it likes best. You'll find it very adaptable. Versatile but not patient."

She glanced at his prick, then turned her eyes directly up to his, unblinking, unchanged.

"I said I've seen a man before."

"Yes, and a good many I'm beginning to think. Just how understanding is this Mr. Harriott?"

"I thought you came to trade."

To put her insolent eyes on something else, the Governor stood. He pushed his trousers off his hips.

"I am the Governor, you ignorant girl, and I have travelled a great distance. You are not the only handsome bitch on this river, and if you think I'll pay in my own department for what I can have right this second for nothing . . ."

"Then you should go."

The Governor looked down as something caught the candle's light. A Bay Company dagger was pointing up at him, the tip an inch from the tender purple of his cock. He leapt back, the fallen trousers strangled his knees, and he fell. The knots of the crude floor hurt him like cudgels. Looking at her past his bare knees, the clump of his clothing, he thought, my pistol . . .

He clambered awkwardly to his feet and jerked his pants up. He flipped the buttons closed. He came close to her and drew his hand back, poised by his ear so she could see the heavy silver ring that would mark her most. The knife was suddenly there, dividing her face so that one doe's eye shone on either side of the double edge.

"You're a madwoman!"

No reply.

"You belong in a madhouse or in an Indian camp. Certainly not in a Northern Department fur fort. Do you honestly believe you can threaten the Governor, with a knife, and I will walk away and put it from my mind?"

She kept hold of the knife but moved it down. She lay it flat between her beaded thighs.

"I said I'd trade but you offer nothing."

"What are you, then? A simple whore? Or does your Mr. Harriott put you out to whore?"

The knife moved again. She scraped its blade across the surface of the stump, carrying the cup, the candle, the silver brooch before it. The candle snuffed. The soft silver of the brooch bounced along the planks and disappeared under the bed.

The knife continued its slow movement and the Governor was powerless not to watch it. This time the point came to rest at the centre of a large flower overtop her breastbone.

"This is what I own," she said. "I can trade it or I can take it because it's mine."

To the Governor's eye, the air between them was thickening. It inhaled like paste. He broke away from her unblinking stare, spun, and marched for the outer door. His feet and legs did not work properly, the feet reaching too far ahead. At the door, he had difficulty flipping the simple latch. All the while, the steel tickled between his shoulder blades even though he had not heard her move from the bed behind him.

Throwing back the door, he ran. He ran into the square, into the smell of dying leaves and the river's fishy reek. His lungs were tight full but he kept on gulping the night air.

※

FORT CARLTON, 1825

The grey hour before dawn. The decorated north canoe was pulled up on shore guarded by an Iroquois. Harriott spurred his struggling mare out of the river and past the man before he could come awake. He rode past the corner of the fort, saw the gate was open, hammered at Small's bloody flanks with the bent rowels of his spurs. As they passed the posts of the gate, Small sank beneath him. Almost slowly, the great-hearted mare ran herself into the ground.

Harriott lost the stirrups, both at once, flew down the mare's neck and over her head. He rammed into the hardpan with his chest and all his wind flew out. His head full of lights, he writhed on the ground for air.

When he could see again, someone with English leather boots was standing inches from his face. He flattened his hands on the ground and pushed, raised himself high enough to see the Governor flanked by his Iroquois. Behind them were the fort women, drunk and laughing.

Then one of the women understood the meaning of Harriott lying there. She threw herself beside him, shouting "Where is my man? Where is my husband? Is my man dead?"

Harriott spat a mixture of blood and dirt and told her that her man, along with the rest, was behind him somewhere. Alive, unhurt. He fought up onto his knees and saw the Governor's arm raised, one finger pointing back over Harriott's head.

"You've killed that horse. I want an explanation."

"I had orders to go to the prairie Indians. From the Edmonton Chief Trader when he passed through. I had to leave the fort undefended."

"So you left your men stranded, also undefended, and came in yourself. That's a ridiculous explanation. You will pay for that horse. She looks like a good one. Now get up and try to resemble an officer."

Harriott's legs were punk. He stood but barely.

"Why are you here, sir?"

"You think I must explain myself to a clerk? No, I must not. What I will say is that I've spent quite enough time at this sorry post."

He signalled crisply for his Iroquois to follow him. He moved towards the gate.

"You too," he said to Harriott. "I have more to say to you."

They started out of the fort, passing Harriott's mare where she lay still in the dust. The Governor called his attention back.

"How often I've heard you praised."

Harriott was hobbling, lagging behind on the trail from the fort gate to the river. The Governor hurled his words back over his shoulder.

"Recommended for promotion I don't know how many times. For some reason I've always known it would be wrong to grant you it. That seems absolutely justified now. Never before have I seen a horse ridden so unmercifully, and mind, it's not mercy I care about but waste. I will not tolerate waste."

"She was my horse."

"You're a Company servant. You have no horse."

"She was mine. Her name was Small."

"Stop arguing with me, you idiot."

"I wanted to protect the fort."

"The women of the fort most particularly, I suspect."

The Governor stopped at the river's edge. He tapped his toe in irritation.

"This young woman, Margaret. You have some personal interest in her."

"Yes, sir."

"Then you have a problem. I spoke to the woman last night and she is mad."

"I don't believe so, sir."

"Then you have a very loose standard as regards sanity. You don't mean to make the woman your wife?"

"As soon as her father consents, yes, I do."

"What a fine impression you make, Harriott. An abandoned trading party, a mad wife, a killed horse. And you expect promotion, I suppose."

"I obey my orders."

"Then obey these two. I was not here and get out of my way. I am near losing my temper, which is something I never do."

The second the Governor was into the centre of the canoe, the Iroquois raced it back into the water. They leapt in over the sides and seemed instantly to be paddling with the current. In the midst of such action, the Governor sat like a stone cat, eyes forward.

Harriott did not wait for them to pass. He ran clumsily up the path, batting the overhanging branches away. Through the gate and across the square. Small's sides were still, her eyes clouded and frozen. He went past her to his cabin and banged open the door. The smell of smoke and rum assailed his nostrils.

In the far half of the cabin, in the gloom and shadow there, Margaret sat curiously straight on the edge of the bed. She wore the wedding dress. Her hair was neatly parted and plaited, not a hair loose. She looked at Harriott when he entered but showed no emotion, not even surprise at the wildness of his appearance.

He approached her halfway, stopped.

"Will you tell me what happened here?" he asked.

"Nothing happened here."

She stood and her face vanished behind a rising curtain of beads. The bead wedding dress came off over her head.

THE BEAD
DRESS

1826–1829

PRO PELLE CUTEM

Dear Editor,

We all wind up as bones one day, whether they travel the ocean or bleach on the ground where you died. But that don't make the pain or struggle of living any less. All these men cared how they turned out, and that meant sadness for those who didn't get where they thought they would be.

One Pound One made Chief Factor in 1826. In the trade they called that getting your second parchment. It happened the same summer as the Governor came back from England, without the wife everybody said he went looking for. What he did get in England was a second governorship to go with his Northern one, and that probably pleased him more. The joke was that the sun could set on the Governor's empire but it was a damn long day.

As a Chief Factor, One Pound One swung more lead. He got Mr. Harriott out of Carlton and set him up in Fort Assiniboine on the Athabasca River. Mr. Harriott's Margaret went with him.

I don't know what to say about Mr. Harriott's country wife. I never had the chance to meet her but he talked about her often, usually when he was drinking and sad. Sometimes it seemed the Governor had the power to make people be what he said they were. No wonder we were all afraid of him.

William Gladstone

FORT EDMONTON, 1828

A man enters a forest clearing. A bird falls dead at his feet. If he ignores the omen and keeps walking, what is he? A man free of superstition? Or a careless fool?

The omen One Pound One brooded over was the death of his interpreter John Welch, which took place at precisely midnight, the moment of New Year's, 1828.

One Pound One had never been the kind to carry on long after someone died. Death was too common, something to shrug off and be glad it wasn't you. So when the Chief Factor turned nervous in response to Welch's death, he was the most surprised observer in all the fort.

Wherever he went, whatever he did, his thoughts would not leave the Edmonton ice cellar. They never stopped seeing the bluish corpse that lay there on a bed of skinned and quartered buffalo, where it must remain until the frost went out and a grave could be dug.

Whatever the relationship had been between One Pound One and Welch, it was not friendship. The Chief Factor could not name Welch's children, nor did he reliably remember that of Welch's wife. He had never been inside the interpreter's cabin and did not recall ever inviting the man to his own rooms for tea or brandy.

The death obsessed him nonetheless. The ominous way it happened and the particular man it killed were portents, and One Pound One feared they might mean his good times at Edmonton were over.

A golden age cut off at New Year's midnight, after which something lasting and dark might begin.

The reason One Pound One felt this way could be traced to events concerning Welch in two separate places and years: the first at Chesterfield House in 1822, and the second at Edmonton in 1826.

On the earlier occasion Welch, a small, wiry and naturally pugnacious man, had picked a fight with a bunch of Big Bellies outside the pickets of Chesterfield during the winter of the Bow River Expedition. He had cheated the Indians in a trade and had been caught with no one to back him up. If the larger and stronger Mr. Pambrun hadn't come along by accident to haul him safely away, Welch would likely have died there and then.

One Pound One had been well aware of this occurrence, and of Welch's escape, but that alone was not enough to make him decide that Welch's life was charmed. Anybody can be lucky once. In fact, his response had been to mark a cross beside Welch's name in the list of *engagées,* a mark to remind him that he shouldn't count on having this man around for long. Likely Welch's temper would get the best of him again and again. The odds were that eventually there would be no hero handy to save him.

At any rate, Welch survived Bow River and One Pound One liked him well enough to employ him as an interpreter afterwards at Edmonton. It was there, in 1826, that Welch did the thing that lifted him out of the ranks of ordinary men, that made him a legend, in One Pound One's mind at least.

In the fall of 1826 some Stoneys had come to Edmonton to trade. They traded a few peltries, then got behind a herd of Edmonton horses by the fort and started driving them away.

A Halfbreed named Lussier was the quickest Edmonton man into his saddle. He gave chase so fast that the first exchange of fire came between the pickets and the trees. It was ball for arrow, and Lussier's bullet found the back of one Indian, who slumped in his saddle but did not fall. Lussier drew his dagger and rode after to finish him, but as Lussier's horse drew even, the Stoney straightened and fought. That Indian fought hard for his life, and only when he was badly weakened from loss of blood could Lussier finish him.

That was just the beginning.

Had the Stoneys not lost a man, they might have taken their horses and gone. Now that the horses had cost them a life, they wanted a better bargain for it.

Though not numerous enough to keep the fort besieged, the Stoneys made it so the horses had to be guarded by day and kept in the fort at night. Still, the thefts continued. Then the Stoneys got too bold and lost a second man, not killed this time but captured. One Pound One locked the Indian in the bastion. For some reason, that Indian's presence in the bastion, singing and carrying on, caused a dread silence to overtake the fort. The moaners and whisperers began to moan and whisper that the Stoneys were preparing an attack. The Indians could not be seen beyond the palisades but they were believed to be there, snaking through the grass, coming for their man, ready to inflict heavy damage on his captors if they could.

That was when the business affected the temper of John Welch. He started his tirade in his cabin. Half destroyed it and put his woman on the run. Then he came out onto the flag square, yelling that no Stoneys were going to keep him hiding in the fort like a frightened child.

Before long, he had gathered a company of the like-minded, and they threw open the gate and marched out. Under every bush and broken sledge, they poked and prodded, until a bayonet thrust into a haystack sent thirty Stoneys flying.

A mad chase began.

Some of the Stoneys ran for the river and a few others turned and fired. In plain view of the fort, three of the Indians were shot dead. On the Company side, John Welch fell with a bloodied breast and a shattered arm.

In all that chaos, smoke and noise, exploding fukes and crying men, Welch lay unconscious and bleeding. But after a bit, he awoke. He climbed to his feet and staggered a bloody zigzag towards the fort.

As Welch approached the Edmonton palisade, he looked up and saw the Stoney prisoner, the one who had started the whole thing, climbing down and escaping. Welch drew his dagger. He let out a yell. He made one last furious rush. "Like a dying grizzly bear" was how One Pound One put it when he told the story. He told it often, his favourite yarn.

After the collision, the Indian fell one way, dead. Welch fell the other way, presumed dead.

But Welch did not die. For several days he lay in a swoon. Then, one morning, he woke up. Just like that, he sat up, produced a great vomit of blood, and lived.

The whole time Welch lay as if dead in the fort, the battle with the Stoneys continued. After the first exchange, in which Welch was shot, the Company had chased the Indians to the river. They expected them to plunge in and swim for it, but instead the Indians vanished into the riverside fringe of trees and bush, and a deadly return fire started up from that direction. In preparation for their attack on the fort, they had dug breastworks. Safe in them now, they took command of the battle.

In truth, the Stoneys were never driven off. They simply tired of the war or were satisfied with the result. When they finally left of their own accord, they had upwards of twenty Edmonton horses running with them. They had severely wounded five Edmonton men.

One Pound One was a doctor's son and the closest thing to a physician at Fort Edmonton. He studied the men's wounds and, after a long deliberation, pronounced most of them fatal. He could see no medical reason for at least three of these men to go on living.

What guaranteed that the story would stick with One Pound One, as one of the strangest occurrences he had ever witnessed in the trade, was this: after Welch sat up out of death's swoon and puked himself back to life, *every one of the other wounded men also began to revive.* Brébant from an arrow in his chest. Pepin, the blacksmith, from a bullet in the haunch. Sinam, the Cree Indian, from a bullet through the shoulder. Even Little Assiniboine, who had been shot clean through the throat, recovered.

Every man, including those assumed lost, rose to do the Company's work another day.

One Pound One was not a superstitious man, and he proved it by not expecting, after these events, that his men would routinely jump up and live after receiving wounds. But according to some other arithmetic, he did conclude that John Welch was magic. To recover from such terrible wounds, coupled with his earlier escape at Chesterfield, seemed to make a case for his having a fiercer grasp on life's cable than an ordinary man. What's more, given the four who survived with him, maybe Welch had the ability to transfer his bulldog tenacity in the matter of staying alive to others.

Though One Pound One despised superstition and tried to beat it out of his men each time he found lucky charms and bags of pagan trash hanging around their necks, it was also true that One Pound One had found his own lucky charm for Edmonton in the person of John Welch. Now, when that same man lay dead in the ice cellar, torn asunder from chest to crotch, it was an understandable shock, an opening to dark forebodings.

Most men would suffer such a feeling to wear off gradually, but One Pound One could not. He lacked that kind of patience. Going about his fort in the first frigid days of 1828, he trailed his woe like a dog with a cut arse. He turned upon himself to snarl and bite. After a week, with the nervous agitation still upon him, he was enraged. He locked himself in his office with a keg of rum and a foot of tobacco. He vowed he would not come out until he had decided who to blame.

One Pound One was a great believer in blame. By blaming, you at least proclaim that effects have causes. Behind most deaths and maimings, there is a human blunder, and if he could just find it in this case, isolate it, he hoped to free himself of the notion that a cloud of black luck had blown over his territory and meant to hang there.

From the moment he started to think this way, the Chief Factor was drawn to Christmas Day, 1827, as a point of beginning. In the chain of cause and effect, the first link seemed on every pass to be the moment on Christmas Day when the two of them, Ted Harriott and his woman Margaret, came by dog-drawn cariole down the portage road from Fort Assiniboine.

One Pound One had gone out to meet them that morning, and the first thing he noticed was the lack of decoration on either Harriott's cariole or his dogs' harness. In keeping with his transport, Harriott himself was badly dressed and stinking of rum. The day was brilliant, so much so you could barely open your eyes to it, and that made Harriott look even worse. He had the death pallor of mushrooms, and he looked at you from deep inside a starved face.

Margaret looked better. Sober, well dressed, pretty. But One Pound

One saw something about her too that made him shiver. Her eyes were bright enough, but One Pound One saw no connection between this avidity and anything going on around her. Same with her laughter, which ignored the joke and sprang forth out of nothing.

Before they sat down to the Christmas feast, Margaret insisted she must change into a better dress. She came to the table finally in such a monstrosity of bead-covered nonsense that One Pound One had to laugh. He couldn't stop himself. The thing must have weighed a stone.

Harriott, meanwhile, acted as though he saw or heard none of it, that his woman's antics along with everything else were a little more than he could follow. While the officers were toasting with wine, brandy and shrub, he somehow managed to keep toasting himself with rum. Maybe he had a keg cached on his cariole that he went to each time he excused himself to piss. He grew steadily blearier as the evening wore on. The map of veins on his cheeks became brighter and more complicated.

What Harriott was that night—ask anyone—was dull. Not one story worth listening to. Not one joke worth laughing at. Just complimentary nonsense about how fine the meal was and how clever the decorations. When the men separated from the women to smoke, he fell silent altogether except when goaded by a direct question.

"What news from Assiniboine?"

"What? Oh. Nothing, nothing really. A quiet place."

He also had a gift those festive days for avoiding One Pound One. The Chief Factor never caught Harriott in the act of avoiding him but he must have been. John Peter Pruden was there, and Henry Fisher from the Mountain House, and One Pound One was able to have private parleys galore with them. But never did a private moment with Harriott present itself.

During the conclave he had with John Peter, that man had also complained about Harriott. The old trader asked One Pound One what he knew of the domestic life of Harriott and Margaret.

"Good lord, John Peter. Your daughter. Your nephew. Why ask me?"

"The nephew has nothing to say and the daughter makes no sense."

Speculation about the couple was cut short on the morning of New

Year's Eve. Before dawn, Harriott had his cariole loaded and his dogs hitched. He bundled his woman into the sleigh and declared himself ready to go. One Pound One had never seen Ted Harriott pass on a regale, but he did that day. He was full of reasonable-sounding blather about weather and having left only one man in charge. He was still firing back lame nonsense when he started his dogs and made his awkward jump onto the sleigh.

One Pound One was not fooled. The reason Harriott was leaving was sitting right there in the cariole, face peeping out of her swaddle of skins, absorbed in something no one else could see.

Their going should have set the mood right, and everyone pretended it had. It was to give the day a rectifying boost that One Pound One allowed the drink to pour even before the winter sun had set. This meant that the usual New Year's allotment of rum was gone well before midnight. To keep the tempest wild, the Chief Factor made up several more toasts out of his private store.

But whatever Harriott and his woman had done to the day was hard to repair. Margaret had touched a lot of the women with a lick of her strangeness. Many men had adopted Harriott's trick of getting joylessly drunk. A dance began, but the jig steps had no heart and the fiddling was off-key. There was not much love between lovers and not much fight between enemies.

As a remedy, a sweetener, One Pound One could think of nothing but to apply more spirits. What else was there? Far from cheering the crowd up, it had the opposite effect. A Hudson's Bay man's gauge is set at a standard measure. He cannot deal with more. Given so much to drink, the louts fell about the place, lamely trying to fight. Men and women puked until the floor was slippery. If you shut your eyes, the sound was an animal din.

Just before midnight, One Pound One supervised a final pouring and left, disgusted. He remembered John Welch coming up to him near the door, drunk as a dog like the rest, wanting to know the time. The Chief Factor had pulled his watch out, held it dangling before the interpreter's swimming eyes. The two hands were about to clap at midnight.

After that, One Pound One crossed to his house and was sitting on the bed pulling off his boots when he heard the cannon blast. Happy

New Year, he said by reflex. He said it to no one, because Louise and his children had stayed behind to dance.

On New Year's Day morning, 1828, the fort slept late, or pretended to. Taken as a whole, the place was like a wounded animal that crawls into a shadow to lick and suffer itself either dead or better.

One Pound One had taken enough drink to make his head pound, but lying in bed was not his way. He dressed and stomped back and forth. No one rose to make his breakfast, so he took his foul mood out of doors into a sparkling morning where the world was coated thick with hoarfrost.

He walked about the fort and the silence oppressed him. For company, he went inside the horse corral and stood among the beasts, their warmth and homely noise. Grunting and nuzzling his pockets for food. But a man couldn't do that all day. He found himself following trails in the snow and reconstructing from them the previous night's events. A piss-yellow bore hole here. A basin of green puke there. Then a big trampled area speckled pink with someone's blood and a more definite trail of red going away.

The reason he climbed to the bastion was that he wanted to see the cannon. In his search for something amiss, for someone to scold, he remembered the midnight explosion. The one responsible would have been in a hurry to get back to the midnight ladies all lined up for kissing. Likely he had left the cannon in a mess.

What One Pound One saw from the bastion doorway did not cause him to shudder or his guts to heave, perhaps because of the almost comical way John Welch was lying plastered against the wall by the force of the exploding gun. Like everything else that morning, the corpse and the cannon were coated in frost, bristling white. Welch's eyes were open wide and the face with its white beard wore a surprised look, as if his parting word with life had been "Oh."

The hoarfrost made the cannon look fuzzy and soft, even along its burst and ragged seams. The crater that was Welch's belly was likewise decorated, the blood itself having grown an old man's beard. We need a new cannon, One Pound One told himself.

He stood a moment longer and imagined what must have happened when the night's revellers heard the blast. They heard it, they cheered, and all the men kissed all the women. But not one of them, the drunken, careless fools, noticed that John Welch did not return.

Finally, then, One Pound One had his chain of events constructed. For him, the death was recorded this way:

> Harriott and his mad wife came to Edmonton for Christmas and New Year's. The trader's drunken sadness and his wife's madness had set the festive days askew.

> One Pound One had tried to put things right with an excess of liquor.

> Drunker than their custom, the men and women of the fort leaned towards destruction. John Welch leaned so far that death reached up and took him.

Clumsily, Welch had set the charge. He probably threw in extra powder for a nice big bang. He lit the taper, lowered it to the fuse. Ignition and an outward wrench too strong for the old cannon to hold. It split and gulfed his midsection in fire, shot his guts full of hot splinters travelling faster than he was as he flew towards the wall.

The sad thing for One Pound One was that, having constructed this chain of events, having affixed the blame, he felt little better. He left his smoking office, the emptied rum keg upon the table, and the doomed feeling and the hectoring questions left with him, barking at his heels.

What kind of year begins with such a midnight?

❧

In the spring of 1828, a cat at Edmonton found two orphaned rabbits. She carried them home and added them to her litter, suckling them alongside the rest. Every man, woman and child at Edmonton, plus all passers through, climbed to the hayloft to witness the marvel.

The scrutiny bothered the cat. She tried to escape it by moving the litter. At the same time, she could not move from the loft she was in because of ravenous fort dogs below. Finally one of her moves was unwise. She stopped above a gap between boards and the nest gave way. The kittens caught themselves by their claws but the rabbits fell through. The dogs erased them, a miracle no longer.

One Pound One decided to send a mating pair of buffalo to England. It had never been done, and he became obsessed with the idea of authoring the moment when the first red-eyed buffalo exploded down a ship's gangplank and routed a crowd on an English pier.

Reasoning that full-grown buffalo would be untransportable on the river, he called for the capture of two buffalo calves. These could be trussed and carried to York Factory in a standard brigade boat. They could be raised there to a more impressive size, then shipped to Gravesend and London.

Early one morning, One Pound One was summoned to the yard where the calves were kept. Each one lay on its side with a feathered arrow through it. There were no witnesses to the slaughter; no one had seen Indians within the walls. Later, One Pound One would hear from his outgoing traders why the Indians feared his plan. If two buffalo travelled the ocean to England, they thought their God would take the rest.

❦

FORT ASSINIBOINE, 1828

The old fort stood within a curve of the Athabasca River with the Swan Hills rising to the north and east behind it. Except when the goods were portaging by horse to and from Edmonton, it was a quiet place. Only four adults lived there and one baby girl: Edward Harriott and Margaret; a Halfbreed labourer named Savard, his woman, Marie, and their infant son.

Savard was nondescript and secretive, no more energetic or talkative than he had to be. Harriott's tendency to treat him as an equal made the man nervous and suspicious. Marie, the wife, was even more silent, and sullen, too. She seldom spoke to Margaret and tried to keep her from touching the child.

Since their Christmas visit to Fort Edmonton, Harriott had been telling Margaret she must go home to her father's family. Clearly the isolation and loneliness were more than she could stand. This suggestion often came at dinner, when Margaret slid before him a plate of charred venison or one of her other specialties: raw meat and stinking rotten meat.

Harriott was drinking these days, working his way through his winter trade goods. When drunk enough, he would command the labourer's wife to cook. The first time he did this, Margaret went for his skinning knife. She was quick and had it unsheathed and poised behind the woman's back before he could disarm her. From then on, when he called Marie to cook, he sat with Margaret at the table and held her by the wrist.

Having the labourer's wife doing chores that had once been hers upset Margaret, but Harriott's telling her she must go home bothered her not at all. Like most of his words, these did not alight in her brain. When she did smile or look fearful, or become angry, she harkened elsewhere, to some drama of her own.

The reason Harriott threatened to return her but did not in fact pack her off to her father's fort had to do with many things, lingering affection and surviving hope being two. He was also afraid of the assumptions others would make about how she came to be so strange. They would likely view it as a product of mistreatment. You can beat an animal until it no longer acts like itself, they might say.

As for John Peter, he would go on blaming the trouble on the original fault of their union. Usually the decayed fruit of incest is the children, but when there are no offspring, it stays on the tree and rots there.

As it was, John Peter would be very unlikely to take his daughter back. After the summer when the Governor secretly came for Margaret, John Peter had returned from furlough in England to find that Margaret had not moved with the rest of his family to Norway

House but had stayed behind at Carlton with Harriott. Furious at such disobedience, he rode up the river to fetch her.

As soon as Harriott saw John Peter in the square at Carlton, he knew what he was after, and he told Margaret to fear not. He would not let her father take her. But Margaret paid no attention. She was already packing. She did not so much as kiss him when she left.

When he got her back to Norway House, John Peter found his daughter changed. He thought it was homesickness for Carlton and Harriott, and assumed it would pass, but Margaret's mother, ever alert to the signs of evil and Windigos, knew it was more. Margaret, their cheerful child, did not laugh now. Instead of talking about Harriott, she spoke of the Governor, unseemly talk of going to his bed if that was the bargain he sought. John Peter thrashed her for it but it didn't change her, except to make her more silent and sullen. Her mother scoured the cattail sloughs and riverbanks for medicine, fed her every possible remedy, but that too was not enough.

Just before breakup the following spring, John Peter came back to Carlton. Behind his horse, he led another on which Margaret sat bareback. When Harriott stepped out his door to greet them, John Peter tossed the halter rope into his hands.

"Take her," he said. "I withdraw my objection to the union."

His own horse was blown, but he didn't stop to change or rest it. He sped back out the gate at a gallop.

During the winter that led up to that day, Harriott had suffered an ache that was one part loneliness and another part some unnameable fear that Margaret was coming to harm. It was as if the pain he'd felt on his desperate ride back to Carlton, when he'd burst the heart of Small, had never stopped. People speak of a second sight that many possess with respect to a lover or a child, an uncanny way of knowing across distance that the other person is sick or dying or in danger. Harriott's pain was that vision unremitting, through every daylight hour and into the night by dreaming.

Now he beheld the result. The beautiful young woman that Uncle John Peter had left on a horse in front of his house was Margaret no longer. Later, with the stranger in his house, Harriott sat at his table and wept.

That fall, news that Harriott had been posted to Fort Assiniboine arrived with the brigade. His orders were to leave immediately. Harriott put Margaret back on John Peter's horse and they rode first to Edmonton, then two days onward to their new home on the Athabasca River.

Whatever was wrong with Margaret became instantly worse. They hadn't been at Assiniboine a week when she threatened to kill herself, then Harriott. She might have, too, except her memory for a plan was short. She would race for Harriott's fuke where it hung on the wall, but arriving would only stare at it quizzically. She might straighten it or lift the corner of her apron and wipe a smudge off the stock.

Variety was not a feature of winter life at Fort Assiniboine. To while away the short days, Harriott hunted along the river and up into the hills. He joined the labourer Savard in chopping wood for the fires. A few Indians came to barter furs and stayed awhile. Dull as the post was, it was out of the ordinary for them.

Even the busy times of spring and fall when the goods were portaging were different only when compared to the rest. Compared to themselves, they were unvarying, too, every task and league of road the same.

There was no comfort of distraction for Harriott's mind, and he did little to help himself. The books he had once loved he read no longer. He seldom wrote to his relations in England and never mentioned books or Margaret when he did. Instead of reading, he watched. If Margaret stared at the fire of an evening, he stared at Margaret, in case a cinder might explode and land on the hem of her dress. He did not trust her to put out a fire if one started.

Another cause for alarm was when she rose as if someone were calling her. That could happen in any weather, and she never stopped to put on a scarf or cloak. Twice she let herself out the fort gate, and in the deep cold with so many pack wolves, Harriott had to fight to get her back inside the pickets and the house.

What Harriott did with all this worry, to tolerate it, was drink. Stupefied with rum, he was less efficient at preventing disasters and so had built a risk into the miserable round of their nights and days.

Sometimes when he was drunk, he would shout at the face that would not hear him. He struck her, too, and that was more humiliating, to see her cower or smile.

The other thing was when he mated with her. Throughout her madness, she maintained her tidiness and her simple adornments. She was neat and pretty. She did nothing to encourage him, was always remote and indifferent when he coupled with her, but he pretended that her thoughts cleared during it. He imagined they were falling backwards, out of their troubled times into the innocence of the past.

Guilt was the dependable aftermath. Thus far, nature had insulated Margaret from conceiving, but unless Harriott left her alone, the possibility existed. He feared a child because he thought it would kill her, or she it. The rest of the guilt was about taking her at all, like a woman unconscious from rum. That she was his woman made no difference, being a kind of lie. This stranger whom he kept and whom he entered when she wasn't looking.

Only one aspect of these days mimicked the old life, something that happened on rare bright winter days when Harriott went hunting. At Carlton, even as far back as when they were children, Margaret had liked to accompany him on hunting forays. She did not look strong but was quick with a skinning knife and able to travel with a quarter of venison on her back. Nowadays, if she saw Harriott take down his fuke and snowshoes, she would often jump up and fetch her own winter gear. At these times, she dressed carefully and properly for the weather, and would check and refurbish her firebag: steel, flint, punk. It amazed Harriott. It was as if she had forgotten she was mad.

Once out on the trail, it could go bad, a miserable business in feet of snow to recapture her if she fled and fought him. Throw her on his shoulder and wallow home under the barrage of fists. But just as often, there would be no problem. The act of moving on snow occupied her in a good way. The logic of a hunting silence extended to her mind and hushed the voices there.

Of all Harriott's fears these days, two stood above the rest. First, he feared that he would be forced to leave Margaret for an extended Company duty. Second, he feared details of Margaret's condition would reach the Governor's ears.

He knew the first was no idle fear because he had let it happen once. At the end of his first outfit here, he'd grown angry over his exclusion from outside life. He joined the eastbound brigade as it came through and went from duty to duty all the way to York Factory. When at the other end of summer he returned, it was to find that Margaret had been putting on her bead dress and going into the woods alone at night. Each time, after a search, Savard and his woman found her curled like a fawn in the undergrowth. If she had a knife there would be nicks along her arms. Marie was very superstitious and said the wounds were to attract a Windigo, that Margaret sought to be devoured. In this way Harriott learned not to leave her again.

As for the Governor, Harriott knew well how that snake could bite. He imagined the Governor prescribing him a choice. Leave the Hudson's Bay Company or get rid of the woman. Even in the Governor's wilderness, they would not kill a woman for losing her wits, but the Governor had it in his power to do something almost as bad. He could pronounce her a burden on Company finances, not able to earn her keep, and insist she be returned to "her people." What he meant was her "Indian" people. That she was generations removed from the last Indian who felt any duty towards her family was not deemed relevant.

Because of the intensity of this last fear, Harriott made himself stupid to the obvious. He clenched his mind to keep from knowing that, with so little else to talk about, a madwoman was the gossip's first choice. In the entire district, he and One Pound One were the only two who did not mention Margaret's strangeness in their letters. All the rest claimed to regard it as their duty.

Liquor and self-deception were Harriott's tools for making Margaret's madness invisible, innocuous. The Christmas season of 1827 was not so bad, he told himself. Others never notice the little peculiarities that seem so big inside a family. In reality, the society of the fur trade was a bog, flat and uniform, from which Margaret's oddity stood out sharply. Lone and striking. Tamarack and strange.

In the end, the suggestion of sending Margaret back was a drunkard's lie. It evaporated the instant it was spoken. Its purpose was to be a lie, an ineffectual pastime beyond which Harriott did nothing, save occasionally to hope.

In the English novels he once read so avidly, women often went mad. They went mad and died tragic deaths that were God's revenge on them for sinning. But there were exceptions. Once, a gentlewoman who had been mad for a year was thrown from a runaway carriage. The axle broke, she spilled out, she hit her head. After being unconscious for weeks, in a stupor from which no one expected her to rouse, her eyes came brightly open. In clear terms, she asked her husband for their baby son.

That Margaret might suddenly wake in this way seemed possible to Harriott, if he could hide her long enough and keep her from harm. Or rather he *might* have believed this. He stood ready to. Possible outcomes for Margaret and himself passed through his mind without cease, new ones every day, just as possible causes and reasons for her madness did. All of it remained within him, as geometric and floral patterns of his own mind.

Whatever anyone might say about Margaret, Edward Harriott was poised to agree, to join in, to raise the lantern and light the way down the appropriate winding tunnel. No one knew this labyrinth better than Harriott, who had been lost in it so long.

❧

YORK FACTORY, 1828

At Council in the summer of 1828, One Pound One surprised himself by having a religious thought. It had to do with Jesus Christ, Pontius Pilate, Edward Harriott and himself.

In this thought, or memory, One Pound One was a boy of ten and he was listening to the priest's Good Friday sermon in their parish church in Montreal. Spring had not yet come despite its being April, and he yearned to be outside doing something more befitting the bright cold day. Teaching a dog to pull or finding a bully to challenge. He supposed he had begun to fidget, because his father had given one of his ears a twist so sharp it almost tore from his head.

He paid more attention to the sermon then. The priest was describing Pontius Pilate's washing his hands of Jesus. The Jews wanted Pilate to take the blame for killing Christ but the Roman was too cagey, maybe even a little moved by the Messiah's holy manner. In full view of the Jews, Pilate washed his hands so they might know that he was innocent of the blood of Jesus.

The connection to the present moment was that the Governor had just recommended a violent change in the career of Edward Harriott and was trying to make One Pound One take responsibility for it. They were going through the list of Northern Department posts, confirming appointments, and the Governor had stopped at Fort Assiniboine to ask a question.

"Are you satisfied with Mr. Harriott at Fort Assiniboine, Mr. Rowand? John? The question's for you."

One Pound One knew very well the question was for him, and the answer should have been no. Mr. Harriott had been slipshod, forgetful and drunk at Fort Assiniboine.

"Harriott? Oh, fine. Steady as he goes."

He could have saved his breath. The Governor had the terrier look and would not stop until his prey lay broken-backed upon the table.

"I don't wish to doubt your judgement, John, but you know that I want more than steadiness from a clerk in charge of an important post. We've always had good men at Assiniboine. Frankly, my impression of Harriott is that he applies himself the minimum. Also I believe he consumes more than his allotment of rum. And we all know that he spends too much time swanning around after that woman of his. Of that particular swarthy idol, what can I say?" The Governor raised his eyebrows as high as he could.

Again One Pound One resisted any urge to reply, left the moment open for the Governor to continue.

"What I want is to test the man. I want to find out once and for all what he's worth. Let's take him out of the Saskatchewan and force him to learn something new. Maybe in Dr. McLoughlin's Columbia District or Connolly's New Caledonia, he could set about proving himself. I have too often been told about Mr. Harriott's smoothness with Indians, Mr. Harriott's ability with languages. Mr. Harriott's this and that. If he is so special, I want more out of him. Do you agree?"

Instead of reviewing the particulars, One Pound One was thinking about Pontius Pilate. He might as well have the same bowl of water before him now. If crucifixion is a man's lot, if he won't hear your advice above his own dismal themes, why persist?

"You have no comment, John?"

One Pound One shook his head.

"You surprise me. You have always been Harriott's champion. Perhaps, having him in your district, you have found him unworthy of your faith?"

Again no answer from One Pound One.

"Very well. Let's plunge him in without delay. I say we send him west immediately with this season's Columbia brigade."

After that, they wrapped up the meeting quickly to accommodate the Governor's departure. He was about to start another of his transcontinentals, leaving immediately so as to reach and cross the mountains before the snow was deep on the Divide. His goal this time was to prove if either the Fraser or Thompson Rivers would serve as a new communication route to the Pacific. He had heard from plenty of others that they were impossible but was following the principle that you don't know a thing unless you test it yourself.

❦

THE TRANSCONTINENTAL, 1828–29

The westernmost part of the Governor's domain, the area between the Rocky Mountains and the Pacific, contained two fur districts: New Caledonia in the north and the Columbia in the south. The latter was named for a great river whose mouth was the destination of the long-journeying English ships. On that river, above its mouth and above danger from tides and storms, was Fort Vancouver, the Governor's destination for the winter of 1828–29.

The Governor had planned the voyage, his latest and perhaps his last transcontinental, to be the most innovative and festive of his journeys. He had an excellent crew of paddlers and what he hoped were promising companions. For playthings and novelties, he had a woman, a Scottish piper and a musical snuffbox. The latter he intended to show off to the Indians by hanging it around the neck of a dog. But as the journey ground on, through the monotonous forests of the Athabasca, over the Rocky Mountains to the New Caledonia headwaters, he found himself hating it.

The woman was Margaret Taylor, the boat captain's daughter, the one with whom he had spent parts of several years. In a moment of sentimentality he had decided to take her with him, to do her a last bit of honour as his longest reigning mistress and mother of several of his bastards. It was his intention to spend the winter after this one in England, finding an English wife, and that meant he must put aside all his old concerns, his bits of brown. He would never be able to say so much as hello to the Taylor woman again.

But instead of accepting the journey as a suitable ending and trying to enjoy the damn thing, or for that matter taking his word that she would be looked after, Margaret Taylor had taken to arguing with him. Craftily she had waited until they were beyond the last post where she could have been abandoned.

By painful coincidence, his other Vancouver-bound travelling companions proved to be boring and annoying as well. Archie McDonald, a veteran chief trader from the Coast, was tedium personified. He gave his opinion on every twist in the river and described every weed and tree by its Latin and common names. If he spotted a twig he did not recognize from one of his books, he was ecstatic and wanted to stop so that he could collect the specimen or draw its picture.

Dr. Hamlyn, a new surgeon bound for service at Fort Vancouver, turned out to be the worst complainer with whom the Governor had ever shared a boat. His aching back (head, arm, leg), water in his luggage, a nail protruding in his shoe; sunburn, windburn, a chafing in his underwear.

Often the Governor wanted nothing more than for their chatter to be drowned out by song, and even here he was frustrated. His best singer among the voyageurs was rendered mute by a sore throat for most of the journey.

The other two novelties, the Scottish Highland piper, Colin Fraser, and the musical snuffbox, had not betrayed him. The reaction of the unworldly northern Indians to both was greatly amusing. One explanation of Fraser's bagpipe was that it was a goose, which by squeezing with his elbow and strangling with his fingers, the Scotsman was able to prompt into this strange song.

When the Governor hung the snuffbox from a dog's neck, the Indians were almost too amazed to speak, though one knelt down and addressed the dog in all seriousness, asking how it came to have this power. But even this joke grew tired thanks to McDonald, who insisted on replaying it for every Indian gathering. The Governor wished finally that he'd thrown the damn thing in the river.

The grand and suitable finale was his testing of the rivers. The Thompson was navigated with sufficient difficulty to disqualify it for all time as a trade route, but at least it hadn't tried to kill him. The Fraser, by comparison, was a boiling cauldron, a whirlpool aimed at hell. It turned the Governor's boat over and slammed it down. Thrashing in its brown deeps, with no knowledge of up from down, the Governor thought his life was ending. But fate, for its own reasons, flung him up again and allowed him to make shore, coughing water for hours but alive.

After all that, the Governor made the Coast and Vancouver in a predictable temper. The greeting by Dr. McLoughlin, District Chief Factor of the Columbia, was unctuous yet superior and did not improve the Governor's frame of mind. McLoughlin had been trained as a surgeon in some bygone year and insisted on the title. He was immensely tall and had the unpleasant habit of standing too close so you had to crane your neck to look up, a habit the Governor hated in a man almost more than any other. McLoughlin's eyes were piercing grey under long white eyebrows that he combed out to ridiculous length like wings. The Governor had never liked the man, but his ascendancy to the throne of the Pacific was a fact of life he had inherited. He had found no solution for it, as yet.

The thought of spending the entire winter with McLoughlin and his travelling companions made the season seem unbearably long even before it had begun. Then Harriott and his damnable woman Margaret arrived. The Governor's first reaction was fury, and it took him a long moment to remember that he himself was the reason for their presence.

He had ordered it at Council. Harriott was such a pathetic sight, with his pallid mildness and meek politeness, so lacking in spirit (while so full of spirits, judging by the colour of his nose and the veins in his cheeks). He looked as though he were being eaten more than he was eating.

As for the woman, she was the same attractive cat that had drawn a dag on him at Carlton, and he hated the fact that the sight of her still made him yearn. But that was before he noticed how entirely mad she was. The Governor had heard the rumour about her lost wits but had not credited it. It was the sort of thing people say—she's mad—but it was seldom so. There was no disputing this case, however. Mad as a St. Petersburg hatter, and the Governor found it satisfying in a way. Revenge not taken but given.

Now that the two were at Fort Vancouver and meant to remain there for the winter, the Governor decided they could at least furnish him with sport. He began by insisting they join him and the other leading families of the fort at all officers' dinners. At these functions the Governor asked after their health, asked for their thoughts on the relatively milder coastal winter, and everything else that it would have been normal to ask normal people. And he went further at times when the brandy was affecting him, adding a little double entendre to the questioning. Harriott was so entirely lacking in defence it was hilarious, and the woman was so off the mark with her every response that it was guaranteed to prompt great shouts of laughter.

Here again McLoughlin showed his perversity when it came to the Governor. He refused to find fun in any of this banter, and when they were in private, the doctor would bring the subject around to Harriott for purposes of praising him. Though Harriott had no experience of coastal Indians, whose ways were so very different than the prairie kind, he was already becoming a favourite with several local tribesmen. Never had the doctor seen anyone pick up the Chinook trade jargon faster. Perhaps the Indians liked Harriott's quiet approach and manner because it was not unlike their own.

Then McLoughlin went further.

After not having seen Harriott or Margaret for more than a week, the Governor asked McLoughlin where they were. Calm as could be, the doctor told him he had dispatched the pair to New Caledonia, where Chief Factor John Connolly was complaining about a lack of decent men. Given Harriott's fast adaptation at Vancouver, he seemed the ideal man to send.

On the face of it there was nothing wrong with what McLoughlin had done. Harriott was his man. New Caledonia was Columbia's sub-district, and as District Chief Factor, the doctor could put whomever he pleased wherever he pleased. But between them they knew it was more. The Governor had been amusing himself. McLoughlin had put his playthings out of reach. Someday, the Governor thought to himself, an opportunity would arise to return the favour.

❧

FORT EDMONTON, 1828–29

One Pound One did not spare many thoughts for Edward Harriott in the winter of 1828–29. He was too busy with the evil events of 1828, a year that had lived up to its portents at every turn. It had been the worst fur season of the Chief Factor's memory and, with any luck, the worst he'd ever know.

By fall, the prairie was raging with fire. The buffalo had either succumbed or stampeded out of the smoke to God knows where. The sun through the smoke was thirsty and wizened. There was bloodshed in the heavens come evening, and from Edmonton's palisade at night, the south sky was so bright yellow you wondered if it wasn't coming for you. If the fire slipped down the opposite escarpment and hopped the river, they'd be burned to the ground by morning.

A certain kind of winter grows from such a fall. By the time the snow put out the fires, the grass was gone. Where there's no grass, there's no buffalo. No buffalo, no Indians. No Indians, no trade.

The Blackfoot crossed the burn only once the whole winter. They came not to trade but to tease. A former Nor'Wester had been hired by the American fur king Jacob Astor to open a fort on the Missouri at the mouth of the Yellowstone. He was another McKenzie, Kenneth, and he

had been a wonderful hunter when One Pound One knew him at the
North West Company, a good trader, too. Now he was said to dress like
a French pansy in silks and brocades. The Blackfoot-speaking Indians
made it sound as though McKenzie was paying liberal price for any old
piece of skin and his stores were stocked with marvels.

One Pound One was certain the old Hudson's Bay Company standard goods were superior but was unable to make that argument owing
to a desperate shortage of supplies. This winter, of all winters, the
Company had starved him of guns. Explain, please, how a trader was
supposed to get skins and meat out of Indians without guns. The
Blackfoot looked in his empty store and laughed. They turned their
backs and rode away.

In such a mood, One Pound One did not think on Harriott often.
If he did, it was with embarrassment more than affection or pity.
Harriott and his woman were at Fort Vancouver where the Governor
had sent them, which meant that the three of them were wintering at
the same fort.

Pretty possibilities. The Governor and Harriott face to face across
the dinner table. At Harriott's side, the bit of brown the Governor had
once fancied so. That young beauty was frothing mad by now, but
maybe the randy Governor wanted her still. Maybe he'd been moving
Harriott around the map of Rupert's Land like a chess piece just so he
could accomplish it.

One Pound One was not capable of enough pity to extend to where
Harriott was now. The Chief Factor's heart was barely big enough for
his own district, where the trade was poor and the hunting poorer. By
the time the Governor came in spring, One Pound One was supposed
to have a working plan for getting the Blackfoot trade back from the
Americans, and that quandary had delivered him into the hands of
Jamey Jock Bird.

Certain people are like the porcupine's quill when it breaks off and
stays beneath the skin to fester and pain. Jamey Jock was that to One
Pound One. Back during the fur war, One Pound One had been on the
rise as a Nor'Wester. His job had been to oppose the Bay Company
men of Edmonton House from the adjacent Nor'Wester stronghold of
Fort Augustus. The old Governor James Bird's family was seldom in

attendance at Edmonton, but his eldest son, James Junior, or Jamey Jock, was there often enough for One Pound One to learn to hate him.

He had a way about him when he walked or rode as if he was a British nobleman, instead of just a Halfbreed. When he looked at One Pound One, a full partner with the North West Company, it was the only time in this country that One Pound One felt belittled. He could not account for why, but Jamey Jock was able, with no more than a look, to make him feel his ugliness, his limp, his coarse manner, his clumsy language. Every lack. And for that alone, One Pound One could never forgive him.

But now, after several pleasant years of never having to see the man in the flesh, the Governor was forcing the two of them together. It had begun with a mention back in the summer of 1825, and now it had blossomed into a letter of instruction. While passing by to the north through the Athabasca country last winter, the Governor had taken time to pen a note and send it to One Pound One by express messenger. As cryptic a nonsense as the Chief Factor had ever seen in print, it read:

> The man of whom we spoke will visit you. Give him all that he asks. Ask him for no explanation. Keep silent about it to all others, including me. All this is of paramount importance.

It was hard to know what it meant, given all the detail it lacked, but at very least it seemed to say that One Pound One was bound to be visited by Jamey Jock Bird. One of these days that haughty bastard would walk or ride in through Edmonton's gate and ask for whatever he felt like having. He could behave with any amount of impertinence. He could be rude and insulting if he cared to, and One Pound One could not lay a finger on him. He must meekly go to the storehouse and fill the list as if he were a wee clerk beneath Jamey Jock's authority.

And that was the worst thing. The letter also meant that Jamey Jock Bird, Halfbreed imposter living among the Indians, had secrets with One Pound One's Governor to which the Chief Factor was not privy. That stung the sharpest.

When Jamey Jock did arrive at Edmonton, in the days leading up to One Pound One's departure for Council, he did not behave in any of the ways One Pound One had predicted. It made sense, too. Why bother to be rude when the greatest insult has already been given? He could be polite as pie, and it only grated all the more.

The Halfbreed arrived on foot, at dawn, a tall, slender figure framed in the gate. No one had even seen him cross the river. He was dressed in his old Bay Company translator's garb. A common cloth cap without a feather. A blue wool jacket missing half its brass buttons. One Pound One offered tea and Jamey Jock accepted, and they talked about the winter and where the buffalo had gone, what the prospects were for beaver from the Missouri country. As for the Americans and the new Blackfoot Confederacy tendency to trade with them, Jamey Jock professed not to like it any more than One Pound One did. He had never wanted the Americans in his country, he said, with their corn liquor and their violence and their easy treachery. He was not without power over the Missouri Piegan, but his power wasn't enough to stop the American trade every time.

When Jamey Jock left Edmonton the next day, he had a huge trading outfit, one of the largest to ever leave that fort, roped onto several pack animals that were also part of the generosity. Indians materialized out of the trees on the south side to help him cross the river, and they were soon streaming through the notch in the forest on the southern rim that was the trail south.

When things like this happened under your nose, it was hard to find time to think of old friends who had moved on and surpassed their usefulness. About all Edward Harriott provided One Pound One's imagination these days was a reminder of what can happen on the Governor's dark side. For some reason none could fathom, the Governor had selected Harriott to punish. It seemed he would never relent, forget or tire. Whatever had ignited that vengeance, however long it would take for its flames to die down, One Pound One preferred the smudge to be out of view. Beyond the mountains was a good place for it.

And if anyone should accuse him of not caring enough about a friend, that person should think again. Who was it gave Harriott his chance to rise in the trade? Who was it ever made an attempt on that sorry man's behalf? Call it fate, inadequacy, bad luck or whatever, Edward Harriott had failed to use the chance he'd been given, and the country was not generous enough to offer again and again.

What was friendship anyway but a drunken kiss? Two slobbering fools with their hearts on their sleeves, convinced that the feelings they've drammed up with Indian rum are of signal importance. Nonsense. A friend is the one who gives you a leg up into the highest saddle. Nothing more than that. At the present moment, an enemy like Jamey Jock was more valuable to One Pound One than a friend like Harriott.

❧

FRASER LAKE, 1829

The snow was too deep for dogs when Harriott decided he would intercept and shoot the Governor on his spring return from Fort Vancouver. It was just cold enough to travel decently on snowshoes when he closed the gate of the fort at Fraser Lake and led Margaret past the Indian camp and down the Nechako River.

Their first camp under the stars began dry, but a wind blew up in the night, a hard westerly that soaked the snow and ate it with appetite. They woke wet and all that day carried the weight of it on their backs.

The wind continued until the snow was rotten. Even in the deepest shade, it sank under every footstep. Snow grown heavy in the trees slid from the branches in sudden dumps. They walked to their knees in sodden drifts, waded sudden rivers. The snowshoes were worthless and they left them in a tree.

The second night, Harriott cut poles and lashed them together like a land raft over the lowering snow. It was so warm they did not need a fire, but Harriott built one anyway and fed it through the night to keep off the wolves. They were exhausted from walking and remained silent until Margaret started vomiting again. Through the night, she continued to be sick.

By morning Margaret was hollow-faced and pale, blue under the eyes. She ate snow and Harriott could not stop her, she was too quick. Her health and the poor conditions meant they travelled only far enough on the third day to have to go through the motions of building camp again.

By the time dark came that night, Harriott had given up. He sat on a robe, wet through. Margaret threw herself to the edge of the skin and heaved from an empty stomach.

By her sickness and the impossibility of moving any distance, Harriott was forced to understand how mad this trip was, not just in view of the weather, but mad from the start. In the best of circumstances, they would have been lucky to make the Fraser River.

Now that Harriott allowed the light of reason in, not one thing about this plot made sense. He had relied on the assumption that the Governor would return east by the Okanagan route, whereas the man was more likely to prefer the Columbia route he'd used in 1826. Harriott had set out with no timetable but the season and the weather, with no compass but the river and the stars. Only a miracle would have allowed him to cross the Governor's path at the moment the Governor was on it.

Harriott understood this now that he'd given up, but he had understood none of it at Fraser Lake when he'd dreamt daily and nightly of a small red hole appearing above the Governor's vigorous eyebrows, above his slightly bulging eyes.

The plan for killing the Governor had come to Harriott at Fraser Lake, but the desire was older. At Dr. McLoughlin's Christmas feast at Fort Vancouver, the Governor, with his mistress beside him, had led endless choruses of laughter at Harriott's and Margaret's expense. Every joke was about them. He suggested that her madness was a ruse so that she could romp from bed to bed and be morally excused. Harriott's drunkenness helped him not to notice. It was all nonsense and cruel, but everyone laughed to prove their servility.

By New Year's, the Governor was still at it. He seldom passed on a chance to mock them. Harriott had gone to Dr. McLoughlin, begging for a transfer. To anywhere, any godforsaken post. Dr. McLoughlin's own dislike of the Governor was probably the key that unbarred the gate and let them out. How angry the Governor must have been to wake and find the mice that he tortured for amusement gone.

Harriott's relief over their escape turned sour again when Margaret escaped at night from one of their camps on the trail north. She started back, for some reason trying to return to Vancouver. When Harriott stopped her, she fought him with all her mad strength. He understood then that he had escaped nothing, that all of this was destined to go on. Faced with a perpetuum, the mind searches naturally for things that can be stopped, such as a man's life if you shoot him.

In their short time at Fraser Lake in the New Caledonia District, it was not wrong to say that Harriott went mad himself. Logic got him nowhere, so why not unleash the mind and let it search for other ways? The Governor had started this. Now he'd made it worse. Maybe the Governor was after all the black growth in Margaret's mind. Maybe he was the chancre in Harriott's head as well. If the Governor could be plucked out and smashed, maybe then it would end. Maybe then Margaret and Harriott would discover themselves sane and free.

Harriott did not sleep that night by the Nechako River, their third night on the trail. He fought the wolves and waited for the light. In the grey dawn, he looked for a long time at Margaret's sleeping face. So sick, so drawn, so lovely to him. At times he felt he had carried her on his back for years. At other times, he loved her. In the whole world, there existed the two of them. Only Harriott cared about Margaret, only Margaret about Harriott.

He reached for his fuke and stroked the wooden stock. Ran his finger around inside the trigger guard. If it were a fiddle, he would like to play on it the death of the Governor. If he could not . . .

Margaret's stomach rose on her again. Barely waking, she crawled to the edge of the raft of poles, rested her forehead on the cruel bark. Nothing left inside her to puke. Harriott reached and rubbed her back. What else to do but bring her home to Fraser Lake, where she could at least lie sick in bed?

Deeper in him played the other tune.

She would trust him even as he held the gun to her chest. He trusted himself to reload and turn the weapon around. As they rested through that day, the melody continued to engage him. By twilight, it had stopped. He had found himself incapable. Morality had no say in it. Delicacy did, and cowardice.

They began their return to the fort that night, when the temperature had cooled and the snow was as stable as it would be. They walked until it was too dark to see. Harriott made a makeshift camp, and the wolves that had been following for days got their courage up to sneak close to the fire. When his yells wouldn't keep them back, Harriott shot into the flash of a pair of luminous eyes, waiting in the moment of deafness and blindness afterwards for a possible rush by the others.

There was no anger in Harriott's heart over the possibility that the wolves would come, no disappointment when they failed to, only a feeling finally that he and Margaret were destined to go on awhile. The killing and eating would continue.

They made Fraser Lake the next day, the weather having changed again and the far shore obscured with a drifting fog. The Indian camp was along the lake edge between the river and the post. Harriott led Margaret to the tent of the woman who served as the tribe's midwife and maker of medicines. Inside her lodge of sticks and skins, the woman told Margaret to lie down and, by the light of a tallow candle, studied her. Then she laughed.

"She's sick," Harriott said, thinking there must be some misunderstanding.

The Indian woman took him by the arm and pulled him. She led him over and placed his hand low on Margaret's bared belly. Hard, smooth, risen. The woman forced her face into a look of sternness. In Chinook, she said, "Don't take her hunting any more."

❧

COLUMBIA RIVER, 1829

The Governor left Fort Vancouver in March. Already the fetid, swampy quality of the coastal air had returned, on the heels of a winter of rain. As he travelled the Columbia River away from the coast, and began to rise from the cedars into the spruce and pine, into the cold sharp air and snow, his heart lightened despite the tough travelling and the summits ahead.

The Pacific Coast: what a harbour for illness, murder, crawling life and rain! Some said it was like England, but the Governor saw it differently. Like Africa or the Amazon. Nature gone berserk.

New Caledonia, the second district west of the Rocky Mountains, where Harriott and his mad damsel had gone, was a higher, cleaner place but in other ways shared the coastal malignancy. People found ways to die in New Caledonia that only Columbians would understand. They saddened, weakened, soddened, crippled; died slow deaths.

It was no different either in the Snake River country, where Peter Skene Ogden, whom the Governor had hired to pursue wholesale slaughter, was the latest example, soon to be the latest tragedy. Starvation and fighting, eating hemlock-poisoned beaver and curing the resulting dysentery with gunpowder and pepper had given him the look of a man about to die. You can only eat fire so long before it eats you.

Ogden for the Bay Company and various Americans were cleaning out the Snake River watershed with great rapidity. When those beaver were gone, it would leave the Missouri headwaters as the final prize. There in the land of the Piegan and Blood, the American fools were paying as much as five of their dollars for a beaver skin when the Company could afford no more than two. Still, the Governor wasn't about to hand it to them without a fight. He planned either to win the Blackfoot trade or to ruin it for everyone, which was his reason for reaching into that unmapped territory and fetching out Jamey Jock Bird. That Halfbreed would be working for them on the Missouri already, provided One Pound One had not bungled his orders.

Dodging ice and fighting the incredible depths of snow, the Governor and his men moved up the valley of the Columbia River. As always the Governor probed the side passes, looking for quicker ways east and west. When they finally crossed the Continental Divide west of Jasper House, the Governor's final thought on the Columbia and New Caledonia Districts was what fine penal colonies they would make after the fur trading was done. At present, only he used them as such. For indolence, cowardice, disloyalty, drunkenness and general lack of pluck—crimes you could not hang or banish for—you could not improve on these districts as places of penance. Men incapable of improvement invariably perished there or went mad.

When he had chosen the West for Edward Harriott, he had chosen well. It was doubtful poor Harriott would ever succeed in scaling the mountains back the other way.

❧

FORT VANCOUVER, 1829

The New Caledonia posts closed for the summer, and the traders gathered for the journey out along Okanagan Lake to Vancouver. Harriott worried hard beforehand whether Margaret would be able to stand the trip, but she was over the sickness part of her pregnancy now. In truth, once they left the mountain forests and found the hot, dry trail by the lakes, she seemed to be one of the few able to enjoy it.

Their procession was slowed by two travois carrying men too ill to ride. A few on horseback were also sick, wincing at every step, sweating in the sun. But Margaret was fine. She sat her horse casually, the bulge of the baby resting on the pommel. In the fresh air, her cheeks bloomed red. Just to look at her you'd think she was cured, that the child inside had chased off her demons. Except that she never spoke. Sometime during their hopeless walk down the Nechako River, words had left her. It was as if she'd never had them.

When they got to Vancouver, Chief Factor Connolly, the uneasy man for whom Harriott had worked this winter, flew into his annual rage. He wanted to return north immediately, and as usual, his kegs, boxes and ironworks were not ready. Ritually, he stormed that he could not succeed in New Caledonia without the quick turnaround this delay denied him. The current year's excuse was that the supply ship the *William and Ann* had not arrived from England. Nothing could be done for him until it did.

For Margaret and Harriott, the reception at Vancouver was

strangely warm, almost regal. The Governor was gone, Margaret was pregnant, and the women of Vancouver flocked to her, eager to perform penance for the ridicule of the season before. The silent Madonna was their celebrity now.

Harriott found it difficult to have Margaret taken off his hands. She had been his charge, his worry, for so long. But benefits accrued immediately. Allowed to work without interruption, he showed an ability that caught McLoughlin's eye again. During the winter he had made a similar good impression on John Connolly. Even with his liking for drink, he was soberer and steadier than most. In private, McLoughlin and Connolly agreed it was a travesty to have such an experienced Englishman in the country without a parchment, and both men knew the cause, though, in their conversations about it, they did not name him.

Near the end of June, still without a ship but upon rumours that the ship was near, they took the final steps towards readying the furs for shipment. It was Harriott's job to see that the men beat the skins vigorously enough to remove the moths before they sealed them airtight in old rum puncheons. That was what they were about when the terrible news came up the river that the *William and Ann,* under a new captain, had entered the Columbia by the wrong channel. The ship had wrecked on the south spit.

It seemed certain that neither the captain nor any member of his crew remained alive. Drowned or murdered was the question. The cargo bales had vanished, and it seemed likely that a nearby tribe of Clatsop Indians had helped themselves.

Immediately, Harriott was part of preparations for maritime war. He and the other officers prepared forty men in four small boats while Connolly went chasing the *Cadboro,* the local supply vessel. All parts of this navy were to intersect downriver and proceed to the Clatsop village.

A relay of messages began. Connolly's messenger went ahead to the Indian village and demanded the return of all Company property. The reply was that the Clatsops would restore what they could and would make up in slaves what they had already consumed. The condition of this cooperation was that the English not land.

By now the Bay Company boats were in the channel offshore of the village and a heavy wind had risen from the sea. The boats were slewing badly in the giant waves and, if they did not make shore soon, threatened to collide and break apart. Even the *Cadboro,* the largest boat, yawned at every seam. None of them would last long exposed to such weather.

The last message to the village was that the Company was going to land. Given full restitution, the villagers had nothing to fear.

While they were disembarking men from the *Cadboro* into landing vessels, the messenger returned carrying the Clatsop chieftain's final response. The Indian had sent a worn-out brush and a blackened scoop, and told the English these were all the goods they would ever see from him. As the message was conveyed, a rain of musket balls whistled in the air and burned the water. Underway for shore, the Bay Company crew fired back. When they crossed into range, an Indian fell dead onshore and, as if that were a signal, the rest of the Clatsops turned for the forest and were instantly absorbed.

Unaccustomed to these damp and brooding forests, Harriott found the sight shocking. First, there had been people running in all directions on the sand; now there was not a soul. Silence and stillness. Except for the smoke from cooking pits and the corpse lying on the beach, the scurry of life might have been imaginary.

The makeshift navy pulled its boats up the soft sand. Half the men took cover behind the boats and kept their guns levelled on the wall of trees while the rest began to search. The Indian war canoes near the buildings contained some of the rum. Two more puncheons were unearthed from the dirt floor of a house. When Connolly could find no more, he ordered the place burned.

Sick from the sea on jellied legs, Harriott watched the fire inch its way. Everything was too damp for a hot blaze, and what the fire did instead was blacken and devour, unleashing a strong smell of the sea.

There would have been so much to look at here on a peaceful day. Immense war canoes with long carved prows. Curved boxes fashioned without nails. The greenish fish-smelling smoke was rolling it all into the sky.

While the wet village smouldered, the men were sent to search for corpses. Along the windward shore, their guns primed in case of ambush, they crunched along, poking sticks into rubbery heaps of sea wrack. In the course of a couple of days, most of the dead were found where the tide had left them.

Dr. McLoughlin had joined them since the military action. After a perusal of the bodies, he chose for the dead skipper the one whose face had been eaten by birds. Two pocket watches were found on the body and these, plus a neck scarf, were bundled up as the official effects of the deceased Captain Swann.

A couple of days of this and Harriott began to feel sick, an illness along his nerves. Trapped between the imprisoning forest and the drowning water, he longed to be back with Margaret. He longed so hard his spirit started pulling from his body. He was desperate to protect her and their unborn child. He did not know how or from exactly what.

The village burned with infinite slowness. The smoke furled into the flannel sky. Every face around him seemed mad and incapable of caring. A village burning and nothing in them all but a slight drumming in the blood, a rhythm for disaster.

Up and down the seashore, Harriott scavenged after death. Death confirmed by discovery, made official by interment, made morally satisfactory by a few words from a tattered Bible. All the while, gripped with panic, he felt a shrieking need to escape.

If the Company is a body, he thought, and the rivers are its blood, he must try to take his family somewhere, across some divide of continents, or across an ocean, where the tainted blood did not reach. Trapped on the corpse-strewn strand in the shadow and stench of the burning village, Harriott made this his vow. He would take Margaret and their child away to where the other world began.

❧

When Harriott returned to Fort Vancouver, he found Margaret calm and well. The women were treating her like a baby, keeping her warm and fed, speaking to her in that musical way some use for creatures who can't talk back.

Harriott asked the women if Margaret could stay with them until after the birth of her child. It was obviously a better place for her than at Fraser Lake, where they might have to deal with the birth alone. Harriott offered a purse to offset expenses.

Then Harriott asked for a meeting with Dr. McLoughlin. In his office, the doctor studied Harriott with shining steel eyes in tiny skin envelopes. The white eyebrows crowning them were as feathers poised for flight. So long living by the sea, McLoughlin had begun to look like a sea eagle.

Harriott explained that he wanted a furlough. He pled his wife's condition. He admitted that he had long considered her incurable and had accepted her madness as their fate. But now that she was pregnant, it changed matters. The child would be born before Christmas, and for the sake of it, Harriott wished to exert himself in search of help for the mother. He wanted to look for that help in the world outside.

What he proposed was that he return from New Caledonia at Christmas and take his wife and child by dog team and snowshoe across the mountains. He would do so in January. His eventual destination was London.

Harriott said he realized the Company owed no financial support to this project. But given his years of service and the quiet life he had led, he had savings with the Company that he was willing to sacrifice. All he asked in return was the grant of time away and permission to put Fraser Lake in other hands for the remainder of the season.

The Doctor's eyes retained their predatory glare. The muscles at the hinges of his jaw worked as if he were trying to free something from his teeth.

"Why January? Why not wait until spring?"

In truth, Harriott was afraid to wait until spring, but he groped for an excuse more plausible.

"Less activity, sir. If I wait until spring, I'd be using resources the Company needs."

As for the cold in January, it could not be worse than winter on the prairies. He and Margaret had done much travelling there in the winter months.

"We'll need luck, I know, but I must take the chance."

The Doctor stared at the table and stroked his jaw. He began citing conditions. The furlough should be limited to half a season, and if Harriott did not return for next year's outfit, his bargain with the Company would be considered broken.

Obviously, if either the mother or the child should fail to survive the birth, all mention of the subject should cease.

Two days later, Harriott departed. Margaret sat in a chair in the home of an interpreter's wife, the prairie woman with whom Harriott was leaving her. Harriott told Margaret he was going and he looked for alarm to rise in her face. But there was none. He kissed her lips and they did not move under his. When he put his hand on the rise of her belly, she smiled.

❧

NORWAY HOUSE, 1829

On the brigade to Council that summer, One Pound One spent much time composing a speech. He wished to inform the meeting, the Governor in particular, of a strange and sinister peace on the prairie. From Red River to the tops of the Rocky Mountains, from Edmonton to the Missouri, not one Indian was at war, and One Pound One did not like it.

Frankly, it went beyond peace. According to his spies, the Blackfoot had herded horses east into the Cree-Assiniboine country this spring. When they got there, they traded them for between two hundred and three hundred guns. They killed a herd of buffalo on their way home and went to Carlton to trade the jerked meat. That was how One Pound One came to hear of it.

Then, when the Blackfoot were back home, the Cree crossed their territory with a second shipment of guns. These they traded to the mountain Kootenai for more horses. The Blackfoot had once blockaded the river above the Mountain House to prevent trade with the Kootenai. Now they permitted one of their enemies to sell guns to the other. Madness.

One Pound One still thought of the Governor as relatively new to the trade. He feared he might not credit these events with their sinister peculiarity. For the first time in years, One Pound One craved the company of Ted Harriott. There was a man who would understand perfectly the gravity and strangeness of the situation.

But Harriott was not on this brigade, nor would he be at Norway House for the meeting. Not even within five hundred leagues of it. One Pound One must face the Governor alone.

Before the meeting at Norway House began, One Pound One had hoped to speak to the Governor, but it was impossible. All the toadies were crowded around, drinking his health and begging for stories about the winter at Fort Vancouver. Then they were ushered into the meeting and One Pound One began to understand how little hope he had of reaching the Governor with any news, especially the important kind.

The Governor was barely recognizable as himself. Perfectly reasonable queries he received with impatience, flippancy and petulance. If anybody made a ridiculous suggestion, he applauded it, and what he liked best of all was a funny story or a joke. As if the purpose of Department Council was to report the year's accumulation of humour.

Adhering to no apparent agenda, the Governor made little decrees as they occurred to him, one of which was to make Harriott a chief trader. Given the tenor of the day, One Pound One thought it might be a joke, too. To be retracted later. *Oh no, surely you knew I was having some fun.*

When they stopped the meeting to piss, One Pound One cornered One Eye, an ancient he generally trusted.

"What the hell is going on?" he demanded, as they faced into a bush.

When One Eye understood what One Pound One was after, he laughed heartily at the other's expense.

"You really don't know?"

"Would I ask if I did?"

"How came you to be so far removed from the Company's gossip?"

How indeed, thought One Pound One.

What came out, finally, was that the Governor was off again to England and this time made no bones about his plan to secure an English wife.

"McTavish and McMillan are already over there," said One Eye, buttoning his flies. "They're looking for women already. English wives are the fashion nowadays, John. You'd better get one or you'll be left behind."

And off went the old monstrosity, laughing as he adjusted himself in his pants. As ugly and hard-boiled a trader as you'd ever find, and even he was infected by the sentimental excitement.

One Pound One had gone to Norway House with one concern. He returned upriver with two. Surrounded by his trippers, he ranted his grievances out loud.

"What if the fashion was a duck's egg smashed on your regent? Would they drop everything and go looking for ducks' nests? What in God's name, in this country, could be more useless than an English wife? Will she chew your leather? String your snowshoes? Run behind your cariole? Make fire out of her firebag? And what becomes of the women they already have? Of the children they've already whelped? I ask somebody and he says, 'The Governor has left his bit of brown at Bas de la Rivière, pregnant again, you know.' As if that were an answer! What a mess! What a bloody awful mess!"

❧

LONDON/FRASER LAKE, 1829-30

McTavish, McMillan and the Governor when he got there each selected a different hunting ground within the British Isles. While the Governor looked for his future wife among the damsels of London, McMillan was in Argyllshire and McTavish was thrashing the gorse in the Highlands. They kept track of one another by letter.

In one of his early letters to McTavish, the Governor described himself as shy and suggested that his years in the wilderness had made him lamentably awkward around the class of woman he was trying to woo. He asked if McTavish might not have a female cousin who would put up with such an old invalid as himself.

At Fraser Lake, Harriott had no way of finding out if Margaret was well. All he had was his rough arithmetic of when the child was due. He must hold on until Christmas.

In his December letter to McTavish, the Governor announced himself in love. A score of years ago, his London uncle had sent for him. He came down from the north and entered the man's sugar brokerage as an apprentice clerk. The same uncle's connections to the Hudson's Bay Company were what brought him to North America. What irony, or fate, that, years later, as a Company Governor, he should return and find his wife under the roof of the same London house? He was speaking of his eighteen-year-old cousin Frances, to whom he had become betrothed.

Harriott worried himself thin, shored up his courage with rum, arrived at Fort Vancouver a day before Christmas. The women wouldn't tell him anything about the birth of his daughter except that she lived and so did his wife. The baby was three weeks old and growing fat at Margaret's breast. Margaret herself was thin and pale but otherwise well, except for her old illness, which remained unchanged. Giving birth had not broken her silence.

The child had no name when Harriott arrived, and the women asked him whether he had one for her. Without having to think, he answered: Margaret.

He began to hire freemen and to arrange equipment for their journey east.

Courtship, marriage. For the Governor and his Frances, the processes had to be tightly compressed so they could take ship for Rupert's Land in the spring. The same necessity sped his two friends into the matrimonial state. McMillan married an Argyll lass and McTavish a miss from Aberdeen. The Governor and McTavish vowed to cement their friendship by honeymooning together on the same return boat.

Harriott and his few men snowshoed to the summit of the Athabasca Pass on a day so cold the trees cracked like cannon. Near the top, he was shocked to hear Margaret singing, she who had not spoken in over a year. It was a lullaby and she kept on and on with it. She would not stop even to catch her breath.

A storm came up as they made camp near the summit, a howling blizzard with snow so dense they could barely see to cut the crooked wood. They made as big a fire as they could, but it seemed pathetic in the swirling snow. When the wind took a breath, the rocks loomed around them.

As the fire descended through the snow, they built a raft of logs over top of it on which to sleep. Something woke Harriott in the night and it turned out to be his baby daughter crying and writhing against his back. Margaret was gone.

He jumped up and yelled to the others to awake. He looked in the pit the fire's heat had made, thinking she had rolled in there, but she had not. He yelled her name but the snow cut off the sound as soon as it was made. Her track was already drifted invisible, and he walked this way and that as far as he could and not be lost. Finally one of his men came with his daughter inside his coat and said, "If we don't go now, the baby'll die."

The Governor and his Frances were married in a suburb of London. It was not long afterwards that they took ship for Montreal. They were a jolly foursome aboard the boat. The Governor was fond of saying that, if he hadn't found the perfect wife in Frances, his next choice would have been Mrs. McTavish.

Harriott put the baby inside his coat against his skin and made for Edmonton as fast as he could. Every mile, he expected to feel her tiny flesh grow cold. But the baby Margaret was the phoenix that rises from the ash. As he passed her into the hands of One Pound One's woman, Louise, she lived.

PIEGAN POST
1830–1834

Mill Creek, 1900

Dear Editor,

I thought you might start disputing what I say sooner or later. But I'll tell you one thing, if the history books are right and the people who told me are wrong, that makes history the only kind of water that gets cleaner the farther downstream you go.

The next part of the story I call the American part because it's when the English Company and the American outfits on the Missouri whittled one another down so small there wasn't any profit left in it for anyone. Old Jimmy Jock Bird was right in the middle where he liked to be or where nature put him.

William Gladstone

FORT EDMONTON, 1830

When Louise took the baby out of Harriott's frost-bitten hands, he couldn't seem to take his eyes off the child. One Pound One pulled him away by the arm.

"Come, Ted. Come and drink. The women know best what to do."

He drew him into his office, where the fire was burning hot, put more wood on and a cup of brandy into Harriott's hands. Poor devil shook half of it onto the floor getting it to his lips.

"You did well to get the child here alive."

Harriott's eyes stared from deep in the skull as from a place of hiding. What they saw One Pound One couldn't guess. Harriott wouldn't look at him or respond to what he was saying. One Pound One supposed he was thinking about his woman, Margaret, dead in the mountains according to what Harriott's crew had to say. While he said the normal consoling things, he believed in his heart that Harriott was better off. What an unlucky shadow that woman cast. The Chief Factor would never forget how she had reversed John Welch's luck and killed him. Harriott was fortunate to have survived her.

So he filled poor Harriott's cup each time it emptied and waited for the shaking to calm out of him. The cheerless booze continued until the brandy rose in Harriott's brain deep enough to drown his thoughts. A mercy.

When in only two days' time Harriott wanted to leave Edmonton, One Pound One did not argue. Let him wander, he thought. Find what he can, escape what he can. The Company should turn a blind eye for

a while to whether he earns his keep, which was what he put in his letter to the Governor and in another to McLoughlin, who was still
Harriott's immediate boss.

"If instead of grief Harriott had a frozen foot we wouldn't grudge
him his rest. He'll work for us well enough another day."

How Harriott spent the time between leaving Edmonton and his
eventual return, One Pound One was never quite certain, in the sense
that Harriott never told him. The evidence was that he camped in the
Athabasca Pass and went looking for his wife's remains. Two men on
an express trip from the west found a recent camp there, though they
didn't see him, and a later group crossing that summit saw a woman's
beaded dress hanging in a tree.

The gossips went around saying Harriott was up in that pass gone
mad like his wife. Some even said Margaret was a Windigo, had been
one in the making for a very long time. If Harriott had met her spirit
in those mountains, wandering huge and ravenous, he was no longer
the same person either.

Damn sure, no one would touch that dress. It would hang where
Harriott had put it until every bead had been prized off by whisky-jacks
and the wolves had eaten the leather.

While Harriott was still up there, a letter came for him, or rather it was
in the mailbag on its way through to the Columbia. A letter from the
Governor. One Pound One snatched it out of the bag and would have
destroyed it in the nearest fire if so many hadn't seen it in the bag and
in his hand. Who it was from and who it was to worried him considerably, and he had to struggle with himself not to open it before
Harriott's return.

Harriott returned to Edmonton in May, just about the time that
One Pound One was putting together the eastbound brigade. The man
looked half-dead of starvation. God knows if or what he'd been eating
in the mountains. When he had a bit of food and drink inside him, the
Chief Factor gave him his letter, which turned out to be no more than
an invitation to Council.

That was odd but not calamitous in One Pound One's opinion.
However, his relief was short-lived. Harriott said he would accept the

invitation. There he was, a skeleton in rags, and wanting to be a dele-
gate to Council.

"Don't be stupid, Ted. I can make an excuse for you. Save you
the trip."

"I'm invited. I'll go."

Then Harriott asked to see his daughter. She was in an upstairs
room near the main chimney. The women had turned it into a nursery.
One of his girls was in there playing with her when they entered. Baby
Margaret was six months old and cute as a button, black-eyed and tan
of skin.

Harriott stood back a pace, making no move to touch her. It
occurred to One Pound One that Harriott had not touched the baby
since taking her from his coat and giving her to Louise in January.
What he did was study her. For several minutes. Finally One Pound
One signalled his daughter out of the room. They left him to it.

That evening over a dram, One Pound One had no choice but to
tell Harriott that the girl's grandparents were back at Carlton and asking to have the child there. Now, with the brigade, was the logical time.

"One of my daughters can go that far and tend her."

"No," said Harriott abruptly. "I can see to my own child."

Again One Pound One did not argue. Give the man his head.

When the brigade left Edmonton two days later, everyone in the
boats and those watching from shore all gawked at the same spectacle:
the famished widower holding his six-month-old daughter before him
in a moss-bottom bag on a cradleboard. Whatever the child's mood,
happy or weeping, Harriott stared at her all the way to Carlton.

One Pound One feared some kind of scene at Carlton, when
Harriott had to surrender the girl. But when the moment arrived,
Harriott handed the girl to her grandmother without comment. His
face, whatever it masked, was unchanged.

Carlton was barely halfway to Norway House, where Council
meetings were now held, and all down that massive river, One Pound
One worried and then worried more. He could not get out of his head
the question of why Harriott was going on this trip. It was not ambition. Harriott had little enough of that at the best of times. And as far
as One Pound One was concerned, the only possibility that left was

revenge. Whatever the Governor had done to Harriott's Margaret, that time when he took his secret journey to Carlton, it marked some watershed. She had begun to grow strange thereafter. On that score alone, One Pound One thought he had good reason to worry as they rode the current east.

Before the final approach to Norway House, they pulled to shore and all the men got out the bit of raiment they preserved in a relatively clean state for such occasions. A fresh handwoven sash. Slicking back their hair and fixing it in place with a clean rag. Then they got back aboard, raised their flags and started a song. They rowed with manly exaggeration around the final bend, and a man or two per boat fired his *fusée* in the air.

As One Pound One began to make out the crowd onshore, he saw an amount of festivity and activity that confirmed the Governor's presence. Even for the Governor, the place seemed gaudy and frantic. It pulsed with an excitement Norway House had probably never experienced before.

When they were closer, One Pound One saw why. In the front row, beside the Governor, stood a white-skinned woman. She was easy to spot because of her lack of colour, even down to a whitish dress. A creature made of snow.

One look at her and One Pound One's month of concern broke open. He jerked himself around in frantic search of Harriott, fully expecting to find that man with his flintlock primed and aimed. So strong was the instinct that it was more of a shock to see Harriott as he really was, slumped between the bales, the only one not looking at all, the only one not focussed on that white space at the Governor's side. His pale, frail, insubstantial English bride.

In this way the first moment of danger passed, but One Pound One's anxiety was far from quiet. After the boats ground to shore he tried to keep one eye on Harriott, but it was hopeless in the scramble. The shouting and shooting, the round of handshaking and embraces. Too soon, One Pound One was pumping hands with the Governor, and then it was the new wife's catlike paw curved in his. He cringed at the idea that she might expect him to kiss it. In her tiny glass voice, she was saying how the Governor often referred to Rowand as one of his steadiest men and most trusted friends.

In the end, One Pound One's attempt to keep Harriott in sight created the moment he was fearing. The Governor saw One Pound One searching around for someone and, looking to see who it might be, found Harriott himself.

"Well, well. There's our Mr. Harriott. Pity about his wife."

At the word *wife*, his own jumped. Someone could have stuck her with a pin.

"Oh, that man's country wife, darling. I told you the story. Madwoman, wandered off. Sad business."

The Governor's Frances. One Pound One felt concern lest someone jostle her. She might break, like a window.

A little dipping sigh escaped her.

"Poor, poor man," she said. "Do you think I . . .?"

The Governor raised his hand to cut her off. Forbidding her to even say the words. There was nothing she could do. Nothing she should even consider doing. He seemed angry at Harriott for having a problem sufficient to cause his wife pain, for making her feel sympathy.

Meanwhile, the direction of so much attention through the crowd had its second effect. A path cleared. To be looked at by the Governor was something the common people could not bear for long. Like keeping your hand in a fire. Thus the Governor had the power to clear a spot just by looking at it. What's more, the force of so much attention broke into Harriott's melancholic concentration and caused him to look up.

The Governor nodded. Harriott cocked his head slightly as if to ask a question. The Governor's wife sniffled, put a hankie to her nose and tipped her head off to one side.

The Governor did not move in the direction of Harriott, nor did Harriott step into the cleared path towards his boss. They stayed where they were and observed one another, like duellists, until the Governor spied, or pretended to spy, someone else he had not greeted yet. His hand shot up, his eyes shifted away, and the whole business snapped closed like a box lid on a spring.

Not only was the moment over, but so was One Pound One's whole anxiety about it. In theory Harriott could still pick up a gun or a knife and murder the Governor, but One Pound One was finally convinced it would not happen. Whatever Harriott wanted by way of expiation for his wife's death, the Governor's life was not the thing. Not now, at any rate.

One Pound One's relief was so great he was almost laughing as he crossed the clearing. That's the thing, he was telling himself. You can't predict Ted Harriott. If all this had happened to One Pound One, the Governor *would* be lying dead on the grass. But what One Pound One would do or not was beside the point. Harriott was different.

The District Chief Factor raised his bulky arm and stretched it across Harriott's bony shoulders.

"Come, Ted. There's a keg of cooled stout here somewhere. Let those fools gape like they've never seen a woman before. We can put our time to better use."

Ft. Vancouver, 1830

Dear Margaret,

They say I should forget you. What I feel is free to remember you. When you died, a shadow your size and shape moved. You were behind it.

Some days I want to die if only because it would be the last death I'd have to witness. When I went back to Vancouver after you disappeared, I lost seven men in the Okanagan Dalles. When I got to Vancouver, half the Indians had died of fever. If people would use their heads, they would run from me. Wound themselves rather than work for me. Why can't they see how much death likes my company?

People wonder why I surrendered Peggy. She is safer where I am not.

Ft. Edmonton, 1830

Dear Harriott,

Here's a reply to your damn letter. We're fools if you ask me to write things so open where any blackguard could look in and have the stuff to ruin us. But I guess that's what we've embarked on. It fits my other plans, mind you, caution thrown to the wind. Thanks to the flood two summers ago when we almost floated off, I have a good start on the new fort and my own Big House higher up. This will be a Big House worthy of the name. Forty by eighty in flat dimension and three storey high above a basement. Big verandas off which to throw the contents of your chamber pot. They're calling it Rowand's Folly already but when you have a wife the size of mine you have to expand your doors. If my dear one could read the above, I'd never eat another meal in safety. Mind you, thanks to McTavish and the Governor and their damn white wives I hardly ever do eat in peace. Louise sees me lift a fork and off she goes. You'll be going to England soon she says. Don't ask me to sew you new clothes so you can make a fool of yourself with white women. They'd never have the likes of you and so on. Will I hear anything different as long as I live? It is a shabby business though. Old Matooskie tossed out like a dry biscuit after seventeen years of faithful service. But you'll never hear me publicly say so. In my opinion ones who call McTavish to account for dumping Matooskie are mad. They think as long as they criticize only him they're out of the line of the Governor's fire. When the circumstances of the Governor's getting rid of his own woman are identical? No, those righteous few are committing suicide and, except for this damn correspondence you've lured me into, I won't follow. They say the Governor is shopping around for a pair of men, one to take care of Matooskie and another for his own old concern. There's gold for someone but I'm glad it won't be me. As you well know, it's best not to get too involved with the man. A better example than even yourself is Colin Robertson. Whatever Colin did to the Governor it's never been forgiven. And the latest punishment is he sent him to cut a road from Red River to Hudson Bay. A mad scheme and it all went wrong of course. The Governor's saying it's all Colin's fault, that he killed his own oxen and lost his outfit. The road was for the produce from the Governor's Red River factories which don't exist and never will. The road business gives him an excuse and one more means to blacken Colin's name. None of which you've heard from me. I'm getting a sore hand,

John

Ft. Vancouver, 1831

Dear Margaret,

I dreamt last night that it was all a mistake. I only thought you'd disappeared on the Athabasca Pass but really you were at Bas de la Rivière with the Governor's mistress and McTavish's.

It was One Pound One told me and I was furious. I said, I'm not their kind to dump my woman out of sight. Then I was in a canoe, overturned, and Peggy's face was before me disappearing into water. If I stayed back she would surface but if I reached for her she would sink.

It is more than one year since I last saw you alive but in my mind I can close my hand and feel the flesh of your arm under the cloth. I can hear you breathing on the pillow beside me.

Ft. Edmonton, 1831

Harriott,

Here we go again, like brainless girls. My God though you made me laugh with your depiction of old Archie McDonald making his Halfbreed wife at Vancouver learn to read and write. Did he really tell her if she doesn't learn he'll toss her out like the Governor and McTavish did theirs? By the way LeBlanc was picked by the Governor to take Matooskie. Donald McKenzie (our old boss at Chesterfield and Matooskie's uncle, remember) wanted one full year of McTavish's salary to go to her. Then Stuart, who's been their landlord over at Bas de la Rivière, decided to stick his oar in God knows why and declared that 200 pounds was a fair sum. So that's what she goes for. LeBlanc gets the 200 after his wedding at St. Boniface and they're barely out the door of the church when he's gone. Spends the day drunk while Matooskie cools her heels in her uncle's parlour. Damnedest thing. Word is now the Governor has selected and paid off another citizen of Red River to marry the boat captain's daughter and raise his children for him. That business will happen right under the Governor's lady's fair nose at Red River. She must be blind or very patient, that one.

John

Ft. Vancouver, 1831

Dear Margaret,

I miss the sun but could not bear to join Peggy in Carlton. I have trouble seeing her even once a year, and so I excused myself from Council and stayed here at Vancouver.

What a fool I was to think I could escape this Company and what ails it. The trade is the god that made us. Where else would any of us go? I could escape the way you did, but I go on living for the chance I might help Peggy somehow.

The only thing that gives me peace is that I have no fear of death. Call it my one asset, and given the way the Company feeds on us, the Governor will probably smell it out and put it to use.

Ft. Edmonton, 1831

Harriott,

I came back from Council filled with news and found more waiting. My writing skills are not up to telling all. To start the Governor's wife is pregnant. She's very sick and hidden out of sight. The Governor looks like the devil and is in a foul mood. I tried to tell him we aren't getting a damn thing out of Jamey Jock and he as much as told me to shut up. Far from cutting Jamey Jock adrift he told me to give him another outfit for the Missouri trade this year. That uncanny Halfbreed was here waiting when I got home so I sent him off with another damn good outfit and instructions to meet me at the Mountain House next spring. I swear I don't know what Jamey Jock has on the Governor but it's something. On another subject this English wife business is turning out a bigger mess than I supposed. A Chief Factor and his Halfbreed woman were snubbed at Moose Factory by McTavish and wife. Then Colin Robertson brought Theresa to Fort Garry for a visit and the Governor treated it as an outrage. I heard the Governor tell the story at Council almost within earshot of Colin. Said he reckoned Colin wanted his dusky maiden to pick up some pointers on civilized life before he took her to England. No damn way was the thing going to happen at Fort Garry in the Governor's wife's divine presence! I had Colin aside for a bit and he swears the Governor said to him and I quote that he (the Governor) "makes a determined stand with respect to non-intercourse in the family way." Holy redeemer! What were those babies then? Virgin births? I did get one thing out of Jamey Jock this last trip. According to him Kenneth McKenzie for the American Fur Company sent a man named Kipp to establish at the mouth of the Marias River. Jamey Jock says Kipp threw a party for a thousand Indians on a single barrel of rum. He took a taste himself and gagged. Bitters hot peppers tobacco ink. But the part that eats my liver is Kipp traded 2500 beaver that week. 2500! I've heard you defend Jamey Jock but I tell you the man's impossible. Gifts galore and he brings more excuses than skins. Now he tells me an American trader gets 2500 beaver in a week on the Missouri with poisoned liquor. It's got to change and it's going to change! If Jamey Jock doesn't make good on this latest outfit he's done for. Meanwhile when you visit next we'll be across a table in my Big House looking at the valley through panes of real glass. The first glass windows west of His Nibs's stone fort are in Rowand's Folly at Edmonton! Seven inches by eight. I brought them on the brigade sunk in kegs of molasses. Not one broken,

John

❧

FORT EDMONTON, 1832

When the ice left the river in the spring of 1832, One Pound One did not travel to Rocky Mountain House for his meeting with Jamey Jock Bird. It was all over the country that Bird had taken his Piegan, and between 3500 and 4000 beaver skins, to Fort Union on the Missouri. He sold them to Kenneth McKenzie.

One Pound One had given Jamey Jock the trading outfit with which he acquired those skins. Hence, they were stolen. They were as surely stolen as if the Halfbreed had broken into the warehouse in Edmonton, taken the pieces and fled.

One Pound One cancelled his annual trip to Council. He arranged an expedition south instead. For men, he selected Henry Fisher, George McDougall and all the toughest Halfbreeds. As for what they would carry, it was knives, guns and ammunition, and a few twists of tobacco for the parleys. Their purpose was not to trade.

What the expedition *was* for, the Chief Factor kept to himself. It was left to the twenty expeditioners to guess. Their impression was formed largely by the colour of their leader's face. One Pound One's bull head was often the colour of ruby port, but since the news from Fort Union, it was black. They were going after Jamey Jock Bird was what they told their wives, and how you get 4000 skins out of the hide of a single man was something they looked forward to seeing.

Before departing, One Pound One laboured two letters to completion. The first was to the Governor, explaining how they'd been betrayed by Bird and that he was going south to avenge it. He laid it on thick, making certain that the Governor understood how foolhardy he'd been to trust Jamey Jock, thinking this would finally cure that condition.

The second letter was for Harriott, who was on his way across the mountains.

Sorry to miss you. Instead of travelling east together I deputize you to represent me at Council. As long as we depend on treacherous middlemen like Bird we're at the villain's mercy. We'll lose every time. When that item comes up, stand fast for a Bow River fort to lure the Piegans. I put in my letter to the Governor that you should boss the place. When dealing with him bear in mind his son born New Year's is sick and expected to die. I can't make this letter longer as I must go to the prairie. When I find Jamey Jock I'll kill him.

❧

THE MISSOURI, 1832

The Milk River canyon had steep walls and a flat bottom. Beyond it, the Sweet Grass Hills resembled a yoke for giant oxen, two arms tapering from a central knob, the whole of it clamped on the south horizon so the load it bore was the world.

When they made it onto the western arm, One Pound One and company met their first Americans. Four free trappers heavily armed, and even they knew the story of how Astor's company had got a fortune in beaver belonging to the English. They didn't palaver long. Maybe they saw the black look on One Pound One's face and wanted to be away from it. They warned that the English should watch themselves, as there had been plenty of killing of late on the Missouri. The Blackfoot were more untrustworthy than usual. One Pound One laughed and waved his flag. The Blackfoot wouldn't kill the English, he said, not to avenge anything the Americans had done.

The trappers knew Jamey Jock but claimed not to know where to find him.

Fruitless weeks of travel followed. One Pound One combed the country with his army and found nothing. Finally he accepted that he was not going to find Jamey Jock here on his home turf, not unless that Halfbreed wanted to be found. He saw that his more important mission was to bring the Blood and Piegan back to the Hudson's Bay Company. With that object, he sought out the summer hunting camps and religious gatherings for another month.

"You call me Big Mountain," he told them, "and just like a mountain I have stood fast for you at Fort Edmonton. You call these flintlocks? See how this hammer is built? This American gun will blow the thumb off you if you try and load it hot."

In every Indian camp he bought an American blanket. As soon as it was paid for, he tore it apart with his bare hands.

"A Hudson's Bay three-point blanket weighs three pounds, guaranteed. You'll freeze to death under this American rubbish come winter."

But the old standards of trade with the Bay Company—fine goods from the Queen's country, fair play and fair prices—were not so easy to sell any more. It had taken a long and bloody war, but the Americans were finally playing the game the Indian way. Why would these Indians cross ten days of hostile country to bring the Bay Company their skins and pemmican? That is, if they could trade satisfactorily with Kenneth McKenzie on their own doorstep.

The only hope was a fort in their country, the Bow Fort that One Pound One had gone ahead and planned, had asked Harriott to fight for at Council. Not knowing if Council had voted for or against his fort, One Pound One went ahead and promised it. The fort would be built on the Bow River near the mountains. This season.

As he became anxious to return home, One Pound One introduced direct insults to Jamey Jock into his daily speeches. In the presence of all the Indians he met, he called the man a liar, a coward and a thief. If what he said wasn't true, he told the Indians, then where was their mighty war chief? Why was he hiding? If Big Mountain was lying, let the Halfbreed war chief come and say so himself.

On a day in mid-August, when they were camped under aspens on a flat beside a brook, and One Pound One was inside his tent lying down and half asleep, he jumped awake to the sound of horses. Indians. He was sure of that even before he heard their cries and the pop of their muskets. He dropped to the ground but nothing came through the tent wall. He could see the shadows on the tent by the time his sentry entered to give the alarm.

"Piegans, sir. Painted up for a fight!"

"Ask for the leader's name and what they want."

After much conversation outside, the sentry returned with the interesting news that it was Jamey Jock Bird and he wanted a parley.

"Tell that powerful war chief of the Piegan, if he wants a parley with Big Mountain, he can come back without his paint on. With his fukes in the scabbard and his bows unstrung."

The sentry went back out. Now One Pound One heard French spoken but got the contradictory message that Jamey Jock made no reply. The go-between, looking even more nervous than at first, said the Indians had surrounded the tent. They had loaded fukes trained on every wall.

Sometimes when One Pound One got angry, he saw a darkness,

like a cloud or a curtain, cross his vision. It happened that way now. For two months he had been waiting to lay hands on Jamey Jock. Now he would do so. Unarmed except for his anger, One Pound One whipped the tent flap aside.

Directly before him, Jamey Jock sat in an Indian saddle on a piebald horse with one china eye. He wore feathers in his hair and more feathers in the forelock of his horse. He was naked to the waist. As the sentry said, the Indians had several fukes, but Jamey Jock carried none. He held a spear, pointed upward, with a fresh-looking scalp dangling.

The two men looked at each other in silence.

"You stole my skins and I aim to take yours in payment!" bawled One Pound One when he could stand it no longer.

Jamey Jock pointed at him, aiming the finger as though it were a gun. "You'll take what you get, One Pound One. Today, that's your life."

Suddenly, Jamey Jock drove his heels into his pony's flanks and jerked it round. Almost overrunning its own front quarters, the horse ran blindly between two close-set aspens. In a gesture completely casual, Jamey Jock raised both his legs above the neck of the horse so they wouldn't scrape.

In the same moment, One Pound One grabbed a fuke from one of his men. He looked for Jamey Jock in the sights but his view filled with horses and leather chests. The Indians had ridden into his line of fire. They crowded tight around him.

One Pound One lowered the gun. He shoved the Indian horses aside and gave the fuke back to the man who owned it. He went inside his tent. It was not the result he'd wanted—Jamey Jock dead—but it was the next best thing. He had faced the Halfbreed and the other had run away. One Pound One was free to go.

❧

FORT EDMONTON, 1832

Harriott had been on the river for months. After breakup on the Columbia, he'd left Vancouver with the Columbia brigade. He stopped at Norway House to attend Council. Because One Pound One had chosen to chastise Jamey Jock rather than attend the meeting himself, Harriott had served as his mouthpiece. Now, because of another of One Pound One's plans, Piegan Post, he was racing back up the river to Edmonton. He chewed with the rhythm of paddle strokes. He breathed to it and dreamt it. He felt clumsier on land than on water.

John Peter's family was back at Carlton, and Harriott had seen his daughter there, a dark-eyed two-year-old now, impossibly pretty. She had jammed her fists under his chin, screamed and fought, until he restored her to her grandmother's arms. The old woman grinned openly to see how weak the father's claim had become.

A thing like that would have shattered Harriott not long before, but a threshold had been crossed somewhere between. He was like a certain kind of sea creature that lives between the ocean tides. If you stab at its flowerlike centre, it winces and grabs at the stick. If you keep at it, the reflex stops. It lies open as if saying, go ahead, stab me to death.

Loved ones, hated enemies, demons of memory: in this old grog shop of a company, they kept up their torments. In a world so routine, force of habit is arguably the greatest force of all. But Harriott had been tortured into quietude. Margaret was dead. The Company sickness ate him a joint at a time. And little Peggy was so distant, even in his arms, that his fantasy of saving her from peril was ridiculous.

Harriott was thirty-two years old. He was seldom drunk nowadays, having barely the energy to find liquor on his own and consume it in quantity. But few would believe that. By now, Harriott was drunk by reputation, and as that condition requires no rum, he was drunk always. Drunk or sober, he could do his work with little effort, and by that margin of utility, he remained worth the Company's while.

The light was dimming on another day when Harriott's boat scrunched onto Edmonton's rocky shore. A cliff stood above him, with One

Pound One's new fort posed majestic on its rampart. No one had thought to bring him down a horse, so he pulled his luggage off the boat and onto the back of a man who ran bent under it up the punishing path.

A second man, a sharp-looking Halfbreed whom Harriott probably did know in some younger guise but could not name, stood by, evidently in charge of his reception.

"You look tired, sir. Are you all right?"

"Fine enough. What's the news?"

They started up the path, the younger man having comical difficulty holding back to Harriott's pace. Harriott had little interest in his instructions but knew this man was charged with telling him. He strained to pay attention, his joints rioting pain at every upward step.

"I took the liberty of choosing horses and men for your trip south, sir."

"Good. I'm sure it's all in order."

"The trade pieces are lined out, ready for the pack animals. If you approve, we can load them any time."

Harriott reached out and stopped the other man.

"Let me catch my wind. Mr. Rowand's not here, then."

"No, sir. He was on the Missouri and now he's on the Bow River, seeing to your fort. Or he might have started back by now. He gave me a map so you can meet him on the trail."

"When do I go?"

"It's too late tonight, sir."

Inside the palisade, the fort was clean as a whistle, the men fearing that One Pound One could return at any moment. Even after a couple of years of operation, the place smelled new, of green wood. A half-built York boat stood under a sheltering roof. Some boys were grooming horses. There was an enormous garden where men and women worked together in rows.

Harriott walked to the front of the biggest Big House in the country and mounted the steps to a broad front veranda. Seeing that the young man was waiting behind him still, he told him to go. "I want to visit the Chief Factor's family. I'm here if you need me."

Finally, a young woman, maybe fifteen, opened the door. She blurted out his name and that allowed him to recollect her. Nancy. Rowand's second daughter, the slender, pretty one, blossoming now into young womanhood. She could not seem to stop smiling, and he was touched almost to tears that anyone would find him so pleasant a surprise.

"Nancy?" he asked to be sure. She gestured him inside and led him into the family dining room, where Louise stood back from some cleaning chore and beheld him. No smiles here, but concern. She stepped forward and held her arms open and he embraced her, barely able to reach all the way around, and then the news against his belly of a child several months inside her. He wasn't sure why it surprised him, as he hardly remembered a time when she wasn't so.

Behind her at the far end of the table a chubby little girl played with a doll. She was whispering to it.

"How is your family, Louise?"

"As you see them. Alexander's in school in Montreal, I imagine Rowand told you that. Becoming a doctor like his grandfather. The others are around somewhere. Henry's hunting. Sophia's in the garden. John Junior I'm not sure." Speaking of how the others were outside seemed to remind her that Nancy and the small one weren't. She shooed them out so that she and Harriott were alone.

"I'll make you tea," she said, turning to the hearth.

"No, Louise. It's too warm. Some water is all I need."

"I'll make supper," she said, already dipping up a cup of water for him.

They had never been comfortable with one another, Harriott and Louise, and it was exaggerated now that One Pound One was not present to fill the silences.

"And Margaret?" she asked, with her back to him, slicing buffalo meat off a cold roast.

It startled him for a second before he realized she meant his daughter, Peggy. "I saw her at Carlton. She's doing well. She doesn't know me."

"No. She wouldn't."

Later, when she had food on the table, far too much for his scant appetite, Louise spoke again, something that sounded like a speech prepared in advance.

"You think you're the kind who won't take another woman. But there is no such kind. The longer you wait, the harder it will be for you to find someone."

"I wouldn't think it would be easy now."

"There's lots of girls if you're not too fussy. Look for one who can bear children and care for you. A family will stop you thinking about yourself."

Having said her piece she stood up, grabbed a few plates and left. He waited, thinking she meant to return, but she didn't. The girl Nancy looked in, but when he glanced up at her, she got nervous and fluttered off. Finally, he went to the place where he always slept and found the bed made and turned down.

As he tried to sleep, the thought of some other woman came to him and immediately he wanted rum. Things that upset him made that urge to drink return, and that's all a woman was to him now: a source of upset. If he could empty his mind or keep it on work he was fine, and that's what he did now. He kept his thoughts on supplies for the trail south until he slept.

Not many hours later, on the back of a good horse, Harriott plunged into the frigid water of the North Saskatchewan. The horse lunged forward until it was no longer touching, then swam with such strength that Harriott stayed in the saddle all the way to the far bank.

The freezing water made him more awake than he'd been for some time, and it brought forth the idea that he was One Pound One's man now. Harriott found he did not mind. In his way One Pound One liked Harriott and valued his mind as a useful annex to his own. The only thing that bothered Harriott was that One Pound One was the last person in the trade whom Harriott could disappoint.

❧

Three days' ride to the south, Harriott's Indian guide spotted the second column, across a distance dotted in aspen bluffs. Harriott could not see the other horses but took the Indian's word for it. The guide said the riders were white men. At this distance, Indians would have looked like elk on account of their spears.

When One Pound One approached closer, Harriott made an effort to rouse himself, tried to be the man the District Chief Factor would want to meet. One Pound One and his horse led a single file, his stout gelding combing the deep grass apart with his chest and raising clouds of grasshoppers and smaller insects. The Chief Factor had grown into a shape almost precisely square, despite a summer's travelling.

Their horses passed noses and they came stirrup to stirrup. One Pound One had his hand out, and though it wasn't held at the right angle, Harriott tried to shake it. One Pound One cuffed his fingers aside.

"The letter, Harriott! Give me the damn letter."

Harriott fetched the Governor's letter out of his coat. The other ripped it open and read. He held it close and read fast. Then he bellowed and threw the paper to the ground. By this, he frightened his horse up onto its hind legs. He clubbed it between the ears with his hat to get it back down.

Finally One Pound One threw his reins to the nearest rider and slid to the ground. He hobbled to where the letter lay and picked it up. He walked away into the grass yelling for Harriott to follow.

They walked twenty yards in before the Chief Factor stopped. He turned in circles like a dog making a bed, then let himself fall, his only way of getting off his feet when there was nothing to cling to. Harriott sat beside him quietly, letting his boss curse and rage awhile. Finally he asked what was wrong.

"Two of the damnedest things I've ever witnessed are in this letter."

He stabbed the crumpled page onto a stalk of grass and stared at it hatefully.

"When I recommended you for the Bow River post, it wasn't to get you killed."

From a long way off, a memory drifted. Another time. A similar warning. When McKenzie wanted to send him from Chesterfield to

the Missouri in the winter of 1822. Harriott had been frightened then.
He felt nothing now.

"Why would I be killed?"

"What I told the Governor was that we must have a Bow River
post or give up all hope of the Piegan trade. What he *instructs* is that
you can trade with the Piegans *only*. No one else!"

"And the others will want to trade."

"Of course they will! They're all there now. Siksika, Sarcee, Bloods.
Cutting poles for a nice long camp."

"And not the Piegan?"

"Not one."

Harriott understood. Refused trade at the new post, the Indians
might burn him out or start a war amongst themselves.

"They must know about the rule," he said to One Pound One.
"That's why the Piegan aren't there."

"Aye. I knew you'd make sense of it. This post is my idea. Now the
Governor dooms it to fail. The way his damn mind works, he'll blame
me."

One Pound One plucked the letter off the stalk, read it again. He
set it down and stabbed it with one finger until it grubbed and tore.

"And goddamned Jamey Jock!"

One Pound One grabbed Harriott by the shoulder.

"You didn't go and get drunk and forget to give the Governor my
letter?"

"I didn't drink. I gave him your letter."

"Did he read it, though?"

"I watched him read it."

"Then how can he say this? 'Jamey Jock is to be regarded as
Harriott's principal ally and given every preference and opportunity in
the trade.'"

Harriott held out his hand and One Pound One gave him the letter. Harriott read it and shook his head. He did not know the answer.
The singing insects were loud in the grass, almost unbearably loud once
he stopped to notice.

One Pound One pulled off his hat and combed his fingers through
his greasy hair.

"What was said of this at Council? Anything?"

Harriott paused to recollect. What came to mind was the Governor drawing him aside to inform him of his assignment to Piegan Post.

"You are One Pound One's protégé," he'd said, eyes bulging. "You'll never be mine."

Harriott kept that back for now.

"The Governor thinks the Piegan will leave the American posts only if the Bow River fort is theirs alone."

"That may be, but what does he think the Bloods will do? And the Blackfoot? Say 'Edmonton's for us, then? Cheery bye, boys.' Who the hell is advising him?"

"He didn't say. Maybe Jimmy Jock."

One Pound One picked up the letter again. He mashed it into a ball and threw it out of sight over the flowered wall of grass.

"He tells me I'm his right arm in all matters of the department. He hints at me as his successor. And then he prefers that goddamned Halfbreed! I let that weasel get away with his life on the Missouri because I thought I had him beaten. And now the Governor, my Governor, grants him powers I don't have. Can you imagine what that does to my authority with the Indians? And yours?"

Harriott said no more. If the Governor had asked Jimmy Jock, Jimmy Jock would have given that advice, insisting that his Piegan be favourites. But why the Governor would listen was a better question.

"This is a bad time, Harriott. You work your whole life to set things up a certain way, and then suddenly it isn't that way any more." One Pound One clamped his greasy hat back on. "Just make damn sure *you* don't trust Jamey Jock. That man is gone. Indian, American, whatever the hell. He's gone to the devil, and he has our Governor in his thrall."

When they were mounted again, their horses pointed in different directions, One Pound One was reluctant to let Harriott go. He pulled on the flesh at the side of his jaw, scowled at the ground.

"Listen, Ted. You can't trade with them, but there's nothing in the letter says you can't give the stuff away. When I get home I'll send more rum. Be lavish with it."

🌿

PIEGAN POST, 1832

Two more days and Harriott and his men came to the Bow River a few leagues east of the fort. The map showed a mountain beyond Piegan Post, probably the square shoulder of rock that faced them as they turned up the valley.

All day up until then, the west wind had torn at them through every gap in the hills. As they entered the valley and turned west, the force of it hit like hammers. On all sides Indians came out of the trees. With exaggerated menace, the men on horseback charged Harriott's column, screaming and waving their fukes and spears. They pulled up so close he could see the whites of their eyes through the black paint that covered their faces. Coming on foot, the Indian women and children hit at their horses' legs with switches of red dogwood and willow.

Harriott's cavalcade moved through them like a slender stream through a bigger, more turbid one. Above the trees, he saw workmen lifting boards to a skeletal bastion as two hook-beaked ravens stood on the picket points and watched. Sharp squeal of green wood as the gate of Piegan Post opened and received them.

When the gate was closed and barred, rattling with rocks and spears thrown from beyond, the crew stepped away from their work to come and look at Harriott. The odd one was familiar. Henry Fisher, that small, neat and able man, was smiling in a friendly way out of his wood-coloured face. Several others looked at Harriott with contempt, either because they knew him or because they didn't and were alarmed that this was the best the Company could offer. Others, mere boys on whose faces life had chiselled nothing, stared at him with something far more disconcerting, something like hope.

When Harriott lowered from his horse, his legs were as water. Not only did he fall but he could not rise after. Sitting in the dirt, he rubbed his legs, trying to restore feeling. If the men knew anything about him, it was probably his reputation for drink, and that must be what they were thinking now. He extended his hand to Fisher, who dragged him upright.

"What's our situation, Henry?"

"You saw them, sir. Must be more than a hundred tents."

"If they were Piegan, that would be good."

"They're not."

"No."

Harriott blinked off the wet that the wind kept bringing to his eyes. Eggshell fort. Half-built bastion perched on one corner like a boy's treehouse. The wind was so loud Harriott couldn't hear the Indians any more, or he couldn't tell what was Indians and what was wind. Then a horse crashed into the palisade from the other side. The wall gave a foot and stayed that way.

"What would you like us to do, sir?"

"I guess you can begin by replanting that post. And keep making the bastion."

"Yes, sir. I made you a house. There. Not much."

"Good enough, thank you. Does the wind blow like this often?"

"Every day."

Harriott went to the little house that Fisher had pointed to. It was made of ripsawed wood, so untrimmed rags of bark hung down the walls. The roof was a few green hides held up by a tent pole, stinking badly. Inside, Harriott found a bed of pine boughs and buffalo hide and fell on it greedy for relief. On the stump beside his head was the other thing Fisher thought he'd need: rum and a cup gouged out of a crosscut branch.

He was considering whether to pour himself a cup when there came a knock.

"Come in, Henry."

Fisher stuck his head in and inquired without speaking if Harriott was all right.

"I'm fine. Come in a minute."

The other stepped in across the threshold, his greasy leathers blinding in the long rays of the sun.

"Close the door."

It yowled shut and Fisher stood waiting.

"Have you heard from Jimmy Jock?"

Fisher paused, then said he had not seen him.

"You've heard from him then."

"A message came in by one of our hunters."

"Saying what?"

"That he's coming."

"Do you think so?"

"No, sir, unless he wants to leave without his hair."

"Why would he bother to send the message then?"

"Trade talk, sir. Trade lies."

"Don't call me sir, Henry, except in front of the men. We've known each other too long. And take this keg away. It's better for morale if their leader is sober."

Minutes later, Harriott saw the world of sleep from its near shore. For a minute he was awake and asleep at the same time, and in that condition he heard the wind stop and a voice from the dreamworld speak. A man's voice called his name. Teddy. What no one had called him since childhood.

🌿

In the days and weeks that followed, the fort was besieged by wind. A gale of wind so strong it seemed it could bowl down the flimsy pickets. Harriott imagined himself blown from the razed fort, bounding over the prairie like a wheel of desiccant weed.

Gale, they called it, and every night by a candle flame sent dancing, he wrote that word in the fort journal. Often he wrote nothing else because there was nothing else.

Like any wind, this one drew breath, and in the lulls, they heard the second din, the Indian noise, its ferocity affected, almost measured, by how much of One Pound One's rum Harriott had doled out through the grate that day.

Jimmy Jock, his principal ally, did not come, nor did any more messages from him. The fort was indeed "Piegan only." Only the Piegan never came there.

At night Harriott gathered his men in the mess hall, all but the ones keeping guard, and they shared the only fire. He lit it and fed it so they would have something cheery to look at. They did not need it for warmth, as the wind they called Chinook brought more than enough of that. The aspens yellowed and were stripped of leaves, but in all other ways, the season would not turn. The buffalo meadow to the south and east stayed brown and naked and looked as it did in August. Not even a fringe of ice grew on the river.

Also every night, Harriott gave the men rum, even as the supply of that item began to run short. It had always been his custom to drink rum in response to catastrophe, so much so that the urge to drink had replaced fear as his response to danger. Now, instead of giving it to himself, he gave it to them. The rum given to the Indians forestalled the end. The rum taken by his men hastened its arrival. Surely when the rum was gone, the story's final chapter would be written.

The faces he looked upon each night were growing gaunt, the cheek flesh sucking in against the jaws and teeth. Heads becoming skull-like as they went partway down the road towards death. The Indians had taken to amusing themselves by following the fort hunters. They would follow quietly as though hunting, too, and then, when the hunter raised his fuke and aimed it at a poised whitetail, an Indian would fire in the air or clap his hands, and the rest would laugh to see the deer bounding away ahead of the explosion of the hunter's gun.

They allowed the odd kill, the occasional feed, and if they didn't and the fort starved too long, they would permit Harriott to break the Governor's rules. They would consent to trade meat for rum.

Then, for three nights in a single week of November, Harriott had a dream. It was a dream of Jimmy Jock hovering over him and saying words about how it was no good staying here; that he had failed and should have the sense to leave.

A week before Christmas, the last rum was consumed. Harriott emptied the last cup into himself, thinking it was more symbolic that way. A day later, his hunters were surrounded by Blood and Blackfoot and they were run like buffalo back towards the fort. In their panic they didn't know if they were being killed, if the guns they heard firing were aimed or not.

When the lookout shouted what was happening, Harriott dispatched riders to bring in the horse guard. Horses and hunters poured through the gate at a gallop, raising a yellow dust out of which they appeared with explosive suddenness. Harriott counted them as they came and, when no more came, they were short three horses, one man.

A Halfbreed hunter called the Little Big Belly had been among them when the chase began but had not finished. Nor had anyone seen him unhorsed or slain.

Now they were besieged in all ways, by Indians and by wind. Nothing could enter or leave, and the iron bar that held the gate was reinforced with spikes across the top so neither side could lift it. Harriott called out through the grate that he remained willing to trade tobacco and cloth, and the Blood and Blackfoot approached with arrows on the string. To make their reply clear, they loosed shafts that struck beside the grate until he lost courage and closed it.

Nothing could enter except the dream.

At first light on Christmas morning, the body of the hunter lay in the dirt before the gate. He was breathing but his scalp was torn away. Manured dirt from the trail had been sprinkled on the blood-beaded flesh beneath. The Indians stood well back and silent, making no move when the spikes were pulled and the gate iron raised. Harriott had the men bring the Little Big Belly into his cabin and onto the bed. He anointed the wound with boiled water. He thought of the last cup of rum that he had drunk and was ashamed not to have it now to quench the poor man's screams.

On a whim Harriott searched the hunter's clothing and found a square of folded paper in a pocket of his moleskin trousers. He took a candle to his rough table and unfolded it there, out of the gaze of others. In letters of vermilion or maybe of the hunter's blood, six words were penned. "I watch you sleep. Go now."

By first light the next morning, Harriott gave the order to pack. When the men seemed about to cheer him, he sharply ordered them silent. Unarmed and unaccompanied except for his Blackfoot interpreter, Harriott walked out the front gate and continued on towards where the Blood were camped. He aimed for the biggest tipi in the half-circle, upon whose door the first rays of the sun were blazing. A young man came out to say that his father would smoke.

Inside, Harriott sat before a tall and elegant Indian called Wanders Far, who it was claimed had earned his name by taking an American fireboat, a paddlewheeler, to the land of the Indians who lived in mounds. The younger man stood directly behind Harriott, and he wondered if the plan might be to take his poor thatch of mousy hair just before he smoked the pipe. But when the pipe stem came, he drew long on it and nothing happened but sweet smoke in his lungs.

He supposed he could ask who had scalped the Halfbreed and, if it was Jimmy Jock, how it came to be that he, for all purposes a Piegan, was allowed through the Blood-Blackfoot cordon to commit this evil. Or, if a Blood had done it, how had a Piegan message come to be in his pocket? As he rehearsed the questions, each one sounded mad, the product of a mind overturned by fear. When he did speak, he chose another topic. He told Wanders Far that he was leaving. He would trade some of his remaining trade goods for food and horses. Otherwise, the same goods would be in the Mountain House, and the Indians could trade skins for them there.

As he expected would happen, the Indian berated him, stood up to do so with many flourishes of hand. If not for the foolish idea of trading only with the Piegan, Harriott could have been trading for skins all along. Now, simply out of stubbornness, he was forcing them to ride to Edmonton or the Mountain House to achieve the same.

It was stupid. The Indian was correct to say so, and Harriott tried to look dignified as he refused to defend the practice beyond saying it was the Company's will, the way you tell a child that any apparent madness in nature is God's will.

"Will you let us pass?"

"Pass to where?"

"The Mountain House."

"And next year?"

"I don't know."

This answer surprised Harriott, even as it came from him. Surely, after this mess, there would be no further attempt to trade at Piegan Post. They would go back to the Mountain House and Edmonton, and accept their losses to the Americans. But he had not been able to say it because out of some dark place inside himself he suddenly believed they would return, strange as that prospect was.

Harriott and his men put their few belongings onto their hungry-looking horses as fast as they could. The tents around the fort came down faster. His men were no match for Indian women when it came to packing, and most of the Indians had gone before the Company train made its Hudson's Bay start from the fort that evening.

The horses, though poor, were adequate to the small amount they had to carry, the few beaver the fort hunters had killed and smuggled in under their saddle blankets. Their trade goods had been mostly rum, and the empty kegs, being light, were lashed high onto a couple of the worst horses. The iron that had kept the gate closed was the heaviest piece, and they made a travois for it behind a strong-hipped grey. On a second travois, the Little Big Belly rode, wearing a poultice of boiled aspen leaves on his scalpless head. He was unconscious now, his life in the balance.

It was hard to gauge the mood of the few Indians who stayed to watch them go. They could not be happy, because of the waste of half a season. They could not be disconsolate entirely, because their plan to ruin Piegan Post had succeeded.

No Indians followed them from the fort, and that by itself was proof of their intention to return to the Americans as quickly as possible. While Harriott and company marched north, the Indians were hastening south.

Harriott's bleak cavalcade had gone but a few miles, close to the place where they would leave the river and turn north, when a Piegan trading party stepped from the trees. It was a large party, maybe fifty tents and seventy horses, but they had almost no skins. They sat and conducted their bit of business.

Harriott asked and looked for Jimmy Jock, feeling a little of the anger One Pound One reliably felt for that man, but Jimmy Jock wasn't present. An old Indian bent almost double came to Harriott carrying another square of folded paper, which he handed over solemnly.

In blood or vermilion, it read "Next year."

🌾

FORT EDMONTON, 1833

Colin Robertson once said of his enemies, they peck me like jackdaws. Finally, the strongest jackdaw had persisted until the old fur trader's skull went crack.

In the fall of 1832, the Governor's old enemy suffered a stroke. A pathetic figure almost incapable of walking, he went to the Governor that winter to beg for retirement on a full share, and he was refused. In the same mail packet to Fort Edmonton came word that the Governor's sickly son had died.

One Pound One read this news at Edmonton and he could hardly contain the foreboding it made him feel. In this changed picture of Robertson (distorted face, slurred speech, dragging leg and useless hand) he saw a possible future for himself. He too might wind up yet on the refuse pile where the Governor threw the men he blamed and the men he did not like.

Colin Robertson was only the most recent and grotesque example of what could follow. By not giving him the money to retire on, the Governor was doing what the Plains Indians did when they stuffed an enemy with grass and left him standing by a trail. The Governor's latest scarecrow was more frightening for being slightly alive.

Edward Harriott was living with One Pound One and family this winter, in the Edmonton Big House. He had come to Edmonton after fleeing Piegan Post, and though One Pound One had encouraged him to come and was pleased at first to have the company, he was beginning to wish Harriott would leave. Rum and grief had addled the man's brain so entirely that he seldom reacted like a normal man. When told of the contents of the mailbag, he professed to be equally affected by the death of the Governor's son as by the fate of Colin Robertson, even though Colin had been like an uncle to him at Carlton.

"Why grieve a child that didn't know it was alive? A child of your enemy's at that. Damn sure Colin Robertson understands the fix he's in. Thirty and more years with the Company and now crippled, and the Governor saying, no, no, Colin, you must work on."

"I don't grieve the child more. It's the combination . . ."

"God's teeth, Harriott! How can there be a combination between an old Chief Factor and a dead baby? Will you never talk sense again?"

In his conversations with One Pound One this winter, Harriott often found himself in this position, at the brunt of the Chief Factor's rages. For the most part, he allowed it, allowed himself to be the means by which One Pound One bled his anger, like throwing open a door when the fire overheats a room.

But today Harriott was not in the mood for it. He put on a coat and scarf and excused himself. The notion of crippled Colin Robertson relating to the death of the Governor's son did have substance, and he wished to ponder it further. Alone.

Inside the palisades, the fort was gleaming white. Cushions of snow sat roundly on each cabin. It had snowed often since New Year's, and given this fine day, the women were baling drifts from the fort. They shovelled it onto blankets that they carried out the gate. One Pound One's fifteen-year-old daughter Nancy was among them. Seeing Harriott, she dropped her end of the blanket to wave. Inside his hat and muffler, Harriott gave a quick nod and hurried on. The girl was pert and pretty, the prettiest of the Rowand women, and her ready friendliness never failed to destroy Harriott's ease. Outside the gate, he dropped his snowshoes, stepped into them, and started east at a duck-like run, hurrying lest she try to follow.

The valley was brilliant in the sunlight, the river shining with ice. Up here the snow was mostly tramped by horses, but Harriott struck a path down one corridor in the trees where the snow was undisturbed. Harriott believed One Pound One had made a mistake putting the fort so high, so far from water in the event of fire, but he couldn't fault it on appearance. As nice a place as he'd ever seen. It took some time before the beauty of it would let him alone with his thoughts.

As he'd been trying to say earlier, Colin Robertson's fate and the boy's death *did* seem related. Renowned as it was for brutality, the trade seemed to Harriott to be getting worse, sadder and more intricately cruel. For all Harriott's efforts, Little Big Belly's head had putrefied on the way back to Edmonton. In his delirium they'd had to tie his hands to keep them away from the wound, and that was how he had died, thrashing and screaming on the travois. In that death and in all the dark events going back all the way to Margaret's death, Harriott had begun to see patterns, designs of danger and catastrophe, small evils interwoven into larger ones. Though it didn't grow simply like a weed but waxed and waned, Harriott couldn't help but watch for and believe in something larger. A final, local apocalypse, like the wave that comes out of the very heart of the ocean and snatches away a harbour or a house that has stood safely for hundreds of years.

Waves and weather was how he thought of it. A minor wounding might start it, then an infection that killed the babies. A murder generally sufficed to end it. Before the force dissolved and pooled, waiting to be stirred up again. Reminding himself of the old woman who forecasts hail out of harmless-seeming clouds, Harriott believed he could feel it coming and that he could tell whether an event was the conclusive violence or one of several preludes.

Next year, Jimmy Jock's note had read, and though it made no sense, it fit the pattern. The scalping of Little Big Belly had ended the season at Piegan Post, but his death brought no appeasement. The dark force was only waiting for its next crescendo, and Harriott, therefore, had more faith in Jimmy Jock's two words on a scuffed note than in all the common sense about Piegan Post that One Pound One repeated daily. A costly failure. An embarrassment to the district and to the department. Closed for certain. Closed forever. Best never mentioned. But Harriott, while purporting to agree, waited for the letter that would tell them the opposite.

Piegan Post would rise again. Harriott would be picked again to lead it. The Piegan-only trading rule would remain as well, being the curse that guaranteed the disaster.

There was no point in trying to explain any of this to One Pound One, who would only tear at himself in an agony of frustration while dismissing it as superstition or as a rum-soaked brain's pathetic attempts to function. But for Harriott, it was neither. If a comparison were needed, the best one was weather: that combination in the air that predicts a storm. But instead of a black tower of cloud or a biting north wind, the pattern here was shaped from old events. To Harriott, this winter looked and smelled very like Chesterfield House, just before he was ordered to lead his men on their frozen walk into the Missouri country. Unless he was mistaken, another pack of wolves was about to give him another flock of sheep to tend.

Returning from his tramp, Harriott felt doomed to meet the Rowand girl, and he did. The women had taken out the last load of snow, and Nancy came running to meet him on the trail. When he took off his snowshoes, she asked to carry them, and to avoid embarrassment, he let her take one. It was not that he disliked the girl. Nancy was lively and attractive. It was more *because* of her prettiness and pleasantness that he needed to keep away.

That night after dinner, when Harriott and One Pound One had retired to smoke, the Chief Factor felt moved to speak of it.

"If I have eyes, my daughter wants you for a husband."

"A girl's fancy."

"Don't pass it off so lightly, Harriott. She's fifteen."

"I'm thirty-three."

"Thirty-three, yes. Not a hundred and thirty-three. Honest to God, Harriott, it would do you good to have a young woman in your life. It's no business a man living alone. Makes you strange and that's what's said of you all over this department. At least in my house, you hear it from a friend."

"I wouldn't want my daughter married to me."

"Don't start with your confounded gloom. Whatever your faults— and I know every one of them—you have two things I want in my daughter's husband. You wouldn't milk me and you wouldn't mistreat her. That's rarer than you think."

"Next thing you'll tell me Louise approves."

"Louise approves of nothing and nobody. Except for possibly you."

"But not as a husband for her daughter."

"It's not for her to say."

The talking stopped for a time as the men attended to their smoking.

"All right," said Harriott. "If, in a year, the girl's mind is made up the same, I promise to take her seriously."

One Pound One looked at him, scowling fiercely. "It's not a disease you're doomed to catch, you know."

❦

The ice in the river below was beginning to shift and groan when the letter came to Edmonton by express cariole. Another year for Piegan Post. One Pound One was so unhinged by the news he went to his office and locked the door. His shade of red still dangerous, he dragged Harriott to his office next evening to talk about it.

"It's those confounded white wives!"

"To do with Piegan Post?"

"White women in this country made no sense, but the Governor and his toads went ahead and had them. Now when his Halfbreed bastards run around healthy as otters and tended by some other man they call their father, the Governor's pure white son lies dead in his grave. But does it stop? No. One mad decision begets another. At the far end is Piegan Post and its Piegan-only rule."

Harriott thought it over and found One Pound One's arithmetic rather like his own for a change. But he tried to put his response in the safe language of strategy all the same.

"Either the Governor knows and wants the post to fail, or he wants it to succeed but is misled."

"There's no virtue in having it fail. Not by anyone's strange ideas. We need back what we've lost to the Americans. Either that or starve. They have a fireboat at Fort Union. And a corn liquor still. We fall farther behind every day."

"Then the Governor must be confused. Maybe his wife's being ill and the death of his son distract him."

"Don't start on me now, Harriott. That would suggest the Governor's grown a heart. You of all people know better. He is misled. You're right about that. And we know by whom. But why is he misled? Whatever the Governor is, he never struck me before as stupid."

Two weeks later, One Pound One went with the brigade to Council, leaving Harriott in charge at Edmonton. As soon as the brigade flags went behind the trees, Harriott ordered a surplus York boat towed from the boat shed to the centre of the yard. While two women caulked it with rags and tar, every other able-bodied person was hauling water up the hill. It took all day until the boat was brimming. Standing beside it, Harriott pronounced Edmonton safer from fire.

The trees pressed out their leaves, the valley filled with green. Mosquitos swam the sky in clouds of thousands while, on a higher horizon, geese streamed north. Each night Harriott climbed to the gallery to study the fading light, the stars, the not-so-distant glow of fires on the prairie.

He bent his head back to watch the white river in the sky that glimmered like the prickling of his skin made visible. Distant thunder rumbled. He was helpless not to think of Margaret. *My life is my own,* she'd said on those nights after the Governor started in on her. *I can take it or I can trade it.* Harriott could hear her voice precisely.

Lately he'd been thinking how simple it would be to come here with a rope. Tie loops on both ends. One over the head, the other over the point of a pole. Then Nancy could find a man less cursed, and Harriott could avoid playing his puppet role in the final demise of Piegan Post.

At the same time as those ideas came, another set jumped in to argue. Who was to say young Nancy would find a safer man? And what kind of leader would replace him at Piegan Post? He imagined Nancy's sweet face twisted in a rough hand. He imagined a simple Company man in charge at Piegan Post, one who would do what he was ordered no matter into what bloody mess it led. Or, worse, a soldier seeking glory. One who would never take the little precautions available.

Harriott kept sleeping each night and rising each morning out of this simple belief that he could help in small ways. It wasn't much, but if the fires did come north on a south wind and a flaming branch leapt the river, Edmonton would have the York boat full of water. It wouldn't make the fort safe, but it would help a little in the panic of that moment. At Piegan Post, he could watch and feel for the rising danger.

❧

A week before it was time to leave for Piegan Post, Edmonton was visited by a Strongwood Cree and his woman. They entered the fort in torn clothing, their hair roughly chopped and dirty. The woman was clutching a baby bundle wrapped so tight there was no aperture for breath.

Harriott saw them from an upstairs window and he felt a clutch in his chest that was out of proportion to the sight. He hurried down to meet them in the square, asking the man in Cree what he wanted. The Indian man commenced a story about how he and this woman had been together for a long time but never any children. His family wanted him rid of her, but he loved her and wouldn't abandon her. Then she conceived and bore this child. Harriott was asked to look at it, and the wrapper when opened released the smell of death.

Harriott stepped back, stared at the ground, tried to think of something to say. One of his men yelled and, looking up, he saw a dagger in the Cree's hand. He thought the Indian meant to kill him, but instead he turned and drove the knife into the woman's back.

The woman's arms sprang apart. The cloth bundle unravelled in the air. The grey, scrunched face of the baby came to rest against Harriott's boot.

The Cree held the bloody knife in the air. He pushed the body of his wife over with one foot so he could see her. He seemed to pay no attention as Harriott's guard loaded his fuke. But when the gun was loaded, that instant, the Indian seized it. He swung away, put the gun in his mouth, tripped the trigger with his toe.

❧

PIEGAN POST, 1833

The journey to Piegan Post ended in a downpour of August rain. Grumbling clouds rolled over the mountain faces and hung on the sodden hills. The fort, when they found it, was standing, but all the plank inside had gone for firewood. The hunters were dispatched to their camps and the work of rebuilding began in the rain.

The Indians stayed away at first, knowing that Harriott had few goods to trade until the brigade from York Factory reached Edmonton. While both sides waited, the fort was made strong. Wood was cut and stacked for winter fires. The men spread out along the mountain foothills and found some beaver houses to work. A few skins to drape over the trading counter, thus disguising the emptiness of the warehouse.

In late September, Jimmy Jock Bird arrived. His long hair was rolled into a ball at the back, shot through with the spike of a feather. A leather shirt draped down over his bare thighs. He rode at the head of a small party of Piegan, dragging one travois slightly swollen with beaver pelts. He banged on the gate with the flat of his hand until he and his party were admitted. Once inside, he kicked his leg over the neck of his pinto and slid down, landing softly in front of Harriott. He extended his hand and Harriott stared at it a moment before taking it.

"How many skins have you brought me?"

"As you see."

"I see not many."

"Twenty-one prime beaver."

"For how many outfits?"

Jimmy Jock shrugged as if all those vanished trading pieces, fukes, ammunition, pots and beads were nothing. He stood before Harriott with long arms dangling, his legs bowed from riding. Harriott waited for an explanation.

"The Americans got to the Missouri camps before I did," Jimmy Jock said.

"Why is that?"

"The Missouri isn't like here. There's no monopoly. The Missouri is lousy with traders."

"Is this the number of your followers?" Harriott nodded at the few boys on their horses, all in attitudes of rest and slumber.

Jimmy Jock ignored the question. "I haven't much time," he said. "The Bloods know that your trading outfit is in Edmonton."

"That's more than I know."

Again Jimmy Jock shrugged off the comment. "Let's trade."

Harriott took him into the mess hall and asked that his boys fetch the pelts onto the rough table there. He brought his account book, and he and Jimmy Jock sat across from one another. Harriott sent everyone away in hopes that Jimmy Jock would be candid.

Harriott opened the account book and directed a candle's light onto it. He opened his ink bottle and dipped his pen. But how to make sense of what was about to occur? Twenty-one skins for an entire outfit, and that was not counting the trade pieces that had vanished the time Jimmy Jock's skins wound up on an American Fur Company counter.

But between them they managed to conduct a trade as if it were within the bounds of normalcy. As he had been instructed to do, Harriott paid again for what the Company had already purchased. When Jimmy Jock asked for another outfit, saying that he would do a big business with it when he got back to his people, Harriott made up that outfit out of every piece he could spare. The only improvement Harriott made on his orders was when he said he would send Colin Fraser and another man back with Jimmy Jock to the Missouri, to observe what happened to the Company's goods.

"You will treat these men as well as if they were your friend the Governor," Harriott instructed.

Giving Harriott the first glimpse beneath the mask, Jimmy Jock smiled. "So little trust, Ted."

"We both know how much less trust is owing."

Within a week of Jimmy Jock's departure, the York Factory trade goods arrived from Edmonton. One hundred Siksika dragging their tent poles followed in their wake. One day more and the first Bloods arrived, claiming to be of a much larger group that would follow. The trees west and east soon bristled tent poles. The drumming began and continued incessant.

Delegations of the tribes and subtribes came to the trading room. Harriott offered gifts while telling them he could not trade. They must continue to Fort Edmonton, where the Company would be more than happy to receive them. They did not argue or tell him their intention was to stay. All this palaver had been done the year before, and the present events were a continuation.

The atmosphere of the Indian camps was also the same as last year but more urgent. It reminded Harriott of the rivers west of the Divide where the grizzly bears gathered each year in anticipation of the salmon. The strongest would stake out their territory at the head of a river or in a rapid, and everything was decorous unless the salmon failed. The fewer the salmon, the more certain the conflict that followed.

One of the delegates from the Blood claimed to have heard that a big party of Piegan was moving north and that a dispute had arisen between them and the Blood.

Harriott began to interpret his orders more loosely than before. His new rule was that he would trade with whomever he pleased unless the Piegan were present. He was giving the Indians reason, if they needed more, to keep the Piegan away.

Still in October, Colin Fraser and the other man who had gone south returned. Their explanation was that a white man had been killed in the Missouri country. Jimmy Jock told them it was no longer safe for them to accompany him.

"And you didn't mind taking orders from Jimmy Jock?"

"He said you had told him to look after us."

In early November the wind switched into the north and a driving blizzard coursed down the hills and filled the valley with hard-shelled snow. Harriott put his men to squaring wood for sledges and building carioles. He traded with the Blackfoot for dogs whose only previous domestic knowledge was how to drag firewood. On the days when they trained the dogs to the harness, the air was thick with cursing and whips and the screams of the freshly educated dogs.

Harriott traded freely with the Siksika and the Blood, and even with the few Sarcee who came, for the Piegan were nowhere in the surrounding country. He sent two emissaries south to find them, to bring Jimmy Jock and his Piegan back.

In December the wind was still out of the north and blowing cold when a fresh rumour drifted into camp of a Piegan advance. The story came from a Blood who said the Piegan had been pushed out of their Missouri camps by the enemy Crow. Without the Blood to support their territorial claims, the Piegan couldn't hold on and were coming north.

On December 13th, with camps of Blood and Siksika still within shouting distance of the walls, a party of Piegan warriors rode up to the gate and demanded to be let in.

🌾

The Piegan were in the hall adjacent to the trading room, a dozen warriors lounging on buffalo robes. They passed a pipe with little ceremony, just for the taste and the feel in their lungs. Once in a long while they talked but the exchanges were brief. Words got in the way of their luxury.

It was four days since they had arrived, and they showed no signs of wanting to return to their camp on the Breast River. Harriott was not certain where the Breast River was, and whenever he asked them, they gestured south and he was no wiser. Otherwise, in accordance with the Governor's rules for trade at Piegan Post, Harriott treated the Piegan like sultans and paid over and over for the two beaver they had brought in trade. When asked why they had come, they were vague. Something about wanting to show the Blood that they had no fear.

When Harriott came into the hall to pay his daily respects, the Piegan started angling for a booze. They'd been drunk twice already, Harriott's idea being to send them home bragging about how much they got for how little. But the strategy made them reluctant to leave. Why walk away from free rum and tobacco before the source ran dry?

At least once a day, emissaries from the other tribes came to the fort to ask Harriott for rum and tobacco. Turned down, told to go to Edmonton, they did not argue. They were not expecting to get what they asked for. They were only confirming the insult.

At night, the drumming in their camps was thunderous, to Harriott's ears the precise sound of rising and tightening danger.

That afternoon, while Harriott supervised the first pouring of rum for the Piegan, the pattern broke. There was silence outside the walls. Shortly, a man came to say the Bloods had gone. Without announcing their intention, they had broken camp and left. Harriott excused himself from the Piegan and climbed to the gallery. He looked at the design of melted tipi circles in the snow, and it was as though a drawstring down his centre was sharply pulled.

He went back to the Indian hall and studied the Piegan. Every one a warrior. While they rested here, their people were on the Breast River without them. When Harriott told them the Bloods had gone, they waved it off as unimportant. They held out their cups. Good. Good that the Bloods were out of the way.

Harriott left again. He found the guard and asked if he knew the direction the Bloods had taken. He said they had started east down the valley on the north side of the river, but a fort hunter who followed saw them cross the river, north to south, once they were out of view of the fort.

Harriott was on his way back to tell the Piegan when he realized it was no good. They were too far into the booze now, into feeling all was well because they felt good. The December sun had gone behind the mountain. The light was weakening and the cold coming on.

Harriott went to his cabin and sat in the windowless dark. His fantasy for Piegan Post had been that some crisis for his men would rise out of the Indian anger, and that his patience or his knowledge, or just his lack of fear, would help them. Maybe he could not stop the bloodshed, but he might lessen it a little.

Now, when the trouble came, it didn't involve his men at all. It would be what the Company called an Indian skirmish, an event of no consequence unless it disrupted the trade. Harriott, by rights, should have felt relief, but the barometer of danger that he had become kept surging inside his skin.

Honest now, he admitted to himself it was not enough. Not enough to sit and watch, lest a cinder fall. He must go and find the source.

Harriott put on a buffalo coat and took his fuke from the wall. He went back outside and made for a knot of men conversing near the gate. Halfway there, Harriott yelled, bent double, grabbed his guts. The men rushed to him, asking what was wrong.

"*Mal de vache*. Must be that fat cow we ate."

Two nodded gravely, while the third laughed, as if shitting yourself was a joke.

"There's a cure. A tea. Do you know how to make it?"

They looked from one to the other. One said it had to do with willow. Made from the leaves. Or was it the bark?

"Get my horse!" Harriott grunted urgently. "Saddle her."

The order was odd. It froze them.

"None of you can make that tea and neither can I. I'm going to the Sarcee."

They understood then. A Sarcee camped downriver had been bragging about his wife's skill as a doctor. One man ran for Harriott's horse. Another offered to go see the Sarcee in his place.

"Who has the *mal de vache,* man? Or did you plan to feed me the cure from your mouth like a bird?"

Harriott groaned, twisted his face, buckled forward. They brought him his horse and saddled it. Another put his fuke in the scabbard. Together they hoisted him on. His last words were that they should not be concerned if he stayed the night. If he found what he was looking for, he wanted several doses. Then he rode out at a gallop, into the faded light where a gibbous moon threaded red like a bloody egg rose out of the northeastern hills.

Harriott started in the direction of the Sarcee camp, towards a pale glow above the trees on the river's north side. Out of sight of his own fort, he veered to the river and looked until he found the trail in the snow where the Bloods had entered the water. He stripped and made a bundle of his clothes and weapons, then plunged the horse in. The water was the temperature of ice, and coming out the far side, he shook uncontrollably and longed for a fire. There was no time. To do any good, he must hurry on the heels of the Blood. He put his clothes on his wet body and continued.

He had not ridden far away from the river to the southeast when he almost blundered into the Blood camp. Where the trees gave way to an east-trending buffalo flat, he left cover within sight of their tents. He hadn't noticed sooner because the camp had no fires. He tucked back into the forest's edge and made a long half-circle to the south and then to the east, coming at length to a point where, as he expected to, he found the trail of many horses.

It made sense. The Blood had left their women, old men and

children. They were proceeding with a war party of men. He had little doubt, but finding the trail convinced him entirely of their intention.

By now, the light was all from the convex moon risen above the trees. The snow gleamed across the flat. The Blood trail was a dense line of prints easy to follow. For the length of the tableland, Harriott galloped his mare, rhythmic grunts pounding from her bellows, the stars jerking on slender strings. He was not dry inside his clothes, and the chill wind stitched needles through his knees.

Near the east end of the flat, the trail bent south and climbed a steep defile. He followed it.

For hours Harriott advanced along the Indian trail. He descended, he crossed rivers, he climbed. At the top of a new rise he emerged from the forest in a stony clearing, the surrounding hills visible on all sides in the moonlight, lowering away from where his horse stood. Two standing stones framed the trail ahead, and the tracks of the Blood horses narrowed between them and down into the next valley.

He swung from the saddle, holding the cantle until certain his legs were set. He tied the mare to the single poplar among gnarled pines, loosely so she could bend the branch and reach the grass.

A flat stone by an old fire circle shone in the light and Harriott went there and sat, bent forward so the blood throbbed in the front of his face. His eyes felt boiled and blind from searching in the dark. One ear and part of his face was numb.

In the first week of Piegan Post last season, he and Munro had taken trade pieces across the river. They had crossed the buffalo prairie same as he had tonight, but instead of climbing they had continued east. They had followed the base of the hills, trending south. That was the only time he had heard of the Breast River, which Munro had said was somewhere to the south. He had not said one day's ride or three, and Harriott had not cared to ask.

Wolves started up howling, one far off and another so close it made his hair rise. He climbed to his feet and pulled his fuke out of the scabbard. His mare murmured to him and he pulled the leather to loosen her cinch. Sitting back down, he worked with his powder horn. Didn't bother with ball and packing, just powder in the bore and in the pan, ready to make a noise if the wolf was sure enough of his weakness to attack.

It was possible he was now on the last ridge to the north of the Breast River Valley and, if so, at a point close to the Piegan camp. The only clue was the hint of grey that was coming to the dark. If the Blood intended to attack tonight, then this would be their chosen time. To hit the camp when they could see and before the Piegan were fully awake.

Harriott decided to believe it was so, which meant his only chance of preventing the attack was to leave his spot and walk down the spine of the hill, through the trees to the east. Then he would turn south into the valley. He must descend to the river and walk upcurrent, hoping to evade the guard. If he made it inside the camp, he would find Jimmy Jock. That would be enough. The Blood would not attack a warned enemy.

Move now, he told himself, and against the restraint of his fatigue, he moved his hands to his knees and pushed. He began to rise, then fell back, arrested by cold steel pressing him hard behind the ear. A dagger flat to his head pointed up through his hair at the edge of his hat brim.

He had heard nothing. His horse was still scrunching grass, unconcerned.

Harriott waited for the knife to move and the only question was what direction. Around to the front to cut his throat, or the shorter path to the soft neck beneath the rear cap of skull. He found that he was afraid. Very afraid. He did not want the pain. He did not want to die. The fear excited him, distracted him. By the time he heard the voice by his ear, he was almost smiling.

"You can talk, Ted, but softly."

Identifying Jimmy Jock's voice, Harriott almost blurted the warning, the one he had crossed miles and night to deliver. Then it came to him how ridiculous that was.

"You know already," he said.

Jimmy Jock met this with silence. Harriott assumed it was the kind of silence that precedes an answer but no answer came.

"Is this the Breast Valley? Is your camp beneath us?"

No answer still.

"For God's sake, Jimmy Jock, it's almost light. They'll attack any minute. Or do you not care?"

"Hush, Ted."

Harriott pushed his head against the knife, forced it to gouge him as he turned to see. The long handsome face. Jimmy Jock close and smiling.

"Poor Ted," he said fondly. "Your uncle should never have brought you into this country."

Another silence until the closest wolf howled.

Jimmy Jock spoke again, softly, as if in prayer. "This day has been coming for a long time. It is necessary so we can all move on."

"What if they kill everyone?"

"This isn't Europe. We're not even enemies. Sometime after you're gone, we'll meet, we'll smoke, we'll be friends again."

"Are you on anyone's side any more, Jimmy Jock? Or is it just whoever pays the most?"

"Let's not waste time saying stupid things, Ted. There's an interpreter at Fort Union who the Americans pay 800 of their dollars per year. Your Governor's price for my loyalty is twenty English pounds. I'm on the side I've always been on. I thought you knew that."

The first fringe of pink had come to the edge of the world. Harriott tried to see into the valley, but a blanket of fog lay in the trees.

"You think you could prevent this. But, even if you could, who will do your holy work tomorrow? It's a weak God who saves everyone so they have the right to starve."

Harriott thought he heard something in the bottom of the valley. Was that a popping sound, a musket? It was hard to say from this high up what was wind and what might be a gun or a human cry.

Harriott stared into the valley even though there was nothing to see but the fog's woolly architecture. Close by his ear, Jimmy Jock's smooth voice began again.

"Last year, I came into your fort at night and watched you sleep. I was very afraid I'd have to come back and kill you. The time has come again, Ted. You've done what you could. Now go home."

Moving slowly, Harriott turned so he could see the shadowed eyeholes of Jimmy Jock's skull very close to his own. He smashed his brow into Jimmy Jock's face at the same time as he reached for the wrist that held the knife. The blow stunned the other man long enough for

Harriott to throw him on his back and crush the knife out of his grasp against the rough floor of the clearing.

Harriott felt Jimmy Jock's body loosen under him. He stared up so calm and unblinking Harriott thought for a second he had killed him. Then Jimmy Jock spoke.

"That was well done, Ted. But I am never alone."

A crash, then a sheet of blue gold.

Then nothing.

❦

From a heavy blackness, Harriott returned to light. Someone was talking.

"I'm sorry, Mr. Harriott. But you have to . . ."

He was in his cabin at Piegan Post, seated on the chair, leaned forward over the table. Under his arm was the post journal open to a page where someone else's hand had written December 18, 1833. Next to his eye, his shirt cuff was blue. He thought he had been wearing the red one. His hand was closed around the base of a pint porringer.

"I don't like to bother you, Mr. Harriott, but the Piegan . . ."

"I know about the Piegan. They were attacked last night on the Breast River. By the Bloods. I don't know how many killed."

It was Fisher standing beside him, and the way he stared down at Harriott expressed something less than admiration.

"I don't know what you're talking about, Mr. Harriott. What I was going to say is the Piegans here in the fort are insulted because you didn't come to them last night or today. They say they'll leave but not before you visit them again. I'm anxious for them to go. Are you able to speak with them?"

"What do you mean, able?"

"You've been drinking."

About to deny it, Harriott again noticed the porringer in his hand. He looked inside and saw it was half full of rum. The black taste was in his mouth. When he raised his head, he was dizzy.

"The last I remember I was far from here."

"The Sarcee brought you back. He said you'd taken his wife's medicine and the two of you had a booze after that. You slept there and he
couldn't wake you, so he brought you in today."

The air was full of webby things. He felt like puking.

"Give me two hours, Henry. Then call me and I'll speak to the
Piegan."

Harriott ground back the chair and stood weaving. He toppled
onto the bed of robes and lay with a fist of pain throbbing behind his
ear. He opened his eyes and Fisher had not left. His tongue was thick
and filled his mouth.

"Leave me, Henry. Please."

Three days later, on December 21st, Harriott was in the yard with the
sledges and carioles, measuring the freight they could carry. Although
no longer certain of any event in the past five days, he believed they
would abandon this fort again soon. He was privately making ready.
Henry Fisher pushed through the main gate and started towards him.
His stride was quick and compact, and the usually impassive face was
troubled.

"Mr. Harriott. Jimmy Jock Bird is upriver about a mile. I said we'd
likely give him an escort in but I wanted to tell you first." Fisher
squinted and frowned even more deeply. "He reports a battle on the
Breast River. He says some Piegan were killed and the remainder are
scattered in the hills."

"I told you that three days ago, Henry. You ignored it then. Now
you tell me it as news?"

"That would be because Jimmy Jock says it happened yesterday, at
dawn."

"How can that be?"

"I checked with Wanders Far. He says the same. Agrees to the day
and the time."

"You're saying I proclaimed it before it happened."

Fisher wouldn't meet Harriott's eyes. "What am I to do with
Jimmy Jock? He says he needs another trading outfit."

Harriott laughed. "Another! You know what I think, Henry?"

"I wouldn't guess, sir."

"I think we're all working for Mr. Bird now. So by all means, bring him in. Don't keep our boss waiting."

The murders on the Breast River had a calming effect on everyone except the Piegan. The camp of the Bloods never returned to Piegan Post, and the drumming of the Blackfoot and the Sarcee seemed less urgent now, more social, even contemplative.

Until Christmas, and for most of the time until New Year's, Jimmy Jock was Harriott's guest. At night he would leave the fort and sneak out through the sleeping Indian villages into the hills. His purpose was to bring back a few of his Piegan so they could bear witness to what had happened to them. They told how the Bloods came riding out of the grey dawn. One old man was killed by an arrow as he stood guard over his horses. Two more, a woman and a child, were shot through a tent wall in the skirmishing that followed.

Before sunrise on Christmas morning, Jimmy Jock brought in two of the warriors who had lazed here in the Indian hall so confidently a week ago. They were too frightened now to share in a Christmas drink. Jimmy Jock ushered them away to their hiding place in the hills after dark.

Harriott had no doubt what Bird was doing. As in a British court of law, he was presenting his witnesses: this one to tell about the attack, that one to recount the tale of Old Head, who'd been in to trade earlier in the season only to be pillaged of his trade goods on the trail out. Each one made the case Jimmy Jock wanted made: that none of his people would trade here; that Piegan Post was of no earthly use to the Piegan.

After ranging about for another couple of days and nights, Jimmy Jock returned to the post on December 28th. The Blood were gone, he said, so he could now make use of the outfit he'd asked for. Without even an expression of irony, Harriott had the pieces assembled according to Bird's careful instructions. Again he sent Colin Fraser south, in the vain hope that his presence would make for more honest use of the goods.

January 1st, 1834. New Year's.

As had always been the Company custom, Harriott served out a few drams per man. They were cheerful, too, his men, having read the omens, the unmistakable lightness of mien that ruled the camps and thus the fort since the defeat of the Piegan. They were having a dance amongst themselves, with a couple of Sarcee women shuffling about in blankets, when Colin Fraser returned.

He brought a keg of gunpowder that Jimmy Jock said should have been rum. Since Colin was there, and some of the men knew he'd brought his pipes to Piegan Post, he was prevailed upon to play. He got his pipes and played some tunes, which finished the job of putting the heart back in the men.

Fisher, whose mind was never far from business, said to Harriott, "There was no such mistake about gunpowder and rum."

"You're right, Henry. There wasn't."

"But you'll let him have it anyway."

"Yes, I will."

On January 8th, Harriott sat down with a candle at his cabin table and opened the post journal for the last time. He read the scribbles opposite the dates since fall. In the back half of the book was the list of skins for which he'd traded and the goods they had cost him. The value of the latter was so much more than the former it verged on laughable, but he doubted the Governor would see the joke. If it had been the Governor's wish to place another black mark against Harriott's name, putting him in charge of Piegan Post had done the job with admirable craft. If his goal had been to get him killed, or to demoralize him further, the Governor had failed.

The truth was Harriott felt lighter in his heart than he had in years. Whether the evil had dissipated for all time, he could not know. Maybe it was only resting again and gathering for another rush. But Harriott was one with the rest in feeling relief to have it over for now. Come summer, he would ride with the Mountain House furs to Edmonton and spend the summer in that fort. When One Pound One was gone to Council, he planned to pay court to his old friend's daughter. He would worry about the evils to come when they came, but he would set the thankless task of soothsayer aside.

All that remained now was to write the final chapter for Piegan Post, and Harriott dipped his pen to do so.

No advantage to be reaped from staying at this place, but on the reverse, abundance of trouble and expense, I have determined on leaving and retreating to old Rocky Mountain House to secure the trade of the Blood Indians there, where we shall be able to bring them more to terms.

In the evening, everything being ready, we took our leave of Piegan Post, which we left to the mercy of the Sarcee. They lost no time in taking possession.

✤

FORT EDMONTON, 1835

In the absence of a priest, they celebrated the union in the old way, with toasts and tears and some reading from the Bible. Harriott had sent a note to his daughter telling her it was too far for her to come, or begging her to stay away. Whichever way she took it, she did not try to attend.

Mostly it was the people of Fort Edmonton who gathered to honour their boss, and most of the excitement came from the bride's sisters. Nancy was the first of their number to take a man.

There was no mistaking her love for Harriott, it shone on her, and he looked pleased as well to have her. She dragged him up to dance and it was a humorous sight, him trying to move in rhythm on his stiffened legs. What stopped the dancing, though, was Nancy's having to cough. She went to the side of the room by a window and stared out with a handkerchief tight to her mouth. Her sisters and Harriott hovered behind. When she finally could stop, she turned to them with a gay smile.

Harriott took the handkerchief from her hand and wiped away a drop of pink foam from the corner of her lips. He parted the fold of the cloth and saw the strands of pink and dots of red inside.

"Don't worry," she said, smiling at him brightly. "I'll make you a good wife."

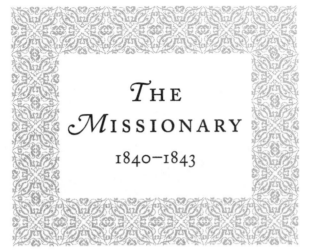

The Missionary
1840–1843

Dear Editor,

Some old-timers say everything bad in this country came up the Missouri River, and there's truth in that. The Blackfoot-speaking Indians fought the Americans to a standstill until they saw the first fireboat on that river. That was too much for them. One of their greatest chiefs went for a ride on it, all the way to the Mandan, and that took great courage because for him he was riding a massive beast with a fire in its belly.

Understanding they were up against a people who owned such a thing, the Piegan and Blood couldn't keep their war against them going. Jimmy Jock had been to England on an even bigger boat and wasn't impressed. He tried to get them to fight on, but except for a killing here or there their heart wasn't in it.

Jimmy Jock's purpose was plain enough. He wanted the Blackfoot country free of white men and everything they built—no traders, forts, missionaries, nothing—which was a tall revenge for them not accepting him as white, but that's what started it, maybe. Later on I believe he was trying to help the Indians by it. When you see what happened after those Indians gave up fighting, you see the soundness of his plan.

Those who couldn't understand Jimmy Jock were ones like the Governor who couldn't believe someone half white and half Indian would ever choose his Indian side. They'd never believe it and that gave Jimmy Jock his advantage over them.

The worst thing that ever came up the Missouri came in '37. It came on a fireboat from St. Louis to Fort Union and it transferred there along with some trade goods to a keel boat bound for McKenzie. It sat in the middle of the river for a time because a trader there had an Indian wife he hoped to keep. If the boat stayed on the river until the weather cooled, he thought they might kill what was on it. But the Blood and Piegan had waited a long time for that boat and they said they'd burn the fort down if the trader didn't allow it to land.

That was the day the smallpox stepped in among the Blackfoot. Before it was done it killed more than half of them.

I heard terrible stories. Where the Old Man and St. Mary's Rivers joined, they called the place "Many Dead." Other places could have been called "All Dead." There wasn't anyone left to do the burying, and the villages and the human remains were left to the wind and the animals. Smallpox kills with fevers and chills and delirium and terrible pains in the head, and some would run into the rivers for relief and die there like buffalo who drown fording a river when it's higher than they remember.

The next year, '38, the country was a false Eden. The prairie grass grew tall and every kind of flower bloomed. With almost no one to bother them, the buffalo walked it slow and covered it for miles, a brown mass just moving. The Indians were weak and so full of sadness they couldn't bother to more than feed themselves. The trade was silent and the ground around the forts, English and American, stood bare.

Jimmy Jock caught the smallpox and it half killed him. It left him with pincushion scars deep into his face. It killed his children and one of his women, and maybe worse it killed his people's desire to keep off the white man. When they saw how they were killed but the white man wasn't, it said they were chosen out of the human race to die. God Himself sided with the whites, and that turned them against their own ideas. It laid them open to whatever the whites would have them believe.

I came into the country about then and I saw what the disease did. Mr. Harriott was less than half the age I am now, but he was old. They spoke of his wife Nancy Rowand as being a girl but she with her consumptive cough seemed old too. But however bad his luck had been, Mr. Harriott never stopped being kind. He never stopped trying to do the right thing.

Next thing up the river after the smallpox was the missionaries. Following disaster as usual.

William Gladstone

❧

FORT EDMONTON, 1840

One Pound One poked his spyglass through a rifle loop in Fort Edmonton's east bastion. The month was October and the valley's north face blazed orange against the black of spruce trees. The glass circle of light skimmed down to the river and framed a lone canoe appearing and disappearing among the trees.

The three men in the boat, two paddlers and a passenger, showed up at this distance as spots of colour. The voyageurs at the two ends had stopped somewhere to put on their red head scarfs and sashes. Their oar flashes were bright and brisk, as if a thousand miles of river were nothing to their bounty of energy.

Normally One Pound One would have cheered them, but today he barely noticed. What he stared at through the telescope was the smudge of black in the boat's middle, which, coming closer, separated into a black hat and a black cloak, with a little white face sandwiched between.

The missionary.

One Pound One slapped his spyglass closed, pocketed it. He took a musket from its lean against the wall and thrust it at the man cowering in the shadow across the room.

"Load it."

The labourer was hunched over with one hand gripped in his goatish beard, the other feeling a luck amulet through the top of his shirt. He lunged to his duty, taking the gun and pouring powder into it from his horn. He spilled plenty. Then he froze at the choice: whether to add a musket ball.

"What do you think? Can I pick him off from here?"

The man's tongue spread thick. The canoe was too far.

"Eh? One squeeze of the trigger and I rid us of this pest before it bites a single soul."

Eyes down, the man drove in a ball and packing, tamped it, added fine powder to the priming pan. He handed the musket back and kept his eyes away until he heard the blast, then checked to see the angle. It was aimed at the sky. The spray of dusty light swirled from the impact.

No fort cannon. No salvo. A greeting insultingly small.

One Pound One handed the hot musket back.

"But I won't shoot him, will I?"

The labourer took a step back. He closed his eyes and braced himself. Surely now would come the kick. Across his face he felt and smelled a tobacco wind as the Chief Factor's heavy form strummed the air. He also heard his master's nickname—light step, heavy pound, light step—across the hollow boards. By the time he risked a look, One Pound One's tricorn gave him a final wink above the plane of the catwalk, then disappeared below.

Several hours later, One Pound One ground meat between his stumps of teeth. He fished a lump of gristle out and flicked it to a dog. Across the table, seen through steam rising off the roast buffalo boss, was his guest. The Wesleyan Methodist missionary Mr. Rundle.

Meticulously, the man was slicing meat into tiny pieces on his plate. Once in a long while, he'd insert one between a narrow opening of lips. Many sighs told how weary he was, even of the need to chew. Every time he spoke, a complaint came out. His fatigue. The lightness in his head.

"Almost a delirium."

The missionary seemed at pains to convince the Chief Factor and his family of the arduousness of his journey. He had started well from Norway House but had grown sick during the last two days.

"A sort of fainting sickness."

Every word shrank him smaller in the Chief Factor's eyes. What would the Indians make of this?

At the same time, One Pound One forced a smile. He had been instructed, all the way from England, to make the best of this missionary, to make him comfortable and to tolerate the confusions he produced in the trade. But when the missionary started in about the Indians, his intention to go out from the forts to their outlying camps on the prairie, it was too much to bear in silence.

"Reverend, listen. There's much bloodshed on the prairie nowadays. Ambushing on the trails. Even torture for its own sake. The smallpox made it worse. The old ones died and the young ones are full of anger."

One Pound One talked around the sharp point and keen blade of his dagger as he worked to free a cord of fat trapped between his teeth.

"Our trade has suffered greatly with the Americans pushing up from the south. It's all disorderly. Their bad liquor and the rest."

"Who . . . who is it that sheds the blood?"

To ask this, the missionary had drawn his thinly encased spine straight. He meant the white fur traders were somehow to blame. It was exactly what One Pound One, in his furies of the past week, had expected. Still, he managed to keep his temper. He laughed.

"Why would a trader kill an Indian, Reverend? If you know nothing about fur trading, maybe you know something about farming. Does a farmer kill his milk cow? Would there be a Hudson's Bay Company here at all if we went around killing our milk cows?"

He had no idea how deep the ignorance ran inside this little man, so he spread it on thick. It was the Indians who killed the Indians, he said. Blackfoot killing Cree. Stone Indians killing Blackfoot. He had even known Bloods to kill Piegans, though those two spoke the same language and had an alliance when threatened. It had gone on forever, before a single beaver or piece of dried meat was traded to a white man.

"But *where* does the killing take place?" The missionary had his cup in a death grip.

Eat him alive, One Pound One was thinking. *Dead within a month and me held to blame.*

But patience was his rule. Carefully, artfully, One Pound One described the prairie for his guest. One day the buffalo were on it like ants on a hill. Next day a place of emptiness. The only cover, grass.

"Out there, Reverend, life can leave you between one breath and the next, and you might never see nor hear nor smell your fate."

One Pound One took a rest from his meal to light his clay pipe, one of several in a line by his plate.

"Do you think for all our guns and horses we are masters on the prairie? When my Governor sends me there, I go, but I count myself lucky to return."

The Chief Factor was looking hard into the missionary's eyes. He leaned forward so the table cut him across his stout middle.

"This prairie you are so anxious to visit is a place we hardly know. The Indians have been there for who knows how long and not a footprint. No houses, no grave markers. Nothing to know them by. Do you see why it's of no use to ask me where the killing takes place?"

"You mistake my meaning."

The missionary's face was pink and glistening sweat. He pushed his plate away. A pile of meat thick in lumpy gravy, a mealy potato, barely touched.

"I refer to the killings near the fort," he said, his voice straining.

"You asked where? The killings near the fort happen near the fort. Why not say what you mean?"

Two of One Pound One's daughters came in to fetch away the dishes. They took the missionary's plate, but One Pound One guarded his with his forearm like a jealous dog.

When the women were gone, One Pound One changed his tone, became almost submissive. He admitted that much of the killing did happen on the lines of travel to the fort. When the Indians came to trade, they were breaking old rules of territory. The area around the forts became a place of murder and plunder. No matter how carefully the traders orchestrated the comings and goings of the rival tribes, it happened that way.

"Then it *is* the trade that causes the violence." The missionary's tone of triumph was high and thin.

"No!" The flat of the Chief Factor's palm slammed the table board. His face suffused with blood, the veined cheeks and nose turning from red to black. "Does a store cause death? If a man buys an axe and puts it in another man's head, do you hang the storekeeper?"

Then, just as suddenly, the Chief Factor was laughing, heartily, as if the anger were just a belch dispelling a momentary discomfort. He pushed his bannock-polished plate away, shouted for tea, stuffed another pipe full and lit it from a candle. He changed the subject as much as he could by saying with real joviality that the missionary should not worry about anything. His mission would soon be going well. There was no need to go out to the Indians because all of them must eventually come to the forts. That was all that he, in his rough way, was trying to get across.

The missionary's eyes had grown bleary, sore from the fire and from One Pound One's incessant pipes. The trader's woman came back and set a mug of tea before him whose strong smell alone brought a wave of sickness. To bed, he longed for bed.

The trader sat smoking around a brown smile, his rust-coloured muttonchops fanning and falling as he took a final lick around his teeth. He lay the pipe aside and stirred milk into his tea with the blade of his knife. All the while, his words kept spilling.

"Soon you'll go to the Mountain House. It's a couple of days by dog team farther up this river. A safe trip if you've got grub and good weather. You'll enjoy yourself there. Mr. Harriott runs it. Chief Trader, in the business almost as long as myself but a very different kind of man. My son-in-law, actually. He's very keen, is Mr. Harriott, for you to come and see his men and his Indians. A religious man. I think you could say that. Some manner of Protestant like yourself."

One Pound One stood up and began his strange pounding walk, back and forth on the far side of the table. He swished his pipe about grandly.

"Converts is no problem. You'll get plenty. Indians love God. All news of God is precious to an Indian. Different style of clothes. New way of speaking and moving the hands in the direction of heaven. They'll be anxious for a translation of your words."

The trader stopped, looked out the door and down the hall to ensure no women were present or near. He scrunched his face, strained and farted.

"And the next time those Indians ride down on their enemies, they'll be feeling strong for the magic of your words. When they make camp, they'll be dancing and singing your words up their spears to the scalps they've taken."

Stopping, leaning, bringing his eyes close, the side whiskers smoking, One Pound One continued in a whisper.

"Do you really have any idea how wild a country you've come to, Reverend? You may think you want mortification of the flesh, but do you even know how a scalp is taken?"

One Pound One reached and drew a wet line with his pipe stem across the missionary's forehead. From above one ear to above the other.

"That's where the cut is made, see? Then, with a jerk!"

One Pound One held his clamped fist before the missionary's eyes.

❦

ROCKY MOUNTAIN HOUSE, 1841

In the great golden eye of a low-arcing sun, the missionary's cariole carved the mushy snow, slashed through the dark, surprising puddles. February in the land of winter and the going was hard because it was not cold enough.

Behind the shield of language, the French driver cursed the soft road and the dogs. He had done so for days. During the last two, Rundle imagined the cursing had expanded to include himself, for he'd been taken by weakness again, the fainting sickness, and could no longer walk his share in the wake of the sled. Like a babe in a decorated cradle, he lay swaddled in a buffalo robe: limp, immobile, dead weight to the four dogs and driver.

Lying with his head back, the missionary tried hard to hear his prayers over the cursing and the incessant barking. The hissing, the swishing, the squealing of the cariole on the ever-changing, unstable road. Then there was the awful whistle and snap of the whip. He peered up through the glued fan of his eyelashes and the whip made its dancing figure against the pale-blue sky. The missionary leaned and looked over the side and there again was the broken trail of bright blood in the snow. God's poor brutes were made to suffer so. The treatment of men was little better.

Ahead, and it must be near now, was the Mountain House. Neither in nor near the mountains, according to One Pound One, the fort took its name from being the last on the North Saskatchewan before the mountains. A hundred yards of churning rapid above the fort was the second reason the explorers had stopped there to build.

When One Pound One had done this describing, the missionary had been surprised at the elegance of the words. In a grassy plain, he'd said, walled on three sides by mixed woods. From the size of its clearing, you could read the age of a fur fort and how continuously occupied it had been. Each winter of use, the meadow grew, chewed back by the sawyers to feed the fort's fires. If the Mountain House stayed closed for any amount of time, the forest would creep back.

Then the cariole burst from shadow into a piercing light, a great openness. Craning up, the missionary saw that they had emerged into a low-relief valley, and as soon as he'd seen it, his snow canoe dropped and rattled across the greenish-yellow river ice. A high grey palisade danced on a ten-foot cutbank. Then a last pull up and they were level with the fort.

At first glance, it was not inspiring. Bastions squatted crookedly on two corners. Stone chimney tops and one roof were all that was visible above the pickets. The roof had a toothless look—rotted by weather, picked apart by wind. Grey and drab was the Mountain House, as befitted a place high on the river beyond which there was no reason to go.

In the clearing beyond the fort, the missionary saw things he liked better. A rough quadrangle of grave markers, surprisingly many, poking up through the snow, with water dripping off their cross-sticks. Against the forest, a tidy row of tipis smoking out their topmost holes.

An explosion of muskets jerked the missionary's attention back, quaked his insides. No matter how often he heard this absurd form of greeting, it made him jump. The fort gate wrenched open, cutting along an engraved arc in the ice, screeching in the slush. Once it opened, Rundle saw a frightened-looking cluster of humanity waiting inside.

A last flourish of whip from the driver and the cariole pulsed under the gate. The knot of people split around it. Then for a moment no one moved. The dogs flattened and began to pant, and a small boy kicked at a thawing pile of horse dung until his mother jerked him away. The only other motion was a young man slowly dragging his cloth cap from his head, down his face, gripping it in a fist against his chest.

At last an older man, walking as if there were no bend in his knees, pushed through the group from the rear. He stepped forward so his boot was inches from the lolling tongue of the lead dog. He removed a worn beaver, smoothed back tufts of mouse-grey hair, then performed an awkward bow in the direction of the cariole.

The missionary could do nothing in reply. In the smother of skins, he found his limbs too weak, too stiff, to move. There passed a suspended moment before the trader understood this, and during it, the missionary realized this was Mr. Harriott, the Chief Trader: One Pound One's son-in-law, who was to be his champion in the service of the Lord.

Rundle tried not to show or feel disappointment. But the seamed and stubbled face, the sad—almost timidly sad—eyes. Dusty coat and stockings darned in unmatched thread. Whose choice of saviour would this be?

Finally, with an attempt at bustle and authority, Harriott tottered up to the cariole. He commanded the driver to help, and the two of them lifted and unbent the missionary.

That evening the missionary sat in front of a smoky fire. Despite the warm weather, the cool of evening had quaked him with chills, and he was wondering why God must present him as such a poor spectacle at each new fort he came to. Humility, yes, but there was need for confidence, too. He wished he had been able to enter here cutting the figure he'd paraded lately at Edmonton: galloping the spirited horse One Pound One had given him as a welcome gift. Or even two days ago, trotting with good stamina behind the cariole. Who would believe it to see him now, his legs covered by a rug and shivering before the fire?

Mr. Harriott had a chair pulled up for himself beside the mission-ary, but he could not seem to stay in it long. Though it clearly hurt him to sit down or rise, he was every half-minute doing one or the other. This time he was up, stumbling to the door, calling for tea.

The missionary's visit had touched off a high excitement in the trader, and Rundle's hope of a quick supper and bed had been snuffed out by it. More of the trader's hospitality had to be endured.

When the trader's woman brought the pot and cups, Harriott awkwardly introduced her. He had neglected to earlier. Now he called her his wife, Nancy. The woman did not quite look at the missionary, and the sound she made was not quite words. Shyness or contempt, Rundle was becoming unsure. Most people seemed to study the floor knobs when the choice was that or look at him.

Nancy was a Halfbreed, that much was evident—the country teemed with them—but not as pretty as many of the women back at Fort Edmonton. Slack-bodied, with the curve of a child under her print dress. Then the missionary revised his opinion. Looking more closely, he saw that she had been pretty at one time. But most of it was tramped out of her now.

By a nod, Harriott gave his woman permission to go, and her quick movement away started a cough. The racking sound of it echoed through the house until Harriott closed the door and cut it off.

In her absence, Harriott explained that Nancy was twenty-two and One Pound One's daughter by his country wife, Louise. Their last child was not baptised. Perhaps, at Mr. Rundle's convenience . . .

The tired missionary muttered that, yes, it would have to be done. The children were the most pressing matter, especially if in poor health? At this Harriott shook his head.

"The child is healthy."

"But that woman," said the missionary. "That cough."

A flush rose from Harriott's collar.

"She has consumption."

"Then we must see to her soul as well."

Rundle was half-conscious that, in his fatigue, something of the pity he should have expressed had gone missing.

"But the Indians," he said, trying to rouse himself. "I will deal with the fort's people, naturally. God's blessing. But my particular interest is with the Indians, who live so distant from the Bible's message. The Chief Factor at Edmonton spoke of certain preparations here for my work among them."

Harriott slapped his knees, pushed himself onto his feet again. Tea slopped on the arm of the chair. "Yes, yes," he said, beginning his painful stroll towards a set of shelves lined with books. He walked there and returned until he was out of sight behind the missionary's chair.

"The tents you saw are Strongwood Cree. I convinced them to wait for you. They've traded all their food and are quite hungry, so perhaps you might see to them soon so they can be off."

The Chief Trader turned and started back for the shelves.

"After they go, we'll fix tobacco for the Piegan. They're from the south. Depending on how things are on the prairie, they might bring the Blood or Sarcee with them."

He went on. When those Indians were in turn gone, he would make arrangements for the Plains Cree and Assiniboine. It all had to be done through messengers carrying tobacco, and he had to be careful that no enemies collided.

"One thing," Harriott said. He was standing facing the wall of books, and Rundle saw a small, spigoted wood cask among the spines. This was the object of Harriott's attention.

"You understand," he began again, seeming embarrassed, "the trade must come first. In the evenings, though, the Indian hall can be yours."

Walking back, Harriott came between the missionary and the fire. There was something pleading in his sad eyes. Would the minister care to join him in a drink? Rundle said he did not mind. In view of his chill and fatigue, he would take some wine.

"I'm sorry, I have no wine here. I have only rum."

"Nothing then. Nothing so strong. But you go ahead, of course."

Harriott threw his tea into the fire and hurried back to the keg. He twisted the spigot and let the cup run full. He drank that off and filled the cup a second time before returning and falling into his chair.

The missionary felt something happen to the man as he sat beside him, though nothing on the surface showed. It was the tension and stiffness leaving the Chief Trader in a form almost palpable. Harriott seemed to occupy ever-widening pools of peace until finally he fell asleep in the presence of his guest.

The empty cup had fallen sideways on his chest, held there in a fold of cloth.

N ext morning, one of Harriott's men carried a small sack of flour to the tents of the Strongwood Cree. The cries of hungry children could be heard across the clearing. Rundle wanted to take the flour himself but Harriott advised him not to. The Indians would not admire a man who ran his own errands. He must observe the chiefs and never act less important than they.

The Indians came to the fort that evening, one chief and a few old men. They trudged into the Indian hall more tired than intrigued. The missionary preached to them and sang, and did more of it again next morning. The moment he pronounced himself finished, they dropped their tipis and disappeared into the woods.

Having spoken to this new Indian flock, Rundle felt hollow, exactly as though he'd done nothing. They had come to him because they were commanded to. It owed to the gun-giving, tool-giving and rum-giving power of the trader, and nothing whatsoever to the power of God. He had accomplished nothing.

The evening of their departure, the missionary cornered Harriott after dinner and challenged him with this interpretation. Harriott looked sad, bewildered. He raised his hands with the palms up, a gesture that asked, what did the missionary expect? That they would come running?

But something of the sort *was* what Mr. Rundle thought. That with God's power coursing through him, a light, a beacon, the Indians might fall to the ground before him, humbled and desirous of the true way.

Harriott's only comment was to confirm that the Strongwood Cree were among the more dependent on the fort, more so than the buffalo hunters to the south. The Strongwood Cree were too far from the Americans to trade there, and besides, the Blackfoot would never allow it. Unable to take their trade elsewhere, these Indians had to more or less do what the Company asked of them.

A part of what Harriott said excited the missionary. "What you're saying is that the buffalo-hunting Indians to the south will not pretend to hear me unless they are ready to listen."

Harriott saw the direction the missionary was tending and did not answer. It was as if he pulled a curtain down between them. But Rundle had made his decision. His real mission, his secret mission, at this moment known only to God, was to bring the message of Jesus Christ to the buffalo Indians of the south.

In the week that followed, no Indians came to the Mountain House. A messenger was out finding the camps, doing the ritual of the tobacco that the missionary only vaguely understood. He used the time to minister to the fort.

First he conducted a marriage: an interpreter named Cunningham to his country wife. Then he baptised some children. Another interpreter, a Halfbreed named James or Jimmy Jock, was visiting the fort. He had an English accent and a reputation as an able translator into Blackfoot, and he said he wanted to bring his children to the missionary for baptism in March.

This was all very encouraging, but Rundle had to work up his prayers on behalf of these people from a resource of duty. He seldom felt the elation that meant to him God's pleasure in his actions.

When he was not occupied with such chores as these, the missionary excited himself with thoughts of the incoming Piegan. He imagined their processions north as a pilgrim's progress towards the blessings of God, blessings that would change their hearts and those of their kind forever. The prayers he offered in respect to these required no urging. The words poured forth, ascended, in a spiralling voice more substantial than his own.

At the same time, the missionary had to deal with others in the fort who were bent on tampering with his mission. For no gain but mischief and crude laughter, they sought to make him fearful. Some of these were even men who came to his services.

During their endless card and dice games, their incessant smoking of an evening, these men never said anything directly against the missionary, and very little directly to him. But while he read his Bible and hymnal, their talk would turn to the prairie Indians and the kinds of outrages they committed. Foolish talk about dismembered bodies, robbed graves, scattered bones, cannibalism. It would be hard to explain how such talk could be boastful but it was, each one trying to be more shameless and grotesque in his story than the last.

When this sort of talk bothered his ability to pray, the missionary would stop reading and silence them with a stare. To this, they inevitably answered with mock apology and servitude.

"Excuse us, Reverend, we forget ourselves. You're so quiet, we forget you're here."

As soon as he began to read, it would begin again.

"That time Bealieu took to the river after that Cree stole his horse. Took a knife in the shoulder, then him and the Indian went under. We give up on him, eh? But damn if it isn't old Beaulieu comes up. And what's in his hand? The Indian's head, clean off at the neck."

The missionary never doubted that it was their purpose to frighten him. As One Pound One had done, these men of the Mountain House sought to frighten him away. But unlike One Pound One, who believed his missionary work was a disturbance to the trade, they had no reason for it save their moral depravity. That which had gradually rotted Europe's heart had crossed the ocean in decaying souls like these.

It should have been a simple thing for the missionary to ignore. What they said was so low that the high mind must surely sail above it. And in his waking hours this was true. It was in his narrow bed, under the strong-smelling robe, in his sleep, that their insidious inventions crept forth and dominated him.

Each night before he slept, the missionary prayed to God for dreams of His garden. Instead, he dreamt of a column of horsemen crossing a burned emptiness. The unshod hooves and the long poles of the empty travois tore up smoking furrows. Through the ashes on the Indian faces, painted symbols shone.

In his dream, the missionary searched these faces closely. He was looking for the goodness all men are supposed to be invested with by God. But the faces were hard and merciless, and he could find no trace of anything but evil.

When Rundle woke from this dream, as he did each time it was hard upon him, he tried to pray but found that the evil dream had more power in his mind than prayer. That was when he felt the downward plunge of despair. For what was he without God but a small, weak man an ocean and the width of a continent away from anyone who cared if he lived or died?

Aloud, he repeated to himself: these images are not of God's making. Nor are they of mine. They come from evil. No other source can make them.

Then, knowing his enemy, he left the half-warm bed and knelt beside it on the raw floor. Again aloud, he said the most familiar of his prayers while deeper still he begged God to find him in this miserable, desolate wilderness where he felt so alone.

Before the morning sun had topped the picket wall, everyone but the missionary knew it to be the day of the Piegan trade.

Then a young Piegan came riding to the fort to confirm it. He entered with a grand, fearless style, as if to say this fort is not a foreign place, it is mine. Harriott gave him a decorated twist of tobacco to take back to his chief.

All was bustling activity after that, with Harriott orchestrating from the centre. His shyness left him and sharp orders filled the air. The storehouse below the bastion was unlocked. Muskets, powder and ball were thrust out to a waiting line of men. The women scurried after their children, herding them inside and slamming fast the doors.

All this motion flowed around the missionary. He took steps in this direction or that but had no idea where he was going or why. Nor would anyone speak to him or meet his eyes. Even Harriott. If Rundle so much as thought about approaching the Chief Trader, he would turn and walk away.

A shout down from the south bastion, then a shout back from Harriott, and all the armed men suddenly ran to the ladders, ascended to the galleries. They sorted themselves in various directions, but the majority massed above the main gate. It looked like preparedness for battle, and the missionary didn't know for sure it wasn't.

Rundle turned to the line of cabins and saw Mary, an English Halfbreed woman who had received his ministry well. Her face was thrust out her door, lit yellow by the sun while her body was back in shadow. She was taking one last look at things before she locked her door. Rundle felt such an impulse to run to her and ask for shelter that he was ashamed.

Right then, he stopped his feet and demanded of himself: What is this feeling? Is it fear? Are you afraid to die?

These would have been simple questions for most people but not for the missionary. In England, he had been asked to consider the question many times. Are you afraid to die? It was part of his training, part of ascertaining if he was worthy.

"No," Rundle said forcibly to the ground at his feet. "I am not afraid to die because death here would be glorious."

This helped. He immediately knew more about the nature of the feeling that gripped him. It was fear all right but not of death. It was a fear of failure, which in turn was a fear of loneliness.

God had invested him with an immense responsibility when he chose him for this mission. If Rundle proved inadequate, God might turn His back in disgust. Being in this place was not easy. Being here without the companionship of God would be a horror beyond imagining.

Rundle ran to the nearest ladder and up it. He scrambled to his feet on the gallery and walked to the rank of armed men over the gate. He did not force his way among them or stand exactly with them. He stopped two paces off the shoulder of the nearest, near an unarmed Scots boy who leaned forward alertly. The boy leaned his chest against the point of a picket, with no greater object than to watch.

In the week that Rundle had been here, the warm west wind had gradually abated. Before blowing itself out, it had swept all the soft snow into piles and muddied the main trail to the fort. Then much colder air had come from the north and frozen everything hard. The rutted mud was ugly grey sculpture fringed in hoarfrost.

The congealed earth, the stillness, the empty clearing and the attentive silence of the men: to Rundle it was as if time had stopped. The sun stood chained in the sky. What broke the silence was a reaction from the men to some change in the picture before them.

Rundle searched the forest edge, the murky frontier between meadow and trees. At first he could see nothing. When he did see the first rider, it was as though the man and his horse came out of the ground. Others sprang into visibility the same way until a long single file of them divided the clearing. The rider on the first horse wore a headgear of feathers and a Company blanket. Below the blanket his legs were bare. The next led a riderless horse, snow-white with ochre stripes across its head.

The young Scots boy began to talk, and although he never turned to the missionary, he interpreted the scene for him. "That one's the chief," he said. "Head chief comes first. Second chief comes second. That horse is a gift for Mr. Harriott."

At the end behind all the men came the women, on foot.

The procession stopped a distance from the fort. Out of range of the muskets, said the boy.

Rundle heard a door slam behind him and, turning, saw Harriott leave his house. His dress was slightly comical. A shining black beaver with a tall pipe, the kind they called a Regent. A black wool coat frogged and piped in white along the open halves and in concentric stripes around the cuffs. On his shoulders were epaulets of gold braid. The stockings hadn't changed, the same ones darned in shades of brown and black. Probably he had no others.

Harriott crossed the parade ground. The gate under Rundle's feet squawked open. Then the Chief Trader came into sight again on the other side. He was guiding his feet carefully among the frozen ruts. The missionary asked the Scots boy what it meant, and the boy said it was by way of compliment. The farther Mr. Harriott went out, alone and unarmed, the more he proved that he trusted the Indians and the greater the compliment.

Rundle was still thinking about this when a burst of gunfire from the Indians jerked him round. As fast, an answering salvo exploded beside him. Through the smoke, Rundle saw Harriott, still making his plodding progress into the meadow. The Scots boy had taken off his cap and had the edge clamped in his teeth.

"Only a salute, sir. Part of the ceremony is all."

All that day, the Indians came into the trading room, one by one or in small groups. Two of Mr. Harriott's men kept a bead on their heads through rifle loops in the ceiling. It had not happened here, but in other places traders had been killed across the counter, usually late in a rum trade. Most of the first day's trade was in rum. When darkness came, the room was closed and the fort's gate barred with iron.

Having avoided him all day, Mr. Harriott sought out the missionary after the evening meal. He led him up onto the gallery so they could oversee the Indian camp. Around half a dozen fires, the Indians were dancing to the music of big drums and keening song. They danced with an intensity Rundle had not seen before, a lifelike pantomime of battle with spear, hatchet and scalping knife.

"I do not understand this, Mr. Harriott. You must enlighten me."

"If I can."

Standing to Rundle's left, Harriott stank of trade rum, and not from spillage save that spilled down his own throat. Conscious of the irony, the missionary forced himself to speak.

"I do not understand this obsession with rum. Rum will not feed or clothe their families, nor help them in any way beyond this night of excess—not that it's helping them now. They might as well be giving you their furs."

"The rum comes from Jamaica. The purchase price there plus the cost of transport . . ."

"You're evading my question, Mr. Harriott."

"I suppose I am. Maybe I don't know the answer. They see rum as powerful. They call it medicine. Some have told me they consider the traders mad to trade such a powerful thing for the skin of a common animal like a beaver."

"And *I* have heard it said that Indians kill one another over this novelty. I was told of a man who froze to death last winter in sight of his own tipi as the result of a treat of rum."

Harriott fell silent. He took hold of the palisade poles, a point in each hand, and blew his pipe smoke in the direction of the Indian fires. In the absence of counterargument, Rundle grew bolder.

"The Company acts as if it has no responsibility in the matter. Because the Indians will trade skins for cheap rum instead of for worthwhile goods, the Company makes the trade and takes advantage of their ignorance. You, sir, take advantage."

"These Indians can trade with the Americans or us, as they like. If we stopped the trade in liquor, they'd soon abandon us."

"So I'm told. But the liquor trade has been stopped elsewhere."

"Where the Company has a monopoly and the American forts are far away and across enemy territory."

As the missionary neared the cliff edge question of why Harriott himself indulged in so much rum, the trader seemed to anticipate him. Suddenly he stood taller on the gallery plank and spoke in a stronger voice. He needed to go now, he said, to ready tomorrow's trade goods.

"The spree will end tomorrow and then they will trade for hard goods. Your business with them can be attended to after that."

He walked to the ladder without farewell and made his difficult progress down it.

As Harriott predicted, the next day's trade was for guns and ammunition, beads, kettles and cloth. Towards evening, the trading stopped and a Piegan chief returned to the Indian hall to hear the missionary's prayers. Four other men and two boys came with him.

Inside the hall the Piegan chief disdained the wooden benches and sat on a buckskin unrolled for him by one of the boys. Quelling his nervousness, Rundle walked to the man and offered his hand. Though the Indian returned the gesture, he did so left-handed. Hoping it was the correct thing to do, Rundle withdrew his right hand and shook the man's left with his own left hand. The Indian nodded, and encouraged by this, the missionary went around to each of the others, shaking them by their left hands. Remembering the procession of the previous morning, he tried to do so in the order of the tribe's own hierarchy.

One old man reached with his free hand and felt the texture of Rundle's clothes. The second brought his face close to the missionary's chest and smelled him. Seen close up, this one had a scar like a velvet lightning bolt from forehead to lip and his cheeks and forehead were a pincushion of smallpox scars.

Coming back to the centre, Rundle broke open his hymnal and sang, his thin tenor wavering in the air. Between this hymn and the next he went to a young man who had a rattle tied to his belt. Rundle pointed to it and mimed shaking it. Through the interpreter he suggested that the lad join in the music if he cared to.

All in all, the Indians seemed pleased by what the missionary did for them that night. He returned to his room exhausted but happy. He was glad at heart that God's work among the feared and formidable Piegan had begun so well.

Someone heard this story: that a piece of paper wrapped in coloured ribbon came from the east. Undo the ribbon, unfold the paper, and the Methodist man of God steps out. It was also said that the Methodist was there to open a trading shop on the prairie, the one the Indians had been requesting for so long. When they found out he brought only news of God, they were disappointed.

❦

By his fifth month in the far west, the missionary had many reasons for thanksgiving. He marked marriages and baptisms in a book, and the list now covered a page. At the end of March, with winter on the wane, he also felt a need to leave the Mountain House. The Indians seldom came in now. Their furs were long traded and hunger had driven them to fan out and hunt. The fort, without them, was a tiresome place.

Every vice thrived here, just as it would in a London slum. The boredom, the repetition, the sheer length of winter brought out the worst. The men talked less, smoked more, and spent most of their time staring into the fire. If they did talk, they were coarse and sharp with one another. Back in their cabins, they were brutal with their women and children. The only remedy they knew was rum, and Mr. Harriott took occasional "pity" on them in this regard.

The moment the rum poured, out would come the fiddle and the jew's-harp. A dance would begin. The French Halfbreed style of violin music was anything but soothing. Skillful enough but incessant and repetitive to the missionary's ears, the speed of the fiddler's fingers mirrored by the dancers' feet. A sound like drumming but created with heel and toe.

How pretty, one might think, how joyful. But the missionary learned to recognize this music as a harbinger of evil. Given rum and a dance, boasting, argument and fighting were sure to follow, usually in that order. When the violence started, he bolted for his room, locked himself in and prayed to God that little blood would spill and no murders occur.

With the Indians, the missionary's work had gone better, but he was far from satisfied there either. His adversary was the same. Again it was the cursed rum that flowed as long as there were skins to ransom it. Rum and more rum. Until the last drop was taken, Mr. Rundle was unwelcome among the Indians.

The Indian drums thundered from sundown through the night, accompanied by heathen chanting, screams and sometimes gunfire. When silence finally prevailed, it was the missionary's signal to invite the Indians to pray. After the rum, after the barter and after the sodden sleep: that was God's place in the trade.

What Mr. Rundle learned from it, each time the cycle repeated, was that he must get away from these iniquitous forts. He must find the Indians in their roving camps, preach and sing to them there, as Jesus would have done. Only beyond the madness of rum could he hope to find an atmosphere of peace conducive to the message of Christ.

On the evening before his departure from the Mountain House, Rundle sat in his room, on the edge of his bed, alone.

His outfit was packed, had been for hours, and his travel arrangements with Jimmy Jock Bird and the other guides were made. They would leave for the south at daybreak. The news of it was all over the fort, and the people, in their easily two-faced way, seemed genuinely sad to see him go. One minute they were listening to him preach, the next minute threatening to cut one another's throats over a dice game, and then, come the third, touching his hem and begging him to stay. A confounding people, and Rundle was not sad to leave them.

As for Harriott—host, ally, principal aide—that man was the most confusing and frustrating of all. Rundle was quite aware of how little he might have accomplished here without Harriott. Possibly he would still be seeking his first convert. Harriott spoke to the Indians and the fort's denizens on his behalf. Harriott ushered the Indians into his presence. Harriott translated prayers and hymns into Cree. (Originally, he had said he would not translate in person, as that could be construed as Rundle's having greater authority, but in fact, he had gone ahead and done it anyway.)

Given what they had accomplished together, one might have

expected the two of them to be sitting together in front of the trader's fire tonight: Harriott asking after the missionary's provisions and arrangements; the missionary thanking the trader for his assistance and offering him God's blessing for all he had done.

But no. Rundle sat alone, ignored since dinner. The meal itself had been entirely silent except for Nancy's coughing. Harriott had made no appearance.

The problem, and it was a great problem, was that a second Harriott existed: a night Harriott so furtive and mysterious the missionary barely knew him. This Harriott was almost certainly in his room right now, separate from everyone, his family included. The only company he would permit were his books, his pipes and his rum.

What had been obvious to Rundle from the start was that the rum trade in this country must be stopped. A solid foundation for God's work could not be built otherwise. Despite Harriott's own drinking, Rundle felt he could appeal to the good Christian nature of the man to help stem the evil tide. But Harriott, who meekly acquiesced to every other request, met this most important one with flat refusal. Without rum, he said, there is no trade. The Indians would take their meat and hides to the Americans, and all here would be lost.

But couldn't he see, the missionary persisted, how the rum debauched the Indians? To say nothing of its effects on the fort's men, and women, too?

Harriott only repeated himself about the Americans and the trade. *Don't come between the Company and the trade* was his way of ending the discussion, any discussion, uttered like the eleventh Commandment.

What the missionary did then was to leave aside the precious subject of the trade. Instead, he persisted in his point about the fort's employees.

"You cannot tell me the people of the fort are at risk of running away to the Americans for want of rum?"

Here, Harriott's excuse was ridiculous. He said he gave out rum to the fort's men seldom. When he did so it was because there were so few other pleasures in life.

"Fighting, debauchery, adultery, murder? *Pleasures?*"

In search of a way to understand this man, Rundle resorted to his most basic teachings. A Methodist believes that salvation is authenticated outwardly by a life of service, inwardly by a peaceful spirit. How then to view the spiritual progress of Mr. Harriott, who by day manifested the outward signs of salvation to perfection and by night seemed to be working just as steadfastly for the devil? As for a peaceful spirit, Rundle had never met a man more darkly and terribly troubled. In no way was Mr. Harriott's a soul among the saved.

But what was also clear to the missionary was that he could not go off from this fort without attempting one more time to help the man. The missionary could not pretend he did not care.

When Rundle pushed open the library door, Harriott's round-shouldered silhouette was framed against the gold and cherry of the fire. A good draft in the chimney had cleared the room of smoke. Rundle coughed to alert the other, then pulled a chair forward to the edge of the hearth beside where the trader sat.

Harriott did not move or speak, nor even turn his head. Shadows danced on his waxy cheek and forehead, and Rundle recognized the look of a man in his coffin.

At last, there was movement, tortoise slow. The trader brought his cup to his lips and drank.

"You're away tomorrow," he said.

Rundle's nerves were twisted so tight by the atmosphere in the room that he began at once to babble. Jimmy Jock Bird had the horses ready for morning, he said. Everything was packed. Dried meat sufficient to start with, though they'd certainly have to hunt much of the way to survive. The guides were all said to be good shots, good hunters. He had several assurances. He had invitations to visit the Crees, the Assiniboines and the Blackfoot . . .

"Be careful of your interpreters," Harriott said, his voice without inflection, his eyes still studying the fire. "Their loyalties are divided."

Harriott had said as much before and the missionary did not agree. Tonight, he felt disposed to argue.

"If you mean Mr. Bird, the man has been quite satisfactory, with the one exception of when he tried to make Munro speak in his place. He has told me since that he merely felt tired of talking to Indians that day and wanted rest. I can understand that. I find talking to Indians tiring as well. In any case, Jimmy Jock has promised to be more active on this journey."

Harriott spoke so quietly that Rundle had to ask him to repeat himself.

"I said that the farther Jimmy Jock is from our Company forts, the more you need to be wary of him."

The missionary struggled to keep his annoyance down. He tried to think of all the good Harriott had done him. He was searching for some way to express that gratitude. Then he could go. While waiting for the words that would allow this, Rundle studied Harriott's profile and saw that the rum had soaked the trader's spirit dark, perhaps darker than he'd ever seen it before.

"Do you think the service of God and the service of the Company can ever be one?" Harriott asked.

"You have proven that yourself, sir. By allowing me to use the opportunities created by the trade to do God's work."

"No," Harriott said. "I do the Company's work and then you do God's. What I'm wondering is if there's ever a moment when the two are the same."

Rundle sighed out his impatience.

"Riddles. I have never been able to set my mind to them. Your two things sound like one to me."

A silence followed but the missionary found he could not leave. He was pinned by his need to thank this man who was refusing the small talk into which such thanks would fit. The longer the silence continued, the more unpleasant it was. The air between them seemed to fill with objects. The missionary's arms grew heavy, swollen with blood. To move or speak, he must swim upward through all this blood and heaviness.

But because it was his duty to make the effort, Rundle did. He asked outright why a good man like Mr. Harriott, an experienced, respected and level-headed man, should be so spiritually troubled.

"Please, you must tell me so that I can understand and help you. Why?"

Harriott's free hand, the one not fixed to his cup, drew up into a fist. It was so tightly clenched the colour left it. For a second Rundle feared the skin could split, the bones could break. Then the fingers flung out wide.

"I have seen and been part of things on this river that I would never forgive if I were God."

The missionary opened his mouth to speak but there was nothing there to say. He was forced to wait out the trader's silence.

"You preach that relics have no power and that their worship is a weakness of popery. But certain relics of this country have great power over me."

"What relics? Don't confuse me, please. Try to be plain."

"Everything is not plain. Will it help you to know that I mean relics of ordinary heathen men? Found in trees, or hanging from a horse's neck, or strewn on the ground."

The missionary's voice was sharp when next he spoke. He no longer cared about courtesy.

"If you can't say anything directly, then please explain yourself by example."

The trader took no offence at the change in Rundle's tone. He thought for a second, then continued as instructed.

"Two winters ago, a trading party of Cree were here. A small band of Blackfoot came in at the same time. We locked the Cree in the bastion to prevent bloodshed. The Blackfoot were belligerent boys with one coyote pelt for which they wanted rum. They came painted for war and were firing their guns carelessly."

He took a sip from his cup, then continued.

"They were pestering us badly, and a man of mine said we should turn loose the Crees. I was angry and without thinking I said, 'By all means, turn loose the Cree.' You understand I didn't mean it to be done. But he took it as an order and raised the plank from the bastion door. There were more Cree than Blackfoot, and they were grown men against boys. The river was frozen hard under deep snow. The Blackfoot tried to escape across it. Most made the trees but a few who had no horses were caught. We listened all night to their screams. When it stopped, we hoped they were dead."

Harriott turned to the missionary, his teeth bared in a humourless grin.

"We avoided that trail for a long time. When finally we had to take it, pieces of the killed men were still hanging in the trees. None of us would touch them. We left them for the wolves and ravens. I noticed later that some of the skin had stayed in the trees and was curled around the branches, tight as a drum."

The missionary was furious.

"Why do you tell me this?" he demanded. "Such a story must have a purpose or it should not be told."

The trader went to drink but found his cup empty. He struggled to his feet and crossed to the bookcase. He filled his cup and sat back down, staring at the missionary, but not as if he actually saw him.

"My problem is that I have always dared to hope. My wife is not my first wife. I was married as a young man to the Halfbreed daughter of the trader at Carlton. He is my uncle so his daughter was my first cousin. She was a great beauty. I had a fierce passion for her and I loved her."

"I am not interested in your lusts," snapped the missionary, the anger welling even higher in him.

"They say I ignored that she was mad when I took her to wife but that isn't true. She wasn't mad then. It was the trade that made her lose her mind. When she became like that, I had to take her everywhere. For a long time I gave up hope, but then, when she bore our child, I did hope again. I couldn't help it. That's how I came to take her over the mountains in midwinter, with our six-week-old daughter at her breast . . ."

"I will listen to no more of this! I have heard the story of this woman before when I was in Edmonton. I do not need to hear it again from you when you are in this condition. I was also told that your daughter was saved. I wonder why you talk only about the dark things and can't spare one word for God's mercy."

"Mercy," the trader repeated. Then he folded his hands, bowed his head and began to mumble. "Smallpox. Thank you, Jesus. Scarlet fever. Bless us, oh Lord. Oh, yes, and thank you, Merciful God, for my second wife and her consumption . . ."

Rundle grabbed his arm and shook him hard by it.

"This conversation is godless! I will listen to it no longer."

The trader lifted his head, his face as close to expressionless as a face can be.

"You asked for examples. I was giving you some. I have more."

Rundle stood. He looked down on Harriott's sparse-haired skull.

"You tell me these things to frighten me! Or to confess to me! Either way, I'll have no part of it. I'm no papist. I don't profess to have the power to forgive you. That's for God, not me. I will tell you one thing before I go. What I have heard speaking here tonight is *rum*. *Rum* is responsible for most of the sinfulness and barbarity of this country, and *rum* has put this evil mood upon you."

Harriott twisted himself around to look at Rundle. He studied the missionary with pale, watery eyes long after his speech had ended.

"How I wish I could believe that," he said mildly. "What I do think is that rum can only let out what is caught within. If there's murder in a man, or despair, does it do any good to cloak it in religion? Or in anything else?"

"Original sin weakens the moral fibre of mankind. The sacrament of baptism erases the stain and communion gives us the strength to resist evil."

The missionary had resorted to preaching, and the Chief Trader did not seem to listen. While the other talked, he swirled the liquid in his cup. When Rundle stopped talking, Harriott raised the cup as in a toast.

"In that case, Mr. Rundle, excuse me while I take my communion."

In slow gulps, Harriott drank his rum. When it was gone he held his mouth like an infant bird's to catch the afterdrops. Harriott's eyes found the fire again. His body assumed the lifeless pose it had held when the missionary came in.

❧

Inside the pales of the Mountain House, the missionary and his guides were mounted and ready. The fort's community had gathered, and Rundle searched among them for Harriott. Finally, just when he had concluded that Harriott was not present and that no final farewell between them would occur, that man came on horseback from behind the line of cabins.

"I would like to ride with you awhile, if I may," he said.

His face had a serenity and a goodwill that bewildered the missionary. In one way Rundle expected an apology; in another, he knew there would be none. What the missionary felt finally, absurdly, was forgiven. But why not accept this smiling face as a gift from God? So he accepted Harriott's offer and they started out together.

Several miles along, in the forest's depth, Harriott said his farewell. "Your mission to the Cree and the Assiniboine is very promising" were his last words as he shook Rundle's hand. Then he went to Jimmy Jock Bird and rode around that man's horse in a full circle. "He comes back" was what the missionary thought he heard him say, before kicking his horse into a canter and riding off. Not until later did the missionary wonder at what Harriott had said to him: the omission of the Blackfoot from his optimistic forecast.

The little company that continued was made up of the missionary, one Canadian named Piché, and two English Halfbreeds, Cunningham and Jimmy Jock Bird. They stayed in the strong woods that day, along a path that wended through wooded foothills and valleys trending south.

The missionary had heard that farther east was open ground, wide-open stretches of prairie. Given the number of dead trees and old snowdrifts on this path, he wondered aloud why his guides did not take that easier course.

Weather, was the gist of the reply. Though it was presently mild, Jimmy Jock was predicting a blizzard. Here they would be safe from it, whereas in the open country where the wind could get at them, it would be a danger.

"Does spring never arrive in this country?" asked the missionary, giggling to signify his joke.

"After the blizzards," Bird said, stone-faced.

In the wake of his guides, Rundle rode hour upon hour. He let his horse drift until they were behind even the remounts and pack animals. His good horse was content to pitch along without guidance, and that allowed the missionary time for thought, time to contemplate what lay ahead.

It was said to be six days' riding from the Mountain House to Bow River, where he was scheduled to meet the Piegan. Between that place and this were the encampments of the Assiniboine and the Cree. All the Indians who had invited him had seemed sincere enough in their desire to have him come to their land to preach.

The fears of a month ago had flown, so much so that he had already composed a letter to the Wesleyan Society in England describing the success of this expedition. It contained the sentence:

> The Blackfoot, so terribly painted in history, will, I believe, be the first on the Plains to bow to the Sceptre of Immanuel.

Premature, perhaps, given that he had not baptised or married any of them, but he *could have done,* that was more the point. He had not because of a reluctance to coax sacraments on those who did not truly understand. What purpose otherwise? It was not, as the Catholics might think, some game in which a scorecard is kept.

Ahead of him, Rundle watched Jimmy Jock, the long back and broad shoulders rolling with the horse's motion. Of his guides, this one would determine his success or failure in the Blackfoot country. The others were sufficient in Cree and Assiniboine, but only Jimmy Jock spoke the language of the Blood, Piegan and Siksika.

Mr. Rundle's eggs were in one basket but that was no cause for alarm. Harriott's concerns and the little business between Jimmy Jock and Munro were small compared to Bird's recent acts of contrition and good faith. In the past month, he had come to the Mountain House with his Piegan woman and four of their children, wanting them baptised. Rundle remembered clearly with what happiness he had sprinkled the rain of salvation on their innocent brows. He remembered too the satisfied smile on the father's face as he did.

❧

THE FIRST CAMP, 1841

Near the night's encampment, a fire raged in the forest, and by the next morning, snow had begun to fall. A V of northbound geese pierced the air beyond a veil of snowflakes the size of feathers. The snow drifted into the smoking forest, the freezing river.

The snow continued heavy into the third day, and there were at times close flashes of lightning within it and quaking thunder, a combination of weather the missionary had never dreamt possible. After crossing the first of the Red Deer River's tributaries, near midday on the 3rd of April, they approached the camp of the Cree. A long procession came out to meet them, led by a chief. Riding past them on his horse, the missionary shook innumerable hands.

The following day they went a few miles farther to the Assiniboine camp, where a similar greeting was given them. The Assiniboine had erected a big tent with a floor covered in pine brush and buffalo robes. Rundle counted them in but grew tired when the number reached one hundred and sixty.

Through his interpreter, he spoke to them that day of marriage and baptism. He taught them to sing "Come to Jesus."

Back and forth between the Cree and Assiniboine. Preaching. Singing. Then, the first baptisms. Nine in the Cree camp on April 6th. The wind of Jimmy Jock's blizzard kept howling around the leather tent while the ceremonies were conducted within.

The timing of the journey began to take effect. It was Easter week, and Good Friday fell on the 9th. The passion and death of Our Lord described. The 11th was Easter, His glorious resurrection, and on the 12th, the floodgates of conversion opened.

Fifty-nine baptisms and five marriages were what he inscribed in his register, and how it must please the Lord! Such proof of the ongoing power of the story of Christ, His earthly life and saintly death. Rundle could see that others were deeply considering his words and would soon abandon their illicit relationships and be married in Christ to their one true wife.

Having made arrangements to meet these people again in July, the missionary departed. Hope exploding in his breast, he rode away from the camp. Boys and girls and yelping camp dogs ran beside him in the deep, fresh-fallen snow.

❧

BOW RIVER, 1841

Travelling south beyond the Cree and Assiniboine camps, the missionary rode to the top of a ridge and saw the fabled prairie for the first time, a hazy blankness disappearing as if in smoke, with no horizon. For a while still they stayed apart from it in the hills between prairie and mountain. They rode in valley bottoms that became progressively more open, more empty of trees.

The disadvantage was that the icy wind blew on their backs and down their necks. The ground was alive with snow snakes writhing through their horses' legs, drifting southeast ahead of them. One night the wind tore the tents down. In a raging darkness, they stood them up again, weighting the edges with stones.

Jimmy Jock proclaimed them two days away from their Bow River destination. When he mentioned a place called Writing Rocks, Rundle insisted they go there. It was in a deep bowl of hills at the end of a twisted valley, easy to miss, and Rundle was most curious to see the drawings for which it was named. As Jimmy Jock showed no interest in guiding him, Piché was the one who took him up the staircase stream to look for them. Before they found anything, the missionary fell climbing a wall of gnarled stone. His ankle twisted so hard he fainted from the pain. Coming back to himself, Piché's face shone above him like a moon.

The wind continued from behind, still a surging blizzard wind. The horses were weakening, and they were so far from forest now that the midday fire had to be made from cakes of dry buffalo dung. When next they stopped, they could make no fire at all. A slimy repast of cold pemmican without tea. No shelter.

Four days south of the Cree camp the guides found the track of an Indian horse, fresh enough to be visible among the drifts. They fol-

lowed the trail hoping it would lead to the Piegan, but where it went
was to a single tipi. For the first time, Rundle felt fear. Had he come
so far only to perish of hunger and cold?

But he should not have doubted his Divine Protector. That single
tent contained a Blood Indian man and woman who, with wonderful
good grace, presented the missionary and his guides with food. Soon
they were seated by a warm fire and dining on fat buffalo meat, even the
prized tongue, which the missionary had never been served by the
nabobs of the white Company.

Put on the right path by these Good Samaritans, they soon came
to a camp of the Bloods, who were themselves on their way to the larger
gathering at Bow River. For these, Rundle held two open-air services,
it being Sunday, but something was wrong. The Indians came and went
as they pleased. They broke into conversation in the midst of his
preaching. He could think of no reason why these people should receive
him any less well than those in previous camps, but they did.

In his journal that night, he wrote that they were "sensible as the
grass they sat on."

He wondered as well if the translation were at fault. In the Cree
camp, there had been a return of the old trouble with Jimmy Jock. He
refused to preach one day, and then by evening had changed heart so
completely as to bring the missionary a plum pudding made by his wife.
Today, with the Blood, Jimmy Jock had translated but seemed to lack
energy. Late in the day, two Siksika emissaries from the larger camp
arrived and Jimmy Jock claimed they were asking how much ammunition and rum Rundle's party had to trade. How could this possibly be
correct? Given his discussions with these Indians last winter, how could
they believe he was here for purposes of trade? And trade in rum, yet?
Preposterous!

In the company of the Bloods, they travelled onward and reached the
greater camp on the Bow River by midday on Monday. The long semi-
circle of tipis in the valley below made the missionary think of a pair of
hands held apart as if imploring the sun to rise. The powerful winds
had blown the plain bare, and all around the tipis horses grazed.

As they looked at the vista, a group of horsemen surprised them, coming over the rise. They were from the camp and they led a white horse, which they wanted the missionary to ride. He was fond of his own horse and almost refused, when an echo came to him from the Life of Christ. As below him people emerged from their camp in a long thin line, he climbed from his horse and let the emissaries help him onto the orange-eyed, snow-white colt. He was remembering how the Jews of Jerusalem had come to Jesus from their city bearing palm fronds.

Blessed is He who comes in the name of the Lord.

In fulfilment of an ancient prophecy, Jesus found a donkey waiting on which he rode into the city over the leaves of palm.

Fear not, O daughter of Zion. Your King approaches you on a donkey's colt.

On his white horse, the missionary descended the final slope of crusted snow and lion-coloured grass. He approached his chosen people.

Next morning, Rundle woke confused. He could hear the wind but felt no pressure against his tent, none of the swelling and flapping he was accustomed to. Coming more fully awake, he remembered that the Indians had pitched his travelling tent inside their own enormous council tipi.

He rose, dressed and made himself neat before stepping out. He had guessed he would not be alone and that was correct. All around, people sat on the ground in wait.

At midday, the council tent began to fill, and soon it was crowded to a suffocating degree. The front flap stayed open and more faces crowded there. Children had removed some of the stones to push themselves in under the sides. In the night the wind had changed from a cold north wind to a warm westerly and had gained much strength. A choking dust had risen.

Rundle wiped his streaming eyes. He squinted in search of Jimmy Jock. The crowd was falling silent and that meant it was time. He found his interpreter seated near a far wall, among some older men, talking. Rundle tried but could not get his attention. Before this became embarrassing, he began alone.

The missionary sang a hymn and the Indians seemed quite interested in the sound. Jimmy Jock, with his hymnal open in front of him, went on talking, more or less through the entire song.

Rundle stopped singing. In English he told Jimmy Jock to be quiet or he would not continue. Bird pointed to the hymnal and said he was showing the Indian where the words were that the missionary was singing.

"That is no way to interpret. If, when I am finished, you would interpret the hymn, I would be glad. But not this way."

Jimmy Jock closed his hymnal with a snap.

Concerned that the Indians were becoming too interested in the drama between the interpreter and himself, Rundle read a prayer and, when he finished, said to Jimmy Jock, "You will please come forward and interpret that prayer."

Jimmy Jock said nothing, nor did he move.

Under the veil of English, Rundle spoke more strongly.

"You dishonour the Almighty, Mr. Bird. The gospel I present is a perfect cure for man, whether civilized or savage, and you stand in its way. You are a murderer of souls."

This, the strongest reproof in his arsenal, fell on Jimmy Jock's ears without apparent effect. The missionary felt the first tickling of panic. Trying to control his face, he asked again.

"Just do it this once."

Bird rose from his place and Rundle assumed he meant to comply. He was thanking God in a prayer when he saw that Jimmy Jock was not coming to the front. He pushed through the crowd and out the flap of the tent.

Rundle quickly returned his attention to the people before him. He forced himself to smile. Under the sound of the wind a terrible silence had gathered. The faces studied him but showed nothing. Rundle reopened his hymnal and began to sing, but he had hardly finished one verse when the dust began carving at his throat. It grated so hard his throat closed and the sound of his singing choked off. He tried to speak but even words would not come.

He sent Cunningham to reason with Jimmy Jock. Cunningham returned alone. Rundle himself went out. Jimmy Jock was standing a short distance from the council tipi, his back to it, the wind tearing at his long hair. As best he could, in harsh whispers, Rundle talked to him.

"These souls are on the road to everlasting misery, Mr. Bird. You have the means of giving them the Word of Life. If you do not give them the Word, you will be accountable on the Day of Judgement, and I will be a witness against you."

Jimmy Jock did not even turn to him. He walked across the camp and into his own tent. By the time Rundle returned to the council tipi, he was entering against a flow of men, women and children leaving. Of these, only the children would look at him. He stood beside the door flap offering his left hand but no one would take it.

Finally the missionary stood alone.

❧

Ft. Edmonton, 1843

It is now the third year of my ministry on the North Saskatchewan.

I send so many letters. To the council of my church and to my family in England. To my direct superior at Fort Carlton. Letters full of religious zeal, enthusiasm and claims of success. The list of baptisms and marriages fills many pages.

As well as that writing, I keep my journal, the official one, because I know the work I do in this country will one day be its history. Let it be known that we, the Wesleyan Methodists, were the first to these forest and prairie Indians with news of Christ.

I write these documents and then, in the loneliness of the night, with sleeplessness upon me, I write this diary that must forever remain secret. Though it be a sin to say, I wish it could be secret not only from men but from God. I wish that because I confide to this document the complete truth, the terrible truth, the unimproved truth that I have no confidence at all in the effectiveness of my missionary work. When two hundred days in the service of Christ can be undone in a minute, that is a difficult conclusion not to draw.

The first, and still most telling, of those moments I owe to

Jamey Jock Bird. (I notice that those who do not like him call him Jamey Jock and that is why I have switched to that convention.) I still wince every time I think of that day in the spring of 1841, when he undid me on the Bow River before the Piegan and the Blood. By the simple act of holding his tongue—withholding his tongues—he created an obstacle that I now believe I will never overcome. I have returned to those Blackfoot-speaking tribes several times, and though they welcome me and listen to me after a fashion, not one of them will take the water of salvation from my hand. Not one will reject his surplus wives and marry in Christ. This I owe to Jamey Jock Bird!

Here in privacy, why not admit my own culpability in the matter? What I learned, in that moment when I could not sing or speak in that giant tipi full of innocent savages, was that I had never made an impression on any Indians because of the news of Christ I bring. If they accepted me or my stories, it was because of the possibility that I was a wizard. When it was shown to them that my powers were less than an interpreter's, they had no interest in me at all.

What then of my work to date? What of my glorious successes during Easter week with the Cree and the Assiniboine? What if they too have taken baptism from me based on some notion that I am semi-divine? Worse still, maybe I knew that and was trading on the deception, exactly like the papist priest who waves his hands over hosts and says, I have made for you a bowl of Christ.

I should have begun steps to remove myself from this place the moment I returned from that so-called mission. I should have accepted and proclaimed that I was unfit. But whether committing the further sin of pride, or because of the phrase learned from my teacher in the faith (Is there anything too hard for God? he used to say) I returned to Edmonton and to my work.

Time can erase almost anything, when there is a strong enough will to forget. Somewhere during that fall and winter, I lost my certainty of failure. I came to see my dismal version of that period as itself a misinterpretation. For didn't Jamey Jock come to me a mere month later with still more of his children to baptise? Innocent as a lamb, as if nothing of negative consequence had ever passed between us. And upon my return visits to the Mountain House, didn't Mr. Harriott work if anything harder in the service of the Lord?

I came to wonder if I had heard any of what I remembered, if I had witnessed any of what my eyes had perceived. I decided finally that I must be succeeding in some way I did not understand, some way known only to God.

By the spring of another year, I had so dispelled my fears that I returned to the prairie. Though as I've written, I did not baptise or marry any Blackfoot-speakers, my visits were not wholly without effect.

In that more hopeful condition, I came back to Edmonton on a summer day in 1842. My health was good, my courage strong, the future optimistic. And what did I find but that Piché, my own guide in the Indian country the summer before, had been to Red River? His French-papist blood had risen in him so that he had brought back a Roman Catholic priest to Edmonton. There he was, Père Thibault, already ensconced, already having completed a sweep of the French Canadians, including many who had been faithfully attending my services for a year.

Several, like Piché, had taken baptism from me, and now had been rebaptised by the priest. My teachings to the contrary, my warnings about the fallacies and idolatries of papism had made absolutely no difference to them. Not as much as a snap of the fingers. A miracle with hosts? Why not?

I went to One Pound One and demanded to know why he had allowed this. He gave me no more satisfaction than a shrug. I pursued him and he became angry, rounded on me and said, "Why is it up to me? Aren't I Catholic too?"

So began another winter of the profoundest doubt in which the Mountain House and Mr. Harriott were my only refuge, the one place the French priests were not invited.

Then another spring and the feeling that I had no choice but to go on. Is there anything too hard for God?

In the tipis of the Indians, I tried and tried. Very slowly this time I began to feel the strength of my mission returning. My decision was to let the priest have his French. I would follow the nomad and baptise him in the cold clear waters of the foothills and prairie as I believed Christ Himself would do.

This was the quality of my thinking as I travelled to the prairies only a month ago, as I stopped south of the Red Deer River to camp.

In the middle of that night I woke to the sounds of violent argument. I looked out. The flat eastern horizon was the colour of roses. In the half-light I saw men taunting each other across a dying fire.

One was Piché. Two days earlier he had appeared out of the prairie to join my travelling party. I had wondered at the time about his motives. I frankly assumed he was there to spy for the priest. His son was with him. All the same, because I am always willing to hope that a man will see the error of his ways, I allowed Piché to remain. When there came an opportunity, I invited him to my tent for conversation. I remember we talked about brotherly love.

But here they were, Piché and son, facing two other French Halfbreeds, brothers, and screaming in rage over some infraction during their night of gambling. I went to them. Stop this senselessness, I said. I remained standing between them and they seemed ready to obey. They left the fire for their respective tents.

I went to my own tent and lay down. I prayed to God to end this evil. But it wasn't long before the shouting resumed. Again I rose and left my tent. The first thing I saw was Piché with an axe in his hands. His son was beside him holding a musket. They were in front of the brothers' tent. Suddenly, the brothers appeared one from each side. They had cut their way out behind. Each had a musket and I had no more than seen this when one fired his ball into Piché's chest. The other fired too and his ball entered the breast of Piché's son.

Piché fell, instantly dead, but his son turned and ran towards me. The terrible ragged wound in his chest. I know it's not possible that I could have seen his heart, but that's what I believed in that moment. His exposed, ragged, bleeding heart. His wild and dying eyes were locked on mine. His mouth, a soft, pink, sputtering thing, said the words "They've killed me." Even when he fell, he came struggling forward on the ground, clawing at the soil with his fingers. His hand stopped just short of my moccasin.

There was an Indian in our camp. He had watched this dealing out of death quite calmly. When Piché's son was finally dead, the Indian picked up the musket that had fallen from his hands. He pointed it at the ground, shook it and laughed. He laughed because the gun was not loaded.

Dear God. How can I possibly go on? When all these horrid visions mock me. Perhaps nothing is too hard for God but I am not God. I am a man, weak and frail even for a man. I fall ill again and again. I wake in the night seized by sweating chills. My back aches until I could cry out.

How often I hear the words of Harriott. His voice swimming back from that night at the Mountain House. Man, evil in his heart. What good to throw a cloak of religion over such an evil core? And wasn't he right?

How my own words about brotherly love must have rung in Piché's ears as he took up the axe to avenge his lost wager! As he bade his son join him so another life could be thrown away with his.

Images of brutality and horror. Like Harriott, I am inhabited by them, am less able every day to see beyond or around them to the shining purity of God. I wake in the night to dreams of ravenous dogs, dreams that have repeatedly torn my sleep since the night in Edmonton a year ago when I prayed before the Aurora Borealis and was attacked. Nearly torn apart for the bit of food my poor flesh could provide.

Is there anything too hard for God?

I will probably stay here and complete my ministry, but I deserve no praise for it. If I stay, it will be because I lack the humility to admit defeat and go.

All these lives I encounter were shaped so long ago. I do not know how long ago or by what force. Mr. Harriott and One Pound One and Jamey Jock Bird. For them, and for all the murderers I have described here, I am simply come too late. Whatever made them the way they are, I cannot undo its handiwork.

THE
ARTIST
1846–1848

Dear Editor,

I guess in this book of yours we're talking about how a place goes from wild to tame. First the Indians have it to themselves. Then traders come to harvest the animals. After that it's the missionaries trying to tame everybody. Artists, white hunters and such want to paint it or shoot it so they can say they did before anyone else. That's the last thing before the homesteaders. I bet it doesn't differ much from Rhodesia to Rupert's Land.

It made me laugh you asking if I met that artist fellow Kane. Truth is I saw him once during my first trip into the country. I was coming in and he was going out. I was sixteen and part of a gang of engagées from Montreal. Our boats and the artist's boat came from opposite directions and pulled up at the same mooring along the river. We ate in sight of each other. I remember he looked like a true frontiersman in beaded leather and all bearded. That he was a painter I guessed by some brushes he had wrapped in a rag and tucked in his sash.

I laid eyes on the Methodist Mr. Rundle on the same trip but farther inland. He was on his way out too.

I had only just come but I badly wished I could leave with them. The bosses and bullies of our brigade were doing everything to smash us on the Company anvil. At the Sault they had locked us in a warehouse so we didn't desert. Another place they made us sleep on the boats under a bridge where a guard carrying a rifle walked back and forth all night. Beyond the Sault they switched us from salt pork to pemmican grease and our guts didn't get the hang of it until Edmonton. Some days there were more asses than oars over the side.

That was my introduction to the colourful life of the frontier. Print that in your newspaper and see how the local parson likes it.
William Gladstone

Ft. Edmonton, 1848

Dear Father,

I am near the end of my journey in the West and I thought I should write to you.

It is my hope that these two years in the wilds will be the making of me. When I was in London in 1842, I witnessed the excitement over Mr. Catlin's paintings of life along the Missouri River. I am a more complete artist than Catlin and my subject, the Hudson's Bay Company in Rupert's Land, is at least as interesting. I expect to enjoy the same success, if not more.

The problem is getting my cargo of sketches and notes across the continent and home. Given the rivers I have already navigated without significant loss, I expect to do so without too much difficulty. At any rate I am anxious to be home and to put on my first exhibition. The HBC Governor who is responsible for my being here promises to buy most of the paintings for his house in Lachine. So it is an assured success provided he likes them.

Sometimes I think back to a decade ago when I was robbed on a Mississippi steamboat and had to paint the skipper's picture as my fare to New Orleans. Nowadays I dream of being the toast of London and Paris, and telling that story as an amusing anecdote. Only time will tell which is more representative of my life.

I know there have been hard words between us in the past and I regret it. Much of the advice you gave me that I seemed to ignore, I have remembered and use to guide my life. For example, your warning as to the "blind hazards of marriage." If I was a married man, my travels would have ended long ago. Without having travelled the West, I would probably have ended my career painting flattering pictures of ugly men and their fat wives.

Your son,

Paul

❧

Ft. Edmonton, 1848

My Dearest,

My work here in the West is almost done. So many pictures and words. I can't wait to lay it all at your feet. I literally limped back into Edmonton before Christmas, my feet being all but ruined and such pain! A common ailment, they tell me, caused by walking too long in snowshoes. Mal de—something. (Don't worry. I have it in a note.) But I'm quite well now and almost ready for my voyage home.

I think you will be pleased when you see what I have, both my pictures and written notes for the book. As you know I am not as good a writer as I am a painter, so I'm counting on your help in the latter area.

The main task with the book will be to make the people and the stories exciting but also palatable. I'm not talking about lies so much as omissions. Leaving out the more bloodthirsty and immoral details.

It's not only this country's Indians who would scandalize. I've seen the white people behave in ways every bit as savage. Here, where the rum flows free, murder is practically commonplace, and seldom punished with anything but primitive revenge. The Company turns a blind eye. For example, a few years ago, Mr. Edward Harriott gave two Halfbreed brothers a bribe of rum to work as hunters at his prairie fort called Piegan Post. Once they'd consumed the spirits, they beat a man to death. The Company was so concerned about the lapse in decorum that the brothers were welcomed at Piegan Post and their contract honoured to the letter.

In other words, I think we'll have to dress the characters up a bit, make them more the wilderness heroes the public will expect and want.

In a sense, the same thing has be done with my paintings of the Indians. Given the rough life they lead, their normal appearance is scruffy and coarse. When I go from sketch to finished painting, I will make them considerably more noble. This is merely practical, for otherwise I wouldn't sell a one!

Getting back to the book, Chief Factor Rowand of the Saskatchewan, my host at Fort Edmonton last year, is a man I must certainly improve. I describe him in my notes as capable, powerful, and quick to both anger and laughter—all of which is true but a great euphemism, particularly the part about anger. In my travels I've never seen a temper to match his. His abuse of language is shocking. He treats men no better than dogs, balls up his fists and knocks them down, kicks their backsides until they can hardly walk.

His style in trade disputes is if anything worse. If in his estimation an Indian is giving trouble, the old Chief Factor is likely to disarm the man by force, then beat him senseless. Far from incurring the wrath of the Indians, it seems to have earned him great respect. They call him "Big Mountain" and "Iron Shirt."

By these names, I probably have you picturing a giant, but the reverse is true. He's shorter than I am. Short and broad, and lame in one leg. The sound he makes walking around his Big House has earned him the nickname "One Pound One," or "Twenty-One Shillings," a joke I like. He owns many fine horses, which he loves more than his children, and every chance, he races them for wagers.

When I first arrived two years ago, I rode to Edmonton from Fort Carlton with One Pound One and a little Methodist missionary called Mr. Rundle. I'm sure I wrote to you about them at the time but I can't remember if I told this particular story. The ride took several days and along the way we lived by our wits and gunpowder.

Then one morning, the missionary announced he was sick and wanted to be left behind. With very little argument, we departed without him. As we rode away, I expressed concern. One Pound One said, "He's lying. It's Sunday and he won't ride. He uses his fainting skill so I won't think him a fool for losing a day."

A Methodist missionary lying in order to observe his faith!

As One Pound One and I continued, our horses became quite worn down. He led us to a horse guard where we got fresh ones. He liked his new horse so much he kept trying to distance me on it. Then, when a prairie fire forced us to cross the river, he plunged his horse in where the current was swift. Seeing that his horse fared well, I did the same.

In no time, my horse was floundering and I was floating off. I barely managed to grab its tail, by which means I made the far shore. I had drifted a great distance by then and swallowed a lot of water.

As I crawled out, One Pound One came galloping along through the trees, soaked to the skin and laughing so hard he could barely stay in his saddle. That I had almost died made it even funnier I suppose.

As for the Methodist, I continued to worry, what with the river so high and fires raging. There was no sign of him the day of our arrival at Edmonton, and that night, as seen from the galleries, the whole prairie was ablaze to the south and east. Next afternoon, into the fort he came, tired and complaining, but basically unhurt and not overly impressed by his survival.

Although it will mock the little man, there is one story I must tell in our book. Rundle has a little cat of which he is absurdly fond, and one day he had it on a string inside his coat as he tried to mount his horse. Many Indians were present and crowding in and suddenly Rundle's horse reared. Kitty fell out of his coat and dropped to the end of the string. Naturally, she put her claws in the first thing she saw, which happened to be the horse's legs! Next thing, Rundle was tossed high in the air and landed right in the throng of his admirers!

There is another man in this area who I find interesting, a Chief Factor named Harriott, the boss of Rocky Mountain House. What intrigues me about him is to what extent he is the opposite of One Pound One. What One Pound One achieves by force, Harriott does by shy diplomacy. I have never heard of him striking a man, and in this country, that counts as unique. When his men take off their hats to him, as is the custom, Harriott likes to remove his own or give it a tap.

I have not seen it but they tell me Harriott has a considerable library at the Mountain House, which is an astonishing thing. Between the Rockies and Red River, most of the books are Bibles, and few enough of those. All of which would make you think Mr. Harriott is an exiled aristocrat, but again, he is nothing of the sort, just a man of ordinary birth who came from England as a boy. His education and manners are all of his own making.

An odd relationship exists between Harriott and the Methodist Rundle. Ever since Rundle came here, Harriott has been labouring in his service, translating hymns and so forth. If you ask about them you'll be told they're the best of friends. But from early on in my observation of them, I got an impression of some deep annoyance. More than once I entered a room and knew instantly they'd been arguing. I gathered it had to do with rum, both the trade in it and Harriott's copious personal use.

All of which brings me to the drama I witnessed here on January 6th this year. One Pound One's son, a spoiled and surly brute, was marrying a pretty Halfbreed girl named Margaret. The Methodist was doing the honours and I was a witness. As you'll see when I get home, I took a sketch of the newlyweds departing by cariole on their journey back to the young man's post.

But here is the peculiar part. Margaret, the bride, turned out to be Mr. Harriott's daughter, not by his present wife but by a previous one who died in strange circumstances in the mountains. Peggy, as Harriott calls her, was just a baby when it happened. Given that Harriott's second wife is the groom's sister, that makes Harriott, by my calculations, father-in-law to his own brother-in-law!

One Pound One was not present, being away on furlough, and in the role of father and host, Harriott got very drunk and melancholy, especially at the dance. This caused a resumption of his dispute with the missionary, but so as not to spoil the party, they took their argument into another part of the house. Being interested, I went out by a different door and crept around to where I could eavesdrop.

What a discussion it was!

At first the missionary was upbraiding Harriott for being drunk, which seemed natural enough, but then he started saying it was imperative that Harriott stop thinking so much about his first wife. If he would do that, he might stop drinking. He might also care more for his second wife and his second family. Harriott didn't accept that evaluation of himself. He replied that he had never mistreated or been disrespectful to his present wife or neglected his children by her.

"If that is so," said Mr. Rundle, "why have you never married the woman before God, or had your first children by her baptised?"

There was a pause before Harriott said in a quiet voice, "The reason is that Nancy and I are married and our first children were baptised."

The missionary was flabbergasted. "Impossible," he said. "I was the first here."

To which Harriott said, "You were not. Two Catholic priests came in 1838. They married me to Nancy and they baptised our children. Except for the most recent child. That one you baptised yourself."

Another pregnant pause and this time followed by the sound of the missionary crying!

"How could you?" he said, all in tears. "After all I've preached about papism and its evils? And your pretence of supporting me?"

Harriott seemed unmoved. "That was before you came," he said. "My wife wished to be married, and One Pound One's family in Montreal are Catholics. I saw no harm in it."

"You are not married!" The Methodist was raving. "A Catholic marriage is no marriage!"

"I married my first wife without any ceremony at all," said Harriott.

"And look what God did! Look how he punished that marriage!" The missionary was virtually screaming. "By madness and suicide!"

"You're wrong," said Harriott, still stone calm. "I'm married to her still and will be until I die. Which means I am married to two women if you're counting sins."

"My heart is broken," said Rundle, sobbing away. "For what evil purpose have you been pretending all these years to be a Protestant man of God? Why have you pretended to help me? So you could mock me?"

"I see no pretence. I did help you, and you were helped."

"But why?"

There was a considerable silence then, except for the missionary blowing his nose, and I thought the episode was over. But Harriott had only been thinking of an answer all that time.

"After the smallpox, the Indians were discouraged. The whites had been telling them their God was no good and the whites had a better one. The way the smallpox attacked the Indians and not the whites, in spite of all the Indians' prayers . . ."

"I fear what you are saying," started up the missionary.

"Then fear it, but I will finish. When I heard you were coming, I thought you might restore their courage. If you could make them believe your powerful God could be theirs, then they might become strong again."

"So the true God and I were just devices to you."

"No. I believed it too. I had the same need as the Indians."

"You had no smallpox."

"But my young wife has consumption. She will not live as long as I do. I married her in hopes of changing my luck, but instead I changed hers. So I did need your God, because just like the Indians, I had lost faith in everything I could do."

"And there you were: brought to God. As I've said to you before, I can't understand why you don't praise God for how merciful he has been to you. Why must you always choose the dark side, when the light is so close at hand? And if I have helped bring you to God's mercy . . ."

"No, Mr. Rundle. That is my point. You asked for it so you

should listen to it. You have tried, and no one should fault you for your effort. But you have not helped me. What you have is not strong enough in this country. Not for the Indians, and not for Nancy, and not for me. You cannot change what is happening to any of us."

"I may not be powerful, but God is. But I will go as you say," said Rundle. "I am leaving soon."

An extraordinary conversation even for this place, and to cut a long story short, I made it my business to find out if Rundle's final statement were true. Next day I cornered him and asked when if ever he intended to leave this country. Quite cheerful and without suspicion, he said that he was leaving soon. He had done his work in God's wild vineyard long enough and it was time to go back to England. Becoming rather silly and giddy, he confided he'd like to find a wife.

I hope you will pardon the length of this letter, my dear. It will take an entire candle to read it. But as you know I use these letters to frame and distil my observations for the book. Odd to think this may be the last of them before I set out to leave this country.

Or it may not be. I have in mind one final foray to the Mountain House, which is closed at present while Mr. Harriott is here and One Pound One is in Montreal on furlough. A few Indians of a kind I have not painted yet are said to be camped there. As well, there is a Halfbreed looking after the fort whose acquaintance I've been wanting to make. A real pirate of the plains by all accounts, by the strange name of Jamey Jock Bird. If anything significant comes of it, I will likely write again.

Yours lovingly,

Paul

🌿

Ft. Edmonton, 1848

My Dearest,

Apparently I have one more letter in me. I have just returned from the Mountain House, where I met the notorious Mr. Bird.

Before I begin the story, I'll give you the same background I had prior to meeting him. His name is Jamey Jock Bird (or James or Jimmy Jock) and his father was once Northern Department Governor here. Despite that privileged position, Jamey Jock went to live with the Piegan Indians, where he married a Piegan woman and acquired some fame as an interpreter and a warrior. The story goes that for many years he was given money by the HBC to coax the Piegan trade away from the Americans who operate along the Missouri. Bird is regarded to be treacherous. The usual reason given is that he pocketed money from the American Fur Company to trade with them as well. He was clever about it and the HBC was never sure if it had been betrayed or not.

Mind you, One Pound One has no ambivalence on the subject. He hates Jamey Jock passionately and claims to have tried to kill him once, except he ran away.

Even Rundle, the Methodist, has a grudge. He blames the Halfbreed for his failure to convert the Blood and Piegan. He says Jamey Jock refused to translate when working as his guide. Harriott tells me Jamey Jock did the same thing to a Jesuit named de Smet.

So there I was, the dog team pulling my cariole into the abandoned Mountain House and about to meet Beelzebub. Smoke was coming out the trader's house chimney, and as we unharnessed the dogs, a tall straight-backed Halfbreed of middle years came out. My driver introduced him as the legendary Jamey Jock Bird.

My first surprise was when he spoke. Having grown used to hearing the English language butchered in dozens of novel ways out here, I could scarce believe I was hearing a good class of English accent and proper grammar too. It seemed impossible to have that sound coming from a leathery Halfbreed, creased by age and scarred by smallpox.

Bird was kind to me from the start and we discoursed on many things. I found him a gifted conversationalist and, frankly, the most knowledgeable man I've met on this voyage. I tried to keep everyone's warnings in mind, but when his Indian wife prepared a plum pudding, my resistance melted.

As we sat together that night, the fort strangely empty and quiet, he questioned me more than I him. I was taking a sketch of him and he asked for whom I was painting. I told him the Governor was responsible for my being in the West and he asked how the Governor was. He said it as you might say, "How's my old friend John?" so I replied, "He's a friend of yours then."

"We never met," he said.

This was the effect of Jamey Jock. He kept me on my heels without apparent effort.

I told him the Governor was fine, showing his age but still active. There was hardly a business scheme in Montreal in which he didn't have some involvement.

Jamey Jock forced me to meet his eye. "I hear companies use him to carry bribes to politicians."

Frankly, I've heard the same but I pretended to be shocked and said I doubted the Governor would do such a thing, or had need to.

"He does not need to," said Jamey Jock, "but he likes doing things that are hidden."

So I asked him how he came to have these insights if he didn't know the Governor.

"I said I never met him, not that I don't know him."

We got out our pipes and smoked for a while after that. It seemed to me that he would not speak again. This happens to me regularly in the West. The acceptable length of a silence is so much longer here. I'm always uncomfortable when others are perfectly at ease.

Jamey Jock broke it by asking if the Governor's wife lived with him.

I affirmed that Frances Simpson had returned from England and was again living with the Governor at Lachine. Before that, although she made several visits, she had been living in London—for, I believe, a dozen years—raising their four children.

"I went and looked at the Governor and his white wife when they lived in Fort Garry at Red River," Jamey Jock said next. "I wanted to talk so I sent him a message. He didn't ask me to visit because our business was secret, but also I know he had a rule about Halfbreeds in his fort. So I spied on him a little. I like to do things in secret too. Their first son was dying at the time and the Governor and his wife were sad. I saw the way the Governor's white wife looked at him. She hated him, maybe for bringing her out here where she would bear children who died."

Jamey Jock took a few pulls on his pipe and then continued.

"The Governor hurt a lot of people in the trade. My father was one. He should have been a senator but, thanks to the Governor, he was a farmer. Only when it came to his wife did the Governor have no defence. She looked down on him and he could not bear it. I wasn't surprised when she went back to England and he let her."

The pudding we ate that night was practically the last food at the Mountain House. Finally this dire shortage drove Jamey Jock, his family and me to make a run for Fort Edmonton. Bird was counting on a food cache halfway, but when we got to the place, it was empty. The cache was made of crossed logs and a starving wolverine, one of the fiercest animals for its size, had wriggled inside. Mr. Wolverine had eaten everything and had grown just fat enough not to be able to leave. He looked as if he could eat us too but Jamey Jock dispatched him. We made a meal of the beast but it was hardly the repast we had in mind.

That night, as we sat around a very poor fire of wet wood and spruce boughs that burned in seconds, I again tried to draw Jamey Jock out. He wasn't as forthcoming when it was I who asked the questions.

I thought to ask him about various people, starting with One Pound One.

"You don't want to know what I think of him as much as you want to know why he hates me. For that you should ask him." And that was that.

I wanted to talk about the Methodist Rundle too, and here, I had a ready means. Back at the Mountain House I had taken a sketch of an old Assiniboine named Mah-Min. He was so pleased with my sketch that he gave me a necklace of grizzly bear claws he had been wearing for twenty-two years! Before I left Fort Edmonton, Rundle had asked me to give the Assiniboines the message that he would not be paying them a spring visit this year as planned. Jimmy Jock was translating for me. When he got to this part, Mah-Min called Rundle "the father of lies."

When I recalled this incident by our campfire and asked Jamey Jock why the Assiniboine had spoken thus, he was impatient with me for the first and only time. "He said he'd visit. Now he doesn't. So Mah-Min calls him a liar. You'd do better if you asked what you want to know, which is, if I'm not mistaken, why I would not translate for Rundle when we visited the Piegan on the prairie."

In the face of such directness and candour I could only admit the truth of it.

"There were two reasons. First, he treated me like a servant in front of my people. The second reason is that the Blood and Piegan cannot be improved by being Christians. I think a church in my country would be even uglier than a fort."

"Very well," I said to Jamey Jock, "if you prefer me to be direct, tell me, how did you earn your title of war chief with the Piegan? By killing white men?"

At this he smiled. He did not seem offended and abruptly launched into a story about the murder of a Gros Ventre chief at a place called Devil's Hole. It happened after the "rendezvous," which is what the Americans call their annual trading party in the mountains. White trappers, what Americans call their "mountain men," bring their winter furs to the traders, who exchange them for trading and trapping outfits, liquor, women and what have you. Some Americans were riding away from the rendezvous—I think this was 1832—when they ran into a war party of Gros Ventre. A Canadian named Godin who worked for the American Fur Company and a Flathead Indian went out to parley. As arranged between them, the Flathead shot the Gros Ventre leader in the back while he shook hands with Godin.

That was the first part of Jamey Jock's story. The next part was a couple of years later at Fort Hall, an American fort on the Snake River. Some Piegans arrived there in the spring and camped on the far side of the stream. They shouted across to the fort that they wanted to trade, but only with Mr. Godin, who was working there at the time. Finally the Canadian waded across.

The Indians had a little fire going and their headman bade Godin to sit. They would smoke a pipe before the trade. The Piegan chief smoked first and then handed the pipe across. The instant before Godin's lips touched the stem, the chief gave a signal and the Canadian was shot in the back. The Piegan chief scalped the dying Frenchman and carved the initials "AJW" on his forehead. They left him in the ashes of the fire for the others to find.

It was quite a story and I assumed I understood why it had been told. "You were that Piegan chief?" I asked him and he nodded.

Having digested this much, I was still not clear on the significance of the initials.

"Why AJW?" I asked.

"Andrew J. Wyeth. He was an American Fur Company officer with the bunch that met the Gros Ventre. Wyeth could have stopped the murder but he didn't think it was his business. I hoped to teach him that it was."

As we sat longer that night with our pipes, then as I made my cold bed under the stars, my blood was running a little cold.

We made our return to Edmonton long after dark the next night, and we were greeted in the square by ghostly old Mr. Harriott, who seemed as though he had outlived the need to sleep. He and Bird greeted each other formally but fondly.

The next day Mr. Bird and family took the trail back to the Mountain House with a cariole loaded with trade goods. I couldn't help but feel the weight of the countless worthwhile stories that must be leaving with him, but I know as well that much of what he did tell me cannot go into my book. I obviously can't write his opinion of the Governor or of the Governor's marriage, nor do I think his opinions of Christianity would help our cause. If I write the final story of how he participated in the murder of Godin, then there will be no sympathy for him at all. Maybe those stories will never be told, and somehow that makes me feel a failure.

So, my dear, another adventure is over, and possibly the last. As I make ready to go, I can't help but wonder if I'll ever return. One part of me longs to do so. Another part fears it would be a disappointment. They have a joke out here about the warm west wind they call the Chinook or Snow-Eater. Something about a traveller going east by cariole at the height of a Chinook. His front sled runs on snow while his back sled drags in mud, all the way. That's my West, I fear. Everywhere I've been and everything I've seen may have disappeared the moment my back was turned.

Meanwhile, my patient darling, I am coming home to you.
Yours,
Paul

DEATH

1848–1867

Mill Creek, 1900

Dear Editor,

I'm sorry to be so slow answering your last letter. Winter settled into my lungs this year and I spent the last month coughing. It's beginning to look like this story will end about where I might have come into it.

That's not such a bad thing. I wasn't on the list of names you gave me back when we started this. When I gave you my suggestions, I wasn't even on my own list. The world and me will have to change a lot before Old Glad's life story is thought of as history.

All in all let's just finish what we started and call it good. The final days of One Pound One and Mr. Harriott. The way it went and ended for Jimmy Jock Bird.

William Gladstone

SASKATCHEWAN BRIGADE, 1848

One Pound One had never been in a worse mood on the river than when he returned from his season of furlough. If he could have made the boat move by kicking each man in turn, he would have done so.

Season of furlough! Season of frustration, more like. Pacing the streets of Montreal for want of anything to do. Visiting the Company's retired veterans, wizened men with blankets on their knees, all hoping to die before their Company savings ran out.

Time spent as well with His Nibs the Governor, who often fetched One Pound One in his carriage as black and glossy as coal for a trot around town and out to his home at Lachine. Now there's a fine property, he'd say, Mr. McGillivray might be pried off that one if you made the right offer.

And so on. You started out grateful but wound up wondering what was his hurry. Did he have a man in the wings groomed and ready for the Saskatchewan? Did he want old One Pound One out of the way?

It had been a fatal mistake, in hindsight, to confide in anyone that retirement was on his mind. How a man almost sixty, with a bum leg and three unwed daughters (like three more bum legs), could fail to be considering retirement, he did not know. Still, he should have kept it to himself. The moment he blurted it out, a whole machinery started up. Every question thereafter, from every source, had the same second question under it:

When will you go?

What made it more difficult was that, having considered retirement for an entire winter, One Pound One wanted *not* to consider it any more. He wanted to erase the whole matter. In Montreal, he had squinted his eyes in an attempt to see his daughters and Louise in the houses and stores, and walking on the streets of that town among the proper snobbish bitches of Montreal with their notions of London fashion and Edinburgh etiquette. The thing was impossible. His women were too big (Louise and his third daughter both topping twenty stone). Their laughter was too loud and their topics too vulgar. Their tempers too hot. Sparks would fly and every time there was a social blowup, One Pound One would be the first one burned.

If he had any doubt about the matter, it came this past winter at a dinner where his son, the Montreal doctor, made a comment about the source of the Governor's occasional ill health so scurrilous One Pound One had been forced to take an oath that it never happened. It was nothing short of a suggestion that the Governor's problem was Cupid's Measles, and he said it with any number of gossips in attendance. And this was the one of his family who was supposed to be civilized. If the choice was the trade versus constant embarrassment, he had no doubts where he wanted to be: back with the horse thieves and drunkards of Edmonton.

Finally, One Pound One understood clearly just how well set up he was at Edmonton. Though the work was often maddening, he was flanked all around with family. His namesake son was at Fort Pitt, with Harriott's daughter Peggy as his new wife, and Nancy was on the other side at the Mountain House with Harriott. If he and Louise, and the spinsters, pulled up stakes, what of them?

John Junior was a good man away from a desk, as One Pound One had often told the Governor, a bit hot-headed and prone to accident but still a valuable hand when there was someone to guide him. And that was the point. That guiding hand had to be One Pound One's, because John Junior would take no orders from any other.

As for Harriott's Nancy, she was so worn out with babies, and with her illness, that at times the women of the Big House had to go upriver to relieve her. How would that service be rendered from Montreal?

For that matter even Harriott still needed watching. No better man with the Indians, though a bit soft according to One Pound One's likes, but he needed his rum more all the time, for the pain in his joints and just generally to keep himself from sinking.

At Council, where One Pound One had just been, one damn fool hinted it was time Harriott took over the Saskatchewan. Now, there was a laugh! Without One Pound One to stiffen him, that sodden fellow would leak through his own floorboards. Run a district, indeed!

The conclusion simply was that One Pound One could not retire. But just when he had made up his mind on the matter, along comes the Governor, sneaking up behind, taking him by the arm and ushering him out. Council this year had been nothing but an insult. The Governor, all concern down at Montreal, averted his eyes from One Pound One at Norway House. Looked at the ceiling and began declaiming freely about all the inadequacies of the Saskatchewan District.

"Perhaps because of the many furloughs taken in Saskatchewan of late, due to age, infirmity and intemperance, returns have barely justified . . .

"If my advice had been taken years ago and Mr. Harriott had been removed to a situation less conducive to his excesses, to a district where liquor is banned, is what I mean . . .

"It has been suggested by this Council—by one veteran Council member that the men we are drafting nowadays are not of the same quality as in bygone years. I would caution this gentleman that men seldom do perform well under the lash. Frankly, we see too many resignations from the Saskatchewan . . ."

What preposterous nonsense! Was it One Pound One's fault, or Harriott's either, that the American traders on the Missouri were thick as flies on a pile of horse dung? That fires (likely set ones) were killing the buffalo and keeping them and the Blackfoot away? That the wolves were proliferating out of control and eating horses at a faster rate than they could breed?

Whole herds of buffalo had been consumed by fire in the fall of '46. They lay down in their thousands to die. The wheel of such a disaster keeps turning. At Council, his Chief Factors told One Pound One that snow had fallen to such a depth during the winter of his furlough that the weakest buffalo could not dig down to the grass. The stronger ones, digging, found nothing but char. They starved and died again. More rotting carcasses, more wolves. When the wolves run out of buffalo carrion, they come for the horses . . .

It took the Governor's particular brand of genius to see through all this seemingly natural disaster and identify the true cause: One Pound One's age, Harriott's intemperance; the bad legs on both of them.

As for the charge that One Pound One was too critical of the men . . . well, the poor darlings. It was not that many years ago (before the damn priests started poaching) that you had men here who could row from dark to dark, who tracked and portaged at a run, who were either never sick or had the good grace to die quickly.

Just looking around the boat on which he sat as he returned upriver to his district, One Pound One had evidence aplenty of the decline in the labouring and paddling class. After watching the poor weak things try to row for half the summer, his intention was to sit down the moment he got to Edmonton and complain again! At length!

Too hard a man!

If there was a single charge that infuriated One Pound One more than the rest, this was it. What other chief factor in the department poulticed his men with milk from nursing mothers' breasts? Who else personally leeched them and lanced their felons? And yet he was seen as too hard because at times he cursed in their gentle ears or knocked one down.

Had none of these darlings heard what the booshwahs were like on the Missouri? An American blackheart named Alexander Harvey beat a score of his men half to death because they complained and got him dismissed. He walked from Fort McKenzie to St. Louis in winter, got himself reinstated, rode the steamer back, and revenged himself with his fists and his knives on every teller of tales against him.

The same Harvey shot a Spaniard he suspected of plotting, right through the head in the company store. Another time, he turned a cannon on a bunch of Blackfoot in his fort to avenge the death of some Negro. It wasn't even the same Indians as committed the murder, but he lured them in and let fly. They say he leapt on the wounded, scalped them himself, and licked the dag clean with his tongue.

That was the standard on the American side of the trade, but the

Governor complained that One Pound One was a man too hard and that the men resigned rather than work for him.

In One Pound One's head, the letter to the Governor began to compose itself:

> All summer I have put up with weak middlemen acting as bowmen and steersmen. With a set of small boys engaged at Montreal who cannot carry a piece. Why did Duplessis not engage the mothers as well as the boys? To take the latter from their mothers' breasts so young is a great sin.

❧

NORTH SASKATCHEWAN RIVER, 1848

Things kept happening on the river that made One Pound One feel he was passing himself, meeting his own past life coming the other way.

In one camp, he met Kane, the artist whose company he'd enjoyed at Edmonton two winters before. Kane's drawings were stowed on a boat in waterproof canvas and he was on his way out of the fur country, out of One Pound One's life forever. When they had first met, One Pound One had been a man with all his power intact. Now, a scant few years later as the artist left, it was gone. Whence, he wondered? How lost?

Farther up the river, One Pound One met a much older acquaintance: the little Methodist Rundle. The missionary was also on his way, to the Bay and England after eight years. The likable elf, foolish to the last, asked One Pound One to convey several messages to his Indians. To ensure this one that God would still recognize him in the missionary's absence. To remind that one that it was no good praying to God if in a week you were importing some relative's widow into your tent and your bed. Also, would One Pound One make sure his replacement knew that the Indians preferred to shake the left hand not the right?

"It's because they wipe their bums with the right one," he whispered in the Chief Factor's ear, then giggled.

Rundle could never get it through his thick head that One Pound One was a Catholic! Not his willing co-evangelist. Well, he was gone now, the little chap, and not the worst sort either.

At Fort Pitt, One Pound One stopped to see his son John Junior, to confront the fact that after all his years of steering a course for the young fool, he had gone ahead and married in his absence, without his consent. And there she was, the self-same little Peggy whom Harriott had delivered into Louise's arms eighteen years previous, after the mother had gone berserk in the mountains and died. The daughter was as beautiful as the mother, and how could you help but fear there might be other things in common between the two?

As for his son: very plump, very pleased with himself.

Then it was Edmonton, pulling for shore with all guns blazing, under the fine-looking fort he'd built from nothing. Harriott stood on shore waiting. What a welcoming party. His old friend, skin and bones, looking even more grey and forlorn than usual. But for once there was a reason. He took One Pound One's arm and said, "Louise."

"Dead?"

"No. She's collapsed. She cannot walk."

"My old colossus," said One Pound One, and he staggered up the path, pushing away the fellows who tried to help him.

❧

FORT EDMONTON, 1848–49

All that fall and winter, Louise could not stand up on her own again, and it took any number of them to move her around the house. One Pound One began to realize that it would never be different, that she was likely off her feet for life.

The setting behind this misery suited it well. The fall was a nightmare of fires that blew down on them from the west, from the burning forests around Lac Ste Anne. They dug up the ground until their arms were weak but they still lost all the cordwood, all the boat lumber and several hay piles. Meanwhile the buffalo stayed away again and it was a winter of living on whitefish that was slightly turned by the time it made the ice cellar.

Out of that bleakness came an old friend. John Lee Lewes, a veteran of many Arctic postings and wonderfully ugly now, paid One Pound One a visit. They drank bumpers of Demerara as of old, but One Pound One could not stop looking at the stump beyond which his friend's right hand used to be. Years ago already now, a gun exploding had taken it off. Lewes's second-in-command had shown the sense to tie up the arteries and to bathe it in a decoction of epinette.

So they talked awhile about how men like that were impossible to find nowadays.

❦

SASKATCHEWAN BRIGADE, 1849

The following summer, One Pound One took his place in the brigade and rode to Council as usual. The meeting was the same nonsense and insults as every year, and he slept through most of it. On the return journey, he met an express boat coming down. The news was written in Harriott's hand and it said that Louise had died, on July 27th. They had buried her in the old cemetery on the river flat.

To no one in particular, One Pound One said, "The mother of my children is no more."

During the rest of the trip, he thought of her, how she'd been. Some had it that One Pound One had fathered children by other women, but it wasn't true. Louise would have killed him with a poker or an axe if he had. Finally, that's what he'd admired best about her. She was fierce. She was as fierce as him.

❦

FORT EDMONTON, 1849–50

The winter was again ushered in by fires. This time they were to the east, around Pitt and down to Carlton. The Indians starved like dogs and the trade was so bad it went backwards. At Carlton, they were eating their own oxen. What can you say of a trading business that cannot feed itself?

If not for the pain all up and down his side, One Pound One would go, even now, and mine for gold in California. But no. His daughters. His sons. His grandchildren. Harriott.

❧

SASKATCHEWAN BRIGADE, 1850

Coming back up the river from Council the following summer, One Pound One's craft rounded a bend in the river and he beheld a sight that carved him like a shard of glass. It was the past returning, and not just any past but the dreadful minutes from last year when the express canoe had borne down upon him with the news about Louise.

Now a boat so little different, a crew so much the same, aimed like a lance at his heart, the middlemen clawing to bring their boat close to his. Whatever it was, One Pound One did not wish to confront it on the water. He signalled them and his own boatmen to the near shore. There was no place to moor, so they stood in water to their knees.

Another man was putting a letter in his hand, his name scrawled on it in the way only Harriott wrote his letters.

I don't want it, he told himself. I fear it.

Finally he stripped the thin seal and read. July 8th. His daughter Nancy. Dead. Harriott had tried to write some consoling sentence but, in his own grief, had stopped partway.

One Pound One in that moment could not stand the weight of his own limbs. Into the water he sat. Its ice-cold caress. Men came rushing and splashing, and he warned them off with an animal growl. He looked down at the paper underwater in his hand. Ink left it in thin strands of black until the paper was blank.

❦

FORT EDMONTON, 1852–53

Between his two family deaths and the spring of 1853, little changed for One Pound One. That is, he took no action while others grew busier and more impatient around him.

It couldn't have been more peculiar to sit so still and wait for others to shift him, but lately he had lost the power to make decisions, at least regarding himself. His remaining daughters were still with him in the Big House: complaining, shrewing, praying. That was part of it. How could a man think in such a din?

One of them was too old and grouchy to marry now. Another was eating her way into perpetual spinsterhood. The youngest looked likely to suffer Nancy's fate, bloody coughing, and she had taken to religion in fear.

In their way, each daughter was lobbying One Pound One for a move. Having no idea how Halfbreeds were cut and snubbed in Montreal, the eldest fancied herself a famous lady there. The two who were interested in men frowned on the lot here and seemed to think it was their father's job to supply better. If he could find none locally he must move them where a better standard prevailed.

His youngest pined only for the nuns, and not even these could One Pound One readily supply. The nearest collection of those magpies was Red River.

One thing he would not do with any of his daughters was risk another with Harriott. He had talked that man into bringing his children to Edmonton, rather than looking after them in the Mountain House alone. That was the reason given, but in fact, One Pound One didn't trust him. Harriott had never tried to do evil one day in his life, but no matter where he went, evil found him. The Mountain House was a good place for him. There was hardly any trade, so Harriott could sit and drink away the days, brooding about his losses.

For One Pound One nowadays, every conversation, every letter, was about this damned business of retirement. He could get no rest from it. The Governor was the worst. He counselled One Pound One to go to Montreal. He counselled him to go to Red River. He asked him to stay on at Edmonton. How could a man reasonably obey?

The thing was you had to have spirit to choose, and lacking it, One Pound One could only go on as before.

What it led to finally was the lowest day of One Pound One's life in the trade. Here in his own fort, he was confronted by a crowd of mutineers. They stopped working and they marched on him. Their ill-spoken leader stood there numbering complaints on his fingers like some jumped-up politician.

"Number one, we want more tea and flour. Number two, we'll no longer pay for horses we use to do the Company's business."

One Pound One pictured himself a younger man, saying *Number three* and charging through them with a horsewhip. But his side ached, and that great ox of a bullyboy that he himself had trained and pampered stood shoulder-to-shoulder with the rest, his fists balled at his sides.

One Pound One did not have the strength to face them down. The bastards knew it, too, or they never would have dared to rise. It hurt differently than to lose your woman or your daughter, but it hurt badly another way. To back down. To pay out their demands.

Just before Christmas, the Governor sent another letter full of useful criticisms. More blame that One Pound One's men were resigning while others refused postings to his district. According to the Governor, the mutiny had been One Pound One's fault. The Governor all but portrayed the Saskatchewan as Eden and One Pound One as driving off the tribe of Adam with a whip.

If anyone in the world was left who cared, One Pound One's opinion was that the Governor had lost all touch with this country. It began with his white wife. Within a very few years of that, the wife was ill and disconsolate over the death of their first son, and the Governor lost all certainty of what he was about. It was in that time, before he took his woman to live in Lachine, that he made his devil's pact with Jamey Jock, which in turn marked the moment when he no longer sought One Pound One's advice on the Blackfoot trade.

His interest had grown fainter and fainter. If he'd ever known the nature of life out here, he'd long forgotten. What it was to ride a sledge into blinding cold in search of an Indian camp—that might have meat and robes, and might not. To watch your woman and Halfbreed children die of spots and a fever cooking their brains.

The Governor was blind to it, and One Pound One feared what sort of man he might choose to be the new chief factor here. Another man in this house that he had built so carefully with his own hands, its galleries and real window glass, and great big hearths to keep you warm. One Pound One was supposed to calmly say, "Very well, it's not mine, it's Company property, it's time," and give way to some fortunate fool who'd done nothing to earn it! Just because the Governor, who knew less now than he did a score of years ago, had proclaimed him too old and too cruel.

Finally the decision was taken out of his hands.

Come the spring of 1853, the Governor left off his gentle prodding and brought out a hayfork. Believing that One Pound One was anchored to Edmonton by his daughters, the Governor asked the nuns at Red River to make room for them. Without any notion of coming between a father and his daughters, the Governor wrote and told One Pound One to get them ready without delay.

In addition, he wrote:

> Harriott's children, being now without a mother and no spiritual counsellor, should make the voyage also. That way, Harriott and perhaps your son from Pitt could undertake to provide for and protect them to Red River, leaving you free to go with the outgoing brigade to Council.

All very neat.

🌿

FORT EDMONTON, 1853–54

Winter again. In Edmonton still.

Alone now. Like a hermit. Except for a woman who came to cook and tidy the Big House. One Pound One did not care about the tidiness but he liked to eat. For that, he needed no utensil save his knife. Wipe it down your trouser leg when you're done. Turn your plate upside down.

But when the eating was over for the day, he found himself alone with not much to do but stare at the fire.

There was correspondence with the ones he still trusted, but these were so few it didn't make much of a pastime. Before summer, he had thought Harriott would figure in this winter, in person or the odd letter, but the Governor had reached in and meddled with even that small plan.

One Pound One should have smelled the rat sooner. The business of bringing Harriott's children to Red River. Motherless blah, blah. Since when did the Governor care whether Harriott or his children lived or died? If One Pound One had used his head, he'd've seen right there that the Governor meant to twist the knife in Harriott one more turn.

Once he got Harriott down to Red River, the Governor didn't let him back. At Council, One Pound One was told that Harriott was "too intemperate to continue" and would be forcibly retired while he still had the funds in savings to do so. What an insult to One Pound One. Whoever heard of retiring a District Chief Factor's relief officer without consulting him? One more proof, if any were needed, of how the Governor had stopped caring about the Chief Factor's feelings or authority a long time ago.

Not even knowing that it would be the last time they saw each other as employer and second-in-command, all there was in parting between One Pound One and Harriott, his longest associate, had been a single overnight mainly spent packing clothes and toys and whatnot for Harriott's children here at the Big House. They took a glass of brandy together at the end of the night, but Harriott was so exhausted by all the packing and travelling he'd fallen asleep in his chair.

That was the picture One Pound One was left with: of a man older than his years, with not one ounce of fat to shield him from the cold or feed him when the hunt failed, splayed in a chair with a cup tipped on his chest dripping brandy through his shirt.

Many times this winter, One Pound One had taken a pair of candles to his desk with the intention of writing Harriott at Red River, the kind of parley they used to exchange, but he never did it. Somehow, the news that came back up the river that Harriott had found yet another woman to marry stopped him.

The thing was, the news didn't come from Harriott. Nothing came from Harriott. It was one of his daughters, now living with the nuns, who told him, and she was all for never speaking to Harriott again as a family policy, because of how soon it was after the death of Nancy. That part, of course, was nonsense. A man with six children can't do without a wife. The longer you wait, the worse it is.

No, the reason he could not write Harriott came from slightly elsewhere. As grandfather to Harriott's children or, more to the point, as a friend, he thought he would be consulted. But far from that, he hadn't even been told. As he wintered in Edmonton, he didn't know whether the marriage was in the past or yet ahead, nor did he even know who the damn woman was.

One Pound One brooded over this into his fire, and what he saw was that the betrayals in his life had come closer with the passage of years. They used to come from far away, from places like the Missouri, from people like Jamey Jock. No one closer would dare. Now the sources were handier. The turning point was when it was the Governor. Then came the young officers who used to cower at his feet. Seeing him tire, they no longer saw a leader. They smelled meat. Then there was the men, their mutiny.

This business of Harriott not writing, not even to tell him that his grandchildren had a new stepmother, had to be a nearly final stage. His oldest friend. Probably that meant the final cut would come from his sons. Unless, in the meantime, One Pound One found a way to betray himself.

If the bears were asleep this time of winter, so too was One Pound One. He roused a bit at Christmas and New Year's, and when letters came. Mostly these were from his daughters, complaints about convent life and the menial tasks they were expected by the nuns to do. He had himself a rare laugh to think of his biggest girl bent over a brush.

But mostly he just rumbled in his chair until the fire went out, until the cold woke him and he walked through the familiar dark to bed.

❧

FORT EDMONTON, 1854

The coming of spring after the loneliest of winters.

Never had spring come to Edmonton so sunny and lush. The green jumped from the ground and swelled into the spaces between shining poplars, almost overnight. Pale green tips on every branch, and the moose stretching to eat them. Spring it was, and that's what it put in One Pound One's lopsided step.

No other season had such power to make a fool of a man. Lusty feelings—ridiculous—and sensations rushing in from everywhere. There you were, inside your broken old body, the randy boy of yesteryear.

Count Lefroy, a scientific observer of some kind, had come through Edmonton in 1844, on his way to the North. Among other things he was collecting stories for a book, as his type always were. From somewhere the Count had unearthed the one about how Louise and One Pound One had got together when young, and he was all aflutter telling it back to One Pound One.

Was it true? he wanted to know.

One Pound One thought hard before he answered. Then, to Lefroy and to himself, he answered: *So be it.*

Lefroy had the first part right, how One Pound One had taken a horse and set out alone to ride. A wild bitch mare that had probably never had a man on her back before. She jumped a few times then took off running. That was fine. She had a comfortable gallop, and there wasn't a fence between them and the top of the world. So why not let her go and see what kind of legs and wind she had? He was not yet twenty and very sure of himself on a horse.

They'd only gone a couple of leagues when a deer jumped out of a bush practically into the side of them. The mare blew up. One Pound One was left hanging in the air.

He still had hold of the rope to her underjaw and he meant to hang on. But the landing! Smack on a stone. And because of the way he came down, with most of his weight above his legs, there were two impacts, the one making the other worse, and a pain that wrote in lightning across his brain.

What he saw when he could see again was his own leg snapped in two, at right angles to itself, and the jagged end sticking out at him through an ugly smile of flesh above the knee. The horse was long gone. It was all he could do to put the bone back inside his skin and make the two parts straight. Then he passed out.

The pain drove him in and out of consciousness all day.

Then he woke to see an ugly big-headed horse pulling a Halfbreed cart towards him. Horse, cart and driver were silhouettes against an orange sky. When they came close, he saw it was Louise.

Here was where Lefroy left truth behind. He had her leaping down, grasping One Pound One in a tearful embrace, confessing her undying love. Then it was him into the cart and home to Edmonton, saved.

In truth, Louise stayed on her cart and looked at him for what seemed a very long time. She had no expression on her face. One Pound One looked back desperately, taking in everything: her long skirt of trade cloth, the fatty arms out her rolled sleeves, bountiful girl even then, a few years his elder. How he was wishing he'd been more courteous in the past. Had he even once asked her to join him in a dance?

She got off the cart at length and sat on the ground beside him. Still she said nothing. That, in hindsight, was the amazing thing. That for so long she said nothing and did nothing. He suspected he was raving, too, raging and begging. Possibly hitting out at her.

Everything was in that silence of hers. She was letting him know it was in her power to go back home, alone. Come dark, the wolves would prevent the story ever being told. As easily, she could fix him up and save his life. But for that to happen, there must be a bargain made.

Somehow in the silence of that afternoon, even the terms were negotiated. That she would be his woman, but that he would be a better husband than the local custom tended to provide. He would never beat her or their children, nor make them work more than was fair. He would not go after other women no matter how much rum he drank. He did not remember exactly how his assent was given, but it was. Every condition agreed to.

Then Louise bathed the wound and splinted him with a stick. She got him up on his good leg, hopped him over and dropped him on the back of her cart. By the time they bounced through the gate at Edmonton, everything was set, without so much as a kiss. That came later and no complaints.

But enough of such damn foolishness. By the amount of ice moving in the river, it was time to pack the furs, caulk the boats and get the horses down from Lac la Nonne. It was time to make the men look lively. He went to let the lazy, mutinous bastards know their winter's sleep was over.

❧

SASKATCHEWAN BRIGADE, 1854

By the time he had the brigade assembled, with a mixed load in every boat and not too much of any single thing in one, One Pound One was champing at the bit. He wasn't sure what his hurry was, unless it was to see his family after Council. His girls had never been easy to live with, but they were no easier to live without. It would also be good to see his grandchildren. He had decided to look up Harriott. He was going to Red River anyway.

So they got on the river and made good time to Fort Pitt. If anyone else had been in charge there but John Junior, One Pound One would have raised hell that the few packs were not ready. Given that it was his son's fort, he accepted it as a ploy to ensure he stayed the night.

Inside John's house, he saw his daughter-in-law. Took a good close look into her eyes when she stepped into and out of his embrace. Ordinary enough, and her answers seemed to go right to his questions.

Excellently pretty girl, too. Possibly prettier than the mother, though his memory there was growing dim.

So One Pound One sat and bounced his grandson on his knee, took a few bumpers of rum with his son, and slept like the dead in the decent bed provided. Truth was he slept too long. Rising late, he dressed quickly and hurried to shore, where John was cracking the whip and most of the few packs were stowed.

It was May 29th. If they got on the river today, it should bring them to salt water on schedule.

Just as One Pound One came on the scene and started to talk to his son, he heard some fracas behind them. He turned and saw two men onshore, one from Pitt and the other from the brigade, squaring off to fight. Filling with wrath and shouting for order as he went, One Pound One hopped down the shingle. The two fools didn't stop, the blockheads, so the old Chief Factor stepped between them. He balled his fist and pulled it back.

And a hammer hit an anvil in his chest.

❧

Mill Creek, 1900

Dear Editor,

I wasn't there the day One Pound One died at Pitt. By then I'd made it a condition of my contract never to row for him again. I was back at Edmonton flirting with the women and otherwise enjoying the boss's absence. When we heard he was dead we broke into the storehouse and stole a cask. We had ourselves as merry a booze as if it had been New Year's.

A story that's seldom told is how the Halfbreed who started the fight at Fort Pitt took one look at One Pound One lying dead and ran. Two days later he was shot to death by a man who said he mistook him for a deer.

After One Pound One died, his family didn't stay in the fur country long. With the £30,000 left to them, John Junior went to Red River and built a fine house for himself and his sisters.

Romantic prospects improved and one spinster married a politician. The huge one married too. She was 24 stone and she married a man of 26 stone. When the two crossed the settlement to visit they did so in separate buggies.

John Junior was a giant too. Twenty-five stone or 350 pounds when he died in 1864.
William Gladstone

❧

RED RIVER, 1854

By the time Harriott heard of the death of his friend, he had been at Red River for some time. He was about to marry a woman named Frances Bunn and was planning the construction of his stone house. The news about John ploughed him with sadness, deep and all the way through. Who had he known better? With whom had he lived more?

He even managed to be surprised that One Pound One had died. The Chief Factor had been the colour of a doomed man for decades, and back then, people used to shake their heads just to look at him. *Poor John, the colour of port again tonight. He won't be with us long.* But when he didn't die, they stopped thinking that he might. Harriott, too.

The only time Harriott could remember seriously pondering his friend's mortality was the last time he had replaced him at Edmonton, when he'd found a letter lying half-written on One Pound One's desk.

> Some of these days, you will hear that we are murdered for want of goods to satisfy the Blackfeet and Piegan. When you hear that I am killed, and Harriott, depend you will regret us but it will be too late. My opinion is no more regarded than a fool's.

More than what the letter said, there was a tone that Harriott found unsettling. A sound of wavering and drift. A weakening. Harriott did imagine then the heart of his friend exploding or a stroke grabbing him by one side of the brain. But when he saw the actual man again, raging and ranting, alive and unchanged, it eclipsed those pictures and he thought of them no more.

As for why Harriott had not contacted One Pound One since coming to Red River, that was something else. A selfish act for which he made no apology. When Harriott found himself on the outside of the trade for the first time since childhood, he realized he was changed in some basic way. He felt lighter and more alert. He was hungrier for food and less so for rum. The other traders who had retired here, the ones who could afford it, took Madeira and port, and Harriott followed their example. Soon he could not stand the taste of rum. The smell alone nauseated him.

Then he found Frances Bunn, a pleasant and handsome Red River woman in her forties, a mother for his brood. When the new house was built, he would be able to draw his and Nancy's six children from their various billets and they would live together again and be happy.

At least once a day Harriott paused in whatever he was doing to thank the Governor. There he had been at the Mountain House, hugged in the latest embrace of sorrow, guilt and rum, brought on by Nancy's death, and just when he felt he would never have the strength to break that grip, the Governor's letter arrived.

At first it read like an order to surrender his children to an orphanage. But in mid-page it changed. Perhaps, in that instant of writing, the Governor had decided it was time to deliver the *coup de grâce*. Rather than deprive the widower of his children's company, another mental beating administered, he could go one step further and be rid of the drunken nuisance forever. By the words of the letter's final paragraph, Harriott was ordered to leave the country with his children, leave it and the trade forever.

When he arrived at Edmonton, where the youngest of his children were living with the Rowands, he did not tell the whole contents of the letter to One Pound One. He thought better of it. Let the news of his forced resignation find the old Chief Factor when the two were not so nakedly face to face.

As for the Governor and his intentions, and what actually came of them for Harriott, it was bound to happen eventually. In an entire career of malevolence, the Governor's weapon of spite had misfired. He had accidentally done good.

At Red River and free of his old griefs and dependencies, Harriott quite naturally began to fear a relapse. That was where One Pound One figured into it. It seemed reasonable that the black depression that had owned Harriott for so long might want him back again. He imagined it like an animal, a black dog, that was back upriver sniffing along his old river haunts, trying to pick up his scent.

It was not out of anger or grievance that Harriott stopped communication with One Pound One; it was out of this fear. He was hiding from his old hopelessness, and he feared that One Pound One, because of how well he knew him, might without knowing it be able to say just the right combination of words to bring it all back again.

When Harriott heard of his friend's death, it did not seem in any way contradictory to mourn. Without bothering to exaggerate him into legend or excuse his worst traits, Harriott grieved the loss of his oldest friend exactly as the man had been. An awkward craft driven by fire, One Pound One had smashed his way upcurrent. He had gone too far and lasted too long and become a kind of wreck in the current of other people's ambitions. If there was fault in that, it wasn't Harriott's job to ascribe it.

❦

RED RIVER, 1860

In the summer of 1860, *Harper's Magazine* sent a writer and a sketch artist to investigate the Metis community at Red River, in the British possessions controlled for them by the Hudson's Bay Company.

The Metis way of living, French and Indian, stewed and compounded over generations, was colourful. They had their own folk dance, a jig, accompanied by fiddle music and mouth harp. In winter they festooned their sleighs and carts with paint and ribbon, raced their dogs and horses. In summer they went en masse to the prairie and hunted thousands of buffalo. It amounted to a frontier originality that *Harper's* wished to present pictorially and in print for its readers.

There was also a political aspect to the story. The Halfbreeds were more numerous in the British Northwest than the whites and Indians combined. For a long time they had possessed the notion that they should govern themselves, and of late they had defied the Hudson's Bay Company's monopoly on trade. A man named Sayers had been tried for illegal trading in defiance of the monopoly and the court had set him free. This act had caused such an explosion of national fever among the Metis that news of it got all the way to New York.

For many Americans, a simmering state of hostility with Britain was considered a requisite of national health. The idea of Britain, or its colonial apprentice Canada, having to fight the Metis to secure its western frontier was bound to be popular.

In any case, a writer and artist were dispatched to rail's end and from there by hired cart to remote Red River. Upon arrival they thoroughly observed, sketched and interviewed the settlement's Metis inhabitants. When they were done with the Metis, they expanded their research in various directions to make sure they did not come home short of material.

It was at this stage of proceedings that they called upon a retired fur trader named John Edward Harriott at his Red River home.

Mr. Harriott's residence is built of limestone, quarried from the native rock and, within and without, was planned by its owner. The cool interior is made pleasant by a few well-selected books on a shelf, house plants in the windows, choice engravings on the walls, riding whips and guns in the hall, tobacco jar and pipes on the side table, and a melodeon, accordion and music box in the room which New Englanders call the parlour.

Harriott's wife served the two young Americans tea, and she and Harriott, and the children around the place, tried not to smile too broadly. Someone had got the Americans up in head rags and Metis sashes around their waists. They looked ridiculous, like dogs in sweaters, and he imagined what a good time the local folk must be having with them.

They were very polite with him, these two Americans, pretending great interest in his life and his career. But at the same time he could smell their impatience. He told anecdotes in response to their questions and, when one finished, the writer would sit with his pen dripping.

"Yes? And then?"

"No. That's all."

Not enough blood and thunder, in other words. For much of the time, the writer wrote nothing, and once, out of the corner of his eye, Harriott saw the sketch artist make a mock flourish with his charcoal over his blank paper. It was a question.

Should I take his likeness?

By some gesture or expression the writer answered no and the artist set his charcoal down.

Harriott began to feel impatience on his side of the bargain, too. Such as when the writer said, "You must have killed a lot of Indians in your time."

"If I had," said Harriott, "with whom would I have traded?"

When the interview petered out entirely, Harriott surprised himself by being truly vexed. Suddenly he hated it that men like One Pound One and his younger self were being assessed and dismissed on the basis of one half-crippled old man in a rocking chair, as judged by two green citizens of New York in comic costume who had likely never hunted a buffalo or steered down a rapid. Transparent politeness alone was keeping them from vaulting up and running out the door.

To their surprise, and maybe his own, it was Harriott who fought to his feet.

"Come along. I'll show you the settlement."

In the afternoon our host ordered his carriage to the door and drove us to the Stone Fort. The horses were a gay pair and the carriage itself a "carry-all," a sober pattern imported from Britain by way of Hudson Bay which is not now in use overseas. With its low heavy wheels, thick substantial whiffletrees and high dashboard, it is the kind of carriage that transported well-to-do English squires from country estate to town half a century ago. Over the bridge and along the road, we cantered at a pace that needed a strong hand on the reins.

It went well until they stood before the walls of the Stone Fort, the one the Governor had named for Nicholas Garry. Standing there, with the Americans expecting an oration, Harriott could think of nothing to say. Walls of medieval thickness. Out of time. Out of place. In his own heart, he felt the ancient tug. Here with his white wife, the Governor had lived, happily for a time, then unhappily, watching their baby son die. But however the episode ended, the Governor had never been punished for what he'd done to Margaret and to him.

"A magnificent building," the reporter gushed.

"Yes," said Harriott, "but what is it for? What was it ever for?"

"Certainly it must have been for protection."

"Against whom?"

The reporter floundered, uncomfortable with this switch of positions.

"Against the Indians? At least one would suppose that."

"One would, but it's not right."

Harriott shrugged and let it go, a conversation he should never have begun.

They started back after that. Harriott left the Americans off in the muddy street close to their boarding house. But he himself did not go home. He continued to drive around the settlement. Friends in their gardens waved him over. He waved back and drove on.

He continued to mull the thing. The intention of the Stone Fort had been mostly for show. Notre Dame crossed with Versailles, a home for a god and a goddess more than for a king and a queen. The thickness of wall? A little Tower of London thrown in to impress and comfort the wife.

The Governor threw up an impregnable fortress around his family. Nothing could get them there. No nasty Indian or Halfbreed. A defence so complete even Colin Robertson and his Halfbreed wife Theresa had been denied entry, refused tea.

What it became finally was different—and more fitting. At the point where the Governor and his wife forsook it for Lachine, the Stone Fort became a hulking tomb, like an Egyptian pyramid. A big tomb for a little boy.

Harriott drove Red River for hours, dogs, chickens and children scattering before his team of blacks. The more angry he became, the faster he drove. The Americans had started it with their damned politeness, but more than that he was furious at the Governor and at himself. For his effect on Margaret, whatever that effect had been: for that alone the Governor should have been made to suffer. Old man or not, he deserved to be driven out of wherever he was right now, from whatever luxury he lived in, out into the street to be stoned like a thief. For that was what he was: a thief of lives and love; of sanity and irreplaceable time.

Harriott's anger at himself was that he'd never put a stop to it. Had he ever really tried? All his attempts were so small and poorly devised, easily deflected. Most often all he'd done was take the idea of murdering the Governor and chase it around his mind, whipping it faster and faster like these horses, but only in a circle, so that when the fit was exhausted, he always ended very close to where he'd begun.

You're doing it again now, he challenged himself, as he thundered along the sticky streets, as women carrying bundles cursed him for a danger and his horses sweated under their harness leathers. His carriage, which had started out gleaming black, was faded grey with dust and mottled by flung slops, striped with shit whipped up by his wheels.

Was this really just another preamble to doing nothing? Would he go home to his chair and his dog and his pipe, and perhaps pour his head full of drink as he had done with this problem so often before?

Out of the corner of his eye, he spotted a false front with a word in red paint on its otherwise grey. *Firearms.* He hauled in his team, the froth of their mouths floating back to melt on his coat. He swerved to the hitching rail.

He tied up and faced the door, which stood open on an interior darkness. When he stepped inside, he could see nothing. The smell was of gun oil, leather and dirt. A match flared and touched a wick, lit a lemon-yellow face shaved shiny and hair gleaming black as a stove. The man's dark eyes held a prick of light in each. Behind him in shadow the vendor's arsenal was protected by padlocked chains through the trigger guards.

"Welcome, sir. Let me guess. The pleasant day has you thinking sport. You desire a bird gun."

"I have enough bird guns."

"I see you have a fine English carriage there. You will be pleased to know that my goods are of finest English quality."

"I want an American gun."

"I have those, too. A buffalo rifle, is it? A Parker?"

"I want an American handgun. If you want to help me, imagine that I want to kill a man with a weapon concealed under my coat."

The merchant blinked several times, then smoothed his waxen jaw.

"Well, then. We are talking about either a pistol or a derringer. A little pepper pot, maybe."

"I don't trust a derringer to fire."

The merchant unlocked another chain out of sight beneath his counter. He started handing up pistols and placing them on the oily board, talking as he went.

"Here's a nice item. Christian Sharps, an American. Known best for his rifles but has a second little company that produces handguns. Or here's Smith and Wesson's lever-action gun. Another more recent one of theirs. The Model 1. You see, it has a revolving cylinder. It fires a very small shell, just .22 calibre, but at the range I think you're talking of, and able to fire several times in succession . . . Then, of course, I have the usual assortment of Colts."

Harriott chose the Smith and Wesson revolver and bought a box of ammunition. He paid with cash, then stabbed the weapon into his waistband so it was hidden under his coat. He turned to go.

"You aren't going to shoot a man today, are you, sir?"

"Not until I reach Montreal."

The merchant laughed and slapped both hands on his counter, probably thinking that, for a man as old and decrepit as this one, Montreal and the moon were about the same distance away.

That day when he got home, Harriott began lobbying his wife. In his head he couldn't stop calling her Miss Bunn. Occasionally he forgot himself entirely and called her that to her face. She liked being Mrs. Harriott and grew very angry at the mistake.

He lobbied her about a move to Montreal. Given the cost of living at Red River, it might work out cheaper in the long run to live there, if they chose their house carefully. Living on savings they had need of every advantage in this regard. Beyond that, he said, it was the location to which the better quality of Company men retired. He hinted at lavish parties in nice houses, hoping to touch some vanity in her. But she was Red River through and through, and that gambit did not work.

Then there was the possibility that Montreal would give his children hope in this world beyond becoming Company clerks and labourers. As ever, Red River was the Governor's harbour for those he didn't care to employ. The ones who had been Metis for generations were perhaps on their way to something better with their buffalo hunts and their independent trapping and carting; their nation talk. But that was no help to his children, who were more like Jimmy Jock: the relatively well born Halfbreed children of a Company officer, but never white enough to make officers themselves. At the same time, they were too white for the Metis to trust or include in the new liberation.

"And in Montreal it would be better?" asked Miss Bunn, who was part Indian herself and, in her forties, no fool.

So Harriott let it go for a few days, but he always returned. He never forgot how he felt the day of the American interview and he never intended to forget. He knew that, when the time came, he could force the issue and his wife would consent, however unhappy it would make her to leave her parents and home. His attitude was that he didn't expect to live that much longer and she could return once he was dead.

Once every week he dismantled his Smith and Wesson Model 1 by lamplight. He removed the barrel and ran cloth and pipe cleaners through the chambers and the slender barrel. He oiled all the moving parts.

On a day in late September, one of Harriott's girls came into the house from skipping and said, "The old Governor's dead. We've made up a song about it."

"Who told you that?" called Harriott, but she was already gone. He got up and went outside, walked to his neighbour's and asked. She had heard it, too.

By the end of the afternoon his parlour was full of old Company hands, drinking brandy, port, Madeira, rum. Some were making toasts to the old man who had ruled them all their lives, even shedding tears to see that great one finally pass.

"He died as he lived," said one milk-eyed former adventurer, referring to the fact that, according to the paper, the Governor had been out at Lachine two days before his final apoplexy, showing off Iroquois paddlers and decorated birchbark canoes to the eighteen-year-old Prince of Wales.

Another old trader, a stringy man with long hairs growing out between his eyes, one who had been passed up for promotion too often to have much love for the Company or its ruling class, noticed Harriott staring off into some sadness. He sat down in the chair beside him and said, "I never thought you'd be unhappy to see this day."

To the man's astonishment, Harriot reached into a wicker stand full of papers beside him and hauled out a firearm, a well-oiled handgun, which he raised and pointed at the ceiling.

"Hold on there, Harriott!"

"It's not loaded."

"What do you think you're doing with it then?" asked another, for everyone was watching now.

Harriott clicked the hammer on an empty chamber, causing them to duck and flinch. Then he tossed the gun back into the basket.

❧

RED RIVER, 1865

By some of Harriott's arguments to Miss Bunn, he convinced himself. After the Governor's death and as his own health grew worse, confining him to his chair on many days, Harriott became if anything more determined to move to Montreal.

The family was in the process of packing for that voyage when Montreal came to him. A Red River lawyer drove to Harriott's house and conveyed him to the local magistrate so he could give testimony in a civil trial taking place in Montreal.

The matter concerned the estate of old Chief Factor Connolly, the sick and complaining boss for whom Harriott had worked in New Caledonia the year of Margaret's death. At that time Connolly's woman had been a Cree, the daughter of a chief. They had lived together a long time, ever since Connolly had been a Nor'Wester at Rat River in 1803.

When Connolly retired from the Company in 1831, he took his Indian wife and their six children to Montreal. A year later he put the Cree woman aside into the convent at Red River so he could marry his cousin. When Connolly died a few years later, his estate went to this cousin and to the two children Connolly had fathered by her.

Now, years later, Connolly's eldest son by his Indian wife was suing for a portion of his father's estate.

Under oath, Harriott was asked to speak to the validity of Connolly's first marriage. He said that, in his opinion, it had been valid. He used his own first marriage for a comparison. In the 1820s he had taken a woman of the country and, though there was no church for a thousand miles, he regarded her as his wife and their marriage as true as one made by a priest or minister.

"But you set her aside?" asked the judge.

"No. She was my wife until she died."

"And you considered that marriage complete with rights and obligations?"

In the end, the Montreal judge found for the plaintiff. Miss Pas-de-Nomme's son received a twelfth share.

❧

To those who asked why Harriott would move now (their implication being when he was so close to the end), he gave the same set of answers. He said it was so his children would know something beyond the fur domain, and so they wouldn't be affected by the Orange zealots currently passing leaflets around Red River. For himself, he wanted medical help beyond cupping, leeching and purging.

All the reasons he gave were true, but they were not quite the truth.

None of them spoke of the restlessness he felt, like a bird before a storm.

Before leaving for Montreal, Harriott paid a visit to his eldest daughter, who had recently been widowed by the death of One Pound One's son. Meeting her father at the door of her handsome house, Peggy was wearing widow's weeds but Harriott sensed there wasn't much grief behind them. She confided that John's will had not been favourable to her and that she was forced to marry again, which supported a local rumour about a military officer said to be paying more attention to Peggy than some thought polite.

As always, Harriott was uncomfortable with his daughter. There were so many things he always thought in her company that he could not say. At every stage of her life, she had been the image of her mother. As a girl, mirroring the cousin with whom Harriott had grown up. Then, as she grew, becoming the living image of the budding woman with whom he'd fallen in love.

What he feared and could not face was that Peggy was now close to the age at which Margaret had died. Soon she would become what her mother never lived to be. It was a kind of cowardice, but Harriott could not bear to stay and see that.

When it was time to go, father and daughter did not linger long at the door. Even though both knew it was the last time they would be together in this world, their embrace was brief, cool, almost formal.

❧

MONTREAL, 1866

Harriott and his family travelled to Montreal by boat. At the Sault, their boat was anchored to the pier beside a boatload of miserable draftees headed in the opposite direction. One pale boy was puking over the gunwale. A bully with a gun stood above them on the bridge.

William Gladstone, Harriott's boat builder at the Mountain

House, had once described a scene like this, from the time when Gladstone himself had been a recruit coming into the country.

A quite different Gladstone had visited Harriott at Red River this past winter. No longer a Company servant, he was there to investigate farming prospects. Nor did he like what he saw. At the time of the visit he was on his way back to the Saskatchewan to try his luck at something else.

Gladstone told Harriott that the Saskatchewan trade was declining to nothing. The Company had stopped the rum and, among other responses, the Piegan had burned the Mountain House to the ground. Without rum, according to Gladstone, the trade was a farce and the New Year's celebration at Edmonton the worst he'd ever seen. It had been comical to see the new Chief Factor going around with commission papers, all but begging the men to renew. Always before, they'd relied on the men's drunkenness, their gratitude for the liquor, to induce their X. This year, able to think clearly, not one man would sign. In this way, Gladstone had left the Company after almost twenty years.

"A man can make a living on his own now, Mr. Harriott," he'd said, "by contracting to the Company or not."

Harriott wished there was a way to tell this boatload of boys, in a way they would understand, that the Company was only their employer, not their god or fate. That with decent luck they would be free men someday.

When his family reached Montreal, Harriott rented a home for them on a nice street with well-grown trees. As winter came he felt a weakness like nothing he'd felt before. He kept it to himself as much as he could, and as soon as it could be done without fuss, he had his son rent a horse and sleigh and asked to be driven up the hill to the cemetery.

Where the sleigh could not continue, Harriott leaned on his cane and his son's arm, and they proceeded slowly through the snow.

"Why are we doing this?" said the boy.

"Don't argue. Just help me find it."

They searched the gravestones, one by one, and found a good many people Harriott had known, most notably Chief Factor Colin Robertson. Robertson had died in 1842, and not of another stroke, as everyone assumed he would. He'd managed a surprising death when, here in Montreal, he'd been thrown from a carriage and killed.

Then at last Harriott found what he'd come so far to see. He asked his son to leave him awhile at the grave of One Pound One.

There'd been so much fuss about his old friend's bones. Somewhere, maybe in his will, One Pound One had asked to be buried in Montreal. Fearing the rage of his ghost, they dug him up at Fort Pitt, boiled him to bones, and sealed him in a puncheon.

They took him the long way around, across to Hudson Bay and over the ocean to England. All to bring him back here, to a hill above the town he'd lived in as a boy.

At least, after his travels, John had a pleasant place. Plenty of trees to make a dappled shade come summer. The broad St. Lawrence below.

Standing there by his friend's grave in the deep snow, Harriott stared up into the blue sky and let his thoughts leave him, out of his painful body, and out of all bonds of place and time. Alone on the gallery of Fort Edmonton on a summer night, he held tight to the points of two pickets, steadying against the white pull of a river of stars. Across the valley to the south, the night was hollowed out by fire, a pulsing gold.

A great fire had coursed northward for days, driven on a Pacific wind, and tonight it reached the south escarpment. Tongues of fire licked among the tree trunks, tortured their silhouettes.

The fire filled Harriott's mind so full he imagined it must be burning everywhere. West to the mountains and south to the arid plain. Southwest to the headwaters of the Missouri and on both banks of every river in between.

Out of the blaze fled the buffalo, red-eyed, the hair on their backs and sides smoking, an immense and final herd. Towards every horizon they charged, until the compass face was empty.

If hellfire burns eternal, earthly fires are never so. They burn to exhaustion, or until the cool rains fall. A pale green rises through the char.

🌿

Mill Creek, 1900

Dear Editor,

It was in the 1860s when Mr. Harriott died. I don't remember the year. They buried him by a Protestant church in Montreal. I remember thinking I should get word to Jimmy Jock, as he was maybe the last one who'd care. But I saved my breath. Jimmy Jock knew everything.

As for the end of Jimmy Jock himself, I don't know what to tell. Some of what I heard I don't like to repeat. They used to say Halfbreed interpreters were in the middle and never on anyone's side. It was just as true that nobody was on their side. The people who liked to play with Jimmy Jock's name did so one more time before the end. They called him Jimmy Jug for selling whisky or drinking it. It was never clear to me which.

In 1877, they had a big treaty gathering of Blackfoot Indians and Mountain Stoneys, on Bow River at Blackfoot Crossing. Jerry Potts was supposed to interpret but some say he got drunk. So they went and got Jimmy Jock out of Fort Benton, Montana, 83 years old and stone-blind. Some say he lied. Some say he didn't know Blackfoot. Both ideas are peculiar, since he'd lived with the Piegan more than fifty years.

A story I believe more, or like more, was one a friend told me about meeting Jimmy Jock years later outside the mountains east of here. His last wife was driving the cart and they were on their way between Browning and Brocket, I don't know in which direction.

Jimmy Jock told my friend how for many years he'd survived by having his wife chew for him. Then she lost the last of her teeth and he assumed they both must die. Just about then a friend visited from Prince Albert and gave them a food chopper as a gift. It was good. It worked well.

Jimmy Jock decided he would live some more.

William Gladstone

ACKNOWLEDGEMENTS

In this novel, I tried to write between the lines of known fur trade history. In researching it, I read as many original documents as I could, and many popular and formal histories, too. I would like to mention J. G. MacGregor's *John Rowand, Czar of the Prairies* (Western Producer Prairie Books, 1978). Many of my stories of One Pound One and Edward Harriott are derived from that source.

I would like to thank Parks Canada for long ago commissioning me to write a guide to Rocky Mountain House National Historic Park, called *Rocky Mountain House* (NC Press, 1985). While researching their copied letters and journals relating to Rocky Mountain House and the Saskatchewan fur district, I conceived the notion of writing this novel.

Another source I would like to acknowledge is the fur trade reminiscences of William Gladstone. To my knowledge his is the only account of the Canadian fur trade in this era left by a non-officer. William Gladstone entered the trade in 1848 as an apprentice York boat builder, and his reminiscences first appeared in print in the *Rocky Mountain Echo* in 1903. They were edited for publication in the *Lethbridge Herald* by Freda Graham Bundy of Pincher Creek in 1958, and were published in book form as *The Gladstone Diaries: Travels in the Early West* by the Historic Trails Society of Alberta in 1985.

I was educated in the town of Pincher Creek. Several friends of my family were descended from, or somehow related to, William Gladstone, including James Rivière, a wonderful mountain raconteur who recently died. William Gladstone was James's grandfather on his mother's side. He never told me stories about his grandfather, but he told other stories I remember and treasure, usually across our kitchen table after buying a truckload of hay. Reading William Gladstone and "listening" to him rage against his brutal bosses in the trade, some of whom are revered figures in the formal history, gave me courage to write a novel that also argues with some of history's assessments.

I also thank Pamela Banting, my spouse, for the beginning of this novel. I don't mean to say she wrote it, but it might never have been written if she hadn't mildly suggested one day that perhaps a novel shouldn't begin with a bunch of men sitting around a table having a meeting. Pamela also published a portion of this book in *Fresh Tracks: Writing the Western Landscape,* an anthology of western Canadian writing published by Polestar Book Publishers in 1998. Srdja Pavlovic also selected a part for his anthology *Threshold* (University of Alberta Press, 1999). Friends Merna Summers, Jan Truss and Gordon Pengilly read early versions of this manuscript and gave me sound suggestions. I thank them very much.

I would like to thank editor Jennifer Glossop for her encouragement and skillful work on this book.

Last of all, I thank friends Matt Cohen, Rachel Wyatt, Edna Alford, Jan Zwicky, Don McKay, Sid Marty, Merna Marty and Andreas Schroeder, who, having heard me read from this book, or at least yap on about it, gave me encouragement and guidance that was badly needed at the time. I'm sure I should be naming other people, too, and I hope they will forgive their omission.

The relationship of the novel to the historical record is something I cannot explain except by annotating every page. The characters are necessarily fictionalized, albeit based on figures from history. The major historical events are as close to the record as I could make them, but most of the specific occurrences in the characters' lives are invented.

Some of the most fanciful-sounding things are true. A cat at Fort Edmonton did find, adopt and suckle orphaned baby rabbits. One Pound One did capture buffalo calves with the intent of sending them to England, and Indians did sneak into the fort and kill them. Margaret Pruden did go mad and walk off into a blizzard on the Athabasca Pass. One Pound One's bones did cross the ocean in two directions en route to their burial in Montreal.

The novel probably contains mistakes I never intended. Some of the things I made up may be true. I leave the rest up to you.